WILD FIRE

Magic slid over the back of my neck, like molten honey, sizzling pleasure on my skin. I gasped into his mouth.

"You're mine," he said, his voice rough. "I'm not letting you go."

"I'm glad we cleared that up."

"Do you understand me, Nevada? I'm not walking away. I thought I could, but I can't and I don't want to."

I brushed his cheek with my fingertips. "What makes you think I would let you go?"

He pulled me to him, and I climbed over, onto his lap. He kissed my neck. Magic swirled along my spine, a heated bliss.

There were blue and red lights behind us.

Rogan growled.

A cop was walking toward us, a flashlight in his hand.

I crawled back into my seat and put my hand over my face.

Rogan rolled down the window. "Yes, Officer?"

WILD FIRE

A HIDDEN LEGACY NOVEL

ILONA ANDREWS

AVON

An Imprint of HarperCollins*Publishers*

WILDFIRE. Copyright © 2017 by Ilona Gordon and Andrew Gordon. DIAMOND FIRE. Copyright © 2018 by Ilona Gordon and Andrew Gordon.

HarperCollins books may be purchased for educational, business, or sales promotional use. For information, please email the Special Markets Department at SPsales@harpercollins.com.

FIRST AVON BOOKS MASS MARKET PUBLISHED IN 2017.

Interior text design by Diahann Sturge-Campbell

Library of Congress Cataloging-in-Publication Data has been applied for.

ISBN 978-0-06-338297-8

24 25 26 27 28 LBC 5 4 3 2 1

TO ANASTASIA AND HELEN.
WE HOPE YOU LIKE THIS ONE.

ACKNOWLEDGMENTS

WE'D LIKE TO thank our editor, Erika Tsang, for her guidance and patience; our agent, Nancy Yost, and the crew at NYLA for putting up with our ridiculous demands; the wonderful folks at Avon Books for helping us turn manuscript into the book; Pam Jaffee for tirelessly promoting the series; Stephanie Stogiera for catching our mistakes; our beta readers for making the book even better; and finally, you, dear readers, for giving Hidden Legacy a chance.

CHAPTER 1

WHEN LIFE HITS you in the gut, it's always a sucker punch. You never see it coming. One moment you're walking along, worrying your little worries and making quiet plans, and the next you're rolled into a ball, trying to hug yourself against the pain, frantic and reeling, your mind a jumble of scared thoughts.

A Christmas wreath hung on our door. I paused with my hand above the lock's keypad. That's right. Today was Christmas. This morning I was at a mountain lodge playing in the snow with the most dangerous man in Houston. Then Rogan's surveillance expert texted him, and now here I stood, six hours later, my hair a mess, my clothes rumpled from being under a heavy jacket, in front of the warehouse that served as my family's home. I would have to go inside and break the ugly news, and nobody would like what was going to happen next. With everything that had happened, we had agreed not to exchange gifts this year. Not only had I missed Christmas Eve, but I was about to deliver one hell of a terrible present.

The main thing was not to panic. If I panicked, my sisters and my cousins would panic too. And my mother would do her best to talk me out of the only logical solution to our crisis. I'd managed to keep a lid on my emotions all the way from the lodge to the airport, during the flight on the private jet, and through the helicopter ride from the plane to the landing pad four blocks away. But now all my fears and stress were boiling over.

I took a deep breath. Around me the street was busy. Not as busy as it had been a few days ago, when I was helping Cornelius Harrison, an animal mage and now an employee of the Baylor Investigative Agency, find out who murdered his wife, Nari, but still busy. Rogan's views on security were rather draconian. He was in love with me, and had decided that my home wasn't assault-proof, and so he'd bought two square miles of industrial real estate around our warehouse and turned it into his own private military base.

Everyone wore civilian clothes, but they weren't fooling anyone. Rogan's people had all gone through armed forces in one way or another, and they didn't wander or stroll. They moved from point A to point B with a definite goal in mind. They kept their clothes clean, their hair short, and they called Rogan Major. When we made love, I called him Connor.

A dry popping sound came from the street. The memory of snapping David Howling's neck gripped me. I heard the crunch his bones made as I twisted his head to the side. In my mind, I saw him fall as I let go, and panic drowned me. I let it wash over me and waited for it to recede. Finding Nari's killer had been an ugly and brutal mess, and at the end I watched Olivia Charles, the woman who had murdered her, be eaten alive by a swarm of rats as Cornelius sang, mourning his wife. I relived her death in my dreams almost every night.

I didn't want to walk back into the world. I just . . . I just wanted a little bit more time.

I made myself look in the direction of the sound. An ex-soldier was coming my way, in his forties, with a scarred face, leading an enormous grizzly bear on a very thin leash. The bear wore a harness that read Sergeant Teddy.

The ex-soldier stretched his left arm and twisted, as if trying to slide the bones back in place. Another dry crunch, sending a fresh jolt of alarm through me. Probably an old injury.

The bear stopped and looked at me.

"Be polite," the soldier told him. "Don't worry. He just wants to say hi."

"I don't mind." I stepped closer to the bear. The massive beast leaned over to me and smelled my hair.

"Can I pet him?"

The soldier looked at Sergeant Teddy. The bear made a low, short noise.

"He says you can."

I reached over and carefully petted the big shaggy neck.

"What's his story?"

"Someone thought it would be a good idea to make very smart magic bears and use them in combat," the ex-soldier said. "Problem is, once you make someone smart, they become self-aware and call you on your bullshit. Sergeant Teddy is a pacifist. The leash is just for show so people don't freak out. Major bought him a couple of years ago. Major is of the opinion that fighting in a war shouldn't be forced on those who are morally opposed to it, human or bear."

"But you're still here," I told the bear.

He snorted and looked at me with chocolate-brown eyes.

"We offered him a very nice private property up in Alaska," the ex-soldier said. "But he doesn't like it. He says he gets bored. He mostly hangs out with us, eats cereal that's bad for him, and watches cartoons on Saturdays. And movies. He loves *The Jungle Book*."

I waited for the familiar buzz of my magic that told me he was pulling my leg, but none came.

Sergeant Teddy rose on his hind legs, blocking out the sun,

and put his shaggy front paws around me. My face pressed into fur. I hugged him back. We stood for a moment, then the grizzly dropped down and proceeded on his walk, his leash dangling on the ground.

I looked at the ex-soldier.

"He must've felt you needed a hug," he said. "He stays in HQ most of the time, so you can come and visit him."

"I will," I told him.

The ex-soldier nodded and followed the bear.

I punched my code into the lock. I had been hugged by a giant, superintelligent, pacifist bear. I could do this. I could do anything. I just had to walk in and call for a family meeting. It was almost dinnertime anyway. On a Sunday, everyone would be home.

I opened the door and walked into the small office space that housed Baylor Investigative Agency. A short hallway, three offices on the left, and a break room and conference room on the right. The temptation to hide in my office almost made me stop, but I kept going, through the hallway, to the other door that opened into the roughly three-thousand-square-foot space that served as our home. When we sold our house trying to raise money for my father's hospital bills, we moved our family into the warehouse to cut costs. We'd split the floor space into three distinct sections: the office, the living space, and beyond it, past a very tall wall, Grandma Frida's motor pool, where she worked on armored vehicles and mobile artillery for Houston's magical elite.

I took off my shoes and marched through the maze of rooms. Garlands hung on the walls. My sisters had been busy decorating.

Faint voices came from the kitchen. Mom . . . Grandma. Good. This would save me time.

I walked past a big Christmas tree set up in the hang-out room, stepped into the kitchen, and froze.

My mother and grandmother sat at our table. A young woman sat next to my grandmother. She was willowy and beautiful, with a heart-shaped face framed in waves of gorgeous red hair and eyes so grey, they looked silver.

Ice gripped my spine.

Rynda Charles. Rogan's ex-fiancée. Olivia's daughter.

"Do you remember me?" she asked. Her voice was breaking. Her eyes were bloodshot, her face so pale, her lips seemed almost white. "You killed my mother."

Somehow my mouth made words. "What are you doing here?"

Rynda wiped the tears from her eyes and stared at me, her face desperate. "I need your help."

I OPENED MY mouth. Nothing came out.

Mom made big eyes at me and nodded toward the table. I dropped my bag on the floor and sat.

"Drink your tea." Grandma Frida pushed a steaming mug toward Rynda.

Rynda picked it up and drank it, but her gaze was fixed on me. The desperation in her eyes turned to near panic. Right.

I closed my eyes, took a deep breath from the stomach all the way up, held it, and let it out slowly. One . . . two . . . Calm . . . calm . . .

"Nevada?" Grandma Frida asked.

"She's an empath Prime," I said. "I'm upset, so it's affecting her."

Rynda gave a short laugh, and I heard Olivia Charles in her voice. "Oh, that's rich."

Five . . . six . . . Breathe in, breathe out . . . Ten. Good enough.

I opened my eyes and looked at Rynda. I had to keep my voice and my emotions under control. "Your mother killed an entire crew of Rogan's soldiers and four lawyers, including two women your age. It was an unprovoked slaughter. Their husbands are now widowers and their children are motherless because of her."

"A person is never just one thing," Rynda said, putting the mug down. "To you she might have been a monster, but to me she was my mother. She was a wonderful grandmother to my children. She loved them so much. My mother-in-law doesn't care for them. They have no grandparents now."

"I'm sorry for your and their loss. I regret that things went the way they did. But it was a justified kill." Dear God, I sounded like my mother.

"I don't even know how she died." Rynda clenched her hands into a single fist. "They only gave me back her bones. How did my mother die, Nevada?"

I took a deep breath. "It wasn't an easy or a quick death."

"I deserve to know." There was steel in her voice. "Tell me."

"No. You said you needed my help. Something terrible must've happened. Let's talk about that."

Her hand shook, and the mug danced a little as she brought it to her lips. She took another swallow of her tea. "My husband is missing."

Okay. Missing husband. Familiar territory. "When was the last time you saw . . ." Rogan had said his name one time, what was it? ". . . Brian?"

"Three days ago. He went to work on Thursday and didn't come back. He doesn't answer his phone. Brian likes his routine. He's always home by dinner. It's Christmas Day. He wouldn't miss it." A note of hysteria crept into her voice. "I know what you'll ask: does he have a mistress, did we have a good marriage, does he disappear on drunken binges? No. No, he doesn't. He takes care of me and the kids. He comes home!"

She must've spoken to the Houston PD. "Did you fill out a missing person report?"

"Yes. They're not going to look for him." Her voice turned bitter. She was getting more agitated by the minute. "He's a Prime. It's House business. Except House Sherwood is convinced that Brian is okay and he's just taking a break. Nobody is looking for him, except me. Nobody is returning my calls. Even Rogan refuses to see me."

That didn't sound right. Rogan would never turn her away, even if I pitched a huge fit about it. I'd watched the two of them talking before. He liked her and he cared about her. "What did Rogan say exactly?"

"I came to him on Friday. His people told me he was out. He was out on Saturday too. I asked to wait, and they told me it was a waste of time. They didn't know when he would be back. I may be naive, but I'm not a fool. I know what that means. Two weeks ago, I had friends. I had my mother's friends, powerful, respected, and always so eager to do Olivia Charles a favor. Two weeks ago, one phone call and half of the city would be out looking for Brian. They would be putting pressure on the police, on the mayor, on the Texas Rangers. But now, everyone is out. Everyone is too busy to see me. There is an invisible wall around me. No matter how loud I scream, nobody can hear me. People just nod and offer platitudes."

"He didn't stonewall you," I said. "He was out of state. With me."

She stopped. "You're together?"

There was no point in lying. "Yes."

"The thing with my mother, it wasn't just a job for you?"

"No. She killed the wife of a man I consider a friend. He works here now."

Rynda put her hand over her mouth.

Silence fell, heavy and tense.

"I shouldn't have come here," she said. "I'll get the children and go."

"That's right," Grandma Frida said.

"No," Mom said. I knew that voice. That was Sergeant Mom voice. Rynda knew that voice too, because she sat up straighter. Olivia Charles was never in the military, but three minutes of talking to her had told me that she had ruled her household with an iron fist and had a very low tolerance for nonsense.

"You're here now," Mom said. "You came to us for help, because you had nowhere to turn and because you're scared for your husband and your children. You came to the right place. Nevada is very good at tracking missing people. Either she'll help you, or she will recommend someone who will."

Grandma Frida turned and looked at Mom as if she had sprouted a pineapple on her head.

"Right," I said. I may not have personally murdered Rynda's mother, but I made that death possible. And now she was a pariah, alone and scared. She had lost her mother, her husband, and all of the people she thought were her friends. I had to help her. I had to at least get her started in the right direction.

"Can I talk to the two of you for a damn minute?" Grandma Frida growled.

"One moment," I told Rynda and got up.

Grandma grabbed my arm with one hand, grabbed Mom's wrist with her other hand, and dragged us down the hallway all the way to the end, as far from the kitchen as we could get.

"Children?" I glanced at Mom.

"Your sisters are watching them. A boy and a girl."

"Have the two of you lost your damn minds?" Grandma Frida hissed.

"She isn't lying," I said. "Her husband is really gone."

"I expect that of her!" Grandma Frida pointed at me with her thumb, while glaring at my mother. "But you ought to know better, Penelope."

"That woman is at the end of her rope," Mom said. "How much do you think it cost her to come here? This is what we do. We help people like her."

"Exactly!" Grandma Frida hissed. "She's at the end of her rope. She's beautiful, rich, helpless, and she's desperately looking for someone to save her. And she's Rogan's ex-fiancée. There is no way Rogan and Rynda won't be spending time together if Nevada takes this case."

I stared at her.

"She's a man magnet." Grandma Frida balled her hands into fists. "They eat that helpless rescue-me crap up. Her husband has been gone for three days. If he hasn't run off, he's probably dead. She'll need consoling. She'll be looking for a shoulder to cry on, a big, strong shoulder. Do I need to spell it out? You're about to serve your boyfriend to her on a silver platter!"

Rynda was very beautiful and very helpless. I wanted to help her. I knew Rogan would too.

"It's not like that. He broke off their engagement."

Grandma Frida shook her head. "You told me they knew each other for years, since they were little kids. That kind of thing doesn't just go away. Rogan's people know it too; that's why they didn't give her any information. You're playing with fire, Nevada. Cut her loose. Let somebody else take care of her. She's a Prime. She's rich. She isn't your problem, unless you make her your problem."

I looked at Mom.

"Third rule," she said.

When Dad and Mom started the agency, they had only three rules: first, once we were paid, we stayed bought; second, we did everything we could to not break the law; and third, at the end of the day, we had to be able to look our reflection in the eye. I could live with Olivia's death. I had nightmares about it, but it was justified. Throwing Rynda out now, when she sat at our kitchen table, was beyond me. Where would she go?

"If Rynda's crying will make Rogan break up with me, then our relationship wouldn't last anyway."

Most of me believed the words that came out of my mouth, but a small, petty part didn't. That was okay. I was human, and I was entitled to a little bit of insecurity. But I was damned if I let it dictate my actions.

"Thank you, Grandma, but I've got it."

Grandma Frida threw her hands up in disgust. "When your heart breaks, don't come crying to me."

"I will anyway." I hugged her.

"Egh . . ." She made a show of trying to knock me off, then hugged me back.

I opened the door to the office and started down the hallway toward my desk and laptop that waited on it.

"It's James," Grandma Frida said mournfully behind me. "He ruined all of my practical grandchildren with his altruism."

Mom didn't answer. Dad had been dead seven years, but hearing his name still hurt her. It still hurt me.

I GRABBED THE laptop, a notepad, and the new client folder just in case, walked back into the kitchen, sat down at the table, and opened my laptop. A few keystrokes told me Bern was home and online.

I fired off a quick email. **Please send me the basics on Brian Sherwood ASAP.** I set the laptop aside and switched to the writing pad and a pen. People minded notes on paper a lot less than a laptop or being recorded, and I needed Rynda to relax. She was already keyed up.

"Let's start at the beginning."

"You don't like me," Rynda said. "I felt it back when we first met in the ballroom. You were jealous of me."

"Yes." That's what I get for deciding to take on an empath as a client.

"And when you walked in and saw me, you felt pity and fear."

"Yes."

"But you are going to help me anyway. Why? It's not guilt. Guilt is like plunging into a dark well. I would've felt that."

"You tell me."

Her eyes narrowed. Magic brushed me, featherlight. "Compassion," she said quietly. "And duty. Why would you feel a sense of duty toward me?"

"Have you ever held a job?"

She frowned. "No. We don't need the extra money."

That must be nice. "Do you have any hobbies? Any passions?"

"I . . . make sculptures."

"Do you sell them?"

"No. They're nothing spectacular. I've never participated in any exhibits."

"Then why do you keep making them?"

She blinked. "It makes me happy."

"Being a private investigator makes me happy. I'm not just doing it for the money. I'm doing it because sometimes I get to help people. Right now, you need help."

The laptop clicked. A new email, from Bern, popped into my inbox. Brian Sherwood, 32, second son of House Sherwood, Prime, herbamagos. Principal business: Sherwood BioCore. Estimated personal worth: $30 million. Wife: Rynda (Charles), 29. Children: Jessica, 6, and Kyle, 4. Siblings: Edward Sherwood, 38, Angela Sherwood, 23.

Brian Sherwood was a plant mage. Rynda was an empath with

a secondary telekenetic talent. That didn't add up. Primes usually married within their branch of magic. As Rogan once eloquently explained to me in his falling-on-his-sword speech, preserving and increasing magic within the family drove most of their marriage decisions.

I looked back to her. "I don't know yet if I'm your best option. It may be that you would be better served by a different agency. But before we talk about any of that, walk me through your Thursday. You woke up. Then what happened?"

She focused. "I got up. Brian was already awake. He'd taken a shower. I made breakfast and fixed the lunches for him and the kids."

"Do you fix their lunches every day?"

"Yes. I like doing it."

Brian Sherwood, worth thirty million dollars, took a brown-bag lunch his wife made to work every day. Did he eat it or throw it in the trash? That was the question.

"Brian kissed me and told me he would be home at the usual time."

"What time is that?"

"Six o'clock. I said we'd be having cubed steak for dinner. He asked if fries were involved."

She choked on a sob.

"Who took Jessica to school?"

She glanced at me, surprised. "How did you know her name?"

"My cousin pulled your public records." I turned the laptop so she could see.

She blinked. "My whole life in one paragraph."

"Keep going," I told her. "How did Jessica get to school?"

"Brian dropped her off. I took Kyle on a walk."

Lie.

"I called Brian around lunch. He answered."

Truth.

"What did you talk about?"

"Nothing serious."

Lie.

"I'm not your enemy. It would help if you were honest with me. Let's try this again. Where did you and Kyle go and what was the phone call about?"

She set her lips into a flat, hard line.

"Everything you tell me now is confidential. It isn't privileged, like conversations with your attorney, which means I will have to disclose it in a court proceeding. But short of that, it won't go anywhere."

She covered her face with her hands, thought about it for a long moment, and exhaled. "Kyle's magic hasn't manifested. I manifested by two, Brian manifested by four months, Jessica manifested at thirteen months. Kyle is almost five. He's late. We're taking him to a specialist. I always call Brian after every session, because he wants to know how Kyle did."

For a Prime, a child with no magic would be devastating. Rogan's voice popped into my head. *You think you won't care about it, but you will. Think of your children and having to explain that their talents are subpar, because you have failed to secure a proper genetic match.*

"Your anxiety spiked. Why? Was it something I said? Is the specialist important?"

"I don't know yet." She would be a really difficult client. She registered every emotional twitch I made. "Did Kyle manifest?"

"No."

"What happened next?"

She sighed and went through her day. She picked up Jessica, fed the kids, then they read books and watched cartoons together. She made dinner, but Brian didn't show. She called his cell several times over the next two hours and finally called his brother. Edward Sherwood was still at work. He had happened to look out the window when Brian had left at his usual time and remembered watching him get into his car. Just to be sure, Edward walked down to Brian's office and reported that it was empty. He also called down to the front desk, and the guard confirmed that Brian had signed out, left the building a quarter before six, and didn't return.

"How far is your house from Sherwood's BioCore?"

"It's a ten-minute drive. We live in Hunters Creek Village. Bio-Core is at Post Oak Circle, near the Houstonian Hotel. It's three and a half miles down Memorial Drive. Even with heavy traffic, he's usually home in fifteen minutes."

"Did Edward mention if Brian was planning to make any stops?"

"He didn't know. He said he wasn't aware of any meetings scheduled that afternoon."

"Did he sound concerned?"

She shook her head. "He said he was sure Brian would show up. But I knew something was wrong. I just *knew*."

All the standard things someone does when their loved one is missing followed: calls to hospitals and police stations, driving the route to look for the stranded car, talking with people at his work, calling other family members asking if they heard anything, and so on.

"He didn't come home," she said, her voice dull. "In the morning I called Edward. He told me not to worry. He said Brian had seemed tense lately and that he would turn up. I told him I would file the police report. He said that he didn't feel there was a need for it, but if it would make me feel better, I should file it."

"How did he seem to you?"

"He seemed concerned for me."

Interesting. "For you? Not for Brian?"

"For me and the kids."

"And Brian has never done anything like this before?"

She didn't answer.

"Rynda?"

"He disappears sometimes when he's stressed," she said quietly. "He used to. But not for the last three years and never this long. You have to understand, Brian isn't a coward, he just needs stability. He likes when things are calm."

That explained why his brother didn't immediately sound the alarm and bring all hands on deck. "Can you tell me more about it? The last time he disappeared?"

"It was after Kyle's one-year birthday party. Edward asked him if Kyle manifested, and Brian told him no. Then Joshua, Brian's father—he died a year later—said that Brian and I better get on with making another one, because Jessica is an empath like me, and a dud can't lead the family."

He called his grandson a dud. Ugh.

"Thank you," Rynda said.

"For what?"

"For your disgust. Brian's anxiety spiked. I felt an intense need to escape coming from him, so I told them that it was late and the children were tired. The family left. Brian didn't come back to bed. He got into his car and drove off. He came home the next evening. That was the longest he had ever disappeared during our marriage."

"Did he say where he went?"

"He said he just drove. He eventually found some small hotel and spent the night there. He came home because he realized that he had no place to go and he missed me and the kids. He would never leave me, and the last time I saw him, he was calm."

Truth.

I rubbed my forehead. "Did you share this with the police?"

"Yes."

And they dismissed her as being a hysterical woman whose husband bolted when the pressure became too much.

"Do you have access to Brian's bank accounts?"

"Yes." She blinked.

"Can you check if there has been any activity? Has he used his cards in the last few days?"

She grabbed her purse, rummaged through it frantically. "Why didn't I think of . . ." She pulled the phone out and stabbed at it.

A moment passed. Another.

Her face fell. "No. Nothing."

"Rynda, did you kill your husband?"

She stared at me.

"I need an answer."

"No."

"Do you know what happened to him?"

"No!"

"Do you know where he is?"

"No!"

True on all counts.

"There are several possibilities," I said. "First, something bad could have happened to Brian as a result of House politics or his job. Second, something traumatic could've occurred during the workday on Thursday that caused him to go into hiding. I can look for your husband. Alternatively, I can recommend Montgomery International Investigations."

When Dad got sick, we'd mortgaged the business to MII, and their owner, Augustine Montgomery, and our family had a complicated history, but that didn't change the fact that MII was her best bet.

"They are a premier agency, and they are very well equipped to handle things like this. You can afford them. You should be aware that Baylor's a small firm with a fraction of MII's resources."

Rynda sat very still.

Someone pounded down the hallway on small feet.

"Mom!" A small boy ran into the kitchen carrying a piece of paper. He had dark hair and Rynda's silver eyes. She opened her arms, and he thrust a piece of paper at her. "I drew a tank! They have a tank in their garage!"

Catalina walked into the room, dark-haired, slender, a small smile on her face. "Kyle wanted to show you."

"That's a scary tank," Rynda said.

"Come on." My sister held out her hand. "I'll show you more cool stuff."

Kyle put the paper in front of his mother. "It's a present for you. I'll draw one for Dad!" He took off at a run. Catalina sighed and chased him.

Rynda watched him go with an odd look on her face.

"I've talked to MII." She swallowed, and I saw a shadow of her mother's ruthless logic in her eyes. "Montgomery turned me down."

Augustine Montgomery declined to get involved. Interesting. I really was her last resort.

"Very well," I said. "I will look for Brian."

She shifted in her seat and blurted out, "I want a contract."

"Okay."

"I don't want this to be an act of charity. I want to pay you."

"That's fine."

"I want things defined and professional."

"As do I."

"And our relationship is that of a client and service provider."

"Agreed," I said.

A door swung open. A thunderstorm appeared behind me and was moving through our house, churning with power and magic. Rogan.

He reached my kitchen and loomed in the doorway, tall, broad-shouldered, his blue eyes dark and his magic wrapped around him like a vicious pet snapping its savage teeth. If I didn't know him, I would've backed away and pulled my gun out.

"Connor!" Rynda jumped up from behind the table, cleared the distance between them, and hugged him.

And jealousy stabbed me right in the heart. He was mine.

Rogan gently put his arms around her, his blue eyes fixed on me. "Are you okay?"

"No." Rynda choked on a sob. "Brian is missing."

He was still looking at me. I nodded. *Yes. I'm okay.*

Rynda pulled away from him. "I didn't know where to go. I . . ."

"I'm going to take care of it," I told Rogan.

"Nevada is the best you can get," he said, his voice perfectly calm.

I checked my laptop: 5:47 p.m. "Rynda, I have some paperwork for you to sign. There are some preliminary things I can do today, but tomorrow I'll go and knock on BioCore's doors. It would make things easier for me if you called ahead and advised the family that I'll be coming by."

"I'll come with you," she said.

"It would be best if I went by myself," I told her. "People may say things to me that they might not mention in your presence. If I'll require access to Sherwood family spaces or other restricted areas, I'll definitely ask you to come with me."

"What do I do now?" She was looking at Rogan, not at me.

"Sign the paperwork and go home. Brian might call or show up," Rogan said. "You're not alone, Rynda. Nevada will help you. I will help you."

"I hate you for killing my mother," she told him, her voice strained.

"I know," he said. "It couldn't be helped."

"Everything is falling apart, Connor. How can it all just crumble like that?"

"It's House life," he said.

Rynda's shoulders stooped. She turned to me. "Where do I sign?"

I walked her through the paperwork, fees, and stipulations. She signed and went to collect her children.

Rogan waited until she was out of sight and stepped close to me.

"She'll need an escort home," I said. "And someone to watch the house." There was no telling where this investigation would lead, and extra security was never a bad idea.

"I'll take care of it," he said, and kissed me. It was a sudden, hard kiss, fierce and hot. It burned like fire.

We broke apart, and I saw the dragon in his eyes. Rogan was preparing to go to war.

"Your grandmother is in the city," he said, and pressed a USB drive into my hand. "You must decide tonight."

He turned and walked away, the memory of his kiss still scorching me.

I took a deep breath and plugged the USB into my laptop.

CHAPTER 2

THE FAMILY SAT at the dining table. I took the head spot this time. A stack of papers sat on my right, covered with a folder. I'd printed out the contents of the USB drive.

My two sisters had taken the chairs next to me, Catalina on my right, Arabella on my left. Catalina, who was a week shy of turning eighteen, was dark-haired, serious, and calm. She liked math, because it made sense to her, and would do just about anything to not be the center of attention. Arabella, still fifteen, was blond, athletic, with bigger boobs and a curvier butt, and calm wasn't even in her vocabulary. She liked forensics and humanities. "Calling people out" was her preferred method of dealing with issues. The high school debate club, which made the fatal mistake of snubbing her because she was a freshman at the time and their roster was full, lived in mortal terror of her.

Bernard, the oldest of our two cousins, sat next to Catalina. Over six feet tall, with shoulders that had trouble fitting through narrow doorways, Bern was built like he broke people for a living. He had wrestled in high school and still went to judo a few times a week, which he claimed he was doing to balance long hours spent writing computer code. When he was a kid, his hair had been the color of straw and curly. The curls were all gone now. His hair had turned dark blond, and he kept it cut short and messy.

His brother Leon was just about his exact opposite. Lean, dark, and fast, Leon alternated between sarcasm, excitement, and total gloom as quickly as his sixteen-year-old body could produce the hormones. He hero-worshipped his brother. He also thought he himself was a dud without any magic. I knew he wasn't, and I was doing my best to keep that knowledge to myself, because there was only one type of job open to someone with Leon's magical talent, and it wasn't a job any of us would've liked him to have. Right now, only Bug, who was Rogan's surveillance expert, my mother, and I knew what he was capable of, and the only reason I told Mom was because his talent would explode into light sooner or later, and if I wasn't around, someone else would have to handle it. Sooner or later I would have to tell Leon.

My mother sat at the other end of the table. She used to be a soldier, but her time as a POW left her with a permanent limp. She was softer now, her brown hair braided and pinned at the nape of her neck. Her eyes were brown like mine. When Dad got sick and after his death, Mom kept us together. I was just now beginning to understand how much it had cost her.

Grandma Frida sat beside Mom. One of my earliest memories was playing on the floor of the motor pool with little model cars, and Grandma Frida, who still had some blond in her hair back then, humming softly as she worked on some giant vehicle. Most people smelled engine oil and rubber and thought *mechanic*. I thought *Grandma*.

Family.

I loved them all so much. I had to do everything I could to keep them safe. This would be a Christmas we'd never forget.

"Victoria Tremaine knows who we are," I said.

The words hit the table like a pile of bricks. Arabella paled. Catalina bit her lip. Bern became very still. Leon, oblivious, frowned at the pinched expressions he saw. Nobody spoke.

Truthseeker talents like mine were very rare. There were only three truthseeker Houses in the United States. House Tremaine was the smallest and the most feared. It had only one member—Victoria Tremaine. And she was coming for us.

"How sure are you?" Mom finally asked.

"She tried to purchase our mortgage."

Mom swore.

"I thought House Montgomery owned our mortgage," Leon said.

"House Montgomery owns the mortgage on our business," Bernard said patiently. "The mortgage on the warehouse was held by a private bank until Rogan bought it."

"To bring everyone up to speed," I said before they could go off on a tangent, "Dad was Victoria's only child. He was born without magic, and she hated him for it. He ran away after high school, met Mom, and lived quietly, so she never found him. But now she knows. She's the only member of her family. Once she dies, House Tremaine will die with her."

"How did I not know this?" Leon asked. "Am I the only one who didn't know this? You guys knew and didn't tell me?"

I raised my hand. "The point is, Victoria Tremaine desperately needs us. She's the only surviving Prime of her House."

"The House is everything," Bern said quietly. "She needs you and the girls to qualify as Primes so she can keep her House alive."

"Question!" Leon said. "If she is the only Prime, how can she still be a House?"

"Every time a new Prime is registered, the Office of Records checks to see if the family has two Primes," Catalina said. "If there are two living Primes, the family is recertified as a House. They don't take away the family's rank until the last Prime alive at the last certification dies."

My sister had been reading up on Houses.

"You know what I can do," I said.

I could do plenty. Being able to detect a lie was the least of my talents. I could crack a human mind like a walnut and pull whatever knowledge I needed out of it. And I didn't have to leave the mind intact.

"Victoria can do everything I do and much more, and she does it better. I'm just now figuring out the extent of my power. She's been trained in the use of magic since she could hold chalk in her hand. She has power, money, and troops we don't. She'll do whatever she has to do to gain control of me and Catalina at the very least."

Grandma Frida put her hand over her mouth.

Bernard was usually calm and steady, like a rock in a storm. But right now his eyes were full of fear. "She can do things with Catalina's talent."

Unspeakable, ugly things. Things that would make my thoughtful, kind sister hate herself.

"And if Arabella's magic is discovered . . ." I didn't finish.

I didn't even want to go there. They would lock her away and keep her sedated for the rest of her life. She would never get to see the sun. She'd never laugh again, never love, never live.

My grandmother wouldn't get her claws on my sisters. I wouldn't let it happen.

Catalina leaned forward, her eyes defiant. "What are our options?"

I checked my mother's face. She was sitting still, her expression grim.

"We can roll over," I said. "That will likely mean that you and I will have to do whatever Victoria says. We'll have to walk away from our business."

Catalina winced. Our parents built Baylor Investigative Agency, and I spent seven years growing it. It wasn't just a business. It was the future and the core of our family.

I had to keep going. "We probably won't see Mom, Grandma Frida, or Bern and Leon again for a while."

That got me a look of pure horror.

"We'd have to obey her and do whatever she wanted. I would be doing interrogations and lobotomizing people." I kept my voice even. They didn't need emotion from me right now. "Eventually Victoria will die. She's old."

And that didn't sound morbid. Not at all.

I forged on. "Eventually we'd inherit House Tremaine."

"How long?" Leon asked.

"I don't know. She's in her seventies. Ten years, maybe twenty."

"Door number two, please," Arabella said.

"I agree," Bern said. "We're not doing that."

"We can fight," I said. "Victoria has more money, more troops, and more of everything."

"But Rogan would help us, right?" Arabella asked.

I struggled with the right words. "Yes. But we can't always count on Rogan."

Strictly speaking, that was a lie. Rogan would do anything and everything to help me.

"We *shouldn't* always count on Rogan," Mom said.

Everyone looked at her.

"This isn't his problem," she said. "It's our problem."

"If we let Rogan save us, we'll be tying ourselves to him," I said. "We'd be viewed as his vassals. We'd have his protection, but we would inherit his enemies, and he has some powerful ones."

"And if your relationship with Rogan sours, things will get complicated," Bern said.

"Yes."

"So we don't want to give up and we can't fight the Evil Grandma. Is there a third option?" Arabella asked.

"Yes. We can become a House."

My sisters and cousins stared at me. I'd brought up this possibility once before, but we were kind of busy at the time trying to solve a murder and accomplishing other important things like not getting killed.

"Whoa." Leon blinked.

"No," Mom said. "There has to be another way."

I leaned back. "Becoming a House would grant us provisional immunity from any attacks by other Houses for three years. That's long enough for us to establish a power base."

"Would Victoria follow that rule?" Catalina asked.

"Rogan says she will. It's in everyone's best interest to protect emerging Houses, because otherwise inbreeding would become a real danger. Apparently, this is one of those rules Primes won't break under any circumstances. It would buy us time to build up our power base and make alliances and do all the things Houses do."

"You can't be serious," Mom said.

"I am."

"She isn't going to obey any rules. That woman is a monster. You can't be that naive, Nevada."

I met my mother's gaze. "Yes, she may still attack us. But she will have to do it in a way that can't lead back to her. Becoming a House would make it much harder for her to hit us." And once we became a House, we could make alliances as equals.

"You're filling their heads with visions of being a House. Why don't you tell them what it's really like? Tell them about Baranovsky."

"Mom is right," I said. "Houses are vicious. You remember

that charity gala I went to in the black dress? It was very exclusive. The man who hosted it, Gabriel Baranovsky, was drinking champagne at the top of the stairs in the ballroom. David Howling froze the wine in Gabriel's throat. He turned it into a blade that sliced Gabriel's neck from inside out."

"Badass," Leon offered.

We all looked at him.

"It's elegant," he said. "The ice melts, and there is no evidence. There are no prints, no murder weapon, there is nothing."

I had to tell him about his magic. There just wasn't any escaping it. That's the way his mind worked and there was no way to rewire him. Maybe I could just get it over with now.

My mother cleared her throat and hit me with a warning stare. It's like she was telepathic or something.

"When Baranovsky choked on his own blood and collapsed, nobody helped him," I said. "Nobody screamed. Hundreds of Primes turned and calmly started walking toward the exit, because the mansion would be locked down and they didn't want to be inconvenienced."

I waited a moment to let it sink in.

"Primes won't care that you are young. They won't be kind. They will try to use us, manipulate us, or destroy us. You could be standing in the middle of the Assembly, and if a Prime summoned a pack of wild wolves to rip you to pieces, I'm not sure anyone would help. This would be our life."

Their faces were grim. I was losing them. I expected that Mom wouldn't be on my side, but I had to at least convince my sisters.

"But if we do this, we can build up our strength for three years," I said. "Victoria is coming for us now. Right now. She's in town. The only reason she isn't attacking us is because Rogan's people are fortified around us. She'd have to go through them, and she doesn't want to start a fight with House Rogan unless she has to."

"Pack your bags," Mom said. "The five of you are leaving."

"Mom?" Arabella stared at her. "We can't leave."

"Out of the question." I knew she would react like this.

"I'm not quitting college," Bern said.

"We aren't leaving you!" Catalina's voice spiked. "We are *not* abandoning you and Grandma!"

My mother put steel into her voice. "You heard me."

"Where?" Grandma Frida asked, her voice so high, it sounded broken.

Mom turned to her.

"Where can you send them so that bitch doesn't find them, Penelope? She knows what they look like. She knows their names. She knows their social security numbers. She can pull the truth out of anyone she meets. Where on the planet can you find a place where her money and power won't reach?"

"Mom," my mother said quietly, looking stunned.

"I told you twenty-six years ago that if you married him, you would pay the price. I told you to let him go. You didn't listen. You raised them to fight. They're not going to cut and run now."

"They will do what I say," Mom ground out. "I'm their mother."

Grandma Frida squinted at her. "Aha. And how did that work out for me?"

Mom opened her mouth and clicked it shut.

"What's involved in becoming a House?" Catalina asked.

"At least two of us will have to undergo the trials and register as Primes," I said. "Most likely it will be you and me."

My sister frowned. "What if I don't qualify?"

"I'll do it!" Arabella announced.

"No," everyone said at the same time.

"Why not?"

"You know why not," my mother said. "Don't make me pull that documentary out again."

My sister took a deep breath. Uh-oh.

"I'm not going to spend my life hiding. Nobody will ever see what I can do!" She pounded her small fist on the table. "I'm going to qualify."

My mother's face told me that I had to fix this fast or she would snap and try to send everyone into exile again.

"You can control your magic," I said.

"Yes!" Arabella said.

"We know this, but nobody else does. People are afraid, because the last person with your magic lost control. The only way they'll accept you is if all of us demonstrate that you have complete control over yourself, and we, as a family, have complete control of you. This takes time. If you give us these three years, by the end of it we'll be established as a House. And then, at eighteen, you can qualify."

"Nevada!" Mom snarled.

"But this also means that for the next three years all of us will be in the limelight," I continued. "And you have to stop acting like an impulsive brat."

"Yes," Catalina piled on. "No more angry outbursts, no more screaming, no more punching people or starting shit online."

Arabella crossed her arms on her chest. "Fine. But you promise me! You promise me right now that if I behave, I'll qualify in three years."

"I promise."

My mother punched the table.

"So that's where she gets it from," Bern observed.

"What's the alternative?" Grandma Frida asked Mom.

"Not getting locked away for life, where they would keep her constantly sedated," Mom growled.

"There are some other formalities," I said. "Everyone who is qualifying will have to give a DNA sample, so they can make sure we are all related. We'll have to submit some paperwork, they will set the date for the trials, then we are tested, and if we qualify, we become a House."

"That's it?" Leon asked.

"Yes." I put my hand on the stack of paperwork. "If we decide to do this, that's it. There is no backing out."

"What if we don't qualify?" Catalina asked. "We'll look like weaklings who wanted to be Primes and fell short. Nobody would do business with us again."

"We'll qualify. I'm a Prime and so are you."

"They might not even know what my magic is," she insisted. "What if I permanently affect people? What if—"

"Oh shut up," Arabella told her. "You made an army of hired killers sit on the floor and listen to your story like they were in kindergarten. And they're all fine now."

"I want to register as well," Bern said. "Maybe not as a Prime, but the last time they tested me, I was ten. I'm stronger now."

Leon dramatically collapsed on the back of his chair. "Rub it in, all of you. You and your magic. I'll just sit here with my dud self."

I opened my mouth and shut it. Now wasn't the time to spring it on him.

"Nevada, there has to be another way," Mom said.

"I don't know what that is," I told her. "And neither does Rogan. If I knew of another way, I would take it, Mom. I promise you, I would. This is the only way we can keep all of us safe."

"If we do this, we'll never be safe," Mom said.

"Things will never be the same if we do this." That wasn't exactly a response to what she said, but I had to keep going. "Which is why we have to vote as a family. We all share responsibility for this decision. Once we make it, nobody complains and everyone has to work together. Does anyone want to add anything?"

Silence.

"Everyone for becoming a House, raise your hands."

I held my hand up. Bern, Arabella, Leon, and Grandma.

"Everyone for running away and hiding?"

Mom raised her hand.

I looked at Catalina.

"I'm abstaining," she said.

"You don't get to abstain," Arabella said. "For once in your life, make a decision!"

Catalina took a deep breath. "I vote for the House."

"Fools," my mother said. "I've raised a pack of nincompoops."

"But we're your nincompoops," Leon said.

I picked up the paperwork bristling with colored flags indicating signature lines. "I need all of you to sign."

"Wait!" Grandma Frida grabbed her phone. "We must take a picture for posterity."

They crowded into the shot around me. Grandma Frida set the phone on a delay and it snapped an image of all of them around me, the paperwork in front of me, a pen in my hand. Cold froze my stomach.

I loved them so much. I just hoped I made the right call.

THE OFFICE OF House Records occupied a short tower of black glass on Old Spanish Trail, across the street from the Bureau of Vital Statistics. The asymmetric building leaned back, textured, its profile odd. As Rogan pulled his gunmetal-grey Range Rover into the parking lot, I saw the front of the tower. It was shaped like a feathered quill.

The setting sun played on the dark glass. Only a handful of cars waited in the parking lot.

"Are you sure he will be there?" I asked.

"Yes."

"It's Christmas Day."

Rogan turned to me. "He will be there, because I called and asked."

I gripped the zippered file so hard, my fingers went white. Last chance to back out.

Rogan reached over, his magic curling around me. He took my hand and held it in his. "Do you want me to turn around?"

"No." I swallowed. "Let's do this."

We got out of the car and walked to the door. It slid open with a whisper, and we stepped into a modern lobby. Black granite sheathed the walls, grey granite shone on the floor, and in the center of the lobby, thin lines of gold traced a magic circle. A guard looked at us from behind his desk and bowed his head. Rogan led me past him to the elevators.

The folder seemed so heavy in my hands. All my doubts bubbled up and refused to disappear.

"Am I doing the right thing?"

"You're doing the only thing that makes sense to keep your family safe."

"What if I don't qualify?"

"You stood toe-to-toe with Olivia Charles, a manipulator Prime, and you won." His voice was steady. "You will qualify."

"Thank you for coming with me."

He didn't answer. He'd made it clear in the past that he expected me to walk away from him the moment our family became a House. He didn't think our magic was compatible. If we had children, they might not even be Primes. He viewed this as the beginning of our end, but he came anyway. He was also in complete denial if he thought I'd let him get away. He was mine. My Connor.

The elevator opened. We stepped into a hallway, with a dozen doors branching off from it, all closed. At the very end of the row of doors, large double doors stood open. We walked toward those doors, then through the doorway, into a huge circular room. Books lined the walls, thousands of books on the curved wooden shelves, three stories high, each floor with its own railed balcony. A grouping of comfortable couches upholstered in dark leather occupied the center of the room. Directly in front of it, between us and the couches, a round counter rose.

An old man sat behind the counter, reading a book. His skin was a warm brown, pointing at a Latin American heritage, his hair was white, and he wore a three-piece grey suit with a tartan bow tie. He raised his head, smiled at us, and hopped off his chair. His eyes, behind large glasses, were very dark, almost black, and shiny like two pieces of obsidian.

"Ms. Baylor," he said, his voice soft and cultured. "Finally."

"I'm sorry to trouble you on a holiday."

He smiled wider, showing white teeth. "Don't mention it. It is, after all, my job. I would've done it anyway. I was in downtown Houston, in the tunnels, when the Old Justice Center fell. I owe you and Mr. Rogan my life."

A man emerged from a shadowy alcove in the side wall, moving silently across the floor. In his mid-twenties, he wore expensive shoes and a sharp black suit, with a white shirt that looked even whiter against his light bronze skin, and a black tie. Black and grey tattoos covered his hands and neck. His dark brown hair, cut short on the sides, but longer on top of his head and slicked back, defined a long handsome face, with intelligent eyes the color of whiskey. He looked dangerous and slightly mournful, like a Prohibition-era gangster at a funeral.

"It's not every day one gets to register an emerging House," the Records Keeper continued. He leaned closer and smiled at me, as if sharing a secret. "Especially one with a truthseeker in it. I'm so very excited to meet you. Michael is also very excited, aren't you, Michael?"

Michael nodded.

The Records Keeper put on a pair of linen gloves and turned around. Behind him a massive book lay on a pedestal under a glass hood. He raised the hood, picked up the heavy volume, bound in marbled leather, and placed it on the counter. An elaborate gold crest decorated the front panel.

"It's beautiful," I said.

"It is. Eighteenth-century Dutch binding. The Houses of Texas have been recorded in this book since before statehood." He opened it gently and showed me an empty page. "If you pass the trials, your House will be written here."

He turned the heavy pages to the red bookmark. Four columns of names written in beautiful calligraphy covered the page. Some were crossed out.

"Are those the people who failed the trials?"

He nodded. "Indeed. Now then, do you have the necessary paperwork?"

I passed him the folder. He opened it, scanning the pages.

"Where is the second witness?" Rogan asked.

"Running late. Given the circumstances, I wanted to make sure to select someone whose reputation is beyond contestation. Someone whose name commands respect. I think you'll be pleasantly surprised."

"A witness to the emergence of a House has certain obligations," Rogan told me quietly.

"Like what?"

"We're expected to offer advice and guidance."

The Keeper checked the signatures and raised his head.

"You've presented us with a conundrum, Mr. Rogan. Finding a suitable test for a truthseeker was challenging, but identifying the younger Ms. Baylor's magic was even more so. I must say, your sister's power is something truly remarkable. It is, of course, a mental branch, but what subset? One would naturally lean toward a psionic, but a psionic who evokes a genuine love has never manifested. Michael and I had to dig very far through our archives and other archives. Favors were called in, access to databases had to be requested, and foreign Keepers of Records were consulted. But we persevered, didn't we, Michael?"

Michael nodded again.

"We had to reach very far, and we finally found what we were looking for in Greece. There is a single House—just one, mind you—whose record showed the emergence of a similar talent. Only in female offspring. The last verified manifestation was in the 1940s. Apparently, there was some unpleasantness."

"What kind of unpleasantness?" I asked.

"The lady in question fought against the Russian Imperial invasion of their small city. The legend states that she placed herself onto a rocky island a short distance from the cliffs and then called an entire battalion of the invading Russian troops to her. She drowned three motorized rifle companies before the few survivors finally managed to reach the rock. She was torn apart. Quite literally, I'm afraid."

Oh, Catalina . . . I could picture my sister on that rock. That's exactly what she would do.

"Dreadful business." The Records Keeper sighed. "The House hasn't had any female heirs since then. A very knowledgeable source has speculated that it was a matter of choice rather than chance."

"They abort female children?" Rogan asked, his voice cold.

"Such is the rumor. The House refused our attempts to reach them for a consult. They're a very reclusive family. Thus, we are left on our own, so after much deliberation, we are creating a new category for Ms. Catalina Baylor." The Keeper paused. "We shall refer to her as siren."

She would hate that.

"It is so very exciting. If this magic endures within your family, this may be the beginning of a whole new subset. The rankings of the rare magic talents may shift. We're bringing in a powerful antistasi Prime for her trials."

Like aegis mages who blocked bullets and physical attacks, antistasi mages specialized in defense, but against mental attacks. Well, at least that should put Catalina's mind to rest.

"Which House?" Rogan asked. "Smith?"

"Alessandro Sagredo," the Keeper said.

Rogan raised his eyebrows.

I glanced at him.

"The best antistasi Prime on record," Rogan explained.

"We're taking no chances," the Keeper said. "Unfortunately, he is otherwise engaged at the moment, so we will have to wait a couple of days. Therefore, your trials will be set exactly one week from now, next Sunday."

A man marched into the room. In his sixties, but still athletic, he wore black pants, a black T-shirt, and a black garment that could be called a sweatshirt in the same way a Porsche could be called a car. It had notched lapels like a suit, the stylish drape of a luxury trench coat, and likely cost more than our mortgage payment.

His skin was a light bronze, his hair wavy and black with a lot of white. He had bold, strong features: a broad forehead, black eyebrows, a prominent nose, and a square jaw mostly hidden by a short beard that was more grey than black. His hazel eyes, alight with intelligence, looked at the world with a touch of humor. When I saw him for the first time, I thought he looked like someone's favorite uncle, who owned a vineyard somewhere in Greece or Spain, spent a lot of time outdoors, and laughed often. That was before I knew who he was.

"Good evening, Mr. Duncan." The Keeper smiled.

My House formation would be witnessed by Mad Rogan, the Scourge of Mexico, and Linus Duncan, the former Speaker of the Assembly that ruled the magical families of Texas. Dear God.

"I'm late, I know, I'm sorry." The former most powerful man in Texas hurried across the room. "Some people insist on being annoyingly difficult. What did I miss?"

"Nothing of importance," the Keeper assured him.

Duncan nodded at Rogan. "Major."

"Colonel," Rogan replied.

The Keeper took out a fountain pen, cleared his throat, and glanced at me, his black eyes sparkling behind his glasses. "Michael, if you please."

Michael stepped forward and produced a high-end camera.

"A verbal acknowledgment is required," the Keeper told me, his tone confidential. "You must say these words to me: I, Nevada Baylor, petition the State of Texas for assessment and recognition of my family's powers. Are you ready?"

"Yes."

My heart was beating too fast.

The Keeper nodded at Michael. Michael tapped the camera's digital screen.

The Keeper raised his pen and looked at me. My mouth had gone completely dry. Somehow I made my lips move.

"I, Nevada Baylor, petition the State of Texas for assessment and recognition of my family's powers."

"I, Linus Duncan, Head of House Duncan, so witness," Duncan stated.

"I, Connor Rogan, Head of House Rogan, so witness," Rogan echoed.

"So noted." The Keeper wrote today's date on the page and added, *Nevada Baylor on behalf of herself, Catalina and Bernard Baylor. Witnessed by Linus Duncan of House Duncan and Connor Rogan of House Rogan.*

"Your petition is granted," the Keeper said.

Michael lowered the camera and set it aside.

"It is done," the Keeper said.

"Congratulations, Ms. Baylor," Linus Duncan told me.

"Thank you for coming to be my witness."

"Well, if you're going to jump into the wolf's den, it helps to have an ally. Even if that ally is old with blunted teeth."

A muscle in Rogan's cheek jerked. He hadn't said anything, but both he and Michael watched Linus Duncan like he would sprout fangs and claws any second.

"I hope you succeed," Duncan said.

"Thank you."

The sound of a woman coming down the hallway in high heels echoed through the room.

"Are you expecting someone?" Rogan asked.

"No," the Keeper said.

Victoria Tremaine walked into the room, two men in suits behind her. She saw me, stopped, and stared. I stared back. I'd seen a recording of her, but we'd never met in person.

She was thin, impeccably dressed, with the kind of face that made people say, "good bones" despite wrinkled skin. High cheekbones, strong yet feminine jawline, narrow nose, large eyes. Given that set of features, most women would look beautiful. My

grandmother didn't. She looked hard and vicious, like a veloci-
raptor in human skin. Even her platinum hair, cut in a pixie style,
did nothing to soften the impact. Vulnerable or unsure weren't
even in her vocabulary. And when she turned to glower at Rogan,
I saw my father in her profile. They had the same aquiline nose.

Rogan stepped forward on my left. Linus Duncan stepped forward on my right.

"This farce has gone on long enough," Victoria announced.
"That child is mine. She belongs to my House."

"No," I told her. "I don't belong to you or anyone else."

"She petitioned the State of Texas for recognition of her powers," the Keeper said. "She's in the book. It is done."

"Linus?" she ground out.

"I'm a witness," Duncan said. "I'm honor bound to protect her,
Victoria. You know how this works."

Victoria Tremaine's eyes narrowed. "I'm taking her out of
here."

"I'm afraid I can't allow that." The Keeper's eyes turned completely black. No white remained.

Darkness shivered in the alcoves between the books and grew,
slithering across the walls, swallowing the light, a living terrible
darkness. An ancient primal thing. Every hair on the back of my
neck rose.

Blue fire sheathed Michael's hands, burning bright against
the rising black tide that smothered the ceiling.

"You know the rules, Victoria," the Keeper said, his voice pure
magic. "You will have no contact with any member of the Baylor
family. You'll make no effort to disrupt these trials. We wouldn't
want any unpleasantness."

Rage shivered in the corners of my grandmother's mouth. She
glared at me. " You will regret this."

Her gaze stabbed at Rogan. "You should've returned my calls.

You think you have her, but you'll never keep her. She'll dump you the moment the Scroll gets a request."

She turned around and marched out, her human Rottweilers in tow.

"Well, that was tense," Linus Duncan said. He opened a billfold, took a card out of his wallet, and offered it to me. It had no name, only a phone number. "In case you need help or advice. Call any time."

"Thank you." I took the card.

The darkness vanished. The Keeper smiled at me. "It was a pleasure to meet you, Ms. Baylor. We'll be watching you. We'll be there in case of any problems, won't we, Michael?"

Michael nodded.

Rogan and I didn't speak the whole way to the car. Outside, the sun had set and the bottomless Texas sky spread above us, an upside-down black ocean studded with stars. We got into the car, and Rogan drove out of the parking lot.

The night city slid past my window while the whole scene kept replaying in my head over and over: petitioning, my name in calligraphy on the page of an ancient book, the raptor stare of my grandmother, the living darkness on the ceiling . . . It didn't seem real, as if it had happened to someone else.

I glanced at Rogan. There was this odd distance between us. He was there, in the car with me, but he seemed contained, as if I were a stranger.

"She called you?" I asked finally.

"She left a message," he said.

I waited, but he didn't elaborate. "What did she say?"

"That if I helped her bring you into House Tremaine, she would give you to me."

"Nice. And was I just supposed to go along with that plan?"

"You would if she had your sisters. Or your mother." His voice was casual. "Holding a knife to your mother's throat would make you very agreeable."

Connor was gone, and I got Mad Rogan instead: cold, calculating, cruel when he had to be.

"And the Scroll?"

"The Scroll is one of the three main DNA databases," he said. "You will be required to submit a sample to the Keeper to prove that you and Catalina are sisters. Once the sample is submitted, you must choose a database. They will sequence your entire family."

"Is it used for genetic matches for future spouses?"

"Primarily, yes. Also in cases when paternity is in doubt."

The gulf between us was getting wider. He was pulling back from me. He was still thinking about children and matches. Was he trying to give me an out?

"Please pull over," I said.

He guided the car onto the shoulder. I unbuckled my seat belt, reached over, and kissed him. His lips were like fire. He didn't respond, but I tried harder, licking his lips with the tip of my tongue, wanting to taste him.

His seat belt snapped free. He caught the back of my head with his hand and claimed my mouth. His magic wrapped around me, mixing with mine. The taste of Connor, the heady intoxicating taste that burned with lust, power, and need, filled me, and I drank it in, melting into it. The strokes of his tongue turned possessive, his fingers tangled in my hair, holding me to him. There was a hint of menace in the way he kissed that warned me that when I tasted dragon fire, I'd get burned and then I would never be the same. It made me want to strip and climb naked on top of him.

Magic slid over the back of my neck, like molten honey, sizzling pleasure on my skin. I gasped into his mouth.

"You're mine," he said, his voice rough. "I'm not letting you go."

"I'm glad we cleared that up."

"Do you understand me, Nevada? I'm not walking away. I thought I could, but I can't and I don't want to."

I brushed his cheek with my fingertips. "What makes you think I would let you go?"

He pulled me to him, and I climbed over, onto his lap. He kissed my neck. Magic swirled along my spine, a heated bliss. I wanted him between my legs. I wanted him inside . . .

There were blue and red lights behind us.

Rogan growled.

A cop was walking toward us, a flashlight in his hand.

I crawled back into my seat and put my hand over my face.

Rogan rolled down the window. "Yes, Officer?"

"Is your vehicle disabled, Mr. Rogan?"

"No," Rogan growled.

"Then you should move along. The road is dark, and you're presenting a safety hazard."

Wow. Apparently we'd run into the one cop in Houston who wasn't intimidated by the Butcher of Merida.

"Ms. Baylor," the cop said. "DA Jordan says hello."

Oh.

"Please move your vehicle for the safety of the public." The cop stepped back. He showed no signs of leaving.

Rogan rolled the window up, we both put our seat belts on, and we pulled back into traffic.

Lenora Jordan, the Harris County District Attorney. When I was in high school, she was my hero. Incorruptible, uncompromising, she served as the last line of the public's defense against crime, especially when committed by the Houses. The first time I saw her was on TV, years ago; she walked down the steps of the courthouse, where a raging fulgurkinetic Prime wrapped in a web of lightning refused to be arraigned on charges of child molestation. Lenora strode right up to him, summoned chains from thin air, and bound him, right there, in front of all the cameras. And then she dragged him into court.

I never thought I would meet her, but I did. She was everything she seemed, and she scared the living daylights out of me. Even Rogan treated her with the kind of respect one affords to a hungry tiger.

"Was that a love tap on the shoulder?" I asked. "To tell me she knows we're filing?"

"Yes. Come home with me tonight."

"I can't. A lot has happened and I need to be with my family. They'll have questions."

"I'll wait."

"I don't know how long it will take."

"I'll wait," he repeated.

I would give almost anything to go with him. He would take me to his bedroom, strip off my clothes, and love me until I couldn't even think anymore. I would fall asleep wrapped in him, with his muscular arm around me, and his hot hard chest pressing against my back, and in the morning we'd wake up and make love again. Saying no hurt. Physically hurt. "Rogan . . ."

"Nevada?" My name rolling off his lips was a caress.

"I just turned my family's life upside down. Everything is in shambles. I need to be there tonight. If one of my sisters knocks on my door at two in the morning, I want to be there to reassure her. If my mom isn't able to go to sleep and comes checking on me in the middle of the night, I want to be there. And I can't do that if I'm over at your place, and you can't be at mine, because you make me moan and scream, and that's not what my family needs to hear."

His face told me he didn't like it.

"What are you thinking?"

"I'm planning to kidnap you until the trials," he said.

"We've tried that, remember?"

"I had the air-conditioning fixed in the basement," he said.

"Is there a nice chain waiting for me?"

"No," he said. "But I do have some handcuffs."

"No," I told him. "Okay, maybe. Who'll be wearing the handcuffs?"

He grinned.

We reached the warehouse.

"I have to go," I told him. I didn't want to.

He opened his mouth and I put my finger on his lips. "Please don't say my name. If you say my name, I won't be able to get out of the car."

He smiled against my finger. It was a wicked male smile, and it made him look both handsome and evil, like a demon.

"I mean it, Rogan. Don't say my name, don't kiss me good night, and don't look at me . . . yes, like that. Don't look at me like that. I have to go investigate your ex-fiancée's husband's disappearance tomorrow, and I need sleep."

I still couldn't move from the seat. He pulled at me like a magnet. It wasn't the spectacular sex and it wasn't his looks, although both helped. It was the way he looked at me when he thought I wasn't watching him. Like I was the center of his universe. When he looked at me like that, I would do anything for him. It scared me that I could love someone that much, so I fought with everything I had to keep every shred of independence I had left.

"I see Caesar's shadow," he said.

I did too. But until we had some evidence, jumping to conclusions did no good. "It does seem like a big coincidence—Rynda's mother dies, then, within weeks, her husband disappears. But, apparently, he has a history of taking off when things get rough, and things are rough for her right now."

He fixed me with his Mad Rogan stare. "If you find the connection between Brian's disappearance and the conspiracy, I want to know about it. Not eventually, not when it's convenient, but immediately."

"Yes, sir. I was going to kiss you good night, but now I can't. It's against the rules to fraternize with my superior officer."

"Hilarious," he said.

I opened the door and climbed out.

"Nevada," he called after me, sinking a world of promise into one word.

I kept walking.

His voice caressed me like a touch. "Come back and let me kiss you good night."

"I can't hear you." I sprinted to my door, got inside, and closed it. It was a big thick door. I couldn't possibly have heard him laughing behind me. I must've imagined it. Yes, that was it.

I walked through the house. The light in the kitchen was on. Voices floated to me. Everyone was still awake and waiting for me.

Tomorrow I would have to go to BioCore and start looking for Rynda's husband. Tomorrow I would see Rogan again. But first, I had to get through tonight. I sighed, squared my shoulders, and went to talk to my family.

CHAPTER 3

IT WAS MORNING. Bright sunlight, cheery blue sky, and a massive headache hammer that pounded the inside of my skull. I'd popped two ibuprofens as soon as I'd clawed my eyes open, because I had things to do today, but they didn't even make a dent.

Last night I came home to all sorts of questions. And once I told them what happened, they came up with even more questions. My mother wanted to know about Victoria Tremaine, Leon wanted to know if he would eventually get a gun when we became a House, Catalina wanted to know about her trials, Arabella wanted to know if Michael was cute, and Grandma Frida said she met Linus Duncan once during the war and wanted to know if he still had that "hot, dark-eyed, Scottish thing" going. By the time I fought them off, it was close to two o'clock in the morning. I went upstairs, took off my clothes, fell into my bed facedown, and passed out. I dreamed of Rogan, woke up an hour later, and couldn't figure out why he wasn't in the bed. Now it was morning, and as I walked into our office, I felt like I was dragging a bulldozer behind me.

Cornelius was already at his desk. He wore a dark grey suit, a white shirt, and a black tie. His blond hair was neatly brushed back. Even at his worst, Cornelius always had a certain style. He was trim, neat, and calm. You'd never guess that the same man sang a horde of rats into devouring a living human being.

Today no rats were in attendance, but Talon, his chicken hawk, perched on top of the bookcase, glaring at me with amber eyes.

Cornelius raised his head from his laptop. His serious blue eyes widened. I was wearing a black Armani pantsuit over an expensive light grey blouse and Stuart Weitzman pumps, which had the wonderful advantage of being comfortable enough to run in, if the occasion required. My hair was straightened and pulled back from my face into a knot. My makeup was applied with all the skill I could muster, considering my headache.

"You look like a CIA agent," Cornelius observed.

"Have you ever met any CIA agents?"

"No. But I would imagine they would look like you."

"This is my inspire-confidence-in-clients look," I told him. "I own two expensive suits. I wear one to the initial meeting and the other when I come to close the case and collect my payment. The rest of the time the suits hang in plastic in the back of my closet."

"Are you planning to impress a client?" he asked.

"We already have a client. I need to impress her House. Her husband is missing, and if his family had something to do with it, I'd like them to consider me a serious threat, so they can focus on me instead of her. I would like you to come with me. It would be a good experience for you, and it would help my credibility."

"Of course." Cornelius rose.

"Our client is Rynda Sherwood. Formerly Rynda Charles."

He froze.

"She showed up here last night," I explained. "Her husband is missing."

Cornelius found his voice. "Does she . . . know?"

"She knows that Rogan and I were present. She doesn't know exactly how Olivia was killed or who did it. I understand if you would rather stay."

"But why would she come to you?"

"Because all of her mother's friends abandoned her, and House Sherwood doesn't seem to be concerned about her husband's disappearance. She truly has no place to go."

"Do you think this is connected to the conspiracy her mother was involved in?"

"Maybe," I said. "Or maybe her husband is a stressed-out workaholic who snapped and decided to disappear for a few days."

Cornelius pondered it.

"I also should mention that I filed to be recognized as a House."

He blinked again. "Congratulations."

"Victoria Tremaine is my grandmother," I continued. "She was none too happy about this development, and while there are rules which prevent her from interfering, I can't promise she won't try something."

"Are you nervous?" Cornelius asked.

"Yes." There was no point in lying. "Given a choice, I would rather hide here until the trials, but I promised Rynda I'd look for her husband."

"You can't hide," Cornelius said quietly. "Your name is in the book. People are watching all of you, but especially you, to see what sort of House you'll become. First impressions matter."

"First impressions?"

Cornelius paused. "When the petition of House formation is filed, it's read before the Assembly and, more practically, it's announced in their internal newsletter."

Great. Every House in Texas would see our name in their email box. "So everyone knows?"

"Yes. This is done to discourage interference from other Houses."

"Will they know what talents we are requesting to be tested?"

"Yes."

So the cat was out of the bag. I had announced myself as a truthseeker to the entire state of Texas.

"You will be watched," Cornelius said. "The way you conduct yourself now is very important."

He was right. Hiding was out of the question. We couldn't afford to look like cowards.

I looked at Cornelius. "Thank you."

"You're welcome."

"Are you in or out?"

He didn't miss a beat. "In. Let me grab a travel cup for my coffee."

BIOCORE OCCUPIED A rectangular building of black glass off of Post Oak Circle, across from the Houstonian. Unlike the towers of downtown, this building was long, eating up a lot of real estate, but only a few stories high.

Cornelius and I parked in front of it. A few weeks ago Rogan had destroyed my Mazda minivan by ripping it in half and throwing pieces at some mages who were attacking us. He'd replaced it with a blue Honda CR-V, which, I discovered after the fact, was armored to the gills. Grandma Frida had tons of fun tweaking it. If we faced magic and bullets, I'd just sprint to my car.

I realized I was scanning the building, looking for hidden danger. My adventures with Rogan had made me paranoid.

I crossed the lot to the heavy glass doors. Talon settled himself on Cornelius' shoulder. Cornelius wore a pinched expression. I couldn't tell if he was concentrating, nervous, or both. This wouldn't do. I needed him to be calm and professional.

"Have you thought of investing in a wooden leg and a tricorn hat?"

He blinked. "No, why?"

I pointed at his reflection in the glass door. He studied it.

"I suppose Talon does very slightly resemble a parrot. I'm afraid I'm not much of a pirate though."

"It's all in the attitude," I told him. "Just imagine that this building is a Spanish galleon loaded with stolen treasure, and you are a captain of a pirate crew."

Cornelius studied himself some more, taking in his perfectly styled hair, his clean-shaven face, and his expensive tailored suit, opened his mouth, and said, "Arrr."

I grinned and pushed the revolving door.

Inside, a sterile, crescent-shaped lobby greeted us: white walls, ultramodern lights, and black marble floors. At the widest part of the crescent, a barely visible outline in the pale wall indicated a double door. To the left of it, two guards in olive green uniforms sat at the reception desk. The guards looked at us and gave Talon the evil eye. We approached the desk. I gave the guards my name and my card and asked to speak to Edward Sherwood. The shorter of the guards picked up the phone and spoke into it quietly.

We waited.

The doors whispered open and a tall man emerged. He was in his late thirties, with brown hair, light hazel eyes, and a square jaw. He moved like a former jock who hadn't quite gone soft, mostly because he didn't know how. The tailored grey suit made his shoulders even wider. You had a feeling that if you stood between him and something that really mattered, he would go through you, and he wouldn't lose his cool, because it wouldn't be personal. He also matched the photographs I'd looked up this morning. Edward Sherwood, Brian's older brother.

Calm eyes, assured walk, no hint of tension in the jaw or in the line of his shoulders. If he had something to do with his brother's disappearance, he was either completely confident that he would get away with it or an excellent actor.

"Ms. Baylor," he said. His voice was measured and calm like the rest of him. "Rynda told me you would be coming."

"Good morning."

We shook hands. He had a firm handshake. The real question was, did he read the Assembly newsletter and would he remember my name?

"Thank you for seeing us on such short notice." I turned to Cornelius. "One of our investigators, Cornelius Harrison."

Cornelius also got a handshake.

"Let's talk somewhere more comfortable. Please follow me." He headed for the door. It slid open at his approach, we stepped through, and it hissed shut behind us. I gaped.

An enormous atrium spread in front of us, a labyrinth of raised beds and planters, so many that the floor formed a curving stone path between them. It had to have taken most of their first three floors. I couldn't even begin to guess at the square footage. You could fit our warehouse inside several times over.

Edward strolled down the path and I moved to keep up with him. Several old trees grew in raised beds, each covered with various mushrooms: a huge mass of white dangling threads that looked like an odd mop or an ultramodern chandelier; turkey tail mushrooms in a dozen colors I had never seen before, from granite grey to vivid green and intense burgundy; a nest of orange snakes that was probably a fungus or maybe an alien from outer space; a huge mass of bright yellow mushrooms, and on and on.

Lichens flourished on the trees. Slime molds in every color in the crayon box stained the bark and massive, moss-sheathed boulders. Some lichens glowed weakly in the shade. More mushrooms grew from the roots: amethyst, indigo, nearly fluorescent green. A mushroom draped in a net of white filaments like a veil. A mushroom that looked like a chunk of Texas limestone bleeding bright red liquid from the holes. On the walls, under Plexiglas, enormous bacterial colonies thrived like abstract paintings.

It was like stepping onto an alien planet. All I could do was stare.

Talon took off from Cornelius' shoulder and streaked between the trees.

"He's overwhelmed," Cornelius said. "My apologies."

Edward smiled as we strolled down the path. "No worries. We bios mages have to deal with our charges' idiosyncrasies. Life is unpredictable."

"Are you also a herbamagos like Brian?" I asked. His background check said he was.

"Yes. But my talents lie with trees. Specifically, fruit trees. Brian rules over fungi. This is his kingdom." Edward raised his hand to encompass the alien landscape. "This way."

He turned right. We followed him around the bend. The mushroom kingdom ended abruptly. A koi stream stretched in front of us, widening into a pond with a rock wall and a waterfall at the far end. On the other side a beautiful garden spread. Fruit trees, some flowering, some bearing golden apples, apricots, and cherries, rose from the planters.

Edward led us across a small Japanese bridge into the garden.

"You're probably wondering why I don't lead the family. Everyone does," he said. "They are simply too polite to ask the question. I'm the oldest and a Prime."

"Why don't you lead the family?" I asked.

"In our family Brian was born with a gold spoon in his mouth. There's significantly more money in fungi-driven pharmaceuticals than in delicious apples."

Edward reached out, and the nearest apple tree leaned to him, brushing his palm with its leaves.

"Does it bother you?" I asked.

"Not anymore."

Lie.

The floor abruptly ended. The path was still there, but instead of stone tiles a green lawn stretched in front of us. Walking on it in heels was out of the question. I'd sink in with every step.

Edward waited, watching me.

I slipped off my shoes, picked them up, and kept going. The grass felt cool under my toes. I had to do this carefully. He was a Prime, and a wrong step would get us thrown out. I owed Rynda some answers.

"Mr. Sherwood," I said. "Rynda has hired our agency to look into the disappearance of her husband."

"It was a shock," he said. "Considering your role in her mother's death."

Right, now that we got Olivia's death out of the way . . . "We would like to ask you some questions. Some topics might be sensitive. Everything you tell us is confidential, but not privileged."

"I'll be as candid as I can. Within reason."

I waited for the familiar nagging feeling, but my magic stayed silent. He was sincere.

"When was the last time you saw your brother?"

"Thursday night a little before six. We spoke briefly about the budgetary meeting on Friday. I asked him if he wanted to attend. He said he would be busy with his research. He left the office. I got up and watched the trees on the other end of the parking lot from my window. It helps me think. I was still in front of the window when he walked out into the parking lot, got into his car, and drove off."

Truth. Off to a good start.

"Are you concerned for your brother's well-being?"

"Yes."

Lie. Spoke too soon.

"I'm concerned for Rynda," he volunteered. "And the children."

Truth.

The path brought us to the curve of the koi pond. Three plain wooden benches, the kind you could find in every home improvement store, waited, arranged in a rough circle. A trellis wove above each, bearing a spray of clematis flowers. Crimson, white, burgundy, blue, the big mixed blossoms sent a subtle, complicated aroma into the air.

"Please." Edward invited me to the bench.

I sat. Cornelius took a spot next to me. Edward chose the bench across from us.

It was so tranquil here. I could sit and read a book in this spot for hours, smelling the clematis, glancing at the pond, and feeling the soft silken grass under my feet. And that was exactly why he brought me here. This was his piece of the kingdom. He was comfortable here, and he counted on the soothing surroundings to soften the conversation.

"When Brian was a young child, he didn't like to be in trouble," Edward said. "No child does, but my brother would become easily overwhelmed. Our father had a harsh view of child-rearing. He was a product of his generation. When my brother did something he knew would put him into our father's crosshairs, he disappeared. He would hide for hours and he was very good at it. At first, everyone would wait for him to come out. Then, a few hours into his disappearance, my mother would panic, sure that this time something bad must have happened. The entire household would look for him, sometimes until morning, and when he was finally found, everyone would be too tired and too relieved for discipline."

"Do you feel that Brian is hiding?"

"Yes."

True.

"Why?"

He leaned back. "BioCore is engaged in high-profile antibiotic research. The average person rarely pays attention to how much we owe antibiotics. They simply take for granted that few people die from infection following surgeries. Strep throat, pneumonia, and UTIs are unpleasant inconveniences, but rarely a cause for panic. Despite extensive travel, we no longer have plagues and epidemics. We've gotten comfortable. It's a mistake."

"Nature always finds a way," Cornelius said.

Edward nodded. "We're facing a sharp rise in antibiotic-resistant bacteria. Our miracle drugs no longer work. This is happening right now, today, this minute. We're losing the battle. MDR-TB, the bacterial strain responsible for tuberculosis, is resistant to a multitude of antibiotics. MRSA, VRE, KPC, the list goes on. I could give you more scary acronyms, which all amount to the same thing. Soon a routine visit to the hospital for a respiratory infection or a relatively safe surgery, like appendix removal, may end your life. The race to find new and better drugs is on. Brian was on the forefront of that. He used his magic to facilitate rapid mutation of the fungi in response to bacterial threats. He was trying to develop new antibacterial agents. It's a dangerous and lucrative field of study."

"Competitive?" I guessed.

"Very. I promised to be candid. Olivia's involvement in Senator Garza's death and the resulting avalanche of negative publicity hurt us. Badly. Brian married Rynda for her mother's business contacts. Right now those contacts are running for cover."

It was as if Rynda had the plague. Everything connected to her mother was tainted.

"Two of our major investors pulled their money. The sum was not insignificant. A large contract, which was all but signed and delivered, went to our major competitor instead. We're having difficulties obtaining necessary virus samples."

"Are you facing a financial crisis?" I asked.

"Yes." He seemed strangely casual about it. "We will survive. These are temporary setbacks. We'll find other investors, and there will be other contracts. But meanwhile, things are very tense. More tense than Rynda was aware."

That didn't line up with Rynda telling me that Brian was calm, but Edward wasn't lying. "Did Brian know about these problems?"

A flicker of something passed in Edward's eyes. Contempt or exasperation? It was too quick for me to nail it down.

"Brian is a genius. His realm is science and research. Financial issues and the day-to-day operations of the company are my responsibility. I made him aware of the situation a couple of days ago. I also let him know that our situation wasn't hopeless. However, as I've mentioned, Brian does become overwhelmed. It wouldn't be out of character for him to disappear and return when the problem has resolved itself. Like I said, he's excellent at hiding."

Brian sounded more and more like a real piece of work.

"Does he have access to cash other than his bank accounts?" Cornelius asked.

"I wouldn't be surprised," Edward said. "He likes to put things away for a rainy day."

"Are you aware of any marital issues between Brian and Rynda?" I asked.

"Rynda works very hard at being an ideal spouse for my brother. She anticipates his needs, and Brian isn't given to emotional outbursts. My brother is quiet and easily hurt, so he prefers calm and routine."

He didn't answer the question.

"Has Brian expressed any dissatisfaction with his marriage?" Cornelius asked.

"Everyone expresses some dissatisfaction with their marriage once in a while," Edward said. "He hadn't said anything lately."

"Could you define lately?" I asked.

"Last couple of years."

True.

"Do you believe that Brian would permanently abandon his wife?" I asked.

"No."

A true statement again. "Does BioCore view Rynda as a liability?"

Edward leaned forward, his gaze suddenly focused. "Rynda is never a liability. She's a woman of grace, kindness, and incredible patience. She's compassionate and intelligent. We are fortunate to know her. She has the full support of House Sherwood."

The real Edward Sherwood finally made an appearance. I'd touched a nerve. He wasn't worried about his brother, but the moment I tried to bring up Rynda, he was ready to bite my head off. Interesting.

"Did you kidnap your brother, Mr. Sherwood?"

His eyes blazed. "I'm not going to dignify that with an answer."

"Mr. Sherwood," I said. "Rynda is extremely upset. She came to me because everyone else had turned her down. I want to resolve this as quickly as possible to minimize her emotional distress. The sooner I can eliminate you from the pool of possible suspects, the sooner we can move on to finding out what actually happened to your brother."

"What makes you think I would tell you the truth? I could be lying."

"I'm an excellent judge of character," I said. "Did you kidnap your brother?"

"No." Muscles played along his jaw.

Truth.

"Did you kill him or otherwise cause him harm?"

"No."

"Did you order or hire someone to make Brian disappear?"

"No!"

"Do you know where he is?"

"No."

"Do you know where he might be?"

"No."

"Has he tried to contact you since his disappearance?"

"No."

Not a single lie in the bunch. I rose. "Thank you, Mr. Sherwood."

Edward got to his feet. He was furious, but his anger was tightly controlled, squeezed by his will like a fist. "Are we done?"

"We are."

He flicked his phone and raised it to his ear. "Margaret, I need you to show some people out."

Margaret escorted us to the exit. On our way, Cornelius had paused by a large tree, the first one we saw as Edward had led us into the inner sanctum. It stood by the entrance, supporting thick clusters of yellow mushrooms with wet glistening caps. Cornelius looked at it for a few seconds, called Talon to him, and we exited the building.

"What do you think?" I asked as we pulled the car out of the parking lot.

"I thought he was being truthful."

"He was. For the most part. He didn't kidnap his brother, and he has no idea where Brian went. He's in love with his brother's wife."

Cornelius nodded. "She married the wrong brother."

"What makes you say that?"

"Do you recall the tree I stopped by? The one with yellow mushrooms?"

I nodded.

"It's called honey mushroom, and prepared the right way it can be delicious. If you prepare it the wrong way, it's poisonous. It's a facultative saprophyte. It kills the tree on which it grows and then feeds on its rotting wood." Cornelius paused. "It's growing on an apple tree."

Brian Sherwood could've chosen any kind of tree to grow his mushrooms on. Instead he chose a fruit tree. And he chose to put it right at the entrance to the atrium where it couldn't be avoided.

"Every day Edward Sherwood has to walk past that tree," Cornelius said. "He feels it slowly dying, choked to death by the mushroom, and he can't do anything about it."

"Thank you. I would've missed that."

"I'm glad I was useful." Cornelius smiled.

"Brian seems to be passive-aggressive in his cruelty," I said. "And he's a coward. He tends to run away any time things get tough and trusts that his wife or his brother will sort it out."

"Why are we driving so slowly?"

"Because Edward Sherwood told the truth. He did see his brother leave the parking lot in his vehicle, which means that if something happened, it happened in the three-mile stretch along this road. I don't want to miss it."

"What are we looking for?"

"Anything out of the ordinary. Broken glass. Chunks of a blown tire."

"What was he driving?"

"Mercedes-Benz, S550, iridium silver metallic finish, which basically means the color of stainless steel."

Cornelius grimaced. "I probably should've known that. I'll do better next time."

I smiled back. "It's my fault. All of the details are in your email. At the beginning of the case, we make a basic info packet, which includes all the relevant information known to us, and Bern drops it in our email so we can access it on our phone. I should've told you this, but we've operated as a family business for so long and I've never hired anyone for a permanent position."

"Do you think Brian was kidnapped?" Cornelius asked.

"Right now I'm leaning toward him abandoning everything and escaping somewhere calm for a few days. His company is on the brink of a financial disaster, his son still failed to manifest magic, and his wife, who was supposed to open the doors to the House elite, is viewed as unclean. He seems to have fooled everyone into thinking that he is sensitive and easily overwhelmed, but the tree makes me think there is some calculation in his responses . . ."

We crossed a bridge spanning a drop. Ahead the guardrail bent slightly, as if hit. I pulled over and got out of the car. A smudge of silver paint marked the bend in the guardrail. I crouched and took a picture of it with my phone. Nothing else was out of the ordinary.

"What now?" Cornelius asked.

I pivoted on my feet. Across the street a brand-new gas station was doing brisk business.

"Now we go and ask them for their security recording."

Three minutes later, we were in the gas station. One of their security cameras did point toward that stretch of the street to cover the exit from their parking lot, and all recordings were uploaded to a server and kept for ninety days. The manager and I bargained. He asked for ten thousand dollars. I asked him if he really wanted me to come back with a cop and a warrant, which would result in him getting no money at all. He told me warrants took time. I told him to Google my name. Then he and his clerk watched Mad Rogan tear downtown apart like he was a demon from hell. We settled on two hundred bucks plus the $19.99 USB stick. Which was highway robbery for 8GB, but I decided to pick my battles.

I plugged the USB into my laptop and fast-forwarded the video.

5:00 p.m.

5:30 p.m.

5:45 p.m.

I let it run at normal speed. At 5:51 p.m., a silver Mercedes slid into view. A black SUV, maybe a GMC Yukon, rear-ended it, forcing it off the road and into the guardrail. A man got out of the Mercedes, presumably Brian Sherwood, although I'd have to ask Bug to enhance the footage to be sure.

Two men stepped out of the Yukon. The driver raised his hand. Brian crumpled to the ground. Taser. The driver scooped him up like Brian was a child and carried him into the Yukon. The passenger got into the Mercedes. At 5:52 p.m. the two vehicles pulled onto the road.

Cornelius raised his eyebrows.

I took out my phone and called Rynda.

"Yes?" She sounded on the verge of tears.

"You were right. Brian was kidnapped," I said.

"I know!" Her voice reached hysterical pitch. "They just called the house!"

CHAPTER 4

BRIAN AND RYNDA Sherwood lived in Hunters Creek Village, in what the real estate listing called a "lovely family home designed for an active lifestyle." They bought the house four years ago, and real estate sites kept archived listings forever. The house sat on an acre. It had six bedrooms and five bathrooms, eighty-five hundred square feet of living space, a pool, a "party cabana," and a wine grotto, which I had trouble picturing. My mind kept serving up something out of a Disney movie, but filled with wine instead of ocean water.

The house also sold for three and a half million, about average for the neighborhood. Driving to it, I could see why. We were surrounded by woods. Birds sang. Squirrels dashed up an occasional palm growing among the oaks. You'd never know Houston was just a two-minute car ride away.

We pulled up to the house. I parked next to a familiar gunmetal-grey Range Rover. Rogan got there before us. Rynda or someone on her security team must've called him. Good. She seemed to listen to him better than she did to me.

"Is that Rogan's car?" Cornelius asked.

"Yes."

"Does it bother you?"

"It does a little." I would have to be a robot for it not to bother me. "But I try to keep things in perspective."

He tilted his head, waiting for me to elaborate.

"Rynda just lost her mother and all of her friends. I have a feeling she must've relied on her husband a great deal, and now he's missing too. She's a mother, and she's laser-focused on surviving and keeping her children safe. She's known Rogan since she was a toddler. He's practically family, and he has the magic and resources to keep her and the kids alive through this. It's natural for her to reach out to him."

"I don't believe she sees him as family," Cornelius said.

"She can see him however she wants. I only care how Rogan sees me."

He told me he loved me, and he wasn't lying. I would've trusted him even without my talent. Rogan was dangerous, at times unpredictable, and always stubborn. Given a chance, he would roll over people like a bulldozer to accomplish his goals. But I could never see him cheating. He was too direct for that. It wasn't in his nature.

The two of us walked to the door. An armed guard blocked our way. Not one of Rogan's ex-military hard asses; this guy looked like a cross between a bodybuilder and a park ranger, his olive-drab cargo pants tucked into desert-tan boots, and his khaki polo shirt stretched tight across his broad shoulders and thick chest. It was obviously custom tailored to accommodate his overdeveloped physique. Around a surprisingly narrow waist hung a thick nylon tactical belt with a pistol in a plain holster, handcuffs, and a handheld radio. Completing the ensemble was a pair of mirrored aviator sunglasses and a ball cap with "Sherwood Security" embroidered above the House crest. High-priced hired muscle.

"Nevada Baylor and Cornelius Harrison," I told him.

He mumbled something into the radio and opened the door for us.

The interior of the house was as beautiful as the exterior.

The place swarmed with similarly uniformed gym rats, all of whom paused to give us their versions of hard stares. We walked through the short foyer into a cavernous family room. Delicate furniture, a beautiful Persian rug, a toy truck, a water gun on the floor, and a child's paintings on the wall in beautiful modern frames. A massive Christmas tree stood in the place of honor, glittering with white and gold.

Rynda stood in the middle of the floor hugging herself. Rogan stood very close to her, one hand on her shoulder. His eyes were warm, and his face was concerned.

She saw me.

"Did you record the phone call?" I asked.

"Yes." She held up her cell and hit play.

A male voice said, "You know what we want."

The recording cut off.

"Did they say anything else?"

"No."

"Do you know what they want?"

"No!" Tears wet Rynda's eyes. "If I knew what they wanted, don't you think I would've given it to them already? They have my husband!"

She wasn't lying.

"Gather the children and pack your bags," Rogan said. "I have a secure base in the middle of the city."

And he just offered to move her into his HQ.

"I'm not going anywhere." Rynda shook her head. "This is my house."

Rogan's expression snapped into a no-nonsense mask. He was about to order her around, and Rynda would balk. She was a Prime. I silently shook my head at him.

"Let's sit down," I said. "Everyone is really upset, so let's just take a moment and catch our breath."

I sat down. Rynda sat opposite me on the ornate sofa. She was breathing too fast. If I didn't calm her down, she'd hyperventilate. I had to break her train of thought.

"Are these Kyle's paintings on the walls?"

She frowned. "Yes. My mother had them framed."

"He's very talented."

"Thank you," she said, probably on autopilot.

"What about the water gun?"

"That's Jessica's. She loves ambushing him with it."

"Where are the children now?"

"In the playroom with Svetlana."

Her breathing deepened.

"Who's Svetlana?"

"She's from the nanny service."

"How did you get the nanny service?"

"All of the mothers in the neighborhood use it. I don't remember who recommended it."

"When did you get the phone call?" I kept my voice quiet and steady.

She checked her phone. "Twelve minutes after ten."

"Do you recognize the voice?"

"No."

"Listen to it again, carefully."

She did. "No."

"Can you think of any enemies Brian had?"

"I told you already, no."

"Rynda," Rogan said, "someone grabbed a Prime off the street in broad daylight. It had to be a rival House. Nobody else would have the balls. Did Brian say anything? Was he angry with someone?"

"Brian doesn't get angry." Rynda sighed.

"Who is his biggest competitor?" I asked.

"House Rio," she said. "But he wouldn't know anything about that in detail. Edward runs the business. Brian grows mushrooms."

Rogan was looking at me.

"Edward is in the clear," I told him.

"Did you think Edward had Brian kidnapped?" Rynda shook her head. "Edward would never do anything to hurt me."

Rynda's cell phone rang.

"Put it on speaker," I told her.

She answered the call and pressed the speaker button on screen. I gently took it from her.

Same male voice, controlled, even. "Give it to us, or he will come back home in pieces."

"My name is Nevada Baylor," I said. "I'm authorized to negotiate with you on Rynda's behalf."

"No negotiations."

"We're trying to meet your demands. We want Brian back home safe. But we require proof of life, so we know we're dealing with the right people. In our place, you would want proof of life, wouldn't you?"

There was a pause. A softer male voice said, "Rynda?"

"Brian!" Rynda made a mad lunge for the phone, but Rogan clamped her down. "Brian, are you okay?"

"Just give them what they want. Please."

The phone call ended.

Rynda buried her face in her hands.

"FBI—" I started.

"No," Rogan, Rynda, and Cornelius said at the same time.

Yes, why wouldn't we call professionals who specialize in exactly this type of crime? That would be silly. "They will call again."

"What if they kill him?"

"They won't kill him," Rogan said. "They went through the

trouble of kidnapping him, which means they want their ransom. If they kill him, they'll have nothing to negotiate with."

I handed her the phone. "Rynda, the next time they call, you have to establish an emotional connection. It's critical. Ask them questions. If they answer, repeat the answer back to them and ask if it's right. Get them to the place where they agree with you. They need to get used to viewing you as being on their side. Use your magic. I know it's hard, but you can't get upset and you can't be hysterical. Make them think that all of you are in this together and that you want them to succeed. Get them to tell you what it is they want."

She took the phone and nodded.

"You will be safer with me," Rogan said. "They're calling your cell. You can take it with you."

"Don't be ridiculous, Connor. I'm a Prime in a house that's built like a fortress and filled with armed guards. My kids are already freaked out, and you want us to move across town into your barracks. No. I'm going to stay right here. We have to stay right here, because we are waiting for Daddy to come home."

Rogan's face promised a storm. "Very well. In that case, I'll put a team on your house."

Rynda looked up at him, and there was steel in her eyes behind all the brittleness. "No, you won't. We have our own security. I appreciate the offer, but no. I'm going to take care of my kids. If you want to help me, please find my husband."

There wasn't anything I could say after that.

Outside I took a deep breath. "Do you want to explain to me why we can't call the FBI?"

"Neumann kidnapping," Cornelius said.

"A rival House kidnapped George Neumann in the 1980s," Rogan clarified. "The FBI went in and lost over forty agents. Nobody was convicted."

"How is that possible?"

Rogan shrugged. "Connections and enough money for excellent attorneys. The FBI no longer gets involved in our kidnappings. This is House business. We handle it ourselves."

Nice. Another perk of being a House I hadn't counted on: when you're in trouble, law enforcement won't help you.

Rogan typed something on his phone. "You should've helped me convince her to leave the house."

"She's a mother and an empath. She knows exactly how scared her kids are. She feels they need stability and a familiar environment. Wild horses couldn't drag her out of that house right now." I rubbed my face. "Can you send a hostage negotiator to help her?"

"He's on his way," Rogan said. "He's also an empath. But we won't need him. Rynda is one of the best negotiators on the planet. She just never had to use it. She'll step up."

"Could you help me understand?" Cornelius asked. "Rynda's mother never hesitated to use her power. Rynda seems almost reluctant."

"Rynda is kind," Rogan said. "She realized from an early age that her magic made others feel uncomfortable. She never wanted to make anyone uncomfortable. We'll know if anyone calls her again."

"Did you clone her phone?"

Rogan winked at me.

"We found the recording of Brian's kidnapping," I said. "I emailed it to Bern. He probably shared it with Bug already."

He stopped typing. "And you didn't show it to me?"

"If I showed it to you, Rynda would've seen it. It would accomplish nothing except wind her up even tighter." I headed to my car.

Rogan caught up with me. "Where are you going?"

"Back to BioCore. I have to convince Edward Sherwood to call

House Rio and get an audience so I can eliminate them as suspects."

"It's not House Rio," Rogan said. "I ran a financial analysis of BioCore. House Sherwood isn't a threat to anyone in its current state."

"I know, but I have to cross my t's and dot my i's."

"I'll come with you."

If Sherwood decided to stonewall me and Cornelius, Rogan would come in handy. It was one thing to shut out Baylor Investigative Agency and a Significant of a minor House. It was another thing to say no to Mad Rogan.

I pretended to mull it over. "Promise not to break any buildings."

He gave me his most polite dragon smile. "I promise."

CORNELIUS AND I used the driving time to brief Rogan on our morning visit there. I parked in the same spot, got out, and the three of us marched to its doors. The two security guards were still at their posts. The shorter one rose. "You're not allowed to be here."

"Please let Edward know that I have information about his brother," I said. "Also, this is Mad Rogan."

Rogan glowered.

The shorter guard paled. His friend picked up the phone and spoke into it in a quick, urgent whisper.

Rogan was examining the door.

"Please don't break it," I murmured.

"I want to see the apple tree with mushrooms."

"If you stand right here, I'm sure you'll see it when Edward comes out."

A couple of minutes passed, then the white doors slid open, and Edward emerged, looking pissed off.

"So you're behind this," he said to Rogan. "And you brought your pet truthseeker with you."

Apparently, Edward had found the Assembly newsletter that told him who I was and who my witnesses were. I wondered how many people knew I was a truthseeker by now. A familiar anxiety pinched me. I'd spent my life guarding my secret, because I didn't want to end up as an interrogator. It didn't matter anymore. Once we were a House, I could fend off any three letter agencies pressuring me to do their dirty work.

"She's nobody's pet," Rogan said. "Least of all mine."

And then he smiled. I knew exactly what happened when he smiled like that. If I didn't spring into action, the building would collapse on Edward's head.

"Don't get upset," I said. "He's jealous of you because he's in love with Rynda and you're her ex-fiancé."

Edward Sherwood turned a lovely purple color. His mouth opened but nothing came out. Cornelius smiled.

Rogan watched Edward with casual interest. "Like I said, nobody's pet. Your brother has been kidnapped. Would you like to see the footage?"

Edward regained his ability to speak and decided that he would, indeed, like to see the footage. We moved to his office, where he viewed the recording. Then he swore and ranted for about five minutes. Words like "arrogant fool" and "told him a hundred times to take a bodyguard" were said. He balked at going to see House Rio, because he didn't want BioCore and House Sherwood to appear weak. Then Rogan opened his mouth and all sorts of financial information fell out, and Edward decided that Rogan was right and they couldn't look any weaker than they did already.

The visit to House Rio took four hours, primarily because their headquarters was across town and traffic was murder. We met with the Head of the House, her three sons, two daughters, and everyone's spouses. Nobody knew anything about Brian's kidnapping, nobody orchestrated it, nobody perpetrated it, and everyone told the truth.

On the way back to our base, Bug provided Rogan with an update. He and Bern had done wonders with the security recording, and tracked Brian's car and the kidnappers' vehicle all the way to I-10 West, at which point they left Houston proper and entered the stretch of small towns and a whole lot of nothing that lay between Houston and San Antonio. The proverbial trail went cold. I asked Rogan to drive so Cornelius and I could review Bern's report. My cousin had combed Brian's social networks and broken into his personal email account. The results were depressing.

"It has to be connected to Olivia," I said. "Brian lived his life without making any waves: he went to work, he came home, he had no affairs, he expressed no strong political or religious views, he made no friends and no enemies."

"So the man is a mushroom." Rogan raised his eyebrows at me.

"Don't be mean. He had one social network account."

"Oh?"

"Pinterest."

"Tell me it's porn. Please."

"He saved pictures of mushrooms to it," Cornelius said helpfully from the backseat.

Rogan sighed. "I don't understand why she married him."

"You told me before that she married him because she needed stability." Something Rogan couldn't give Rynda even if he tried.

"Let me rephrase. I don't understand why she stayed married to him. This isn't stability, this is a slow suffocation." Rogan turned onto our street, guiding the car past the security booth. "Rynda wanted to be loved. She needed to be loved. She needed someone who would take that extra step to support and shield her. Most of all, she needed someone to step up and be there. Instead she got this prick who torments his brother and runs away at the first sign of trouble, leaving her to pick up the pieces."

"It's not too late. You could be that strong supportive man for her." And it just fell out.

Rogan parked the car in front of the warehouse, turned, and looked at me, his blue eyes incredulous. "Are you jealous?"

"Nope," I lied.

He glanced back at Cornelius. The animal mage raised his hands, palms up.

Rogan pondered me for a long second and laughed. I managed to get out of the car without slamming the door. There was an unfamiliar Volvo parked in our lot. We had a visitor.

The Volvo rose in the air and gently landed in front of the warehouse door.

I turned. Rogan leaned against the Honda, his arms crossed on his chest.

"I like that you're jealous."

"Rogan, put the car back."

"Come to dinner with me tonight and I'll consider it."

Yes! "No. I don't negotiate with terrorists."

"If you don't go to dinner with me, I'll have to do something drastic like stand by your window with a boom box blasting some ridiculously sappy song."

"Where would you even find a boom box?"

"I'm sure I can scrounge one up."

I pretended to think it over. "Pick me up at six o'clock."

"Seven," he said. "It's five now and you'll be busy for the next hour at least. Have fun giving your samples."

What samples?

The Volvo rose and slid back into its place. It had a custom plate ATCG105, which told me nothing.

Rogan walked away, heading toward his HQ.

Cornelius opened the car door and cautiously peered out.

"Yes?" I asked.

"Checking to see if it's safe to come out."

Everyone was a comedian. I sighed and went into my office.

A MAN WAITED for me in our conference room. Bernard sat with him. He looked up from his laptop and gave me a little wave when I came in.

The man was about forty, with the build of a marathon runner—lean, tall, long-legged. He wore a conservative black suit over a black shirt with a sleek black tie. His hair was dark and combed back from his face, the frame of his glasses was black too, and against all that darkness, his light blue eyes stood out.

"Nevada, this is Mr. Fullerton of Scroll, Inc.," Bern said. "He says he's here to get our DNA on behalf of the Office of Records."

Anxiety shot through me. Sooner or later, Arabella would have to submit to DNA testing, and I had no idea what would happen next. Monsters hid in our bloodline, and once they were found, it would be too late to do anything about it.

Mr. Fullerton rose and offered me his hand. I shook it. He had a firm, dry handshake.

Behind me, Cornelius walked into the hallway and paused before the doorway to the conference room.

"Good evening, Mr. Harrison," Fullerton said. "How is your daughter?"

"Good evening," Cornelius told him. "Matilda's well."

"I'm glad to hear it."

Cornelius glanced at me. "I had to go through genetic testing twice, first as a child, and the second time as a father. Would you like me to sit in on this with you?"

"Yes. Please."

Cornelius nodded and took a seat at the table.

Fullerton and I sat as well.

"Catalina should be here as well." I picked up my phone and texted my sister.

We waited. A couple of minutes later, Catalina walked through the door and took a spot next to Bern without saying a word.

"As you are aware, Ms. Baylor, you must submit a genetic sample for everyone who is qualifying with you," Fullerton said. "The genetic sampling done by the Office of House Records is very basic. They ascertain only that you and everyone who is testing with you under prospective House Baylor are related and their familial status matches the one you indicate. In other words, they will test to determine that you and Catalina are sisters and that Bernard is your cousin."

"Do they ever make mistakes?" Catalina asked.

"The OHR is extremely thorough," Fullerton said. "But human error is always possible. That's why all OHR results are also independently verified by a third party, usually one of the genetic archives, which is where I enter the picture. I represent Scroll, Inc., the largest genetic archive in North America. Today I'm here to obtain the genetic samples for the Office of Records; however, I also would like to take this opportunity to present our services to you. The testing we provide is considerably more extensive. We create a comprehensive genetic profile, a snapshot of your family. We test for all known predispositions to genetic diseases. At your request, we can trace the roots of your bloodline. We can also suggest potential partners who would be most likely to produce offspring with the magic talents you specify."

Rogan's specter rose in my mind. *We're not compatible, Nevada* . . . I wondered how much he really cared about it. Maybe more than he admitted. Brian Sherwood could barely handle that his son wasn't a Prime.

"But it's not a guarantee," I said. "This genetic matching doesn't always produce the . . . the child one wants?"

"Magic is a poorly-understood phenomenon," Fullerton said. "Through our projections, we can greatly increase the likelihood of a child within a particular branch. Mathematically speaking, we have an eighty-seven percent success rate when it comes to predicting what branch of magic the child would fall into—elemental, mental, or arcane. This is a broad statistic. The actual chances depend on the specific match."

"How does this work?" Catalina asked.

"If you choose to employ us, I will collect blood samples. I will transport them to our lab, where your DNA will be analyzed. The results of that analysis are sealed. We cannot be compelled to disclose them even by a court order. You have complete control over the information we will provide. If another House wants to consider you as a prospective match, they may request your profile, which contains basic information. You will be notified, at which point you may accept or reject the request. We won't release anything without your approval. If consent is granted and the other House finds the results intriguing, they may request an in-depth profile. Again, it's up to you to allow it or reject it."

Fullerton paused and leaned forward, his blue eyes focused and clear. "We safeguard your genetic information. If we become aware of any attempt by an unscrupulous agency to collect, analyze, or sell your genetic samples or results of their analysis, we will pursue them with extreme prejudice."

"You will sue them?" Catalina asked.

"We will kill them," Fullerton said.

My sister glanced at me.

"It's standard practice," Cornelius said quietly. "Any of the larger registered agencies will do the same."

"Your privacy is of paramount importance to us," Fullerton

said. "We take any attempt at DNA theft very seriously. By law, I'm obligated to provide you with the list of our rivals."

He opened a file in front of him and passed me a piece of paper with a list of companies on it.

"I do hope that you will consider us. As I mentioned, we are the largest archive in North America. We've sequenced over sixty percent of all US Houses, including House Rogan."

Funny how he mentioned that.

"If you are interested in a particular bloodline, we can process your request with greater expediency. If we don't have a profile for a House, we will work with whatever agency has sequenced it, which may add a few days to the processing of the request. We will take care of your House, Ms. Baylor. We pride ourselves on our discretion."

"What if another House wants access to records for reasons other than making a match?" I asked.

"We will forward you their request for approval."

"What if it's a very powerful House?" I asked.

"It doesn't matter," Fullerton said. "All Houses have the same rights, all of them have the same contracts, and all of them pay the same fees. If you are a wounded House with only one Prime or a flourishing House with ten Primes, in our eyes you're equal."

"How much is the fee?" I asked.

"A fifty-thousand-dollar establishing fee for the first year and then twenty thousand annually. After the first year, each additional DNA profile carries a twenty-thousand-dollar fee as well."

"Fifty thousand dollars?" Catalina made a choking sound.

Fullerton didn't say anything.

Fifty thousand dollars. I couldn't remember if I had ever written a check that big. It was one-sixth of our annual operation budget and our rainy day reserve combined. I glanced at Cornelius.

"You're paying a little extra for the security and the convenience of the largest archive," Cornelius said. "But fees from other archives are comparable."

"Bern?"

"I vote we get it over with," he said.

"Catalina?"

"If we have to do it, this is fine."

I rose, went into my office, and got out the firm's checkbook.

CHAPTER 5

I STOOD IN front of my bathroom mirror and inspected myself. I wore a pale green dress that clung to me and a pair of light black sandals with tiny sparkles. The sandals gave me about three extra inches of height. Rogan would still tower over me, but now I would be three inches closer.

My hair and Houston's humidity never got along too well, so I straightened it, and it fell in a smooth, shiny curtain, framing my face. My makeup was perfect: mascara, blush, powder, lipstick; everything was just the way I wanted it. I always hated wearing foundation, and even my face cooperated today. No breakouts.

The dress was a little plain. I needed something sparkly to off-set the low neckline. I didn't have anything on hand, so it would have to do as is.

I checked my phone. Almost seven.

Last touch-up on the hair. A tiny squeeze of the perfume bottle and . . . done.

I grabbed my purse and clicked my way down the stairs from my loft apartment to the media room. Leon and Arabella were playing WWF on TV.

"Yeah!" my sister roared. "Take it, take it, take it."

On the screen, her female fighter was smashing the chair over Leon's beefy fighter's head. Grandma Frida sat in the corner of the love seat, sipping tea.

I cleared my throat.

Everyone paused the game and looked at me.

"Eleven out of ten!" Arabella declared.

Leon held up two thumbs.

"Now this is a proper 'you can't have my man' dress," Grandma Frida said.

"Who is going to take her man?" Arabella asked.

Grandma Frida squinted her eyes. "Rynda Sherwood."

"Grandma!" I growled.

"What?" Arabella whipped around. "Why didn't I know this?"

"She isn't trying to take my man. Her husband is missing. Besides, Rogan doesn't want her, he—"

My phone chimed. Rogan. Yes!

I flicked my finger across the surface.

Something came up. Give me an extra hour.

"Oh no," Grandma Frida said. "Oh no, no, no. That was something bad. Did he cancel?"

"He didn't cancel. He got held up."

"You look worried," Grandma Frida said.

"Mhm." Nothing short of a true emergency would've kept Rogan. I didn't have a good feeling about this.

"Did he say where?" Grandma Frida asked.

"No." For all I knew, he texted me between throwing a bus at someone and bringing down an office building.

"I bet he's with Rynda." Grandma Frida set her cup on the table so hard it clinked. "You should call that woman and tell her to back off."

"Yeah, you should call that bitch out," Arabella said.

"First, she isn't a bitch. She's a client with a missing husband. Second, butt out of my love life."

"Call her out," Arabella said.

"Tell her Rogan is yours!" Grandma Frida pumped her fist.

"Don't let her take your man!" Leon declared.

We all looked at him.

"I was feeling left out," he said.

"Butt. Out. I mean it."

I clicked my way out of the media room and headed toward my office. That was the only place they wouldn't follow.

There was probably a perfectly reasonable explanation for why he got held up. And when he showed up, I would ask him about it. If he got a lead and didn't tell me . . . He would regret it. Cooperation went both ways.

Cornelius was still in his office, reading something on his laptop and drinking coffee, bathed in the soft yellow light of the lamp in the corner. His door was open. I knocked on the glass. "You're still here."

He looked up from his laptop and smiled. "Matilda is spending the night with Diana."

Progress. A few weeks ago Cornelius' sister barely acknowledged the fact that her niece existed. "Is it their first time?"

Cornelius nodded. "My sister is nervous." He raised his phone. "I have six texts so far. I had to remind her that she's a Prime and the Head of our House."

Prime or no Prime, five-year-old girls were scary. I babysat my sisters when they were that age. It still gave me nightmares. "Are you nervous?"

"No. I have faith. They will work it out. But meanwhile, I thought I would read more on the case. I would like to be good at this. I like doing this, even if I have none of the qualifications to do it. At least not yet."

"When I started out, I thought I had no qualifications." I leaned against the wall. "I thought it would be like the movies or that TV show *Justice and Code*. I would be busting through doors wearing an armored vest and chasing people down. In reality, even cops rarely do these things. You know how most murders get solved? Someone reviews a hundred hours of CCTV camera footage, spends a week talking to people in the neighborhood, gets a few tips, and then quietly arrests his guy."

"Patience." Cornelius mulled it over.

"A lot of patience. Being thorough and meticulous. Sometimes you end up following someone for weeks, just for a twenty-second shot of him working bench press, taken through a gym window, to prove that he is cheating on his workers comp." I shrugged. "Most people would find it boring."

"Is that why there are always books in your car?"

I nodded. "I still love it, even if it's boring."

"I think I might too," he said.

I smiled, went to my office, and sat at my desk. The clock mocked me: 7:16. No new messages from Rogan.

Not good.

This whole mess with Rynda's husband disappearing smelled bad. When I thought about it, I got a sinking feeling in my stomach, like I was standing somewhere high and peering over the edge. It was just too coincidental that her husband got kidnapped after her mother died.

In theory, it made sense. Once Olivia was out of the picture, her connections and influence vanished. Former friends now actively tried to distance themselves. House Sherwood was disoriented and trying to get its bearings in the new social climate. If Brian had enemies, it was the perfect time to strike.

That was precisely the problem. Brian had no enemies. His company was swaying back and forth, like a giant on sand legs. Even his direct competitor wasn't interested in pushing it over.

Kidnapping for ransom was a rare crime in countries with robust law enforcement. In the US, it was extremely rare. The problem was retrieving the ransom. It put the kidnapper or their accomplice in direct contact with the family and law enforcement lying in wait. With all the different means for the Houses to track people, starting from hiring experts to using their own private security, kidnapping was too high-risk. Besides, the Houses would do everything in their power to avoid paying the ransom. It wasn't about the monetary cost. It was the loss of power and influence.

You would have to be desperate to kidnap the Head of a House. Unless you were also a Prime. Or several Primes connected to a conspiracy behind the attempts to throw the country into a state of unrest so an empire could be created, a new Rome. The people behind it were tired of democracy. They chafed under the accountability and legal constraints that democratic society brought. They were already in positions of power because of their magic and wealth, but it wasn't enough. They didn't want to govern with their every step scrutinized; no, they wanted to rule with absolute power, never to be criticized or brought to answer for their offenses under the law. They wanted an empire, led by a modern-age Caesar.

Olivia Charles was one of those people. We'd stumbled onto this conspiracy when Adam Pierce attempted to burn down Houston, trying to destabilize it. When that failed, the conspirators concocted a different, less obvious plan. They engineered the assassination of a US senator, which Olivia Charles and David Howling carried out, and planned to use it to put political pressure on their opposition within the Assembly. When that didn't work as planned, because Rogan and I interfered, they tried to use the incident to inflame unrest. In the end, both David and

Rynda's mother died for their cause. We still had no idea who Caesar was. Whatever Olivia and Howling knew had died with them.

Olivia Charles had been a pillar of the Houston elite. When she was involved with anything, including the secret conspiracy to overthrow the social order, she ran it. She wouldn't settle for anything less. It would be beyond naive to cling to the notion that Brian's kidnapping was an isolated incident, but I had to keep that possibility open. Dad always warned against jumping to conclusions too soon. That's how mistakes were made, and in our line of business mistakes had real human costs: reputations, marriages, and sometimes lives.

I should check on Rynda. All of this was tying me in knots, and I was a stranger. Her husband had been kidnapped. In her place, I'd be losing my mind. I picked up my phone and dialed Rynda's cell.

Ring.

Another ring.

Ring.

Something was wrong.

Ring.

Ring.

You've reached Rynda Sherwood. Please leave a message after the tone.

Shit. I jumped up and marched to the front of the office, where I'd left my spare sneakers in the break room.

"What's wrong?" Cornelius asked from his desk.

I kicked off my shiny pumps and pulled the old shoes onto my feet. "Rynda isn't answering her cell."

"Perhaps she didn't hear it ring," Cornelius said.

"It's the number Brian's kidnappers used for their ransom calls. That phone is the most important thing in her life right now. She would have it on her at all times." And I was the person she had trusted to fix it. She would take my call.

Cornelius got up and grabbed his jacket.

I SPED DOWN I-10. The beltway had been clogged all to hell, and the I-10 was a nightmare, but this time of day the surface streets were even worse. There were about eleven miles between our warehouse and Rynda's house and I was driving like a maniac.

Cornelius took his cell from his ear. "Still no answer."

We'd called Rynda three times in the last two minutes.

"Please try Edward Sherwood."

"No answer on his cell."

"Try BioCore."

If people would just get out of my way, we could be there in fifteen minutes.

"I'm trying to reach Edward Sherwood," Cornelius said into his cell. "It's an emergency concerning his sister-in-law."

A white truck cut me off. I braked, avoiding slamming into its back by two inches.

"Cornelius Harrison. She's in danger. . . . I'm a Significant of a House. I'm telling you that the wife of the Head of your House is in danger. Do your duty and send assistance."

Cornelius glared at the phone, incredulous. "Edward already left, and this genius says he has orders to keep me from entering the building. He hung up on me."

The traffic parted in front of me and I strong-armed my way into the right lane. We tore down I-10 and took the Wirt Road exit, flying through it like a bullet. I made a sharp right onto Memorial Drive and raced down the street. Trees flew past us, dark creepy shadows in the early night.

I pressed the voice button on my steering wheel and pronounced each word clearly. "Call. Rogan."

My phone, tethered to the car's stereo, obediently dialed Rogan's number.

Ring.

Please answer.

Ring . . .

"Yes?"

"Rynda isn't answering her phone."

He swore. "Where are you?"

"Two minutes from her house."

"Who's with you?"

"Cornelius."

Rogan swore again. "Why didn't you take backup?"

"What backup, Rogan? Edward isn't answering his cell either."

"I have twelve people in my HQ."

"They're your people. I can't just walk up to them and order them around."

How exactly did he think that would work? *Hi, I'm Rogan's girlfriend, I need you to come risk your lives for his ex-fiancée whom you didn't want to let into your base before . . .* Yes, they would drop everything and rush right over. They were his people, not mine. They had no loyalty to me.

There was a pause. "I'm on my way. My people will be coming to back you up. Be careful. Don't charge in there and get killed."

The line went dead.

I made a left onto Rynda's long, winding driveway. The headlights plucked a prone body in a Sherwood Security uniform from the darkness. He was sprawled across the driveway, hands outstretched. Something crouched over him, something furry, with a hunched-over back and paws that looked like hands with fingers and long claws. It glanced up. Two pairs of watery yellow eyes glared at me, set one under another on a nightmarish face above a mouth filled with a forest of needlelike deep-water teeth. Wet, bloody flesh hung from its jaws.

I rammed it. The armored CR-V slammed into the body, crushing the creature. The impact reverberated through the car. A wet thud hit the undercarriage. Something scratched at the metal. I slammed on the brakes, reversed, and backed over it. Bones crunched. I stomped on the gas pedal and we rolled over it again. If it was still alive, it wasn't happy. I sped forward.

"Was that a summon?" I asked.

Cornelius swallowed, his light eyes opened wide.

"Cornelius?"

"Yes."

A summoner mage had reached deep into the arcane realm and pulled that thing out and nobody knew how many more. Average and Notable level summoners could summon a creature but it vanished the moment they lost focus. Significants could summon several, and when Primes reached into the arcane realm, whatever they brought back stayed in our world permanently until they banished it back. Rogan and I had come up against summoned creatures before. They were hard to kill. I should've checked on Rynda sooner.

The front door stood wide open, spilling warm yellow light onto two bodies crumpled in the doorway. A man and a woman, their green uniforms stained with red. Something had eaten their lips and ears.

I slid the CR-V as close to the door as I could, shut off the engine and the lights, popped the glove compartment open, and grabbed my Baby Desert Eagle and a spare magazine. Twenty-four shots. I had my backup Sig in there too.

"Cornelius, have you ever fired a gun?"

"No. I don't feel comfortable with guns."

Scratch that idea. The last thing I needed was him getting uncomfortable and shooting me in the back by accident.

"There are seven creatures in the house," Cornelius said. "I feel them moving."

"This is an armored car. You're safe here."

"I'm not staying behind. I have to at least try to be useful."

"I thought animal mages had no power over summoned creatures."

"I never tried to make friends with one."

"I don't think they want to make friends." I was pretty sure they wanted to kill us and devour our corpses.

"I'd like to come," Cornelius said. His mouth was a thin firm line. His jaw muscles were locked. His gaze was direct. I knew that look. I'd seen it before on Rogan, Leon, and my own father. It was the look of a male who'd made up his mind and would not allow logic, reason, or arguments to interfere with his chosen course of action. If I left him in the car, he would follow me. I couldn't really stop him and I had no time to argue.

"Stay behind me."

He nodded.

I slipped out of the car, brought my gun up, and walked to the door, forcing myself to pay attention to the bodies. The guards were dead. Very dead, beyond all help. Someone had taken their weapons. The odor of blood hit me, salty and awful, mixing with something else, an odd stench that reminded me vaguely of ozone during a storm. I swallowed down bile and stepped over the corpses into the brightly lit foyer.

Blood marred the expensive marble tile, bright red against the soft cream hues. A few long, fading out smudges—someone had slipped frantically in his own blood, trying to get away. A bloodstain with feathered edges, as if someone had pressed a paintbrush against the floor—someone's bleeding head met the marble tile. A long swipe—whoever had fallen here was dragged into the living room and he or she had tried to grab on to the floor with bloody hands. Please don't let it be Rynda or the kids. Please.

I padded along the wall, avoiding the bloodstains. I was so glad I dumped my pumps for the sneakers. Best decision of the night.

The vast living room opened in front of me. The overturned Christmas tree lay on the floor, pointing like an arrow toward the center of the room, where, twenty feet away, two creatures crouched on their haunches over another dead body splayed out on the Persian rug. About five feet long from head to the base of a prehensile tail, they had the build of a sleek greyhound, but there was something simian in the way they sat on their haunches, picking at the body of a young man with their black paw-hands armed with long white claws. Their stiff, greyish-blue fur stood straight up like bristles on a boar. Their heads, round and crowned by bat ears, swiveled toward me.

The man they were eating looked barely twenty. Death had frozen his face into an expression of utter horror. He had known he was about to die. He probably felt it as they ate him alive. Anger swept through me. They wouldn't be eating anyone else.

Summoned creatures or not, they looked similar enough to our animals, which meant their eyes were close to their brain. Brain was an excellent target.

I fired.

The gun roared. The first shot tore into the left creature's muzzle. Missed. The second took it in the right top eye. The bat-ape stumbled back.

I turned and fired at its friend. Bullets punched into the second beast's face, ripping through bone and cartilage.

Two shots.

Three.

The bat-ape collapsed facedown.

The first beast jerked on the floor, gripped in spasms, painting its own blood onto the rug. I carefully stepped over the body and put another bullet into the back of its skull just in case it decided to get up. Six rounds gone.

Cornelius touched my shoulder, pointed to the right, toward the kitchen, and held up one finger.

Something thumped above us. Echoes of faint voices floated down.

If we went up the stairs and the thing in the kitchen decided to follow, we'd be in a lot worse shape. Being attacked from the rear wasn't fun.

I moved into the kitchen, slicing the corner. A dark shape leaped at me from the kitchen island. I squeezed off a single shot before the bat-ape landed on me. My back slammed against the floor. All of the air rushed out of my lungs. The beast tore into my shoulders, pinning me down. The awful mouth gaped open, the needle teeth like the jaws of a trap about to enclose my face. The odor of ozone washed over me.

Something smashed into the beast, knocking it off me. I rolled on my side. Cornelius stepped over me and bashed the beast's head with a frying pan.

The bat-ape tried to rise.

He bashed it again, then again, bringing the frying pan down like a hammer. Blood splattered the walls. The bat-ape shook and lay still.

Cornelius straightened. I got off the floor and looked at the mangled corpse. Cornelius hefted his frying pan, pondering the body.

"But you don't like guns?" I whispered.

"This is different," he whispered back. "This is how an animal kills. This feels more real."

My new employee was a closet savage, but I wasn't going to complain. I would take this surprise savagery and be grateful. "Thank you."

He gave me a solemn nod.

I left the kitchen and crept up the stairs. Cornelius followed me.

"Any luck with making friends?" I whispered.

"No. Their minds are very primitive. It's like trying to bond with an insect. All I feel is hunger."

Ahead, the staircase turned in a grand sweep. A low eerie growl came from deeper within the house. All of the tiny hairs on the nape of my neck rose. A voice floated back, urgent, female, but too low to make out the words. Rynda.

We rounded the bend and I moved deeper into the house toward the sound. I glanced at Cornelius. He held up four fingers. Four creatures. I only had four bullets left in this magazine. I'd need a lot of firepower in a hurry. I ejected the magazine, slid it into my pocket, and put my spare in. Thirteen shots, twelve in the magazine and one in the chamber. I'd have to make them count.

A short hallway turned to the left, bringing me into the second living room.

". . . bleeding out. There is no need for violence," Rynda said. Her voice trembled.

"Give me the file and all your problems go away." Male voice.

"How do I know that you won't kill us?"

"You're playing for time, thinking that whoever fired that gun downstairs is going to rescue you."

I pressed my back against the wall by the doorway. I couldn't see into the room, and once I got in there, I'd have to act fast.

"I've been doing this a very long time. Nobody is coming to save you, Rynda."

Cornelius closed his eyes and opened them slowly. They were very blue and luminescent, almost catlike.

"Your knight in shining armor is clutching at his guts on your floor. Apparently, you don't care."

A man moaned.

"Stop it!" Rynda yelled.

"Keep going the way you're going and I'll make you watch as they eat him alive."

"Leave him alone!"

"Fine. Pick a kid. I'll do one of them instead."

"You wouldn't dare, Vincent."

"You know perfectly well that I would. Just give me the fucking file. This mother's last stand is getting tiresome. Here, I'll pick for you. That one."

"Mom!" a little girl screamed.

I lunged into the room. Someone pressed pause on the world, the room crystal clear in a split second. On the left, a dark-haired man in black clothes with his arms crossed on his chest. The summoner Prime. Vincent.

A creature waited next to him, indigo blue, with a spray of ghostly black and paler blue rosettes and spots across its fur. At least two and a half feet tall at the shoulder, six feet long, with a thick neck crowned with a fringe of tendrils, a short wide muzzle with dagger teeth, and wide paws as big as my hand. It reminded me of a tiger.

Two bat-apes crouched by Vincent, one by his feet and the other on the table behind him. On the right, fifteen feet away, the third bat-ape sat over Edward's body. Edward lay on his back on the blue rug. A wet wound gaped in his stomach. The third bat-ape was digging in it with its claws. Edward's eyes were open and filled with pain.

Rynda stood behind Edward, her arms around her two children, her face a bloodless mask.

If I killed Vincent, it would cure everything that was wrong with this picture.

"Run!" I barked, and fired.

The world snapped back to its normal speed in a roar of gunfire. The bat-ape by Vincent's feet jerked upright, throwing itself into the path of the bullet meant for the summoner. I'd missed by a tiny fraction of a second.

I pumped three bullets into the bat-ape. Its head jerked with each impact, but it still stayed upright.

Four.

Five.

Rynda didn't move. She just stood in the same spot like a deer in headlights. Damn it.

The creature by Edward leaped over his body and charged me. I pivoted and put six bullets into its skull. It toppled over. I spun back. The first bat-ape sprawled on the floor, dead. The last bat-ape had taken its place, blocking Vincent.

Only one shot left. I put it into the bat-ape's left lower eye, ejected the magazine, brought the other out . . .

"I wouldn't," Vincent said.

The feline beast snarled, a strange sound that was half pissed-off tiger and half the deep bellow of a sea lion. The fringe of bright blue tendrils, six inches long, rose in a collar around its throat, the thickened ends glowing with bright blue. His huge maw gaped open, his dagger teeth an inch from Rynda's daughter.

"This was fun," Vincent said. "Drop the magazine."

I opened my hand and let it fall to the floor.

"Put the gun down."

I crouched and lowered the weapon to the floor.

"Kick it."

I gave the Baby Desert Eagle a nudge with my foot. The gun

slid across the floor to the left side. If I threw myself down, I'd be able to grab it. If I could get close enough to Vincent, I could shock him.

The last bat-ape, Vincent's new meat shield, crouched, revealing the summoner. Vincent was about Rogan's age, handsome, dark brown hair, a square jaw, dark eyes, and the perfect amount of scruff on a dimpled chin—generations of all the right genes in all the right places.

If I lunged at him, the bat-ape would tear me apart.

Vincent rolled his eyes. "I can't believe I have to say this. You there, dashing male secretary! Drop the frying pan."

The pan clattered to the floor behind me.

Vincent smiled.

That languid, assured smile told me everything I needed to know: none of us would walk out of here alive. He would kill me and Cornelius, then he would finish off Edward, Rynda, and the kids. Vincent was one of those people who derived pleasure from wielding power over others, and there was no greater power than life or death. He would toy with us, like a cat with an injured bird, then he would kill us.

"The next time someone tells you to run, Rynda, you should take their advice," he said.

I should've been terrified, but instead I was angry. "Takes a lot of balls to terrorize two children."

He glanced at me. "Another idiot with moral scruples. What is it today? Would you like to volunteer instead?"

"Yes." I had only one shot at this. I pushed my magic out and gripped him in its fist.

Shock slapped Vincent's face. He tried to move and couldn't. His mind writhed in the grip of my will. Holy shit, he was strong.

I shook, straining to hold him, trying to claw at his mind. His will clashed with mine. It was like trying to hold a fire hose with the full blast of water jettisoning out of it. He was a Prime and his power was off the charts. It took all of my willpower to contain him. I couldn't even move.

I had to ask questions. If I didn't, he would overpower me. Questions would force him to conceal the truth and drain some of his power.

My voice came out deep, every sound dripping with magic. *"What's your name?"*

Damn it. Should've asked something more useful.

His face shook with the effort of trying to break free.

The two summoned animals stared at him, confused.

My hold was slipping.

Now, Cornelius. Now. Do something. Rynda, run. Save yourself. Come on.

He bared his teeth. He let his creatures feed on people. He was going to murder Rynda's children, who had no say in any of this. Rage erupted in me, boosting my magic. My will crushed Vincent's.

A raw, guttural snarl tore out of him. "Vincent Harcourt."

Pain blossomed at the base of my neck and rolled down in a heavy wave, like molten lead. My teeth rattled. The strain ground down my bones, as if someone took a cheese grater and drew it across my spine.

"What do you want from Rynda?"

The world wavered. Blackness swirled in the corners of the room, threatening to expand and swallow me. I couldn't pass out. I had to hold on to consciousness.

Beads of sweat dotted Vincent's hairline. A tremor shook him. His mind opened slightly, and within its depth, I sensed the solid wall of a hex. I had done something like that before, but I had created the illusion of it. This was the real thing, a trap saturated with magic.

"Her . . ."

My power brushed against the hex, and I almost recoiled. It felt familiar. It was set by a truthseeker.

". . . mother . . ."

My grip slipped. Agony exploded in my brain, and I stumbled back from the impact.

"You fucking bitch," Vincent snarled.

The bat-ape charged me, swiping with its hand. I jerked back, but its claws grazed my leg, painting a red-hot line of pain across my left thigh.

The massive cat-thing jumped in front of me, shockingly fast, knocking the bat-ape aside. The smaller creature flew from the impact, landing on my gun. It tried to rise, but the cat-monster pounced. A massive paw rose, claws flashed, and the cat-monster ripped the bat-ape apart with a single swipe. Thick red blood poured on the floor.

"What the fuck!" Vincent snarled.

"The pact is made," Cornelius said, his voice distant and otherworldly.

"The hell it is. It's mine!"

Magic snapped out of Vincent, gripping the cat.

I dove left, trying to push the bat-ape off my gun. The heavy body refused to move. My hands slid in the blood.

Cornelius and Vincent stood face-to-face, the cat creature crouching by Cornelius. Magic churned between the two men. I couldn't see it, but I felt it.

I put my legs into it, heaved the beast aside, grabbed my blood-soaked Baby Desert Eagle, and spun around, scrambling to grab my magazine.

Cornelius opened his mouth and sang out a long note that sounded like the howl of a cat.

Vincent clawed the air with his hands. The magic swirled

away from Cornelius, sparking in the empty air. A dark knot of smoke formed above the floor, shot through with lightning. He was about to open another portal.

I slapped the magazine into the gun. *Got you, you bastard.*

Rynda screamed. Power erupted from her in a torrent and slammed against Vincent.

I fired. The gun roared twice.

He jerked a fraction of a second before I squeezed the trigger, his face contorted with raw panic, and went through the window in an explosion of glass shards.

No.

I jumped to my feet and ran to the window. A well-lit backyard stretched into the night, the pool perfectly still. My first shot had grazed his shoulder. My second had gone wide. I was aiming for his head. If Rynda hadn't done whatever she did . . . It didn't matter. Vincent was gone.

Rynda collapsed on her knees in front of Edward's body. The kids wailed. Edward raised his head and tried to say something.

Rynda grabbed his hand. "Don't speak. It will be okay."

The blue cat creature rubbed its head against Cornelius' hand.

Vincent got away. I wanted to throw my gun against the wall. I didn't, but I really wanted to. Instead, I pulled out my phone and dialed 911.

ROGAN'S PEOPLE BEAT the paramedics by four minutes and they brought Dr. Daniela Arias with them. When they found us, I was pressing Cornelius' bundled jacket against Edward's wound, the kids were wailing despite Rynda's best efforts to calm them down, and the monster cat was making demonic noises Cornelius claimed was a form of a purr. Cat wasn't an accurate description. There was something feline about it, something reminiscent of the broad powerful tiger, but its nose was a complicated thing of four nostrils, and the fringe of tentacles that ringed its neck moved on its own. The beast looked at me with an understanding, as if it was a lot smarter than any Earth animal. It was just odd. Really odd and unsettling.

Rogan's people stabilized Edward, moved all of us into the upstairs living room, which was free of the nasty-smelling corpses, assigned a man with a Beretta tactical shotgun to guard us, established a perimeter, and began a systematic sweep of the house and the grounds. Cornelius and his new pet went to help.

While they did that, I called home, told Bern what happened, and then did a quick search on Vincent Harcourt. Vincent, the only son and heir apparent of House Harcourt, Prime, Summonitor, which was the official term for summoner mages. No convictions, no criminal records, worth around fifty million dollars. Summoning didn't have great applications in the real world, but the Harcourts clearly had done well for themselves.

Rynda held Edward's hand until the paramedics took him away.

"He'll make it," Daniela said. "The damage wasn't significant. The main danger is infection."

"Thank you," I told her.

She squinted at me.

Dr. Arias and I didn't see eye to eye. She'd tried to warn me that my relationship with Rogan was a very bad idea, and I didn't listen to her advice. I'd also threatened her. Considering that Daniela was at least eight inches taller than me and built like a woman who could stop a horse in full gallop by grabbing it, in retrospect, threatening her wasn't one of my wiser decisions. But I wanted to be with Rogan and I wouldn't let anybody stop me.

And he was still missing in action. Worry gnawed at me.

"Is any of that blood yours?" Daniela asked.

"Some."

"So you have an open wound and you're covered in blood from the arcane realm."

"Yes."

"Were you planning on letting me know about it?"

"Yes."

"When?"

"Right now." She would kill me for sure.

"How is it that nobody else has any blood on them?"

"Uh . . ."

She reached into her bag and pulled out a giant bottle of water and another of alcohol sanitizer. "Let's see it."

I hiked up my dress. Three bright scratches tore across my left thigh. "Just scratches. Also shoulders." I was pretty sure the claws had punctured me.

Daniela sighed and got out a syringe sealed in plastic and a vial.

"What is that?"

"Antivenin. The creatures secrete venom on their claws. Does it hurt?"

"No."

"It should." She tore the plastic off the syringe and stabbed it into the vial through the seal on top. "It will hurt in about ten minutes if the venom is neutralized."

It hurt like someone stabbed me with a hot poker. My thigh was on fire. My shoulders burned. It took her about fifteen minutes to thoroughly sanitize my wounds and seal them with a skin adhesive. None of it was deep, but it hurt like hell.

Then she started cleaning my hands and legs. By the time I was released, I felt like I was scrubbed with one of those green scouring pads used to get dried-on crust out of pans. My skin was clean. My dress was another story. There was no way to expose the shoulders without taking it off completely. We had to cut it. That hurt almost as much as the antivenin.

"Done," Daniela said.

"Thank you."

She squinted at me again.

I got up and moved to where Rynda and the children sat on the love seat. The kids were curled up around her. Kyle had finally fallen asleep. She'd covered him with a blanket. Jessica was almost there too, her face sleepy, her eyes closing, tucked into the corner of the couch.

I sat across from them on a footstool, trying not to wince. Rynda glanced at me. She looked like she'd been through hell and back.

"Walk me through it," I told her.

"Right now?"

"Yes, please."

"We were getting ready for bed. I went to use the bathroom and while I was in there, Jessica came and told me that Kyle ran away. We started looking for him. That was when Edward arrived."

Her voice broke. She sniffled.

"He wanted to apologize. He felt bad, because he thought Brian was just off on one of his hiding sprees. He helped me look for Kyle. We found him in Brian's office. He refused to go to bed, because he wanted to wait until his daddy got home. I heard gunfire downstairs, so I locked the door. Then one of those things went through the window. Edward grabbed a chair and hit it. It ripped into him and then he collapsed on the floor. Then Vincent came."

Truth. "Who is Vincent?" I already knew, but it didn't hurt to have her take on it.

"Vincent Harcourt of House Harcourt. We went to school together. He was a bully and he grew up into a despicable bastard."

"That's a bad word," Jessica said, her voice sleepy.

Rynda kissed her hair. "He is a very bad man."

"What did he want?"

"A file. He wanted one of my mother's files. I told him I don't have any of her files. The estate is still in probate. I don't even have access to her house. He didn't believe me. He said he knew for sure I had the file."

"Do you have any idea what he might be talking about?"

She shook her head. "No. He had one of those things snap its teeth an inch from my children's necks. I would've given him everything."

"Did your mother interact with Harcourt?"

"I don't know, okay!" Rynda's voice rose. "I don't know what my mother was involved in. Everyone assumes I do, but I don't know anything! She didn't share. She didn't ask for my advice. Will you just leave me alone? Just for a few minutes, for the love of God!"

Truth.

"She saved your life," Daniela said over my shoulder. "She's trying to find your husband. Maybe you could stop being uncooperative for a few minutes and make an effort?"

Rynda opened her mouth. Nothing came out.

I could've hugged Daniela. She'd break me in half, but it would be worth it.

"I thought we were going to die," Rynda said in a small voice. "Is that what you wanted to hear?"

"What happened at the end?"

"I emanated. He felt everything he made me feel. All my fear. All of my desperation. I don't do it often. It's a very violent thing to impose your emotions on others. I just couldn't think of anything else to do."

"Thank you."

I stood up.

The guard at the door stood straighter. Rogan walked into the room.

Rynda ran past me and threw her arms around his neck.

Oh for goodness' sake. Really?

"It was awful," Rynda said.

"You need to pack," Rogan said, gently hugging her back. "I'm taking you and the kids out of this house."

"Okay," she said.

He didn't say anything else. She stood for another long moment hugging him, then her hands dropped, and she took a step away.

Rogan turned to me. He took in my sneakers, my ruined bloodstained dress, the bandages on my legs, and then I was in his arms.

CHAPTER 6

ROGAN PACKED ME into his Range Rover. I told him I was fine driving my own car, but he pretended to not hear me. Cornelius somehow managed to pack the cat creature into a Ford Explorer by laying down as many seats as he could. He informed us that the cat was a he and that we would call him Zeus.

Rynda finally recovered enough to call the Sherwood chief of security. Before we left, several people in Sherwood House uniforms showed up to secure the house, led by the chief himself. Cornelius decided that would be an appropriate time to mention we had called BioCore and he had hung up on us. Rynda slapped the security chief. Rogan's people confiscated Sherwood computers, loaded Rynda and the kids into an armored car, and our small convoy of five vehicles headed back to base. Two of Rogan's ATVs led the way, Rynda and Cornelius were sandwiched safely in the middle, and Rogan and I brought up the rear.

It was just me and Rogan in the car. I liked to watch him drive. He did it with calm assurance, focused on the road. I liked the lines of his muscular arms, the way he tapped the wheel with his left thumb at long stoplights, and the way he kept glancing at me as if reassuring himself that I was okay in the passenger seat. I didn't like the darkness in his eyes. I'd seen it before. It was a bad sign.

"Is it because of me?"

He didn't answer.

"Are you brooding because of me?"

"Brooding implies marinating in your own self-loathing," he said. "I don't brood."

"Then what are you doing?"

"I'm planning to kill Harcourt."

Rogan didn't tolerate threats, and Vincent Harcourt was a threat. I didn't want to think about how close I'd come to dying tonight.

"He was really strong. I clamped him with my magic and lost him after only two questions. Ten, fifteen seconds max."

"Summoning is a will-based talent."

So was truthseeking. That explained why Vincent was so difficult to hold.

"Victoria Tremaine would've melted his brain," I said. "I barely managed to hold him for a few seconds." And I was spent. I had very little magic left. The familiar fatigue of overextending was settling in.

"You did more than anyone could ask. You bought more than enough time for Cornelius to deploy his iron pan and for Rynda to escape."

"Cornelius was trying to make friends with Zeus. Rynda was in shock."

He didn't say anything, but the darkness in his eyes turned deeper.

"Rogan, I'm in one piece. More importantly, the kids are okay."

"If Cornelius had walked up and brained that bastard while you held him, we would be having an entirely different conversation. Neither of them had the presence of mind to pick up a weapon or run away."

"You can't blame Cornelius. He was fascinated with the cat. It was a compulsion, Rogan. He doesn't think the same way we do and he stepped up in the end when it counted."

"You need better backup."

What I needed was someone to teach me the ins and outs of my magic. Truthseekers were rare and they guarded their secrets. I was practicing, but I've barely begun to scratch the surface.

"Vincent's mind was hexed. It felt familiar. I think it's the same kind of wall I put into Augustine."

A week ago Victoria Tremaine had zeroed in on Augustine, the Prime who owned the large investigative firm that held the mortgage on our business. Augustine had helped me to save a little girl from slow death by arranging for me to pry open her kidnapper's mind. Victoria had come to find out the identity of that truthseeker. To keep Augustine intact and to save myself, I'd put a wall in Augustine's mind. It was a ruse, a fake hex, but it had looked real enough and there was no way to find out if it was false unless Victoria actually attacked Augustine. She decided not to risk it.

"Was it false?" Rogan asked.

"No. The one in Vincent's mind was real."

"Better backup," Rogan repeated, nodding to himself. "Someone trained. Someone who will put your safety first."

"Like who?"

"Like me."

"What are you saying?"

"I'm saying that from now on I'll come with you. Just like before."

"Connor . . ."

He took my hand and squeezed it with his strong fingers. His voice was ragged. "I should've been there. I was at the wrong place at the wrong time. You could've died. It scares the hell out of me."

I squeezed his hand back. "I didn't die."

He held my hand.

"Where were you?" I asked.

"Bug found one of the cars exiting a rural road. He couldn't see the license plate, but he swore it was the same vehicle. I took a few people and went to check it out."

He thought Brian might have been held somewhere on that road. "Any luck?"

"There are five ranches on that road. He could be at any one of them, assuming that's where they dropped him off. It's connected to the conspiracy, so the trail will be well hidden."

"What could be in that file?"

"I don't know," he said. "But if it exists in Rynda's computers, Bug will find it."

"Bernard would find it faster."

"Fine. They can look for it together. I'm sorry I wasn't there."

"I'm not upset that you weren't there. I was doing my job. I don't blame you for anything, Connor. Except not telling me that you had a lead. That wasn't cool." I lowered my voice, trying to match his. "When you have a lead, I want to know about it. Not eventually, not when it's convenient, but immediately."

He didn't rise to the bait. Apparently, he was determined to blame himself.

"So, are we still on tonight? For our dinner?" I asked.

"Hell, yes. We're on for tonight. We're on for tomorrow. We're on for the foreseeable future. You're not going anywhere without me."

And here I thought he was being romantic. "Would you like to wrap me in bubble wrap?"

"If I can find the bulletproof kind."

"Rogan—"

"I mean it." He checked the rearview mirror. His eyes narrowed.

I turned to see a massive black Jeep Wrangler closing in behind us. Heavily modified, it sat high on a lift and oversize tires. Custom bumper, light bar, and a grille made to look like fangs with a big *M* in the middle. The Jeep looked ready to bite our bumper.

I reached for the glove compartment and pulled out my Baby Desert Eagle. I'd bummed some ammo from Rogan's guys.

The Jeep flashed his lights at us.

"Someone you know?"

"House Madero. Probably Dave Madero." Rogan's gaze gained dangerous intensity. He was calculating something in his head.

"Why is he flashing his lights?"

"He's warning us that he's about to use an EMP cannon." Rogan pressed a button on his steering wheel. "Rivera?"

"Major?" Rivera's voice said from the speakers.

"Drive on without me. I have something to take care of."

"Yes, sir."

Rogan took the Kempwood Drive exit. The Jeep followed.

"We're not running?"

"No. The EMP cannon would stop the vehicle in the middle of the lane. The road is busy. I'm not taking chances with you in the car."

Rogan shifted into the far right lane. A narrow strip of grass, bordered by a wall of trees that was the edge of Agnes Moffitt Park, rolled by us.

"Madero is a gun for hire," Rogan said. "He can harden his skin with a layer of magic and he is supernaturally strong. I saw him take a hit from an SUV at sixty miles per hour. It folded around him. Shooting him will do no good. The bullet won't penetrate, but just to be on the safe side, he also travels with an aegis."

A protector mage, capable of projecting a shield of magic that would absorb gunfire. Great.

"What did you do to Dave Madero?" I asked.

"He isn't here for me."

Victoria Tremaine. Alarm shot through me.

The wall of trees ended. Rogan made a sharp right onto Hammerly Boulevard. The Range Rover jumped the curb, and Rogan drove across the grass onto the wide lawn and brought it to a stop.

The Jeep came to a stop about forty feet behind us. Darkness had fallen, but the lights of the streetlamps flooded the park with light.

The driver door opened and a man stepped out. At least, he was vaguely man-shaped. He had to be seven feet tall. He wore loose black pants and a black T-shirt. Hard muscle slabbed his chest and monstrous shoulders. His enormous arms rippled. His biceps had to be as big as my thighs. His blond hair was buzz cut to a mere memory. He looked like a caricature of a human, an action figure of a bodybuilder come to life.

"Is he real?"

"Yes." Rogan shut off the Range Rover.

The passenger door opened and a blond woman stepped out. That had to be the aegis.

"If I get close enough, I can shock him."

"No, you can't. You spent all of your magic restraining Vincent. You shock him now, you'll die too."

Rogan swung the door open.

"Stay in the car."

"Rogan!"

He jumped out.

Stay in the car, my foot.

I popped the door open, circled the car from the hood, and sighted Dave Madero with my gun.

"Her grandmother wants to speak to her." Dave Madero sounded the way he looked, his voice deep and unhurried. "Your magic won't work on me directly, Rogan. Nothing else here will do enough damage. Give the girl to me and we'll go our separate ways."

"No."

"I get it. You don't want to look bad. But I'm going to get her anyway and take her to her grandmother. She said to make sure she's alive. She didn't say in what shape and she didn't say anything about you. Those things are up to me. You give me the girl, she won't get roughed up."

I really wanted to shoot him.

Rogan didn't answer.

"Suit yourself."

Madero's skin bulged, turning a darker, flushed red. He started toward Rogan, slow and confident. Rogan watched him. He shouldn't have gotten out of the car. He could do terrible things to a human body with his hands, but kicking or punching Dave would do no good. Rogan would just hurt himself. I would do anything to keep him from getting hurt.

The aegis behind him stepped forward, a gun in her hands. She was my age, red-haired, and her eyes were uncertain. She watched Rogan with apprehension.

I had to neutralize her. Rogan already had his hands full.

I sighted her and channeled my mother. "You shoot, I'll kill you."

"I'm an aegis."

"I know. I never miss."

She opened her mouth and closed it. I did my best to look like I meant business, because I did. She couldn't shoot and maintain her shield at the same time. The moment that gun came up, I would fire and I would hit her to save Rogan.

"You can't—" she began.

"Test me and you'll find out."

She stayed where she was, gun pointed to the ground.

Dave Madero rolled his shoulders and moved forward, circling. He was at least ten inches taller and probably twice as heavy as Rogan, who towered over me. Rogan's body was corded with hard, flexible muscle, but next to Dave, he looked like a teenager who had yet to fill out.

Rogan moved too, with easy natural grace, focused on Dave. His whole body realigned itself, transforming him from a civilized man who had been driving a car just a minute ago into something else, something savage and almost feral. He moved toward Dave with a predatory anticipation. The hair on the back of my neck rose.

Dave must've realized he was being stalked and slowed.

"You sure you want to do this?" he asked. "It won't be pretty. You think we're gonna fight, you gonna punch, maybe throw some kicks. She'll be impressed. It's not gonna work like that. I don't know what kind of training you have, but whatever it is, it's not gonna be enough. This isn't the dojo. We're not gonna shake hands and bow. And your girl will be worse off when you lose."

"Stop talking." Rogan's voice was iced over. "Show me."

"Fine. Your funeral."

Dave swung. It was a slow, wide right haymaker. Rogan leaned out of the way.

Dave threw a left. It fanned Rogan's chest with plenty of space to spare.

"Slow," Rogan said.

Dave rolled his eyes.

"Every generation you breed bigger, slower, and dumber," Rogan said.

"Keep talking. We'll see what kind of noises you'll be making when I make you swallow your teeth."

They moved in a circle.

Dave snapped a fast right hook. Rogan moved out of the way like his joints were fluid.

"When the other families want a big oaf, they call you and here you are. Any job, any time. Kidnapping. Pain. Theft by brute force. *Brute* is the key word. You're a House of Blockheads."

Dave locked his teeth. Rogan hit a nerve. He was pissing Madero off on purpose.

"Soon you'll breed out what little brainpower you have."

"Done?" Dave growled.

"Almost. Just wondering when you will start wearing leashes. This generation or the next?"

Dave hammered a shockingly fast jab. Rogan dodged by a hair. Jab, jab, hard right.

Rogan kept moving. Dave was backing him into the Jeep. The aegis saw it and scurried to the side, keeping the gun ready.

Dave drove a long straight jab, but palm up, turning it into an uppercut. Rogan ducked. Dave unleashed a crushing hard right. Somehow Rogan dodged and Dave's fist hammered into the Jeep. Metal screeched. The hood buckled from the impact. Dave growled and shoved the Jeep back with his left hand. The vehicle rolled thirty yards back, all the way to the tree line.

Cold sweat drenched me. If Rogan took just one punch, even a glancing hit, it was all over.

"The fight's right here," Rogan said.

"You made me hurt my baby," Dave said. "That's extra. I'm gonna kill you for that."

He wasn't joking. He would actually kill Rogan.

Dave charged like an enraged bull. He pounded after Rogan, erupting in a whirlwind of punches.

Jab, jab, cross.

Left jab. Right uppercut.

Left hook, right cross, left hook to the body.

The hook grazed Rogan's side and he flew five yards, landed hard, then rolled to his feet. Fear punched straight through my chest and down into my legs.

Dave chased him. Rogan backed away, trying to dodge a wild barrage of punches. Dave was on him, swinging, his breathing labored and heavy. His face turned purple. He was sucking air in shallow gasps.

Jab, overhand right, hook, cross.

Rogan stepped into the punch, sliding between Dave's arms, wrapped his left arm over Dave's right, catching it in the bend of his elbow, so the giant man's forearm rested on Rogan's shoulder. He locked the fingers of his hands together and twisted, throwing all of his weight to the right. A loud pop echoed through the park. Dave howled, a raw, terrible cry of pure pain. He sounded like an animal screaming.

Rogan moved away. Dave straightened, his face contorted by rage. His right arm hung useless at his side. Rogan had snapped his elbow like a twig.

The aegis shivered in place, her face pale.

Dave charged, reaching for Rogan's throat. Rogan backed up at the last minute, sapping the speed out of Dave's attack, moved in, turning all the way to the left, so his right arm slid over Dave's left, and bent his elbow, trapping Dave's arm in his armpit. Rogan's fingers locked on Dave's wrist. There was another sharp pop. Dave screamed and collapsed on the ground, his wrist still in Rogan's hand. Rogan moved his left leg over Dave, clamping the man's arm between his legs, stepped all the way to the right, and twisted again. Another crack. Dave was screaming his heart out. The aegis shrieked like a dying bird.

"Rogan, stop," I called. "That's enough."

"Are you done?" Rogan asked.

"Fuck you!" Dave spat.

"Dave!" the aegis cried out.

"The man isn't done. He's still got two good legs left."

Rogan picked up Dave's left leg, pulled it straight, and rolled back, sitting around it, so his right leg was locked over Dave's thigh. He would snap Dave's knee.

The aegis flung her gun across the lawn and looked at me, her face desperate.

I ran to Rogan and dropped on my knees by him. "Enough. Please. *Please.*"

"Is it enough?" Rogan asked.

Dave moaned. He was purple like a plum now, his breathing so fast, he wasn't getting in any air.

I put my hands on Rogan's steel-hard calf. "Please. He can't even talk anymore. He can't tell you to stop."

Dave raised his palm and slapped the ground.

Rogan released his leg and stood up in a single fluid movement. His voice could've frozen over the Gulf. "Don't come after her. She won't stop me next time. Tell your brothers. You come after her again, I'll go through your House until none of you are left."

Dave deflated slightly, his skin turning a more human color. Sweat drenched him. He sucked in air, leaned on his side, and vomited.

The aegis knelt by him, a water bottle in her hand.

I wrapped my hand around Rogan's arm. "Let's go home."

We got into the car. I slid into the driver's seat, started the Range Rover, and drove back to the street before Rogan decided to go back.

He leaned back in his seat, his face calm. He had to be hurting.

"Are you okay?" I asked.

He nodded.

"How bad is it?"

"I'll live."

Dave was in the wrong place at the wrong time. Daniela once told me that Rogan hated feeling helpless more than anything. He would go to any length to avoid it. My going into Rynda's house while he was across the city made him feel helpless and scared. He needed to let it out. He needed to hurt someone, and Dave had presented himself as a threat to me. Rogan broke him and would've kept on breaking if I didn't stop him.

The Belize War had changed Rogan. It changed everyone, but it had torn him apart and he had to remake himself to survive. He served as the army's ultimate weapon. He would walk into a city, reach into the deepest part of his soul, where the magic was wild, and let it out, and the city would crumble and fall around him. He inspired fear. They gave him scary names. The Butcher of Merida. The Scourge of Mexico. Huracan. As if he weren't a man but some terrifying legend come to life. And then he ended up in a jungle, miles into enemy territory, with soldiers depending on him for their lives. Using magic would've saved him but his soldiers wouldn't survive. So he didn't use it. He walked them out of that jungle, but very few people knew what those weeks in Belize had cost him. He would never again fit into the civilian life. Rogan would never be "normal." He left the military five years ago, but it made no difference. He was still in.

"Did I scare you?" he asked.

"Yes."

"I'm sorry."

"You didn't have to go toe-to-toe with him."

"Yes, I did." Understanding dawned on him. "Wait. You were scared for me?"

"Yes!"

"I've seen him fight. When he armors up, he can't sweat. He has a limited time frame before he starts overheating. The more he moves, the hotter he gets."

"It was still dangerous."

"I didn't rush into the fight. It was a calculated risk," he said.

Oh well, that makes everything better, then, doesn't it? "You could've picked up a tree and smashed him with it."

"That would take care of Dave, but not his family. House Madero doesn't understand telekinesis. They understand brute force and broken bones. I sent a message and I made it simple enough so even they won't misinterpret it."

Well, he had a point. They wouldn't misinterpret it. They wouldn't work for Victoria Tremaine again.

"There is a difference between self-defense and torture. I understand why you broke his arms. But there was no need to break his legs."

He didn't say anything.

"Occasionally there will be times when I'll be in danger," I said.

"I know."

"There may not always be a Dave handy."

"I know . . . I'll learn to deal with it. But I will protect you, Nevada, no matter what it costs me."

He simply stated it as fact. Oh, Connor.

"I'm glad you stopped me," he said. "I wasn't when I was doing it. But now I'm glad."

I was probably the only one who could. If it was one of his guys, he would've just kept going. And the next time, if I wasn't there, he would break Dave's legs.

I understood why Rynda was trying so hard to ingratiate herself to him. She was in panic mode and she knew that if Rogan cared about you, he would stop at nothing to keep you safe. If he and I ever had a family . . .

Children? Was I really thinking about having his children? I pictured what Rogan's children might be like. Smart, and beautiful, and deadly. And impossible. They would be little demon children, getting into everything, trying everything, and not understanding the word *no*.

His eyes had iced over again. When Olivia Charles had killed his people, Rogan went into a grim place. There was nothing there except the absence of light, ice, and revenge. I had dragged him out of that darkness, and I would never let it have him again.

We passed the checkpoint and I parked the car in front of his HQ. He released his seat belt and studied me. The air in the car vibrated with his tension and energy, all of it dark.

"Some things I can't help," he said.

"I know."

"But I'll try."

"That's all I ask."

I looked into his dark eyes and saw the edge of a storm brewing. He was focused only on me. Nothing else existed. I had the dragon's undivided attention. Breath caught in my throat.

He leaned forward. He was going to kiss me.

Anticipation gripped me, mixed with a hint of instinctual alarm.

His lips touched mine. His kiss scorched me. I gasped and let him in. His tongue claimed my mouth and I tasted him, the unique flavor that was Rogan, male, harsh, and irresistible. His hand cradled the back of my head, his fingers sliding through my hair. He drank me in, possessive and seducing.

Magic touched the back of my neck, its velvet touch pure ecstasy on my skin. It slid down my spine, setting every sensitive nerve on fire.

My seat belt slid open. I sat there, dazed, as he got out of the car, walked to my door, and opened it. Rogan held out his hand. I took it. His fingers wrapped around mine. He led me into the building, through the downstairs, usually filled with his men, but now empty, up the stairs to the second floor, past Bug's observation station, a crescent wall of computer screens, past his own office, to the back, where another stairway led up to the third floor. We walked up, he opened a metal door, we walked inside, and it clanged shut behind us.

An open space spread before me, a wide stretch of sealed concrete floor. A big bed stood on the left, on which someone, probably Rogan, had thrown a grey wool blanket. On the other side, to the right, a glass screen curved, probably hiding a shower and a bathroom.

The right wall was normal drywall, painted deep grey. The left wall was glass. Heavy three-foot squares of smoky glass climbed up thirty feet to meet at a sharp angle above us. I'd seen this building a dozen times and I'd never realized that the glass cap on top of it was transparent. It seemed solid black from the outside.

I walked to the window. Outside, the evening had birthed a night. The stars spread above us, glowing sparks of jewel-fire against the velvet blackness. A hoard that was the envy of any dragon.

Rogan wrapped his arms around me, my back to his chest. I heard him inhale the scent of my hair. His long hard length pressed against me. I leaned into him. He made a rough male noise that spoke of hunger and need. It made me weak in the knees. He brushed my hair aside and kissed my neck. Tiny electric shocks dashed through me. Magic danced over my skin, hot, slow, and deliberate. The muscles on his arms were tight under my fingers.

His hands slid over my breasts, caressing, teasing. A jolt of pleasure rolled through me. I gasped. I wanted more.

The zipper on my dress slid down. It fell around my ankles. His warm hand slid down over my stomach. Lower. Please.

My bra came unhooked. He slid the straps over my shoulders, eased the cups off my breasts, and I let it fall to the floor. His fingers slid over my nipples. The sudden burst of sensation was so intense, I jerked in his embrace.

He kissed me right below my right ear, setting my nerves on fire. I looked down on to his hands gliding across my stomach and saw dark smudges. Summoned creature's blood.

"Rogan . . ."

"Yes."

He kissed my neck again. I could barely talk.

"I'm covered in blood."

He stopped and spun me around. "Are you hurting?"

"No. I'm just dirty."

He looked down at the dried blood on my stomach. "I can fix that."

He took my hand and we crossed the floor to the glass screen. A shower waited, three walls of tile bristling with faucets. He turned the knobs, and crisscrossing jets of water erupted from the walls. Steam rose. I slipped my underwear off and walked into the wall of water. It felt like heaven. Instantly I was soaked. The water dragged my hair down, plastering it against my chest and back. It ran dark, then almost immediately clear. I scrubbed my face, banishing the last traces of makeup, and turned around.

He stood in front of the shower, watching me, as if mesmerized.

I stepped through the water toward him, letting the jets spray my breasts and my stomach. Water ran down between my legs, wetting the curls of hair where they met. I was already wet inside.

Rogan swore.

"What?"

"You're so beautiful."

He pulled off his shirt and dropped it. He was big and golden, his body all hard muscle, honed to lethal efficiency. His broad shoulders and powerful chest slimmed down to a flat, hard stomach. I wanted to run my fingers across the hard ridges of his abs. His pants followed the shirt, revealing muscular legs. He was erect and ready, the full length of him massive and straining. He stood naked in front of me, towering, all brutal power and strength. His eyes were full of lust.

I opened my arms.

He came through the water for me. We collided. Magic whipped around me, swirling on my skin, a hot velvet pressure that flowed like liquid over my neck, my breasts, into the creases of my butt, gliding between my legs . . . He kissed me, hard and possessive, his arms around me. Our tongues tangled and I tasted him again. It was like being drunk.

I wrapped my arms around him. The cables of muscle on his back were steel-hard under my fingers. His hands roamed my body, stoking the fire. A wet ache hummed between my legs, a heavy pressure that demanded him. I kissed him back, desperate for more, and pushed him against the wall.

He grinned at me, a male smile, not just sexy, but carnal. He was like a dream come to life. I slid my hands over his chest, over his abs, down, over the thick girth of him. He groaned. The ache between my legs was unbearable now. I needed him inside me.

I pumped, squeezing, draped myself against him, my nipples pressing against his wet chest, and slipped down. My mouth closed around him. He barely fit. I sucked. Rogan growled and hauled me upright. His hands gripped my butt and he heaved me up, onto his hips. His hand slipped between my legs, dipped into the wet heat, and stroked the sensitive bud. Pleasure shocked me. His magic spilled over and joined his fingers. It was too much. I arched my back and rode his hand.

He pushed my back against the cool tile. I felt his thick shaft press against me. He thrust all the way, right into the center of the ache, and we were one.

He thrust again and again, in an unrelenting, maddening rhythm. Climax burned through me, wiping out everything. He kept going, as he drove himself into my heat. I opened my eyes and saw him looking at me. I clung to his shoulders, kissing the strong column of his neck, his jaw, his lips. A shudder rocked him and he emptied himself. The tidal wave of his release reverberated through his magic, sending me tumbling into ecstasy again. I draped myself over him, boneless and limp. The pleasure was so intense, I almost cried.

"You're everything to me," he said into my ear.

I wanted to tell him that he was everything to me, that I wouldn't let the darkness have him, that he never had to worry that I would give up and walk away. But the echoes of our shared pleasure stole the words, and so I said it the best I could.

"I love you."

SOMETHING WAS BEEPING. I stirred and raised my head. Next to me Rogan swore, gently lifted my arm off his chest, and rolled out of bed. We had collapsed there after the shower, barely bothering to towel off, and I had dozed off on his chest, exhausted, happy, and safe, with his arm around me. Sleeping next to him was like coming home.

I blinked until my vision was no longer blurry. Rogan fished his phone out of the pile of his clothes by the shower and answered it.

"Slow down." He moved back to the bed and held the phone out a couple of inches from his ear.

Rynda's high-pitched voice emanated from the phone, punctuated by a child wailing. ". . . can't calm him down. Please. *Please.* I need your help. Please, Connor."

I groaned and collapsed back on the bed.

"I'm busy," Rogan said.

"If you just talk to him, he's only four, please . . ."

Rogan looked like he wanted to throw his phone against the wall. "I'll be right there."

I slapped a pillow on my face.

The pillow disappeared and he leaned over me. "Wait for me."

"Let me guess, it's another crisis only you can solve?"

"Kyle is panicking. I put her and the kids in the building north of us. It will take me thirty seconds to walk over."

"We just had sex, and now you're taking off to see your *ex-fiancée.*"

"I'll be back. We're sleeping in the same bed tonight. I mean it."

I waved at him. "Go."

He pulled on his jeans and a T-shirt. "Wait for me."

He opened the door and left.

I exhaled. It's not that Rynda was consciously manipulating him. It was more that she relied on other people to fix her problems. First her mother, then her husband, and now Rogan. She was the kind of person who would see a pot overflowing on the stove and come and tell you about it, instead of picking it up and moving it off the burner. And then she would be proud of herself for acting quickly in a crisis.

Rogan, on other hand, would solve the problem. That was what he did.

I checked the small digital alarm clock on the nightstand: 10:03 p.m. I thought it was much later. I must've just fallen asleep when Rynda called. Except now I was wide awake.

I studied the starry glass ceiling above me. The night was so beautiful from here. It would've been even more beautiful if Rogan was here with me.

I'd left my phone in my car. I had meant to grab it, but so much had happened.

The room spread in front of me. No shelves, but a stack of books sat on the floor near the window.

10:10 p.m.

I got up and snagged the top book off the stack. *Monsters Inside Us: A Case Study of Magically Induced Metamorphosis*. Well, that was a mouthful. I dragged the book with me to the bed, turned on the lamp, and leafed through it. Magic did strange things to human beings. A century and a half ago, when the Osiris serum was first developed, it was given out like candy. Nobody knew exactly how the Osiris serum did what it did. Some thought it created new powers. Some said it awakened the dormant talents we had repressed. But how it acted was less important than the results. Some people took it and gained great power. Others turned into monsters. Those magic-warped had to be destroyed.

Now, years later, the instances of monsters were rare. I'd met one, Cherry. She was an addict and she sold herself to some institute run by a House. They had exposed her to something and now Cherry spent her days in the murky waters of the Pit, a nasty flooded area of Houston, eating frogs. Part of her was more alligator than human.

10:19 p.m. Thirty seconds, huh.

I wrapped the blanket around myself and flipped through the book. I knew a lot of these cases. The case of German Orr, the real-life minotaur. German was a sicko, who could transform himself into a bull-like beast. While in his minotaur shape he was extremely well-endowed, and he used his talents to star in some seriously gross porn. He was arrested on bestiality charges and went to court, arguing that this was magical discrimination and his rights were being violated. He lost, was jailed for six years, and then left the country.

Jeraldine Amber, the Bangor Banshee. When Jeraldine used her sonic magic, she transformed into a strange pale creature with black eyes and watery white hair. She was normal in all other respects, and while her talents passed to her children, the ability to metamorphose didn't. Or so they claimed.

10:35 p.m. Seriously, Rogan?

I turned the page. The Beast of Cologne. I knew this story so well, I could write a book on it. Misha Marcotte, a Belgian woman, discovered her talent in her early twenties. She could assume the shape of an enormous beast, a creature out of a nightmare. She was practically indestructible in that shape, but she had no control over it. Once she metamorphosed, she would go berserk. The Belgian Armed Forces in cooperation with the French Légion de Sorciers, the Sorcerer Legion, had tried to evaluate her skills, and during her third transformation, she permanently lost her humanity. She crossed the Belgian-German border and rampaged through Cologne, nearly leveling the city, until they finally contained her. How exactly they managed to do it was a secret, but the dominant rumor was that the Germans drowned her in the waters of the Rhine. She was a cautionary tale for anyone with the power of metamorphosis.

There were rumors that she had reverted to her human form, survived the drowning, and was being kept alive somewhere under constant sedation. I believed it. The Primes would never throw a talent away, not while they hoped to glean some knowledge or increase their power from it.

I slapped the book closed. 10:48. I'd been waiting for him for almost an hour. Enough was enough. I couldn't just sit here, pining in the dark by myself, naked. I had family to check on.

I got up off the bed. The thought of putting on my blood-smeared dress turned my stomach. No, thanks. He had to have some clothes around here.

I searched the room. The glass curve of the shower extended a few feet past the shower itself, and behind it was closet space. Shelves supported stacks of neatly folded T-shirts and sweatpants, and a rod held a couple dozen hangers, offering everything from shirts to ridiculously expensive suits, precisely organized and quickly available. Military habits were hard to break.

I grabbed a T-shirt. It came to mid-thigh on me. I stole a pair of sweatpants. Predictably, they were a little tight on my hips and way too long. I rolled them up. Good enough. I kicked the remnants of my dress, my bra, and my underwear into a pile on the floor. I really liked that bra, but there was no way I would be walking out of his place with my bra in my hands. With luck, nobody would see me, but I didn't want to take chances.

I slid my feet into my beat-up sneakers and padded out the door and down the staircase to the second floor. Bug sat in his chair, absorbed in the glow of nine computer screens arranged in three-by-three formation on his wall.

He blinked at me. Bug always looked like he'd lost his sandwich and needed desperately to find it, because he was on the verge of hunger jitters. Before Rogan enticed him to come to work for him, Bug had been in bad shape. The swarm the military pulled out of the arcane realm and bound to him was supposed to have killed him in eighteen months. Only volunteers became swarmers, usually for a big payday. Bug never shared why he did it or what he spent the money on. Somehow he survived past his time. When I met him, he lived in an abandoned building, which he had booby-trapped. Skinny, dirty, paranoid, trading surveillance for an occasional hit of equzol, a military-issue drug and the only thing that would "quiet" the swarm according to him, Bug had one foot in his grave. Napoleon, a bastard son of a French bulldog and some adventurous mixed breed, was the only thing that kept him grounded.

Rogan had plucked him out of his hidey-hole. Now Bug had filled out, his dark brown hair was neatly cut and clean, and he wore decent clothes. He seemed calmer. His paranoia had receded. He could carry on a conversation without twitching. Napoleon, also clean and a good deal plumper, snored by his feet on a little couch, upholstered with red fabric and Île-de-France motif.

"You're leaving?" Bug asked.

"Yes."

"Don't leave," Bug said.

"I've got to go."

"What do I tell him when he comes back?"

Did Rogan tell him to keep an eye on me? "Tell him whatever you want, Bug."

I crossed the floor, turned the corner, and descended the staircase. The lights were on. Half a dozen of Rogan's ex-soldiers, four men and two women, carried on a quiet conversation. It died when they saw me.

I recognized Nguyen Hanh, an Asian woman who worked as Rogan's head mechanic, and Michael Rivera, Rogan's second-in-command. About mid-thirties and Latino, Rivera had a great smile. He usually smiled after he shot someone.

"Are you leaving?" Rivera asked.

"Yes." Kill me, somebody.

"Why?" Nguyen asked.

"Because I'm going home."

"But the Major isn't back yet," Rivera pointed out.

"I realize that."

"You can't leave. He said he would be right back, and we're supposed to keep you safe while he's gone. If you leave, we can't keep you safe," Rivera said.

"You can still keep me safe. I'm going to my house across the street." I pointed through the wide open double door at the warehouse. "You never close these doors anyway, so you can watch me walk twenty yards to my house."

"He'll be in a bad mood if you leave," a dark-haired man said.

Rivera looked at him for a second, then turned back to me, smiling up a storm. "Maybe you could wait for him?"

"No, I really can't."

I walked straight at Rivera. He stepped aside, I marched through the doors and headed toward the warehouse.

"It's because of the Sherwood woman," another male voice said behind me.

"Of course it is," Nguyen said. "I said when she first showed up she'd be trouble."

I crossed the street, punched the code into the lock, entered the office, and locked the door behind me. I had had one hell of a day. I had left my phone in my car, my gun in Rogan's car, and I had no underwear. Walking around without underwear felt odd. Being without my phone was even more odd. There was probably some sort of deep conclusion to be derived from the fact that losing my phone disturbed me more than losing my underwear.

This wasn't me. I always had my phone and my gun. And underwear.

I eased the interior door open. The warehouse was quiet. A lonely light glowed at the very end of the hallway in the kitchen. With four teenagers in the house, someone was always raiding the fridge during the night, and we usually left the light fixture over the table on for the midnight snackers. Tonight I heard no voices.

It was a few minutes past eleven, and on a school night everyone would be in bed by then, but we'd decided to keep everyone in until the trials. Where were they?

I tiptoed down the hallway, took a right, cleared another short hallway, and peeked out at the Hut of Evil, a small building within the building where Bern reigned supreme with all his equipment. Faint voices floated down to me.

". . . right . . . he's on top of the building . . ."

"Got it."

Right. Team Baylor was making the world safe from alien zombies one cyber shot at a time. At another time, I would get right in there and join them, but tonight wasn't that night.

I leaned a little more and caught a glimpse of Bern. He wasn't wearing his gaming headset. His face, illuminated by the glow of the monitor, looked haggard, the eyebrows furrowed. He was focused on whatever was in front of him at the cost of all else. Probably going through the contents of Rynda's computer, looking for the file the kidnappers wanted.

I turned around and padded into the kitchen. When he found something, he would tell me.

My cell phone lay on the kitchen table, illuminated by the lamp like a lure. Cornelius must've brought it in. Ha! I picked it up. One thing recovered.

A missed call. I flicked the icon and listened to the voice mail.

"This is Fullerton at Scroll, Inc. Please call me at your earliest convenience, no matter the hour."

All the muscles in my stomach tensed into a tight hard ball. It was past eleven. He said as soon as possible. I called the number.

He picked up on the first ring. "Hello, Ms. Baylor."

"Hello, Mr. Fullerton."

"The analysis of your DNA is completed. Your familial relationships are verified, and you are clear for trials."

I exhaled.

"We've received two requests for your basic profile. Under the circumstances of the impending trials, I felt I had to notify you as soon as possible."

"Let me guess, House Tremaine?"

"That's one of them."

"Denied." Victoria wouldn't be getting her claws on any of my information.

"Noted."

"Is the second from House Rogan?" What do you know? Rogan did care about the genetic match after all.

"No. House Shaffer."

"House Shaffer?" Of the three truthseeker Houses in the US, House Tremaine was the most feared, because my evil grandmother did business with the brutality of an axe murderer. House Lin had the most members. House Shaffer was the middle of the road and I knew very little about it.

"Yes. Should I deny or accept the request?"

"Why would they be asking about my genetic profile?"

"There are numerous reasons," Fullerton said carefully.

"You're an expert and this is brand-new to me. I'm just asking for a guess."

"The basic profile can be used for a number of things. It doesn't contain enough information for in-depth planning. However, it is very useful in eliminating the possibility of familial relationships."

Oh. "Do you feel they are trying to make sure that we're not related to House Shaffer?"

"That would be my expectation. Truthseeker talents are very

rare. As a gesture of goodwill, they've made their basic profile available to you, should you choose to peruse it."

"Have you examined their profile?"

"Yes. House Baylor and House Shaffer are not related."

I pondered it. If I didn't grant their request, they would wonder if I'm some sort of illegitimate relative. If I let them have access to the basic profile, they would quickly realize that I wasn't anyone's love child and leave us alone.

If only it would be that easy. The block in Vincent's mind was put there by a truthseeker.

I felt like I was playing a game of chess blind.

"Let them have access to our basic profile."

"As you wish."

"Thank you."

"My pleasure, Ms. Baylor. Have a lovely evening."

I hung up. Too late for that.

What I needed now was a nice long nap . . . I turned. Mom was leaning in the doorway, her arms crossed.

I had no underwear, but I was wearing sweatpants. She couldn't possibly see through my sweatpants and ask me where my underwear was and why I was sneaking into the house in Rogan's clothes.

"What was that about?"

"Another truthseeker House wants access to the summary of our records. Fullerton thinks they want to rule out the possibility of a familial relationship."

"What do you think?"

"A summoner attacked Rynda tonight."

"Cornelius told us."

"I sensed a block in his mind. It was put there by another truthseeker." I leaned against the table and crossed my arms too. "Brian's kidnapping is tied to the conspiracy to create New Rome. Vincent, the summoner, told me that whatever ransom they want from Rynda is connected to her mother, and her mother was in this conspiracy up to her eyeballs. We also know that when the conspiracy first started to show itself, with Adam Pierce trying to put together pieces of an artifact which would make him powerful enough to burn down the city, the location of the artifact segments was entrusted to a certain family. Their minds were shielded with a protective hex. A truthseeker had managed to peer under that hex, just like I had done, to get the information Adam needed."

"And you think this other House . . ."

"House Shaffer."

"House Shaffer is involved?"

I sighed. "I don't know. The hex was very powerful. It would take a Prime to get past it. It's logical that it would be one of the three truthseeker Houses within the United States. They have the most skin in this game, which means it's either Lin, Shaffer, or Victoria Tremaine. Our genetic profile couldn't have been up for more than a few hours, and the moment it went up, Shaffer jumped on it. So I let them have the summary. Let's see what they will do with that information."

"Was that really wise? What if they share it with your grand-mother?"

"Let's say they do. It will confirm what she already knows. We're her grandchildren." I shrugged. "You know she had Dad's DNA sequenced the moment he was born. She can probably pre-dict our genetic makeup based on that alone."

My mother frowned. "This worries me. This is the world your father escaped, Nevada. He'd done it for a reason. He hated it. It's dangerous and he didn't want to have anything to do with it. He didn't want his children to be a part of it."

I felt so tired. "What do you want me to do, Mom? We're caught in this conspiracy. The only way out is to expose it. It's a big tangled knot and the truthseeker is a string that's sticking out. I'm pulling on it."

"I don't want you to strangle yourself with that damn string. We should've never filed to be a House."

"Well, it's too late for that, isn't it? Mom, I'm trying to survive and keep everyone safe. You keep criticizing me, but there is nothing else I can do. You and Dad must've known that one day our grandmother would find us. What was the contingency plan?"

She didn't answer.

"That's right. There wasn't one."

My mother's face turned a shade paler. "We could run."

Not that again. I was so done with this.

"No. You and Dad could run, because it was only the two of you. But we can't. There is me, Catalina, Arabella, the boys, you, and Grandma Frida. That's seven people. Where are we going to go? How will we hide seven people? Should we split up, so Victoria can get the weakest of us and then use that person as a bargaining chip? You know that's a bad idea. Your plan was to hide forever. Well, it doesn't work like that. A magical talent will break into the light. It's inevitable. It's a part of who I am. I'm a Prime truthseeker, just like my grandmother."

Her expression turned harsh. "That's not who you are."

"Yes, it is. I'm our best hope. It's now up to me to keep the girls and Bern and Leon safe. Except you and Dad hid us so well that now I'm untrained. I have never even used an arcane circle until this year. I hadn't even known that I had other powers besides being a living lie detector. It's all on me now, and I have no weapons to fight with. You did the same thing to Catalina and to Arabella, and now you and I are doing it to Leon. You can't stuff us into a glass box and keep us from using our powers, Mom. We will lose our minds. How about instead of criticizing me, you just help me? Because I need help."

I turned and stomped out of the kitchen through the other entrance.

I LAY IN bed. I'd abandoned the sweatpants as soon as I stomped into my loft, slipped on a pair of underwear, and climbed into my bed, still wearing Rogan's T-shirt.

When we sold the house and moved into the warehouse, my parents built me a loft apartment—a bedroom and a bathroom, accessible only by a wooden staircase. I could retract the last ten feet of it, which effectively frustrated my sisters' attempts to bug me when I wanted to be left alone. I even had a window for my bedroom. It was a cozy space, my retreat from the world, my favorite place, where I ran away to when I was tired and overwhelmed. Right now it seemed empty. My bed seemed too big and empty too.

How in the world did I get used to sleeping next to Rogan so fast? I could count on the fingers of one hand the number of nights we slept together.

He didn't ask for my DNA profile. I couldn't decide how to feel about it. It depended on why he didn't request it. Did he not request it because he loved me and didn't care if we were genetically compatible, or did he not request it because he wasn't thinking of anything serious like marriage?

Did I want to marry Mad Rogan?

Marriage meant exclusivity, but in the world of Primes, affairs weren't just common. They were almost normal. I would do almost anything to stay with him, but sharing him with anyone else was beyond me.

Something knocked on my window.

Maybe it was a bat.

Knock. Knock. Knock.

I climbed out of the bed and walked to the window. A small grey rock tapped the glass from the outside. Knock-knock-knock.

I looked down. Rogan stood on the sidewalk.

Well. Think of the devil.

I pulled the latch up and opened the window. The rock streaked to the ground.

"I'm trying to sleep."

"I said wait for me."

"I did. I waited for an hour. Then I had to go home."

"You're mad at me."

Thank you, Captain Obvious. "Why would I be mad at you? Is it because as soon as we had sex, you jumped out of our bed and rushed to see your ex-fiancée and was gone for almost two hours?"

"One hour."

I checked the clock by my bed. "One hour and twenty-two minutes."

"There was a hysterical child on the other end of the line. When I got there, his sister woke up and started crying. Then Rynda cried."

"Did you soothe them to sleep?"

He gritted his teeth. "I made sure they aren't crying."

"Great. Then the problem is resolved. I'm going back to bed."

"I asked you to wait for me and you didn't."

"Why would I stay there, Rogan? You weren't there. I have my own bed right here."

"What exactly did you want me to do? Was I supposed to listen to her scream and tell her to fuck off because I would rather stay in bed with you?"

"So now I'm the bad guy?"

"Well, yes, a little bit. I went to do something nice and you got mad about it. You're overreacting."

Ooh, no he didn't.

"Nevada, as the Head of a House, there will be times I will have to get out of bed, no matter what we're doing, and go take care of things."

"Taking care of your ex-fiancée is House business?"

"I've known her since we were children."

"Mhm."

"She's practically family."

"And what am I?"

He realized he'd walked into it.

"As it happens, I'm also about to become a Head of a House. You're right, sometimes things do come up, and we have to leave and take care of them. I'm not just going to lay all sad in your bed waiting for when you decide that you're done blotting another woman's tears. I have profile requests to evaluate and kidnappings to solve."

"What profile requests?" he growled. "Who?"

"Not you, if that's what you're asking. You didn't check on our genetic compatibility."

"Who, Nevada?"

"Do you think if you snarl enough, I'll tell you? You're not that scary, Rogan, and I don't respond well to intimidation. Maybe you should lather up some spit."

"Who was it?"

He was like a dog with a bone. He wouldn't let go of it until I told him, and it had very little to do with what I wanted to fight about. Fine. "House Tremaine and House Shaffer."

"Did you say yes?"

"Not to Tremaine."

"You said yes to Shaffer?"

"Yes."

He lapsed into silence. His face arranged itself into a cold mask. "You're right. You are becoming the Head of your House. Might as well start planning now."

Oh, for the love of . . . "They asked for my basic profile to eliminate the possibility of familial relations, because they're worried I might be a Shaffer love child."

"They asked for it to ensure that there are no complications preventing a match," he ground out. "That's the first step."

I leaned through the window and savored the words. "You're overreacting."

A door swung open somewhere and Catalina called out, "Mom says that you should either have sex or stop arguing, because it's past midnight and all of us are trying to sleep. Figure yourselves out!"

The door slammed shut.

"That's okay," I hissed. "We're finished talking. Just one question before I go: in your expert opinion as the Head of a House, when Rynda called you, was it a true emergency? Was it something that absolutely couldn't be resolved without your presence, or was it another opportunity for her to make sure that you're emotionally engaged to take care of her and her children if Brian doesn't make it? And if it was a true emergency, why didn't you ask me to come with you?"

I slammed the window shut. There. I got it out.

He stared at me through the window, turned, and strode across the street.

That's right. Just walk away.

I threw myself on the bed. Well, that went well.

Something thudded outside.

Now what?

I got up and went to the window. He stood in the middle of the street. A stream of pallets and huge tires flew past him, stacking themselves on the ground under my window.

I just stared, mute.

The stack grew with ridiculous speed. He was building a ramp to my window.

I pulled the window open again. "Are you out of your mind?"

His face was grim. "No."

"You're expending a huge amount of magic doing this."

His expression told me he didn't care.

The flood of tires ended midway up; the pallets stopped too. He'd run out of building materials.

The door opened again. "Mom says—" my sister started.

A fire escape ladder tore itself off the building across the street on my left and wedged itself in the stack. Several cement bags landed on its base, anchoring it.

Catalina shut the door without another word.

He walked up the ramp, climbed the ladder to my window, and held his hand out to me.

"What do you think you're doing?"

"I'm kidnapping you back to my lair. You're sleeping in my bed tonight and all other nights."

"Is that so?"

"Yes."

"And do I have any say in this?"

"You always have a say. If you say no, I'll leave."

He wore his Prime face, inscrutable and detached. But his eyes gave him away. He was barely in control and hanging on by the tips of his fingers.

We could either work through this mess or I could sit in my room and steam in my own hurt feelings. I grabbed his pair of sweatpants, pulled them on, stuck my feet into my slippers, and put my hand in his.

My cell phone rang.

WHO THE HELL would be calling me at midnight?

I raised my finger. "One second."

The phone streaked across the room and held still in front of me.

I took it and answered.

"Nevada Baylor."

"There you are," Vincent Harcourt said.

"Hello, Vincent." My voice was so sweet, you could drip it on pancakes. I put him on speaker. "So nice of you to take time away from terrorizing children to call me."

"I had a spare moment."

His voice set my teeth on edge. So smug.

Rogan took my hand. Together we walked down the ladder, then the ramp toward his HQ.

"I see you filed for trials."

It wasn't enough he had almost killed Rynda's children, Edward, and a houseful of people. No, he decided to call me in the middle of the night to rattle me.

"Do you think you can be a Prime?"

"You tell me. How did it feel when you couldn't move and stood there shaking, trying with all your will to keep me out of your mind? Did it feel like I'm a Prime?"

Heat flared in Rogan's eyes. He smiled, low and lazy, looking at me as if we were in the middle of a ballroom and I wore a ten-thousand-dollar gown instead of his T-shirt.

"Touché," Vincent said. "Too bad you won't make it to trials. You might have been interesting."

"Is this the part where you threaten me?"

"No, this is the part where I educate. You don't know how the game is played, so I'll explain it to you. You're dead. Your mother is dead."

In my head I saw my mother lying in place of Edward Sherwood, a bat-ape creature digging in her stomach. You bastard.

"Your cute sister is dead."

He would pay for this.

"Your other sister is dead."

Other? He took the time to opine on the cuteness of my sisters while threatening to kill them. *Oh, I wish he was within bullet range. I wish.*

"The two fools who live with you are dead."

We walked into the HQ. Rivera, Nguyen, and two others from before, the blond woman and a dark-haired man, were still there. At the sound of Vincent's voice, Rivera came to life like a shark sensing a drop of blood in the water. Rogan shook his head.

"The animal mage is dead . . ."

"You're wasting my time," I said. "Just say everyone I know and love is dead. It's more efficient."

He laughed quietly. "You're mouthy."

"And you're a psychopath."

"You say it like it's a bad thing. It's practically a requirement for people in our position."

"Yes, well, David Howling did it better."

"Rogan won't always be there to do your dirty work."

"Rogan didn't kill David. I did. He fought me for his life and lost. The next time we meet I'll pull every dirty secret out of your mind and lay them out in the open. When I'm done, you'll curl into a ball and weep, just like all the others. That's how you threaten, Vincent."

Nguyen blinked. Rivera took a careful step back.

I passed the phone to Rogan. My fingers shook and the phone trembled slightly. He took it and I curled my hands into fists.

"She's right," he said. "You need to work on your delivery."

"I'm so glad you're there, Rogan. It saves me a phone call."

"I'm always here for you," Rogan said, his voice deceptively light. "It's been too long. We should get together."

"I was thinking the same thing. You're overdue for a visit."

"Can't wait." Rogan smiled.

"You can't kill all of us, Rogan."

"But I can kill you, Vincent. Don't worry about the others. You'll never know how it will turn out anyway."

"We'll see. Your cousin sends her love."

"Tell her I've missed her."

The phone call cut off.

Rogan turned to me. "House Harcourt disavowed Vincent about an hour ago. They claim to have no idea where he is or what he's doing."

"How convenient."

"I thought of going over to the House Harcourt compound in the morning." His tone was still light. "I could knock on their door and you could ask them some questions. Would you like that?"

"Yes. Yes, I would."

Rogan looked at Rivera. "Make the arrangements."

"Yes, sir."

Rogan led me to the stairway. I walked up the steps. "He knows that we've identified him. He will expect retaliation."

"Yes," Rogan agreed as we crossed the second floor. Bug saw us and didn't say a thing.

"If I were him, I'd attack the base as soon as we leave."

"I've accounted for that possibility."

"What if he attacks tonight?"

"He won't." Rogan led me to the staircase to the third floor. "He performed a high-volume summon tonight. With summoning, the totality of the matter coming through is what counts. One large creature is equal to several smaller ones. Vincent summoned nine beings tonight and then expended energy and magic manipulating them, defending against you, and fighting Cornelius for control. He won't risk attacking tonight knowing that I'm here. He needs to recharge."

"What about Cornelius? He's an isolated target."

"Cornelius is staying here tonight, in the same building where I put Rynda. Matilda is with his sister and brother at their family ranch. He called them while en route. They are coming over in the morning to view Zeus."

"When did you find this out?"

"When I got up to deal with Rynda. I would've told you about it if you didn't leave in a huff."

We walked through the door into the bedroom.

"What will attacking the Harcourts do to Brian? Brian is our first priority."

"Nothing," Rogan said. "I don't believe Vincent cares, but even if he did, he botched an attack on Rynda. As you said, the retaliation is expected."

He shut the door and turned to me. I stared back at him.

"Let it out," he said. "You've been holding it in since the phone call."

"He threatened my family," I ground out. "I watched him let a creature eat a man while he was still alive, in front of his niece and nephew. He enjoyed it, Rogan. I saw it in his eyes. He would've killed us all, even Rynda's kids. I know he's a monster. And then he calls here and pretends to be urbane and charming and wants to have a polite conversation. He's like a serial killer who butchered a person in plain view, washed his hands, and went to a costume party."

"He's a psychopath. He always was one."

"There is a disconnect there, Rogan. He did horrible things and he doesn't even realize how screwed up it is. He doesn't feel bad. This can't be the first time he did this. How did he get to the age he is without someone realizing what he is?"

"He's a useful asset to his House," Rogan said. "His usefulness outweighs his unsanctioned excursions. They punish him, they talk sternly to him, but in the end they need him. Other Houses knowing that Vincent exists is enough to keep them from attacking Harcourt."

"This is what bothers me." I spun around and began to stalk back and forth. If I didn't move, I would explode. "What kind of world is it where Vincent is necessary? Where he's an asset. Where Dave can just kidnap people off the street and nobody will do anything about it? Don't you see how terribly fucked up this is?" I stopped. "And I'm about to drag my sisters and cousins into it. I'm scared, Connor. I'm scared out of my mind."

"When you are in it, you have no idea it's not normal," he said quietly. "I didn't realize until I joined the army that everyone didn't live like this. This is what we're fighting against. If the conspiracy succeeds, Vincent will get free rein."

All of the fight went out of me. I sat on the bed. "The further I go, the less choices I have. We're not even a House yet and already I have to make sure we look strong enough to not be attacked. Everything I do from now on has to be dictated by getting more magic, more power, more wealth, just so we can survive."

He knelt by me, resting his hands on my arms.

"If I don't do this, my own grandmother is going to crush us. I'm not just responsible for making sure I put a roof over my family's head and food on the table. I'm now responsible for their lives. I want to murder Vincent Harcourt before he lets his beasts tear my mother into pieces. I killed David and I have nightmares about it, but now I want to kill Vincent, because I have no choice. Even the choice of my husband has to be calculated based on some genetic bullshit that says Rynda is a better match than me . . ."

I'd said too much. I clamped my mouth shut.

"Do you love me?"

The question caught me off guard. "Yes."

"Do you love your family?"

"Yes."

"Would you do anything to protect them?"

"Yes."

"Then it doesn't matter, Nevada. Nothing's really changed. I love you. You love me. We're together. I don't care about genetic matches. You told me before it didn't matter. Did that change?"

"No."

"Then we're okay." He slid his warm hands down my shoulders and took my hands in his. "Every world has dangers. There are muggings, shootings, car accidents, drug addictions, abusive relationships. It has nothing to do with being a Prime. This is life. The only difference is, now you can see the dangers more clearly."

He squeezed my fingers.

"Your grandmother was a threat to you before you were even born. Your father didn't run away from her because she was a loving and caring mother. He found your mother and married her without any genetic matches. You are at least as strong as Victoria Tremaine. The difference between you is education and experience, and you can get both."

I took a deep breath.

"It's all coming too fast," he said. "A lot happened in the last two days. You met your grandmother, you registered for trials, you dealt with Rynda, you fought Vincent and almost died. You need time to sort through all of this. But you are here tonight, and nothing will touch you while I'm with you in this room. I promise that I won't leave no matter what the hell happens and if I go, we'll go together."

I put my arms around his neck and hugged him. The warm strength of him felt so good. Reassuring.

His arms closed around me. "I've got you. It will be okay. I've got you."

We stayed like that for a long time.

CHAPTER 7

"WAKE UP," ROGAN said in my ear.

My eyes snapped open. I flailed for a second in the sheets and sat up, blinking.

He watched me with an amused grin. He was already up and wearing dark pants and a loose T-shirt. The morning light streamed through the window wall. I had overslept.

Morning. Harcourt. All remnants of my dreams fled. I was wide awake.

"Arabella dropped this off for you." He put a large suitcase on the bed.

I unzipped the bag and threw it open. Baby Desert Eagle and four magazines, underwear, sweaters, jeans, socks . . . a Ziploc bag with my toothbrush, deodorant, and makeup. Condoms in bubble gum flavor. She would pay for this.

"You have a weird look on your face," he said.

"I'm trying to decide if this means I'm kicked out of my house." Considering the fight I had with Mom last night, I wouldn't be surprised.

"Now that would be an interesting development." He crossed his arms. "You have no place to go."

"This isn't funny."

"It's hilarious. The stuff of rom-coms. Disowned by her family, thrown into the arms of an obsessive, paranoid billionaire . . ."

I threw a pillow at him. It stopped three inches from his face. He pushed it aside with his fingers, leaned over, and kissed me. The pillow landed back on the bed.

"I'm your only hope. Face it. Your only chance to strike out on your own and take over your family business, eventually destroying your evil grandmother."

"I already run my family's business. And I don't want to destroy Victoria. I just want her to leave us alone." I climbed out of bed and realized he wasn't wearing shoes. A piece of chalk lay on the table. The last time he was dressed like that and had chalk with him, he performed a ritual to recharge his magic. "The Key?"

He nodded. "I'll need the power. The documents for a Verona Exception were filed with the DA this morning."

The Verona Exception meant the State of Texas acknowledged the conflict between Houses and washed their hands of it. It would give Rogan free rein to attack the Harcourts on Rynda's behalf.

"Was it granted?"

"We'll find out in the next hour or so."

"You didn't go personally?" Lenora Jordan, Harris County District Attorney, wasn't Rogan's favorite person. He thought she was dangerous, which was why he preferred to deal with her directly.

"I told you I would stay with you."

He did. If he promised, he would stay with me. It was as simple as that.

"Besides, if I went personally, Lenora would've spent some time explaining the folly of helping Olivia Charles' daughter to me. I'm disinclined to tolerate a lecture. I sent a team of lawyers. I have things I need to do."

"You don't think House Harcourt would meet with us? Like House Rio?"

"House Rio are researchers and botanists. House Harcourt is a combat house. They think they can win this fight, but even if I rolled up to their doors with a thousand soldiers, they would still fight me. They can't afford to appear weak."

Yes, they couldn't afford to appear weak, and Rogan couldn't afford to not retaliate after Vincent's attack, and I couldn't take the chance that he would go after my mother, my sisters, or my cousins. Because none of us could afford any of that, we would all go to war. People would be injured. Some might die. If everyone just set aside their pride, none of this would be necessary.

"How well do you know Vincent?" I asked.

"Well enough. He was a couple of years behind me in high school. Had a reputation as a bully and a penchant for cruelty."

"The timeline of this doesn't make sense to me. Brian's kidnappers called to negotiate. We've told them that we have every intention of cooperating. Usually there is a slow escalation of negotiations. Instead Vincent shows up and smashes the whole thing with a hammer."

"He got impatient," Rogan said. "As I said, Vincent isn't much on waiting and planning. Rynda frustrated him, so he decided to apply his particular brand of pressure."

"But why not just show up at their house and hold the kids hostage from the start? Brian and Rynda would've given him anything he asked for. Neither of them is a combat Prime. Why go through kidnapping Brian? It doesn't seem like Vincent's style."

"That's because it isn't. Somebody has him on a tight leash for this particular operation." A dangerous light crept into Rogan's eyes. "He got loose last night."

"Who has enough power to restrain Vincent Harcourt and make him stick to a plan?"

"That's what we'll have to find out."

Rogan tilted his head, obviously thinking.

"Yes?"

"House Harcourt has one battle strategy: they summon a horde of monsters from the arcane realm and throw them at their opponents. It will be bloody and chaotic."

"I haven't changed my mind. Vincent threatened my family."

"Will you let me put you in a ballistic vest?"

"Yes." I eyed the chalk in his hand. "Do you have another piece?"

He smiled. Another piece of chalk streaked across the room and hovered in front of me. "What do I get if I give you this chalk?"

"Dinner. You and me tonight." I deserved the nice dinner he promised me. I would wear nice clothes and pretty makeup. Also, I realized I was starving. I hadn't eaten since yesterday's lunch. I'd have to see if Rogan stocked any supplies in his kitchen downstairs.

"Done."

I kissed him and grabbed the chalk out of the empty air.

ARCANE CIRCLES WERE used for everything, from fine-tuning a mage's power to channeling magic into a particular spell. They had to be drawn by hand or they lost their power, which was why most Primes trained in circlework as soon as they could hold a piece of chalk in their fingers. I wasn't most Primes. Drawing a circle on the floor was remarkably difficult. Drawing a charging circle was somewhere between the seventh and ninth levels of hell. It started as a large circle, with a smaller circle inside, three small circles inside that inner circle, drawn side by side so they formed a triangle, and then three outer circles exactly opposite of the inner circles. It took me twenty minutes and by the time I was done, my back hurt and I had said enough cuss words to make Bug, who came to hang out with me, raise his eyebrows.

At least I got to raid Rogan's kitchen counter and devour an apple bear claw before I started.

Finally, I stripped down to a sports bra and spandex shorts to maximize the charge, stepped into the circle, and sat. My power shot through the circle. The chalk lines pulsed with white and faded. Magic flowed to me, sluggish at first, then a steady current, slipping into my body. I relaxed and closed my eyes.

"This one is crooked," Bug advised.

I opened my eyes and looked at the circle he was pointing at.

"It will be fine."

"You could've just asked the Major."

If Rogan had drawn the design, it would've taken him three minutes and all the circles would have been perfect. "I have to draw my own circles."

I glanced to the left. The second floor had a wide industrial door, which opened onto a large square patio of sealed concrete, flooded with sunlight. The doors stood ajar and I could see Rogan. He'd drawn circles on the concrete and moved within them, lunging, kicking, and striking, his large muscular body graceful and flexible. His grace wasn't that of a dancer but of an assassin trained to lock onto his target and pursue it at all costs. His feet were weapons; his hands cut like blades, then struck like hammers, breaking his invisible opponents. The Key of House Rogan was a warrior key, and when he moved through it, the savage, fierce thing that made him Mad Rogan surfaced and took over. It scared me and pulled me like a magnet, which is why I drew my charging circle here, so I could watch him.

I was hoping to watch him in privacy. But Bug parked himself on the sofa right behind me, with Napoleon tucked under his arm and the laptop resting on his lap. Ogling Rogan under these circumstances would be slightly creepy. I closed my eyes and tried to concentrate on the magic emanating from the circle like heat from the asphalt on a scorching Texas day.

"Is everything okay?" Bug asked.

"Mhm."

"You and him are on good terms?"

"Mhm."

"So you're talking?"

Damn it. I opened my eyes and looked at him over my shoulder.

"Good communication is important in a relationship," Bug said.

"Everything is fine."

"You're not fighting anymore?"

"No. I'm trying to recharge. I need to concentrate."

Bug nodded solemnly.

I turned back, savored the glimpse of Rogan, and closed my eyes.

"How's the sex?"

"Did you honestly just ask me that question?"

Bug and Napoleon scooted further away from me on the sofa. "We just want to know that everything's okay."

"We?"

"Uh . . . Napoleon and I."

Lie. "Bug, turn that laptop toward me and don't you dare hit any keys."

He hugged the laptop. "No."

"Is that Nguyen and Rivera on the other end?"

"No."

Lie.

"Here, I'll say it really loud so they can hear. Are you ready? Butt out of our relationship!"

"Okay, okay!" He waved his arms.

"If you really want to help, brief me on the Harcourts."

"What's there to brief? Owen Harcourt, sixty, Ella Harcourt, fifty-five, Alyssa Harcourt, twenty-three, and Liam Harcourt, eighteen. Everyone is a Prime summoner. It's going to be a bloodbath."

"Fine. I'm going to concentrate now, so hush."

I closed my eyes. For a few minutes, blissful silence reigned and I sank deeper into the stream of magic.

"Incoming," Bug announced.

I turned. Rynda came up the stairs, crossed the room, and sat on the other sofa. She wore black designer jeans and a pink silk wrap blouse that demurely covered her breasts while simultaneously dipping far between them. Bug pretended to ignore her. Napoleon gave Rynda the evil eye.

Rynda studied my circlework and very carefully didn't say anything. *Yes, I know. It's crooked.*

I sat quietly. Minutes stretched. Bug typed on his laptop, hitting the keys so loud, I could hear him from several feet away.

"Are you going with Rogan to fight the Harcourts?" she asked.

"Yes."

"Is that wise?"

"Rogan will need my help when we question them."

"The Harcourts have a reputation," Rynda said. "It will be brutal. You're not a combat mage."

"Thank you for your concern. I'll be fine."

She fell silent, then glanced at Bug. "Could you get me some coffee?"

"No," Bug said.

She blinked.

"I'm a surveillance specialist, not a waiter," Bug said, his diction perfect, his voice flat. "The coffee is on the kitchen counter over there. Help yourself."

She opened her mouth and closed it.

"Nevada?" Bug said.

Don't do it, don't do it . . .

"Would you like some coffee?"

"No, thanks." Ass.

"Because I'll totally get it for you."

Rynda got up and walked to the kitchen counter, glancing in Rogan's direction for a moment.

"You're being cruel," I murmured.

"Sue me," Bug whispered back.

Rynda came back with a cup of coffee and sat on the couch. Bug resumed his aggressive typing. Rynda studied him for a long moment and cleared her throat. Bug showed no signs of moving. All this tension was distracting me.

"Is Kyle feeling better this morning?"

She startled. "Yes."

"Glad to hear it." There. A little less tense.

"I didn't realize you were there when I called Connor."

And we're back to awkward. Great.

I smiled at her and watched Rogan through the window.

"I understand that you and Connor have a relationship," Rynda said. "But I need him more than you right now. I hope you understand."

Oh no. No. "Rogan and I have something." I kept my voice as gentle as possible. "You are not a part of it."

"I've known him a lot longer than you."

"And I understand that Brian is gone and you're scared. But Rogan won't be anyone's plan B. He isn't a backup option."

"Is that a threat?"

I sighed. "No. I'm not going to threaten you. You're my client and you've been through a pressure cooker. This isn't a 'back away from my man' conversation. I'm simply telling you that what Rogan and I have is genuine. I don't blame you for trying and if you somehow succeeded, I wouldn't be as angry with you as with him. That's not my point."

Her lips were pressed together so hard, they were almost bloodless. "What is your point?"

"Suppose for a moment that you get Rogan to somehow become involved with you. Then what?"

She didn't answer.

"Were you relieved when he broke the engagement?"

"That's a private matter."

"You were relieved, because you didn't really want him. He is volatile and frightening. You want the security his presence provides, but you don't love the man who creates it." But I did. I loved him and all his volatility.

"You don't know me," she said. "You don't know the first thing about me."

"You asked what my point was. Here is my answer: if you continue to rely on others for that security, you will never find it. You're a Prime, a woman, and a mother. Make yourself secure. Take charge of yourself. My circlework may be shaky and crooked, but it's mine. I taught myself how to do it by studying books and now I'm using it. I didn't ask Rogan to draw it for me, because I didn't have to."

Rynda rose, her coffee in her hands, walked over to the open doors, and stood on the left side, watching Rogan power through the final motions of the Key. He finished and walked into the room, nodding to Rynda. "Morning."

"Nobody here likes me, Rogan," she said, her voice soft and broken. "Your people don't like me."

"They don't have to like you," he said. "They will, however, protect you and your children with their lives."

"I feel like an invader."

"You're not an invader. You're here at my invitation."

She hugged herself. "Can I talk to you? Privately."

He invited her to the patio with a sweep of his hand. She walked into the sunshine, and he followed. They strode to the edge, Rynda saying something, an urgent look on her face.

"I can tell you what she's saying," Bug said.

"Thanks, but no."

"It would just take a second. Two keys." He raised his laptop and waved it at me. "It's not rocket surgery."

"No."

Bug heaved an exaggerated sigh. "Don't you want to know?"

"No."

"Why?"

"Because it doesn't matter. I trust Rogan."

I closed my eyes and let the magic flow into me.

"NEVADA?" ROGAN'S VOICE pulled me out of the deep well of magic inside the circle.

I opened my eyes. He was crouched by me. He wore an army combat uniform, but instead of the familiar camouflage pattern or the darker woodland/jungle variant, his uniform was black and grey. A black tactical vest hugged his chest. A sophisticated communication set curved around his neck in a collar-like shield, with the thin filament of the mic stretching to his lips. Another man stood next to him, about my mother's age, probably Japanese, broad-shouldered, but not bulky. Greying hair, trimmed so short he was almost bald, a short neat beard and mustache, and piercing dark eyes. He wore the regular urban camo ACU and he held himself like he'd spent the best part of his life in some sort of uniform.

"We got the Verona Exception," Rogan said. "Are you ready?"

Magic coursed through me, strong and potent. I felt tighter, more focused. I would've liked another couple of hours, but it would have to do. I got up.

Bug held up a stack of clothes for me: socks, boots, the same uniform as Rogan, but instead of black, my ACU was patterned in shades of grey and beige. The urban variant. Also a helmet.

"Are we going to war?"

"As close to war as we're allowed," Rogan said.

"I have my own clothes."

"If you wear this, you'll blend in with the rest of my people and lower the probability of you being singled out as a target."

I eyed his black uniform. "You don't mind being singled out."

"I don't. I'm wearing this so they will key on me. I'll have a personal aegis."

I could stand there and argue about the uniform, or I could just put the ACU on and stop holding everyone up. I took the stack. The older man watched me carefully.

Rogan offered me my phone. "Also, your mother has called several times."

"Did she say what she wanted?"

"No, but it sounded urgent."

Great. I took my phone and escaped into his office to get dressed and to call Mom.

She answered on the first ring. "What's going on?"

"Rogan is going to attack House Harcourt."

"He has two modified armored personnel carriers up front. I'm watching his people load them. He's packing enough firepower to start a small war."

"That's the plan. Harcourts are summoners. There will be a lot of otherworldly creatures."

"Are you going with him?"

I braced myself for an argument. "Yes."

"I'm coming with you."

"Mom?"

"You heard me."

She hung up.

I finished getting dressed, tightened my ballistic vest, put my helmet on, and walked out.

"My mother will be joining us."

Rogan didn't miss a beat. "Glad to have her."

We went downstairs. A group of Rogan's people in combat gear waited by the two armored personnel carriers, some in urban ACUs, some in older style camo. I had a feeling they just wore whatever felt familiar. The third vehicle, a massive heavy expanded mobility tactical truck, idled behind the two transporters, its cargo in the long, reinforced bed hidden by a green tarp.

Rivera appeared by my side and handed me a rifle.

"Ruger AC 556. Three modes of fire: semi-auto, three-round burst, and fully automatic. Major thought you might like it."

I took the weapon and checked it over on autopilot.

My mother exited the building, carrying her Light Fifty, a Barrett M82 Sniper Rifle. Leon trotted next to her, like an overeager puppy.

"He's coming with me," she said. "I need a spotter."

"Thank you for coming with us," Rogan said.

I remembered to pick my jaw up off the floor and climbed into a personnel carrier.

RIDING IN A personnel carrier was about as comfortable as riding in a tank. It felt like sitting on a bag of potatoes while it bucked and jumped over every tiny bump in the road. The carrier had two rows of seats along the walls, facing each other. I sat next to Rogan toward the front. My mother and Leon rode across from us. The older Japanese man sat quietly on the other side of me, watching Leon and my mother. Further on my left, within the depths of the carrier, uniformed bodies and helmeted heads filled the space. The hum of human voices hung in the air as Rogan's people talked. Fragments of conversation floated up, interrupted by sudden peals of laughter.

An odd expression claimed my mother's face. The corners of her mouth had turned up slightly. The frown wrinkle between her eyebrows that had been permanently there for the last three days smoothed out. She sat relaxed, calm, and perfectly at peace, as if she was riding to a picnic at the beach. There was something almost meditative about her gaze. Next to her, Leon could barely stay in the seat. If he could, he would've jumped up and bounced around the carrier.

The older man next to me touched his headset and said in a deep, calm voice, "All right."

My helmet's comm system channeled his voice into my ears.

All conversation stopped.

"This is for the new people and those of you who didn't pay attention. House Harcourt occupies a fortified facility. It's U-shaped, with left and right wings protruding. The entrance is located between them. There is only one approach, through the front door, through a corridor between the two wings. This is their killing field. When we enter it, the shooters from the two wings will fire. The front gate will open, and the Harcourts will release the MCM."

MCM stood for magically created monsters. My memory served up the mouth of a bat-ape gaping at me, about to sink its teeth into my face. A chill rolled down the back of my neck. I sat up straighter.

"The snipers, including Mrs. Baylor and her spotter, will disembark prior to engagement and take positions at the Magnolia Apartment Towers, buildings A and F. They will concentrate on taking out the shooters in the two wings of the Harcourt building. Upon arrival to the Harcourt building, the carriers will form a barricade. You will position yourselves behind that barricade. The Major will be behind you working on his circle. Melosa will shield the Major. Tom and Li Min will provide top shield for the line. House Harcourt relies on blitzkrieg tactics. They will send wave after wave of creatures trying to overwhelm our defense. We will hold that line until the Major finishes the circle and deploys the grinder."

What the hell was the grinder?

"No matter what nightmare comes out of those gates, you will hold the line. Am I clear?"

A chorus of voices exhaled at the same time. "Yes, Sergeant."

"Major and Ms. Baylor are VIPs. You will keep them alive. Do you get me?"

"Yes, Sergeant."

The sergeant settled back and looked at me. "My name is Heart. Stay on me, Ms. Baylor."

I nodded.

The carrier rumbled. Moments built into minutes. Rogan reached over and took my hand. He didn't say anything. He just held my hand in his.

"What's the grinder?" I asked him quietly.

"A House Rogan spell."

House spells were of the highest order. They unleashed incredible magic, but required a lot of preparation and complex circles.

Leon was grinning to himself.

"Don't do anything unwise," I told him.

"I won't." He rubbed his hands together. His smile looked positively evil.

"We'll need to talk after this." I looked at my mother to make sure she got the point.

"Is Heart your real name?" Leon asked the sergeant.

"It's the name I chose."

"Why?"

"Because I care too much," the sergeant said.

Leon decided to shut up.

I had been in a firefight before, but this sitting still while riding to one was completely different. The urge to jump up, scream, do *something* hummed through my body. My rifle felt too heavy in my hands. My adrenaline was up and the fight hadn't even started. My mother was still in her serene place. Sergeant Heart on my left had an almost identical expression on his face. Rogan on my right was smiling quietly to himself. At least Leon hadn't gone to his happy place.

My cousin fidgeted in his seat. "Why don't we just shoot a rocket at the building? It would be faster and easier."

"Because the Verona Exception obligates us to avoid unnecessary loss of life," Rogan answered. "When you blow up buildings, fallen debris and explosives don't discriminate between combatants and civilians."

"What would happen if we did it anyway?" Leon asked.

"Your sister and I would be hauled before the Assembly and forced to explain ourselves. Depending on our answers, we would be released with a fine, jailed, or killed."

"But you're Mad Rogan. A Prime."

"Primes have rules," I told him. I was learning them, and none of it made me happy.

"Weapons check," Heart called out.

I checked my rifle. I had a thirty-round magazine and three more in the pockets of my ACUs. My helmet felt too heavy. Sweat gathered on my hairline.

Heart leaned toward me. "Don't worry. It will be fine. Watch me, watch what the others are doing, follow orders, and you will survive this."

I pulled my phone out and made a group text message, tagging my sisters, Bern, and Grandma Frida. I love you so much.

That's it. There were other things to say, but that would have to be enough. I turned off the phone and put it away.

The carrier came to a stop. My mother rose and nodded to Leon. He unbuckled his harness and went toward the side door. I had this terrible feeling that I would never see them again.

My mother fixed the sergeant next to me with her sniper stare, distant and cold. "Keep my daughter alive."

"I will," he told her.

"I love you," I said. "I'm sorry."

"I love you too. Don't forget to breathe."

My mother exited the vehicle, the door slammed shut, and we were off again.

Rogan's phone rang. He answered it and put it on speaker.

"Liam, what a pleasure."

"As I said, we don't know where Vincent is. So I suggest you turn your transports around and go back the way you came."

"I prefer to ask your father in person."

"Not going to happen."

"I must insist."

"No, you mustn't. We have four Primes in residence. Do the lives of your soldiers mean so little to you? They think they're going to come in here and kick our asses. We both know it's not going to happen. If you care about them, take them home."

"Your concern for my people is touching. If you want to avoid bloodshed, open the gates and we can talk like civilized people."

"No. You're not coming in. You're not talking to anyone. Don't come here with your bullet-meat soldiers and threaten us. Nobody is scared, Rogan. If you persist in your idiocy, we'll wipe you off the face of the planet."

"That's a big promise." Rogan smiled.

"Suit yourself. Your funeral."

Liam hung up.

Rogan slid the phone into an inner pocket and squeezed my hand. "Hold on."

The vehicle made a sharp turn and my insides went sideways. The back of the carrier dropped open, turning into a ramp. Rogan was already moving, lost ahead of me behind bodies in fatigues. Sergeant Heart thrust himself into my view and barked, "Follow me! Move!"

I grabbed my Ruger and got the hell out of the carrier.

OUTSIDE, THE BRIGHT sunlight slapped me. Bullets buzzed by us like pissed-off bees, striking the top of the armored carrier with metallic pings. The space directly above us pulsed with blue as the two aegises shielded us with magic.

"Move!" Sergeant Heart roared.

I dashed forward, following the line of ex-soldiers. They grabbed the edge of the armored plate on the side of the carrier. Metal clanged, sliding into place. The armored plate split and its bottom half dropped down, forming a platform attached to the carrier's flank.

"Up!"

I jumped onto the platform and pulled myself up between the other soldiers. Servomotors whined and the platform rose, carrying us up. Rogan's people grabbed the top half of the armored plate, still attached to the carrier. Metal clanged again, and the armored plate slid up. Heart reached in front of me, yanked on a lever, pulled a rectangular shutter open within the plate, and secured it. I was looking through a window, two feet wide and one foot tall. The top of the armored carrier was right in front of me and I could rest my rifle on it.

A concrete yard stretched in front of us, bathed in bright sunlight. Sheer walls rose on both sides, and ahead, about two hundred yards away, another wall towered. Within it a massive door loomed, painted black, like the door of some giant castle.

Next to me, Heart called out, "Okay, boys and girls, weapons ready. Safeties off."

I slid the selector switch on my rifle to full auto.

A chorus of voices barked back. "Roger, Top."

"Rodriguez, range to target."

A male yelled out, "Two hundred and eleven meters."

"Fire on command."

Heart leaned next to me. "We work in teams of two. I'm your teammate. When I give command to fire, you fire. When you're out, say 'Out!' and take two steps back. If you jam, say 'Jam!' and take two steps back. Understood?"

My heart was beating too fast. "Yes."

The massive door split in the middle, showing a glimpse of complete darkness.

"Hold your fire," Heart ordered.

My hands shook. I took a deep breath, all the way to my stomach, held it in for a few seconds and slowly let it out, concentrating only on breathing.

The gap widened. Something stirred in the ink-black darkness. In . . . and out. In . . . and out. It wasn't working.

The doors swung open. A pale spindly leg thrust into the sunlight, a sickly mottled grey, the color of old concrete.

"Hold it," Heart said next to me, his voice echoing in my helmet.

A creature stepped into the open. It stood on four spindly legs, bent backward like those of a grasshopper, its knobby knees protruding up. Its body hung between them, little more than a sack of flesh. There was no head, no eyes, and no nose. Only a mouth, a round cavernous mouth, lined with rows and rows of conical teeth all the way around. It was a monster designed to feed.

The creatures stumbled in the sunlight. Another emerged from the shadows, then another, and another.

We were two hundred yards away. That meant, considering the door, that they were . . . the size of a small car.

The first beast froze. Two long, feathery whips snapped upright from its shoulders, like antennas. They turned toward us. A sea of feathery antennas sprang up. Oh dear God.

"Hold it," Heart said.

The creatures charged.

They came at us in a ragged pale mob, rushing in a whirlwind of legs, their mouths gaping open.

"Range!" Heart called out.

"Two hundred meters," a male voice called down from the left.

Sweat sheathed my palms.

"One ninety."

My mouth went dry. Waiting was torture.

"One eighty."

I glanced over my shoulder. Behind us, shielded by a blue sphere of Melosa's magic, Rogan was drawing a complex arcane circle with chalk.

"Eyes front!" Heart barked.

I spun back to the horde. The stench of ozone hit me, the same one that I smelled in Rynda's house.

"One seventy."

I sighted the beast directly across from me, a big ugly creature. Shooting it in the wrinkled bag that was its body probably wouldn't do much good. The skinny legs would be a much better target. I moved the selector to three-round burst.

"One sixty."

My breathing deepened. I focused on the legs.

"One hundred and fifty meters."

"Fire!" Heart roared.

I squeezed the trigger. The first burst went wide. I sighted and fired again. The beast's left leg crunched and broke. I sighted the second front leg and fired. The creature collapsed.

The second beast took its place. I sighted and squeezed the trigger. Screw the Harcourts, their beasts, and Vincent's threats. I was my mother's daughter and I did not miss.

Bodies piled in front of me. To the right someone lobbed a grenade. The explosion scattered the bodies. Yellow ichor and pale guts flew.

I switched to full auto. I was in the zone now, and it was faster.

The gun clicked.

"Out!" I took two steps back.

Heart stepped into my place, thrusting a fresh magazine at me. I released the empty one and slapped the new one in. A woman ran up to me, snatched the empty magazine out of my hand, and held out a full one. I took it.

"Out!" Heart barked, and took two steps back.

I shoved the full magazine at him and took his spot.

The creatures kept coming, scuttling over the corpses. The two massive .50 cal guns mounted on top of the carriers came to life and spat thunder and death, chewing through the advancing horde.

More beasts poured out of the gates: smaller yellow creatures that looked like skinny cats with wolf heads; bloodred raptor-like things moving fast on two thick legs; a six-legged horror sheathed in glistening thin tentacles that writhed like earthworms, its top half erect as if it were some nightmarish version of a centaur . . . They came and came and came. Time lost all meaning. Only two things mattered—shooting and calling, "Out!"

The space between the carriers and monsters shrank. Barely thirty feet separated us now.

I unloaded the last of my magazine into a tentacled monstrosity. "Out!" I stepped back, ejected the old magazine . . .

I grabbed the new one from the runner, slid it into the weapon . . .

A huge blue cat that looked just like Cornelius' Zeus lunged onto the top of the carrier and charged us. Heart fired, point-blank, his rifle spitting a stream of bullets. The cat snarled and rammed the armored plate. It bent. It shoved its massive paws through the window, trying to rake at Heart with its claws.

I threw myself against the armored plate, thrust the rifle through the window, pointing it almost straight up, and sank a stream of bullets into the cat's throat. Blood splashed on me. The great beast collapsed, the light fading out of its beautiful eyes.

"Out!" Heart and I yelled at the same time.

No runner came. I pulled a spare magazine out of my pocket. Heart did the same.

Creatures piled on top of the carrier, snarling, screeching, clawing, slipping in the blood. We fired point-blank.

A woman screamed on the right.

A tentacle whipped through the window and wrapped around Heart's arm. He jerked a knife out and hacked it in half.

Last magazine. We were overrun.

Magic moved behind me like a tsunami. The armored carrier under me slid. I grabbed on to the armored plate. The two massive vehicles slid to different sides like the two halves of a door opening wide.

I turned. Rogan stood inside one of the most complicated circles I'd ever seen. It glowed white.

The animal horde abandoned the carriers, streamed toward him, and crashed against the boundary of the circle. Rogan had drawn a high-level spell. The amount of magic he'd fed into the circle was so high, its outer boundary no longer existed in our world.

The green tarp covering the cargo of the truck flew aside. Three long metal cylinders lay in the back of the truck, each thirty feet long and twice as wide as a telephone pole. Rogan raised his arms in a classic mage pose, palms up, elbows bent. The cylinders shot straight up and spun in place. Dozens of blades slid out of the metal shafts. The cylinders turned sideways, forming a triangle, two on the bottom, one on top, rolled over each other and cut into the beasts. Severed limbs flew.

The grinder.

The blades swept through the horde, mincing flesh. Blood drenched the pavement, pooling in puddles under the heaps of cut-up bodies. The air smelled like blood and ozone.

Someone retched. I couldn't even vomit. I just stared at it, mute. The slaughter was so bright, so vivid, there was no defense against it.

The flood of creatures stopped. In the back, in front of the gate, a knot of magic formed thirty feet above the ground. Black, shot through with violent lightning, it churned, growing larger and larger. Something strained within it, stretching at its boundaries from within.

The blades mopped up the last of the beasts and hovered near it, waiting.

Magic pulsed. The invisible blast wave hit me in the chest. My heart skipped a beat. For a torturous second my lungs locked up. I staggered back and managed to draw a hoarse breath in.

The darkness tore. A colossal foot landed on the pavement, thick toes splayed wide. The armored carrier shook.

Another foot, thick purple-red, its texture rough. Thick claws, each the size of a car, dug into the pavement.

My mind refused to accept that something that large could be alive.

A giant beast landed in front of the gates. It stood on all fours, its legs spread wide like those of a charging Komodo dragon. Thick horn spikes studded its purplish hide and united into bone plates on its shoulders. Its head resembled that of a snapping turtle, but a forest of teeth filled its mouth. Angry white eyes stared at us.

The blades moved toward it and ground against the beast's side. A grinding noise lanced my ears.

The beast swatted at the blades, knocking them aside. The cylinder flew, spinning. The gargantuan creature raised its front left leg and stomped toward us.

Boom. The carrier shook.

Boom. Another step.

The blades scraped along its sides and dove under its stomach. No effect. The beast opened its mouth and bellowed, an unearthly lingering sound. The sonic blast hit us. If it wasn't for the helmet, I would've clamped my hands over my ears.

Boom.

We had no cover. The armored carrier wouldn't hold it. If the creature stomped on it, the vehicle would be a metal pancake. The wall was behind us. Everything else around us was gore.

"Fire at will!" Heart's precise voice snapped in my helmet. "Everything you have. Light it up."

Boom.

"Belay that," Rogan's voice said in my helmet.

One of the bladed cylinders fell to the ground. The other two rose, spinning so fast, the blades became a blur. The cylinders streaked to the beast and punctured its eyes, drilling their way into its skull.

The creature screamed.

In the circle, Rogan's whole body shook as if he were trying to lift a great weight. The light of the circle faded, its power exhausted.

The blades burrowed deeper.

Rogan snarled.

The blades sank in all the way and disappeared into the creature's skull.

Not enough. It was still moving. It was still—

The colossus trembled. Its head pitched back. It staggered forward and collapsed. The pavement cracked under its weight, breaking in big chunks, like ice on a frozen lake.

I let out a breath. My legs gave and I sat down on the platform.

Heart crouched by me and patted my shoulder. "You did good."

I realized something wet was on my cheek and touched it. A tear, tinted with alien creatures' blood.

"Look at it," I whispered. "It's awful. So much death. Why?"

"House warfare," Heart said, and patted my shoulder again.

I took off my helmet. Someone handed me a wet washcloth and I cleaned the blood off my face. Rivera appeared next to me, as if by magic, and I gave him back the rifle. The battle was over.

I pulled out my cell phone with shaking bloody fingers. There were two messages from Catalina and Arabella, demanding to know what was going on, one from Grandma Frida asking if I was feeling okay, and a smiley face from Bern.

I dialed Mom.

The phone rang.

She picked it up.

"Mom?"

"We're okay. Are you okay?"

I almost cried. "Yes."

"Good." She hung up.

Rogan walked out of the circle. His face was haggard. He walked like his whole body was sore. He was looking at me. I walked toward him. We met halfway among the gore. He hugged me to him, tight, hard, and kissed my hair.

We walked together to the gates. Rogan's people formed around us. We entered the dark building. There was nothing there. It was basically a cavernous hangar, reinforced steel walls and a concrete floor, empty except for the stench of ozone and signs of many animals crammed into a small space: clumps of alien fur, a few torn-off tentacles, and puddles of urine. We crossed it to a door on the far left, walked through a short hallway with the same concrete floor and reinforced walls, and through another door.

I blinked. An expensive black and red Persian rug ran over a beautiful floor of golden wood. Paintings decorated the tall walls. It was like suddenly stepping into a palace.

Rogan nodded, and the core of our force peeled off to guard the entrance, moving past us to secure other doors, leaving only Rogan, Rivera, Heart, and me.

We walked through the hallway to a wide-open door and entered a large room. The floor was golden wood, shielded by another Persian rug, this one in the calming shades of white, beige, and brown, glinting with what might have been touches of real gold. Inside, a gathering of expensive couches waited, arranged around the coffee table. Delicate and ornate, with the weathered curved wooden frames supporting shimmering dark grey cushions, it was at once elegant and inviting. If the Sun King had built Versailles in the twenty-first century, he would've picked this set.

A family rested on the furniture. An older man slumped back in a chair, a handkerchief pressed to his nose. Owen Harcourt. A woman in her mid-fifties, with mahogany-red hair, thin, wearing a blue pantsuit, sat next to him, gently patting his arm. His wife, Ella. Another woman, this one about my age, and with the same rich mahogany-red hair, leaned forward on the other couch, her hands clenched into a single fist. That would be their daughter, Alyssa. The youngest of the four, Liam, from the phone call, with dark blond hair and a pale face, looked like he could be one of the college friends Bern occasionally brought home when they ran short on cash and needed a home-cooked meal.

Liam saw us and jumped off the couch, his gaze fixed on Rogan. "You bastard!"

"Sit," Owen said.

"Father—"

"Sit. We lost. You're the future of the House. Don't give him a reason to kill you."

Liam landed back on the couch, his mouth a thin slash across his face.

Ella looked up at us. "We've removed our people to avoid further bloodshed. You won. But Vincent is our son. You'll get nothing from us."

"He attacked Rynda Sherwood in her house," Rogan said. "He slaughtered her guards, he critically injured her brother-in-law, and then he tortured him in front of his six-year-old niece and four-year-old nephew. He would've killed the children."

"You don't know that," Alyssa snapped.

"I do," I said. "I was there."

She didn't even look at me. Clearly, I wasn't important enough to warrant an answer.

"Bring on your tortures." Ella crossed her arms on her chest. "We are ready."

Rogan sighed, pulled out a piece of chalk, and offered it to me. I took it.

The beautiful Persian rug slid aside. I crouched and drew a simple amplification circle. They watched me. I stood inside it and concentrated. Before I started, I had to assess their strength.

My magic washed over them. I sank into it, looking for a way to fine-tune it. I had done this once before, with Baranovsky, another Prime, when I was looking for Nari's killer and trying to pull the information out of his mind. My magic moved, shimmering in my mind's eye. Come on . . .

There. The magic fell into place with an oddly satisfying inaudible snap. In my head, the four of them glowed with pale, almost silver light, each mind a spot of darkness.

Strong-willed. Every single one of them. They were exhausted, but their mental defenses were strong. Who would be the most likely to know about Vincent? It had to be the father. Owen was the Head of the House. He would want to keep tabs on his son.

I wrapped my magic around Owen, letting it saturate him. He stiffened. Wow. His mind was a wall. If I barreled through with brute force, he would fight me every step of the way. I wasn't sure there would be a mind left after I was done.

"Today!" Liam snapped.

"Hush," I told him. "I'm trying to make sure you still have a father when I finish."

The Harcourts glared at me.

"Who is this loser?" Alyssa demanded.

His wall was strong. Hard, dense, heavy, like granite. But granite was also brittle. Hit it the right way and it fractured. I needed to hit it the right way.

Like a wave. A wave that battered the pier.

I felt an urge to draw a wave within the circle. I had never seen that anywhere before. But I needed it. I needed the pattern. The magic wanted it.

I crouched down and let it flow through me. The white line stretched from the tip of my chalk, a perfect sine wave all the way along the inner boundary of the circle.

Ella Harcourt gasped.

Magic punched me, strong and pure, like a clear mountain spring.

"*Where is Vincent?*" the voice that came out of my mouth didn't belong to a human being.

Liam stared at me, his eyes horrified. Owen's will fought mine, and I sent the first wave into him. It smashed against his mental wall and cracked it.

"A Tremaine!" Ella jumped to her feet, disgust and horror on her face. "You brought a Tremaine here? Are you out of your mind? This is too much even for you!"

"Oh God." Alyssa clamped her hand over her mouth. "Oh God." Liam turned white.

"I love my father." Alyssa swallowed, words coming out too fast. "He's the only one I have. Please, please don't take him from us. Please!" She spun around. "Mom!"

"We'll tell you whatever you want," Ella said. "Just make that abomination release my husband."

Rogan turned to me. "How would you like to proceed?"

They were looking at me, a mixture of panic, disgust, and utter desperation on their faces. I was the monster in the room.

"Abomination?" I asked. "You forced hundreds of creatures from another world into a needless slaughter to protect your sick psychopath. He let his summoned creatures eat people alive. I watched one of them dig in Edward Sherwood's stomach for juicy tidbits while two children hugged their mother, too scared to cry. Your precious Vincent called me and promised to murder my mother, my baby sisters, my cousins, and my grandmother. But I'm an abomination? What the hell is wrong with you? Are you even human?"

Owen moved within the grip of my magic. Words came out of him slowly, with great effort. "House . . . Harcourt . . . no . . . ill will . . . to . . . your . . . family."

Liam covered his face with his hands. His shoulders trembled.

"Let him go," Alyssa begged. "Please let him go."

Ella Harcourt took a step back. "Please."

I pulled my magic back to me. Owen collapsed in his chair, breathing deeply.

They all crowded around him, as if trying to shield him from me. I felt sick.

"Where is he?" Rogan asked.

"We don't know," Ella said.

"She's telling the truth," I told him. "Vincent kidnapped Rynda's husband. He wants something from her. What?"

Owen shook his head. "We don't know."

Damn it.

"He didn't do this on his own," Rogan said. "Vincent isn't one for elaborate schemes. He prefers brute force. Someone is pulling his leash. Someone with enough power to keep him in check."

"I agree with you," Owen said.

"So you know who that is?"

The patriarch of House Harcourt drew himself up straight in the chair. "Do you think that if I had any idea where my son is or who he is with, I wouldn't have taken steps? We don't serve other Houses. We stand on our own. Do you think I would allow my heir to fall under the influence of another Prime?"

"Alexander Sturm," Liam said.

Everyone looked at him.

"He's with Alexander Sturm. Sturm has a collection of medieval swords. He owns an Oakeshott XIIIa sword, a Grete War Sword. It's a precursor of a Scottish claymore. The one Sturm has is supposed to be the true sword of William Wallace. Vincent sent me a picture of him with it two days ago."

Owen and Rogan swore.

CHAPTER 8

ꟼ SAT IN an armored carrier. Outside, Rogan's ex-soldiers were loading the grinder's cylinders onto the transport. It took twelve of them to safely lift and carry one. Rogan lingered with the Harcourts. Apparently, there were some papers to sign. We all had engaged in a massive slaughter, and now we had to formalize it. That part of House warfare never made sense to me. I'd never forget the moment when Rogan and Cornelius bargained over who would retain the right to kill Cornelius' wife's murderer and then drew up a contract spelling out their agreement.

Even inside the vehicle, the air smelled like gore. If I bent forward, I could see the remains of the bodies.

Rogan climbed into the carrier and sat next to me, leaning against the bulkhead, his helmet off, his eyes closed. For a while we sat next to each other.

"Did you get the papers?"

He nodded. "They signed a no-retaliation agreement. They legally acknowledge that they were at fault and promise to not pursue the matter further."

"Is it going to stick?"

"Yes. If they break it, the sanctions from the Assembly will be severe."

I nodded and looked away.

"Are you okay?" he asked.

"No."

"Tell me."

"Do you think they made these monsters up cut of nothing, or is there an actual place, another world, they pulled them from?"

"Nobody knows."

"So much death, Connor. For so little."

He reached over and squeezed my hand.

"Is that how people will see me?" I asked. "An abomination."

"That's how they see your grandmother. About two decades ago Victoria Tremaine went on a rampage," Rogan said. "It was before my time, but I asked my mother and she remembers it."

I glanced at him.

"What?"

"Your mother? I thought you were estranged?"

He frowned. "No. I talk to her every week."

"Why isn't she . . . involved in all of this?"

He shrugged. "She doesn't want to be. My mother survived more assassination attempts than several heads of state put together, played the House politics, and after my father died and I came back to take over, she decided that she was done. Can you blame her?"

I glanced at the bloody pile of animal body parts. "No."

"As I said, my mother remembers your grandmother's reign of terror. Victoria Tremaine cut a wide swath through the Houses. Primes would disappear and then turn up babbling, their minds fried. People would be snatched off the street, hauled before her, and interrogated. Those who survived called it mental torture. It took them a long time to recover. Some never did. My mother thinks Victoria must've made a deal with the feds, because they let her go on unchecked for far too long. Rumors said she was looking for something, but nobody who'd managed to escape her claws was in any shape to talk about it."

"She was looking for my father." The timing was about right.

"I think so." Rogan stretched his shoulders. Something popped in his chest. He grimaced. "You're not Victoria, Nevada."

"But I am. Did you see how they looked at me?"

"Yes. They are afraid of you."

"Terrified. They are terrified and disgusted."

He grinned, a dragon baring his fangs. "Yes."

He didn't seem upset by that. I'd terrified the Harcourts. I was the terrible abomination, and they were willing to spill their darkest secrets just to keep me out of their minds.

Oh.

"Is it going to get around?"

"Possibly. Your name was on the Verona Exception packet." He looked unbearably pleased with himself.

It would get around. By tonight, the movers and shakers of Houston would know that future House Baylor took their root from Victoria Tremaine. The number of Houses who were considering taking us down once our grace period was done just got cut by a good percentage.

"She will be livid. Now everyone will know that we're rebelling against her."

"Livid, yes. Also proud," Rogan said. "You walked in and made a combat House with four Primes submit without lifting a finger. Your grandmother will quite enjoy that."

He looked like he was enjoying it too.

I leaned closer to him. "What about you, Rogan? Are you afraid of sleeping with an abomination?"

He smiled, his blue eyes light, raised his hand, and brushed a loose strand of blond hair from my cheek. "When we were at the lodge, and you were dancing in the snow, I kept wondering why it wasn't melting. You're like spring, Nevada. My spring."

Rivera stomped up the ramp into the carrier. "We're good to go, sir."

"Move out," Rogan said.

"Yes, sir."

Rivera stomped out and barked, "Move out! We're done here."

I pulled my phone out. Dead. I should've charged it this morning. There goes my intelligence gathering.

"What's the deal with Alexander Sturm?" I asked, as the transport began to fill with people.

"He's a Prime," Rogan said.

You don't say. "What sort of magic?"

"He's a dual fulgur and aero Prime, highest certification in both."

Holy crap. Alexander Sturm controlled both wind and lightning. "Nice name."

"His great-grandfather legally changed his name when he established the House," Rogan said.

The big vehicle rumbled into life. We were off.

"How powerful is he?"

Rogan's face snapped into his Prime face, neutral and calm. "When I was two, my father met with some other Heads of the Houses to discuss the strategy they were going to push through the Assembly in response to the Bosnian conflict. They met in a concrete reinforced bunker, sunken twenty feet into the ground, because some of them were paranoid about surveillance."

"Okay."

"Gerald Sturm got upset that he wasn't invited. He created an F4 tornado and held it in place for eighteen minutes. The tornado partially dug out the bunker, ripped off part of the wall and the roof, and hurled it over a hundred feet. Maxine Abner was sucked out through the gap. She was a hopper and she managed to pulse-jump away, but the fall broke both of her legs."

"What happened then?"

"Eventually, Gerald ran out of steam. When the tornado died, there were nine pissed-off Primes. Gerald had to pay restitution and publicly apologize. But my father never forgot sitting in that bunker while the sky roared above. Neither did anyone else who was there. Alexander Sturm is more powerful than his father." Darkness crept into Rogan's eyes. "We'll have to adjust our defenses."

The carrier stopped. My mother boarded, followed by Leon. She was still calm, her face serene. Leon had a dreamy look on his face. The last time I saw it, he was seven and we took him to Disney World.

"How was it?" I asked.

My cousin smiled at me. "Glorious."

Mom rolled her eyes.

Rogan's phone rang. He answered it.

"Slow down, Rynda, I can't understand you. . . . Okay. Put it on ice. We're on the way."

He hung up. His face was grim. "They sent her Brian's ear."

The ear came in a Ziploc bag in a plain yellow padded envelope. It was addressed to Rynda and me and dropped off in front of the security booth on Gessner Street. She left the ear in the bag. I did the same, except I slid the bag onto a piece of white paper to examine it.

The ear was Caucasian and had been severed in a single precise cut, the kind an experienced surgeon might make with a scalpel. The cut bothered me. Things weren't adding up.

We were in Rogan's HQ on the second floor. The moment we arrived, people ran up to the carrier with urgent looks on their faces and Rogan took off with them, which left me to deal with the ear.

Rynda had been waiting all this time in the tender care of Bug, who was looking slightly freaked out. At least they had the presence of mind to get a cooler and fill it with ice.

"It's not going to get fixed, is it?" Rynda asked, her voice dull. "We're not going to get through this okay."

"You will," I told her. "Did Brian have pierced ears, scars, tattoos, anything that would let us confirm it's his ear?"

"Please don't ask me if it looks like my husband's ear," Rynda said in a small voice.

"Are you registered with Scroll?"

She blinked, taken aback. "Yes?"

"Please request DNA analysis on the ear. Let's confirm it belongs to Brian."

"Why would they send me someone else's ear?"

And that was the million-dollar question.

"I'd like to be thorough."

She rose. "I'll make the call. I'm going to go check on the kids now. They don't know. Please don't tell them."

"I won't."

I watched her go down the stairs. She seemed so frail now. I half expected her legs to give out. That poor woman.

I puzzled over the ear some more.

Bug sidled up to me. "What's the deal with the ear?"

"I'll tell you, but you have to promise to keep it to yourself."

"I can fill this room with things I keep to myself."

"I mean it."

"Cross my heart and hope to die."

"Sit down."

He sat on the couch. I took a pen off the coffee table. "Let's say you're restrained, so hold your hands together."

He clamped his hands into a single fist.

I showed him the pen. "Pretend this is a knife." I grabbed his head with one hand and moved to "cut" his ear. He jerked away.

"See?"

"This doesn't explain anything."

I picked the bag up gently and showed him the ear. "One precise cut. No tears, no jagged edges, no nicks. He would have to be held completely immobile while this happened. Why immobilize someone's head like that? You can just hack the ear off."

"Maybe they sedated him."

"Why? He's a botanical mage. He isn't dangerous. Why go through the trouble? I don't know about Sturm, but Vincent for sure would want to torment him. He gets off on control and fear. Besides, sedation is dangerous. You never know when the person might have an adverse reaction to it and die."

Bug pondered it.

"There is another thing," I told him.

"What?"

"Look at the ear."

He peered at it and gave it an intense once-over. "I don't see it."

"I don't either."

He squinted at me. "Will you just say it, Nevada, you're driving me nuts."

"When you nick your ear, it bleeds. A lot."

"Yes. All head wounds bleed, so?"

"Where is the blood?"

He stared at the ear. "Huh. Did they wash it?"

"If you wanted to terrify a man's wife into paying a ransom, would you send her a bloody mutilated chunk of flesh that was hacked off his head, or would you send her this perfectly clean, surgically removed ear?"

Bug blinked. "So what does it mean?"

It meant one of two things. Either Brian was dead or it wasn't his ear.

"And?" Bug asked.

"And I'm going home to think about it. Did you find anything on Rynda's computers?"

"No. Bern and I have been through them last night. He's digging deeper today. There is nothing there. Pictures of the kids, a fungi database, Rynda's holiday recipes . . ." Bug waved his arms. "So much domestic bliss, I could puke."

"Tell me if you find something, please."

"No, I was going to keep it all to myself, but now that you asked me, I guess I'll clue you in." Bug rolled his eyes.

"One day your face will get stuck like that," I told him.

"Is that all you've got?" he asked.

"I've had a hard day. Don't test me, Abraham."

He opened his mouth and closed it with a click at the name. *That's right. I do know your real name.*

"That's playing dirty."

"It is."

"How did you know?"

"I'm a truthseeker, remember? I could fill this whole room with things I know and keep to myself."

I tucked the cooler with the ear under my arm and headed down the stairs. It was finally time to go home.

In theory, successful kidnapping hinged on the victim being kept alive. In practice, things went wrong. Vincent, freshly pissed off from failing to intimidate Rynda, could've stormed into wherever they were keeping Brian and killed him in a fit of rage. Or they did try to sedate Brian, and he died. Or he could've made a break for it, and they accidentally killed him. The last possibility seemed remote. By all indications, Brian wasn't the type to run or take a dangerous decisive action. He would likely comply with all of their demands, relying on other people to solve his problems, the way he relied on his older brother to handle the business issues and on his wife to shield him from domestic struggles. Brian led a charmed life. He wouldn't jeopardize it. Not only that, but the people who grabbed him off the streets were professionals: they forced him to stop, nabbed him, and took off in seconds. They left no traces of themselves behind, and Bug still couldn't find them. Professionals would have kept him alive.

If this was a punishment for our attack on House Harcourt, the ear would've been a lot bloodier.

If it wasn't Brian's ear in the cooler, we were in entirely new waters. Maybe cooler heads prevailed, and Alexander Sturm and Vincent Harcourt decided not to mutilate a Prime of another House. Vincent would do it for fun, but, really, how much of an accomplishment would it be to cut off Brian's ear? *We snatched this helpless mushroom mage off the street, beat him up, and chopped off his ear. We are total badasses, fear us.* If they had gotten their hands on Rogan, that would be one thing. But doing it to Brian would only generate derision from other Houses.

If they really meant to terrify Rynda, they would've sent her Brian's real ear.

That left only one possibility, and I really didn't like it.

I punched the code into the door, stepped into the warehouse, closed the door, turned, and froze.

Zeus stood six inches from me. His massive head was level with my chest. Turquoise eyes regarded me with mild curiosity. He took up the entire width of the hallway. An enormous tiger-hound from another world with teeth the size of steak knives and a fringe of tentacles at his neck.

It occurred to me that I was covered in dried blood.

I held very still. I could jump back and slam the door shut behind me, but it would cost me a second to open it. A second would be more than enough for Zeus.

"He's friendly," Cornelius called out from the conference room. "He just wants to say hello."

"Cornelius . . ."

"Just treat him as a poodle."

What was wrong with my life and how did I get to this place?

Slowly, I raised my hand and offered it to Zeus. He sniffed my fingers and nudged my palm with his wide nose.

"He's nudging me."

"Try petting him."

I brushed my fingers up Zeus' wide nose and over the blue fur on his forehead. He made a low rumbling noise that could've been a purr or might have been a sign that he was hungry. His tentacles moved, caught my hand, and released. He stared at the cooler in my other hand.

"No."

Zeus blinked his mahogany eyelashes.

"No. You can't have it."

He opened his mouth—it split and it just kept going and going—and licked his lips.

"Absolutely not."

I sidestepped him and carefully edged into the conference room. Bern sat at the table in front of his laptop. Fatigue overlaid his face, tugging at the corners of his eyes. As I entered, Cornelius turned away from the kitchen counter, brought two cups of coffee over, and set one in front of Bern.

"Thank you," my cousin said.

Cornelius sipped coffee from his steaming mug.

Zeus nudged my ribs with his nose and looked longingly at the cooler.

"Is there something edible in there?" Cornelius asked.

I opened the cooler and showed the contents to them.

"Oh," Cornelius said.

Bern blinked.

I closed the cooler and put it into the fridge, next to my stash of Juicy Juice.

Zeus sighed.

I poured myself a cup of coffee and sat down opposite from Bern. He stared at me over the laptop, his face grim.

"I've been over the contents of Rynda's computer three times. I've gone over all of his correspondence, and I've analyzed the fungi database for hidden patterns. It's not a code for anything. If the file exists, it's not there."

"Thank you for looking," I said.

"I didn't find anything." Bern sighed.

Zeus parked himself in front of me and stared wistfully at my coffee.

"He likes you," Cornelius said.

"Has Matilda seen him yet?"

"Not yet. With everything that went on, I asked them to delay their visit until tonight."

I got up and looked in the fridge. Juice, a bunch of old grapes I should've tossed three days ago, a pack of mozzarella string cheese sticks sealed together into a block with plastic wrap. That will do.

"Can I give him cheese?"

"I do believe he's a mammal, so yes."

I tore several cheese sticks off the block, came back to my seat, opened one, and offered it to Zeus. He pondered the cheese for a long moment and opened his mouth. I deposited the stick into it.

Zeus chewed thoughtfully.

"Bern, would you mind looking through Brian's personal correspondence one more time?" I asked. "If you're too sick of it, I can get Bug."

"No, I'm not sick of it." Bern sat up straighter. "What am I looking for?"

"I would like to help as well," Cornelius said.

The arcane tiger nudged me. I fed another stick to Zeus. "I need to know if there are any hints that Brian Sherwood may have collaborated with his kidnappers."

"Why?" Bern said.

I explained to them about the ear. As they listened, the frown on Bern's face deepened.

"I believe it isn't Brian's ear," I said. "It's possible that Brian is innocent, and they somehow immobilized him and very carefully sliced his ear off, but I don't think they would go to the trouble. It's also possible that they decided not to mutilate him."

"But?" Bern asked.

"It requires more preparation," Cornelius said. "They would have to find a fresh corpse they could mutilate. Far simpler to just cut off Brian's ear, and Alexander Sturm would have no problems slicing off an ear or a digit to make a point. He is . . . direct."

I nodded. "Assuming this is Brian's ear, it means they had an anesthesiologist and a surgeon ready. While I don't doubt that Sturm's money would buy both, it's a complication they don't need. Two more people aware of the kidnapping, extra risk to Brian's life by putting him under, and so on. Far easier to just hack off his ear and be done with it. However, if Brian was an accomplice in his own kidnapping, they would leave his ears alone."

I gave the last stick to the tiger-hound and wiped my hands against each other to show him that I was out.

"Are you sure of that?" Bern asked.

"Knowing Primes, they probably signed a contract, and they would stick to it."

Cornelius grimaced. "Sadly, that's accurate. We are a society of tigers. We are exquisitely polite and formal, because if we don't spell out all of the rules from the start, an accidental misunderstanding will have fatal consequences."

Tigers and dragons, oh my. And me without my ruby slippers. But then, who needs ruby slippers when you can lobotomize people on the fly? I sighed.

"So I'm looking for any connection to Sturm or Harcourt," Bern said.

"Or anyone else we know for a fact to have been involved in the conspiracy," I said. "Howling. Rogan's cousin."

Her face flashed before me. For a second I was back in the car hurtling down the street as Rogan spun the wheel to avoid hitting Kelly Waller and the throng of small children she used as her living shield. Kelly Waller betrayed Rogan. She couldn't get what was coming to her fast enough for my taste.

I turned to Cornelius. "You know this world better than us. Anything out of the ordinary could be important. A lunch in a place where Brian normally wouldn't be seen. A function a man of his standing wouldn't attend."

"This will be very interesting," Cornelius said.

"Do you want me to bring Bug in on this?" Bern asked.

"No."

"Can I ask why not?"

"Because Rynda is working very hard on Rogan, and Bug resents her for it. If he thinks that Brian did cooperate, and we don't know yet if he did or not, he may blurt it out at the point he thinks it will do the most damage."

A chime sounded through the office. Someone was at the front door.

"That must be Scroll to pick up the ear." I jumped up. "Hold on, I'll just be a minute."

I headed for the door.

"Nevada . . ." Bern called after me.

"One moment." I checked the camera. A blond man in a dark suit stood with his back to me. I had expected Fullerton. Interesting.

I opened the door.

The man turned toward me. About thirty, he had a strong masculine face, so handsome it might as well have been chiseled out of stone. Square jaw, full lips, beautifully defined nose, and smart green eyes under the sweep of dark eyebrows. His blond hair, a few shades lighter than his eyebrows, and cut to a medium length, artfully framed his face, emphasizing its power. The effect was stunning. If I had seen him in a mall or on the street, I would've discreetly turned for a second look.

"Hello," he said. "Are you Nevada Baylor?"

"Yes."

He smiled, showing white teeth.

Wow.

"I'm so glad to finally meet you. I'm Garen Shaffer."

Oh crap.

I HAD TO say something.

"What a surprise." Oh great. That was brilliant. "Please come in."

Before Rogan sees you and decides to squish you with a random tank he has lying around somewhere in his industrial garage.

I stepped aside to let him pass. Zeus seized this opportunity to thrust himself in the space I vacated and give Garen a once-over.

Garen froze in place.

"Ignore him." I nudged Zeus with my hip. He refused to budge. "He's a recent rescue. We haven't had a chance to train him. He isn't used to strangers." What the hell was coming out of my mouth?

"Houston animal shelter?" Garen asked, a little spark in his eyes.

"No. A summoner House, actually. Go see Cornelius."

The massive beast twitched his ears.

"Zeus," Cornelius called.

The tiger-hound turned and hurried into the conference room with liquid grace.

Garen stepped inside. I shut the front door and led him to my office. Sooner or later someone would report to Rogan that a person from House Shaffer appeared on my doorstep. Most likely they reported it the moment he drove up to the checkpoint. The consequences would be interesting.

I sat behind my desk. Garen Shaffer sat in my client chair. I touched my laptop. It came on. A message window from Bern opened.

> Garen Shaffer, heir to House Shaffer, truthseeker Prime.

Better and better.

I put on my professional smile and clicked the small icon in the corner of the laptop, enabling recording. We had a hidden camera positioned on the shelf behind me. We'd had some trouble with clients who displayed selective memory, and it was amazing how quickly threats of lawsuits faded once we presented a recording of them saying the words they claimed they couldn't remember.

"What can I do for you, Mr. Shaffer?"

He leaned back, throwing one long leg over the other. "I've come to hire you."

Lie. This was a test.

"That would be a lie, Mr. Shaffer. Care to try again?"

"Would you mind?"

"No."

Magic accreted around him. "I'm thirty-one years old."

My power pressed against the magic wall and slipped through. "True."

The magic wall grew denser.

"I have three sisters."

"Lie."

Magic spilled out of him like water out of a geyser. It wrapped him in a cocoon of power. How the hell did he do that?

"I'm the only child."

The cocoon looked impenetrable. My magic wrapped around it. The wall of power held tight. If I hammered against it with brute force, we'd be locked in a fight, his will against mine. He was strong. Very strong. Possibly stronger than I, although we wouldn't figure it out until we clashed. A part of me really wanted to find out.

Ignore the wall. Imagine it's porous. Imagine it's not there.

He narrowed his eyes.

His wall was stone, but my magic was water. It slipped through the cracks. All I had to do was guide it and let it flow . . .

Lie.

"I think we should stop." I leaned back.

The wall vanished. His magic wrapped around me. "Are you trying to appear stronger than you are or weaker?"

"Neither. I just don't want you to know."

"Why?"

"I don't trust you." I waved my hand in front of my face, as if clearing smoke. "Please keep your magic to yourself."

He smiled. His power vanished.

"Why is there a cooler in the fridge?" Arabella called from the conference room.

When did she even get a chance to get in there? "Leave the cooler alone. Stay out of the fridge."

"Sister?" he guessed.

I made a face at him.

"I have one myself. They are difficult at times."

Arabella stuck her head into my office and showed me the Ziploc bag with the ear. "Why are you dressed like a soldier? Is that blood on your clothes? Also, why is there a human ear in the fridge?"

Argh. Just argh.

Garen's eyebrows crept up.

"It's evidence," I ground out. "Put it back in the cooler."

"Fine, fine."

She went back into the conference room.

"I would very much like to take you to dinner."

I made a show of looking down at my ACUs. "Today wouldn't be a good day."

"What about tomorrow?"

I raised my head and pretended to consider it. "Unfortunately, I'm in the middle of something, so I can't promise I won't stand you up."

I felt something, a light click, like he'd flicked his fingers against my palm. Was it his magic working? Is that what it felt like?

"That's okay. I'm a very patient man."

True. He was flirting with me.

"Okay, I'll go to dinner with you if you answer a question."

He leaned forward, his green eyes fixed on me. "It's a deal."

"Do you feel a click when I spot-check your answers for truth, and if so, does everyone or is it a truthseeker thing?"

"That's three questions."

Two could play the flirting game. "Do you want me to come to dinner with you or not?"

He pretended to consider it. "You drive a hard bargain. Yes, no, and it is a truthseeker thing. We call it pinging. There is nothing like coming home late in a damaged car and having both parents ping you in stereo as you answer their questions. Tomorrow at six?"

"Where?"

"Bistro le Cep. They tell me that's the best place in Houston for quiet conversation."

I had no idea where that was. "Very well. Tomorrow at six."

We both got up. He held the door of my office open for me. I walked him to the outside door and watched him get into a black Cadillac. The car reversed and rolled down the street, unmolested.

Arabella came up to stand next to me.

"He was pretty."

"What was that all about? You never interrupt me while I'm with clients."

"Bern texted me and told me to do it. He said you and he sat completely still, staring at each other for ten minutes. He thought something might have gone wrong and said I should check on you."

Smart move. Garen would consider Bern with his wrestler build and judo shoulders a threat. But Arabella, barely five feet and maybe one hundred and ten pounds wet, would seem harmless. Garen had no idea how close he'd come to being crushed to death.

Ten minutes. Must've been when I was trying to find a way through his wall. Felt like a few seconds. I wonder if that's what Augustine Montgomery felt like. Over a week ago I was trying to convince him to let me shield his mind from Victoria Tremaine, and I pulled some harmless but private information out of his mind. He never realized it happened until I told him. It was like a chunk of time simply disappeared from his memory.

Cold sweat drenched my hairline.

I spun around, ran the few feet to my office, and grabbed my laptop.

"What?" Arabella demanded. "What is it?"

The image of me and Garen sitting across from each other filled the screen.

"What can I do for you, Mr. Shaffer?"

"I've come to hire you."

I clicked to fast forward. Frantic gestures and teeny voices. Blah-blah-blah . . . There.

Garen and I stared at each other. I zoomed in on myself and turned the sound up.

Nothing. I sat completely still, like a statue. So did he. No movements. No words. Just quiet staring. All my secrets were still mine.

I collapsed in the chair. I was suddenly so exhausted.

"Nevada? Are you okay?" Arabella grabbed a tissue box from the corner of the desk and thrust it at me.

I touched my face and realized I was crying.

"I think you're stressed out," my sister said. "I have a pack of cigarettes I've been hiding from Mom for when Catalina and I get stressed out. There is one left."

"Mom is going to kill you when she finds out."

"She won't find out if you don't tell her."

I got up and hugged her.

"Are you okay?" my little sister asked.

"No. But I'm going to be. We're all going to be."

My laptop screamed at me. Bug's face filled it. "Get here! Now, now, now!"

I sprinted out the door to Rogan's HQ, Arabella at my heels.

I RAN THROUGH the first floor, pounded up the stairs, and burst onto the second floor. Rynda stood next to Bug, her face pale, her phone to her ear. Kidnappers.

". . . scared me. I'm very scared."

She listened for a moment. "My husband is everything to me. I'm going to give the phone to Ms. Baylor. She's authorized to negotiate on our behalf." She handed the phone to me.

"This is Nevada Baylor."

"Good," a cultured male voice said on the other end. "Perhaps we can finally get somewhere."

"You broke the rules of engagement," I said.

Bug's fingers danced over the keyboard and the man's voice echoed through the room.

"Oh?"

"We had an understanding, and you broke it."

"What kind of an understanding, Ms. Baylor?"

"You want your ransom. My client wants the father of her children safely home. You trust that we won't involve authorities and that we will surrender the ransom, and we trust that you will keep Brian safe and allow us time to prepare the ransom. You made a demand, you gave us no chance to respond, and then you sent Harcourt to attack Rynda and her children in her house. And now you sent us a severed ear. This is a severe breach of trust."

There was a long pause.

"The Harcourt incident was unplanned," the man said finally. "It won't be repeated."

"Is Brian still alive?" I asked.

"Yes."

"We would like proof of life, please."

"Very well."

The phone went silent. Rynda clenched her fists.

"Hello." Brian's quiet voice echoed through the room.

Bug pushed a mic toward Rynda. "How are you?" she asked, her voice breaking.

"In pain," he said.

"Did they treat your wound? Did they bring in a doctor?" Rynda asked.

"Yes, but it still hurts. Please give them whatever they want."

"I love you," she said. "I'm trying, honey. I'm doing everything I can. Please hold on for a little longer."

"I love you too," Brian said. He sounded dull, his words devoid of any emotion. Maybe it was his ear, and he was in shock.

Rynda clenched her hands into a single fist. She looked like she wanted to scream.

"Now that we've gotten that out of the way," the kidnapper said, "let's get back to business, shall we?"

"It would help us a great deal if you told us what we're looking for," I said.

"You cannot believe that Rynda is that naive."

"I don't need to believe anything," I said. "I'm a truthseeker, and I'm telling you that my client has no idea what you're asking. The most I got out of Vincent, before he dove through the window, was that it's something connected to Rynda's mother."

Another pause. Vincent mustn't have told him. Ha.

"That should be good enough," he said.

"We're looking for a needle in a haystack and we don't even know if it's a needle. It could be a pen or an apple. We've gone through Brian and Rynda's computers. We didn't find it."

"It's not in the computer." A note of irritation crept into his voice. "It's somewhere in the house. Or outside of it, in a personal safe deposit box, or wherever else Olivia stashed it."

"You want us to find we don't know what in we don't know where."

"And you'll find it, if you want Brian to survive."

"Could you at least give us time?"

"Very well. You have forty-eight hours."

I had expected twenty-four.

"I suggest you make good use of it. I hate to see children cry because they miss their parent, don't you? If I don't have what I need in forty-eight hours, I'll deliver their father to them in pieces."

The disconnect signal filled the room. Bug turned the feed off.

"Someone needs to squish him," Arabella said. Red tinted her cheeks. She clenched her teeth. He really managed to piss her off.

I turned to Rynda. "You don't have to worry about Brian for forty-eight hours."

"But what happens at the end?" She hugged herself.

"We'll deal with that then. Have you called Scroll?"

"Yes. They're on the way."

"Good. I need you to take this evening and think back over the past few weeks. They seem to be absolutely sure that whatever they want is in your house or somewhere where you would have access to it. Did your mother give you anything as a keepsake? No matter how unimportant? Ask the kids."

She sighed. "I'll do that."

"I can talk to the children."

"No." She held up her hand. "No, I'll do it."

"Thank you."

She went down the stairs.

I turned to Bug, held out my phone, and typed a text to Bern, holding the phone so Bug could see what I was typing. I didn't want to take any chances that Rynda or someone else would over-hear.

> Talked to kidnapper. He's absolutely sure that whatever we're looking for isn't on Brian's computer. Could we check if Sherwood computers were accessed using Brian's credentials from some unusual location?

"On it."

I leaned to Bug and whispered, "Could you please check the route Brian took to work and find out how many cameras are facing that street?"

Bug blinked and ran to his workstation.

My cell rang. Please be something good. I looked at it. Rogan.

Here we go. We'd have to discuss Garen Shaffer. I knew this would happen sooner or later. "Hello?"

His voice had the calm, collected overtones of a Prime. "You promised me a dinner."

My mind made a 180-degree turn and it took me a second to catch up. "Yes."

"I'll pick you up in an hour and a half. Cocktail attire."

Cocktail attire meant there was probably a reservation. I was wearing bloodstained ACUs.

"Do you need a dress?"

What was he up to? "No. I have one."

"See you at seven."

I exhaled and trudged back down the stairs to take a shower and get dressed.

Behind me Arabella spoke into the phone. "Catalina, what are you doing? . . . Can you cancel that? Nevada needs help."

* * *

"DID HE SAY what this was about?" Grandma Frida asked for the twelfth time.

"No."

I sat at the kitchen table and tried to work on my laptop. Bern and Cornelius were still going through Brian's correspondence, so I decided to scour his mushroom Pinterest account.

When you waited for an important phone call, ninety minutes seemed like an impossibly long time. When you had to go from blood and gore to some sort of presentable, ninety minutes was nothing. Luckily for me, my sisters had mobilized to help. The moment I stepped out of the shower and wrapped the towel around myself, Arabella attacked my hair. Catalina appeared with an airbrush I'd bought her last Christmas, because she kept worrying about her nonexistent acne, and told me to sit down and not move my face. I was dried, styled, and had a liquid mist of makeup sprayed at my face. I drew the line at contouring. If I gave them free rein, I'd come out of my bathroom with skull-like cheeks and Cleopatra-style wings on my eyes. But because of them, I had finished in record time.

Now Rogan had to show up.

The word of his previous failure to appear must've spread, because the entire family found their way to the kitchen one by one. Bern was reading a textbook in the corner. Grandma Frida sat next to me and attempted to knit something that was probably a scarf but looked like a brilliant attempt at a Gordian knot. My mother rearranged the tea drawer, which she's never done since we've had one. Arabella sat across from me, her gaze glued to her cell phone. Catalina sat on my left, texting furiously. Zeus lounged under the table by my feet, and Cornelius was drinking tea across the table. Even Leon wandered in and leaned against the wall, waiting.

Nobody was talking.

"Just out of curiosity," Cornelius said, "if Rogan doesn't arrive, will all of you skin him alive?"

"Yes," everyone except me said at the same time.

I sighed.

The doorbell rang.

I clicked the key on my laptop. The view from the front camera filled it. A woman stood at the door, wearing a dark pantsuit, her silvery-blond hair caught in a ponytail. A little girl with dark hair stood next to her holding a large white cat. A large Doberman pinscher dutifully guarded both of them. Diana, Matilda, her cat, and Bunny.

"Matilda is here," I said.

"Oh good." Catalina got up and went to open the door. A few moments later, Cornelius' sister and his daughter made their way to our kitchen.

"Daddy." Matilda held out her hands. Cornelius got up off his chair, crouched, and hugged her. Arabella discreetly took a pic with her phone. I couldn't blame her. Matilda was too cute for words.

Matilda blinked. She looked a lot like her late mother, Nari Harrison, but her expression, serious and somber, was pure Cornelius.

Behind her, Diana frowned. "What is that?"

Matilda's eyes widened. "A kitty."

"I have a surprise for you." Cornelius smiled.

Oh. He hadn't told them.

Zeus shifted under the table, a massive furry shape, and his huge head poked out half a foot from Matilda's face.

Matilda opened her mouth, her eyes wide.

"Oh my God," Diana said.

Bunny froze in place, clearly unsure what to do.

Matilda held out her hand. Zeus nudged it with his nose. She backed up, and the huge beast squeezed all of himself out. He was a foot taller than Matilda. She gasped.

196 • ILONA ANDREWS

The blue beast lowered his head, and Matilda hugged his furry neck. "He's so soft."

My sisters snapped simultaneous pictures.

"He is beautiful . . ." Diana crouched and scratched under Zeus' chin. "The eyes, Cornell. Like jewels. How did you even manage this? This isn't possible."

"Feel him," Cornelius said.

"I do. That's remarkable."

The door chimed again. I checked my laptop.

Rogan stood at our front door. Behind him a gunmetal-grey Mercedes-Benz E200 waited, its lights on. Rogan wore a black suit. He was perfectly proportioned, and unless I stood next to him, it was easy to forget how large he was. The suit emphasized everything, from his height and long legs to his narrow flat waist and broad shoulders. He'd shaved. His short hair was brushed. He looked every inch a billionaire.

He was definitely up to something.

"He's here!" Grandma Frida announced.

My family forgot about the tiger-hound and crowded all around me.

"Hot!" Arabella declared.

"He's going to propose." Grandma Frida rubbed her hands together.

"Mother!" my mom growled.

"He isn't going to propose. We're going to dinner. Let me up!"

I managed to escape the table.

"A date?" Diana asked, smiling.

"A dinner," I said.

"You look like a princess," Matilda told me.

"Thank you!" I hugged her, but she had already forgotten about me. Zeus was much more fascinating.

I marched through the office to the front door and walked out into the Texas winter, where Rogan was waiting for me. He tilted his head, and I saw the exact moment heat sparked in his eyes.

"You look fantastic," he said.

I wore a black dress, an Adriana Red original, from an up-and-coming Houston designer. I bought it for three hundred dollars last year, when her boutique store had just opened. Two months later a young star wore her green gown to the Emmys, and suddenly Adriana became a fashion name. I couldn't afford her anymore—her prices had tripled overnight—but as far as I was concerned, I was wearing her best work. The dress was simple, but it glided down my body in a controlled cascade, emphasizing all the right curves while still making me look elegant. Its hemline fell a couple of inches above the knee, the perfect length to show off my legs while still remaining professional. The V-neck plunged a little lower than was strictly appropriate for a business dinner, but I wasn't having a business dinner. My hair fell on my back in soft waves. My shoes gave me four inches of extra height. My outfit wouldn't take any fashion prisoners, but nobody could find fault with it.

Rogan's eyes had turned hot and dark.

"You look great too," I told him.

"The dress needs a little sparkle." He pulled a rectangular black box out of his pocket and opened it. A beautiful emerald lay inside. A little larger than my thumbnail, the stone caught the light from the lamp above the door and shone with breathtaking green tinted with a hint of blue. It dangled on the pale gold chain like a tear.

"Yes?" Rogan asked. There was a slight wariness in him, as if he expected things to go terribly wrong any second.

"It's gorgeous," I told him honestly.

He took it from the box. I held up my hair and he slipped the chain over my neck. The stone settled on my skin, a radiant drop of light.

"Just for dinner though," I told him. "I can't keep it."

"I bought it for you," he said. "I meant to give it to you for Christmas."

His face told me that rejecting the necklace would be rejecting him. Yes, it was an expensive emerald. I was probably wearing fifty thousand dollars on my neck, which was more than all of the jewelry I've owned in my lifetime put together. But then he had more money than he could count in a lifetime, and if he wanted me to wear the necklace, I would.

"Thank you."

He smiled, a satisfied dragon.

"If you keep looking at me like that, we won't make it to dinner," I told him quietly.

"Then you better get in the car."

He held the door out for me and I slid into the heated interior of the Mercedes.

FLANDERS' STEAKHOUSE SAT at the top of a twenty-story building on Louisiana Street, just southwest of the theater district, and it took full advantage of the view. Floor-to-ceiling windows presented the spectacular expanse of the night sky, below which Houston spread, glowing with warm yellow and orange against the darkness. Freeways curved among the towers, channeling the current of cars seemingly through mid-air. The floor, ceiling, and walls offered soothing browns, and the delicate chandeliers, wrought iron spirals supporting upturned triangles of pale glass, softened the décor even further. I'd gone out on a few business dinners, and most Houston steakhouses catered to executives with business accounts. They ran either straight into rustic Texas, with longhorn skulls and cow pelts on the walls, or they resembled gentlemen's clubs, where one had to be a card-carrying member. This was nice.

It finally hit me. We were on a date. Our first real date.

An impeccably dressed host led us through the restaurant, past well-dressed patrons. Some of them had to be House members, because as we moved past them, they saw Rogan's face and stopped what they were doing. I got a few stares as well, some surprised and puzzled, some openly curious, especially from women. Women watched Rogan wherever he went, and I was getting the once-overs as they tried to figure out what was so special. That was fine. They wouldn't ruin the date for me.

We arrived at a secluded table covered in chocolate-colored cloth. Rogan held my chair out. He didn't make it slide out for me with his power. No telekinetic fireworks. Tonight it would be just me and Connor.

I sat. He took his place across from me, with his back against the wall, a spot that would conveniently let him watch the entire restaurant for incoming danger.

A waitress appeared at our table as if by magic. Menus were placed in front of us.

"Wine?" Rogan asked me.

Why not. "Yes."

"What do you like?"

I liked Asti Spumante. It was sweet and bubbly and it cost five dollars per bottle. "Red. Not too dry." Here's hoping I didn't make a fool of myself.

Rogan ordered a wine from the list. The waitress bowed her head as if she was granted knighthood by some royalty and glided away.

I grinned at Rogan from above my menu.

He grinned back. The set of his shoulders relaxed slightly.

I stared at the menu. Oh my.

"I'm starving. I haven't had anything to eat since I stole a bear claw from your kitchen this morning."

"You didn't steal it. All my bear claws are yours."

I studied the appetizers. Roasted Portobello mushroom ravioli. Tenderloin carpaccio. Chilled seafood cocktail.

"Is something wrong?" he asked me. There it was, that weary caution in his eyes.

"I'm trying to decide what I can order that has the smallest chances of me spilling it on myself."

He laughed quietly under his breath. "I've never seen you spill anything on yourself."

"That's not true. When we were climbing through the Dumpsters into the high-rise on Sam Houston, I spilled rancid spaghetti all over myself."

And why did I just mention rancid spaghetti. I sighed.

"That doesn't count. You stepped on it."

More like rolled in it, but now wasn't the best time to point out that distinction.

The waitress appeared again with a bottle of red wine. She dramatically opened it and poured a little into two glasses. There was some sort of ceremony here I remembered from the movies. You held the glass a certain way, swished the wine inside, smelled it or something. I raised the glass and took a small sip. It washed over my tongue, warm and refreshing.

"It's delicious," I said.

Rogan nodded at the waitress. She beamed and stepped aside. Another waiter appeared. A bread basket was placed on our table containing several small loaves, crunchy and fresh from the oven. Small heated plates of two types of herbed olive oil followed. The aroma of freshly baked bread made my mouth water.

"Appetizers?" the waitress asked.

I hit complete decision paralysis. "You pick."

"Carpaccio," he said.

I had ordered carpaccio the first time we ate together, in Takara, when he was trying to convince me to work for him. He remembered.

The waitress nodded and we were alone again.

I took a swallow of my wine. The tension of the day slowly seeped out of me.

He reached over and covered my hand with his, lacing his fingers with mine.

"Hey," I told him.

"Hey." He smiled and Mad Rogan went away. Connor was looking at me. We might as well have been alone in the whole world.

"Thank you. I needed this after today."

"Thank you for coming with me. It doesn't always have to be blood and gore. It can also be this."

"This is very nice."

"I'm glad you like it."

Carpaccio arrived. I ordered a double-thick pork chop, and Rogan went for a dry-aged rib eye.

The carpaccio tasted divine. We ate it with crusty bread dipped in olive oil.

"You were in mortal danger this evening," I told him.

"Oh?"

"My whole family waited in the kitchen for you to show up. If you stood me up, there would've been hell to pay."

He grinned. "Your family likes me. I would charm them into sparing my life."

"I don't know. They were pretty determined."

He leaned forward. "But I can be so charming."

Oh yes. Yes, he could. It's not hard to be charming when you are that smoking hot. I had to pace myself.

The restaurant wavered around me, receding. The light changed, growing soft and golden. I was in bed with Rogan. Neither of us was wearing a shred of clothes. His big hand slid up my thigh . . .

I pulled back from the projection just enough to see him looking at me from across the table.

"Be careful," I told him, and licked the wine off my lips. His gaze snagged on my tongue. "You might set the tablecloth on fire."

He looked on the verge of getting up and dragging me out of the restaurant to have incredible sex in the car. And I would totally go with him.

The projection vanished, like the flame of a snuffed-out candle.

Rogan's eyes iced over. He picked up his glass and leaned back as a man approached our table. Tall and broad-shouldered, he wore a custom-tailored suit with casual elegance. His skin was dark brown, his hair cropped very short, and a precise narrow goatee traced his jaw. I'd only met him once, but he'd made an impression. It was the eyes. You looked into them and knew this was a dangerously smart man.

"Rogan."

"Latimer," Rogan said. "Chair?"

Michael Latimer nodded. A chair moved by itself from the nearest empty table and slid to ours. Latimer sat.

"The Harcourts reached out to me today," he said. "They offered a strategic alliance on very favorable terms. Do I need to worry about you, Rogan?"

True.

"My business with them is concluded," Rogan said. "Except for Vincent."

"You have plans for Vincent?"

"Yes."

"Do those plans hinge on him no longer breathing?"

"Yes."

Latimer leaned back. The chair creaked slightly. "They've given up. They don't think they can protect Vincent."

"Agreed. They know they'll be vulnerable without their biggest gun," Rogan said.

Latimer raised his eyebrows, thinking. "Good information to have. Enjoy your evening."

He rose and looked at me. "The offer stands. Any time, any place."

"Thank you."

Michael Latimer walked away.

Rogan turned to me. "What offer?"

"When Augustine took me to Baranovsky's gala, Latimer saw the bruises on my neck and mistook me for a domestic abuse victim. His aunt distracted Augustine, while he offered to walk me out of the gala and take me to a doctor and give me a safe place to stay."

Rogan leaned to the side to look after Latimer. "Michael Latimer?"

"Mhm. He wasn't lying."

"Interesting," Rogan said.

Our waitress appeared by our table with our food.

My pork chop was incredible. I decided that I didn't care if I spilled food on myself. I did care if other people saw me shovel the food in my mouth as if I were a cavewoman, so I forced myself to cut painfully small bites.

"We should have dessert," Rogan said.

I eyed my pork chop. My plate had enough meat to feed me for two days.

"What's your favorite dessert?" he asked.

"I don't know what it's called. I had it one time when I was maybe nine or ten. Mom was deployed, and Grandma Frida and Grandpa Leon took my sisters and cousins to Rockport Beach for three days. I was supposed to go, but I got sick and spent the first day throwing up in Dad's office. I was so miserable. Everyone was at the beach, and here I was sleeping in the office next to a bucket. On the morning of the second day I kept down some crackers and by the evening I was so hungry. Dad closed a big case, and he took me to some restaurant to celebrate. I don't remember what I had for dinner, but Dad said I could have whatever I wanted for dessert. So I ordered something called the treasure box. They brought it out and it was this big cube made of chocolate. I tried it with the spoon and the top broke. The chocolate was paper thin. There was this amazing cream inside mixed with raspberries and blueberries. It was the best thing I've ever eaten." I smiled at the memory. "Your turn."

"Chocolate mousse," he said without hesitation. "I craved it in the jungle. No idea why. Never liked chocolate much before. Some days when we were starving, I'd wake with the taste of it in my mouth, thinking it was real. When we walked out, they put us into helicopters and brought us to Arrow Point, the base in Belize. I stayed awake until they got us to the hospital. All these people were running around, frantically trying to make sure I didn't die on their watch. At some point someone asked me what I wanted. I must've told them, because when I woke up in the hospital bed, it was waiting for me."

I wanted to hug him. I had to settle for reaching out and gently stroking his hand with my fingers. "Was it good?"

"Yes. It was."

A young woman walked up to our table on tall needle heels. She was about twenty, with light blond hair, twisted into a complicated arrangement on the back of her head. Her skin was flawless and her makeup expertly applied. She wore a black cocktail dress, but unlike my simple number, hers consisted of artfully sewn strips of ghostly black silk, each strip shot through with a streak of gold. The dress screamed money. She knew she was beautiful and she was used to taking it as her due.

She ignored me, her gaze fixed on Rogan. "My name is Sloan Marcus of House Marcus."

Rogan pondered her.

"We're the third largest telekinetic House in Texas," she said. "I'm a third-generation Prime. I'm twenty-one, in good health, and free of genetic diseases. I'm a graduate of Princeton. You interest me. My profile will be available to you on request."

She just propositioned him right in front of me.

Rogan nodded. "My companion is much too polite to explain the facts to you, Sloan, so I'll have to take it upon myself. She and I had a rather trying morning, and, having washed off the blood and gore, we came here for a quiet meal. You're interrupting it."

Color tinted her cheeks. She wasn't embarrassed. She was angry at being rebuffed. "I don't believe you understand. I said, my profile will be available to you."

"I don't think he wants to see your profile," I told her. "He hasn't even looked at mine, and we're sleeping together."

She condescended to look at me. "Primes marry other Primes."

I smiled at her and kept eating.

Sloan raised her chin. "Nobody says no to me."

"Lie," I said.

"How dare you?"

"It's a fact," I told her. "Someone says no to you a lot. You lied about being twenty-one as well, but it was a good speech, so I didn't interrupt."

Rogan laughed quietly.

"Who do you think you are—"

"Leave us," Rogan said. His voice had a tone of unmistakable command to it.

Sloan opened her mouth. Rogan's magic splayed out around him, an invisible but violent current. The dragon had opened his wings.

Sloan stumbled back, her face shocked, and hurried off on her impossible heels.

Rogan's magic vanished.

"Have you ever checked if you and I are compatible?" I asked.

He frowned. "I'd have to get Tremaine records for that. Do you think your grandmother would give me access?"

"I doubt it. Although you never know with her. Didn't she promise me to you?"

"Yes."

Now was as good of a time as any. "Garen Shaffer came to see me today."

Rogan's face was relaxed, almost casual, as he cut his steak. "The heir."

"He asked to have dinner with me tomorrow." I cut another tiny slice of the pork chop. "I said yes."

Something crunched. Rogan kept eating, his expression perfectly calm. The thick window glass beside us developed a hairline crack all the way across the top corner, just above Rogan.

"Thinking about the future is important," Rogan said, his voice neutral. "I understand why you want to keep all possibilities open."

Oh, you fool. "A truthseeker was involved in breaking through the hex and helping Pierce to find the artifact. A truthseeker also created a barrier in Harcourt's mind. We haven't yet been confirmed as a House, but the moment our profile went up, Shaffer jumped on it. I'd like to know more about him."

"That's as good of a reason as any."

"If he's working with Harcourt, he may know where Brian is kept."

"Sounds logical." He was cutting his steak with surgical precision.

"I'd like you to watch."

"Of course." He froze with his fork in midair. "Run that by me again?"

I spoke slowly. "I'm going to record the conversation with a hidden camera and send live feed to Bern. I'd like you to watch it."

He just stared at me.

"Going to see Shaffer carries a risk. He did something today in my office that made it difficult for me to recognize if he was lying. He was testing my magic. There is some possibility that he will try to do the same thing with me as I did with Augustine. If you hear me start to confess things, please call me. I'm hoping a phone call will be enough of an interruption, but I can't be sure."

"So you don't mind if I listen in on your date?"

"It's not a date."

"Your dinner appointment."

I sighed. "If I minded, I wouldn't ask you to monitor the conversation."

He came to life like a shark sensing a drop of blood in the water. "What if I come with you and just get a different table?"

"No."

His eyes narrowed. "You're clearly concerned. I'm also concerned about your safety. If you allow me, I can be near in case things go wrong."

"No."

"Why not?"

"Because the moment Shaffer puts his fork down the wrong way, you'll storm in there and slice off his head with his silverware. Or some loose change in your pocket."

"I won't need silverware or anything else. If he hurts you, I'll wring his neck with my hands."

I pointed my fork at him. "And this is exactly why you will give me your word that you will maintain some distance."

"How much distance?"

"Lots."

"Can you be more specific?"

"Rogan, stop."

He took a swallow of his wine. His expression didn't change, but his eyes did. They grew guarded.

"Sturm," he said quietly.

I pulled my magic to myself and let it out, drenching the table in it.

A man walked up. He was about six feet tall, lean, and pale, with eyes the color of coffee grounds. His dark brown hair framed his face in soft waves, long enough to brush his neck. He'd shaved that morning, but now stubble peppered his jaw, and he didn't seem to care. He had an attractive face, but not handsome. Where Augustine's features had the perfection of beauty, and Rogan's spoke of power, Sturm's telegraphed focus. He was a man who would patiently plot and think of a strategy. His eyes said he'd be ruthless in its implementation. Watching him wasn't really a choice, it was a compulsion. He tripped some instinctual alarm deep inside my brain that said, *Danger*, and my survival dictated I had to keep an eye on him to see what he'd do next.

"Rogan. Fancy meeting you here. What a lovely surprise," Sturm said. His voice had a slight rasp. If wolves could assume human form, they would sound just like that. Come to think of it, he looked like a wolf too. A patient, vicious, smart wolf.

"Sturm," Rogan said, as if he didn't have a care in the world.

Sturm landed in the spare chair. I drank my wine and moved my magic, one thin strand at a time, to wrap around him.

"I thought you became a complete recluse," Sturm said. "A hero damaged by war and withdrawn from us ordinary mortals.

Yet here you are having a steak at Flanders', in presentable clothes even, and your date is wearing the Tear of the Aegean around her neck. How wrong I was."

The Tear of the Aegean?

"Assumptions can be dangerous things," Rogan said.

"Indeed. A man can often assume that he is in the right, only to find himself unexpectedly on the wrong side of history." Sturm smiled. "I'm glad to see you out and about, Rogan, enjoying the finer side of life. This is, after all, what being a Prime is all about. Comfort. Wealth. Power."

"Duty," Rogan said.

Sturm rolled his eyes. "You're no fun. What do you think about all this, Ms. Baylor?"

"It's nice. My pork chop was delicious. The wine is also excellent."

Sturm bared his teeth in a sharp grin. "Your pork chop. That's priceless. You're delightful."

"That's right. Have you ever met Vincent Harcourt, Mr. Sturm?"

"Of course."

I wrapped the strands of magic tighter around him. "Does he strike you as an erratic man? The kind who can ruin a carefully structured plan by failing to follow simple orders?"

Sturm laughed his lupine raspy laugh. "You haven't even been certified as a Prime, Ms. Baylor, but you play the game so well. Doesn't she, Rogan?"

Rogan didn't answer. He took another small swallow of his wine.

"A man in our position has to play the game well, as Rogan will tell you, Ms. Baylor. Otherwise we risk losing everything. People who work for us. People we love. Before you know it, we find ourselves cowering in a tiny bunker while the tornados of fate roar overhead. But then sometimes the tradition of losing runs in the family. How is your nephew doing, Rogan?"

Rogan smiled. The window beside us cracked with a lovely musical crunch.

That smile meant murder. I reached out and put my hand on his wrist. "Please don't."

"Ah." Sturm smiled again. "The civilizing influence of women. What would men do without it?"

I turned to him. "Some men are too thick to realize that when they push too far, other men may murder them without any thought of consequences. Such men would be wise to remember that consequences won't matter to them, because they would be dead."

Sturm glanced at the window. The hairline cracks framed extremely sharp glass shards. If the window shattered, the shards could slice him to ribbons, especially if they were precision-guided by a Prime telekinetic.

"I see I've overstayed my welcome."

"No," Rogan said. "Stay. Chat a bit more. Let's catch up."

"Sorry, but I do have to be going." Sturm rose. "Think about what I said, Rogan. It's not too late to walk on the right side."

He walked away.

"What am I wearing, Rogan?" I asked.

His face looked pained. "A shiny rock."

True. Fine. I pulled out my phone and typed "Tear of the Aegean" into the search window.

Tear of the Aegean, a diamond measuring 11.2 carats and rated as Fancy Intense Green Blue, was recently discovered in an ancient shipwreck off the coast of Argos. The Tear of the Aegean is only the third of all known diamonds to possess a blue-green hue, others being Ocean Paradise and Ocean Dream, making it one of the rarest diamonds in the world. (Blue-green color is common in artificially enhanced diamonds and achieved via various irradiation methods; however, it is exceedingly rare in nature.) The Tear of the Aegean was recently sold to a private collector for $16.8 million.

I choked on empty air.

"Do you want to stay for dessert?" he asked.

"No."

Our waitress appeared, as if summoned.

"We're ready to go," Rogan told her. "Put the window on my bill."

We walked out of Flanders' and got into the car. Rogan drove through the night city.

"Why?" I asked finally.

"Because I love you."

"Sixteen million dollars."

He didn't say anything.

Houston's glowing lights slid past the window.

"I wanted to show you the other side of being a Prime," he said. "The benefits of it."

"You mean the benefits of a stuck-up asshole in an Armani suit threatening us or the part where some random woman throws herself at you?" Ouch. Okay, that wasn't fair.

"The difference between her and Garen is practice. She'll get better with experience."

"Garen didn't come on to me."

"He will."

I sighed.

"I wanted tonight to be just about us," Rogan said. "Free of killing and gore. Just you and me. No Prime business."

And instead there was a never-ending parade, at the end of which Alexander Sturm came to gloat. And I pointed it out. Oh, Connor.

"It can be peaceful," he said. "We're at war right now, but we won't always be."

He turned onto our street.

"Will you drop me off at my house?" I asked.

He brought the car to a smooth stop before the warehouse. I reached for the chain around my neck.

"No," he said, steel in his voice.

"I can't. It's too expensive. I . . ."

"I bought it for you," he said.

If I forced him to take it back, he would toss it out of the window and drive off. I could see it in his eyes.

"Okay. Don't wait for me. I'll be a little bit."

His face shut down.

I stepped out of the car and punched the code into the warehouse door.

Mom and Grandma Frida were still in the kitchen, bickering about something in low voices. The moment I walked in, everything stopped.

I took off the chain and put the diamond on the table.

"Ooo, shiny." Grandma Frida stared at it. "What is it?"

"It's sixteen million dollars."

I landed into a chair. My mother and grandmother stared at me, mute.

"Sixteen million dollars?" Mom finally found her voice.

"It's a green-blue diamond. There are only three in the world. I tried to give it back to him and he refuses to take it. We're just keeping it for a little while. Can we put it somewhere safe so I can give it back to him when he feels better?"

"Did he propose and you turned him down?" Grandma Frida demanded.

"No. He didn't propose. It's a Christmas present. It was a nice dinner." It wasn't Rogan's fault that Sturm ruined the end of it.

My mother rubbed her temples. "Where would we even put it? We don't have a safe."

"I can put it into the spare ammo lockbox and you can keep it in your bedroom," Grandma Frida said.

"Let's do that. And please don't tell my sisters." The last thing I needed was them taking selfies with the Tear of the Aegean. I got up and went to the fridge. Let's see, eggs, whipping cream, butter . . . We had chocolate chips somewhere here.

"What are you doing?" Mom asked.

"I'm making chocolate mousse."

"Now?" Grandma Frida asked.

"Yes."

Thirty minutes later, with the diamond safe under my bed, I grabbed my favorite sleeping T-shirt out of the laundry, stuffed it, my laptop, and a packet of makeup wipes into a canvas bag, grabbed the baking pan with six teacups filled with mousse and a small container of freshly whipped cream, and walked over to Rogan's HQ.

Bug was still at his station. His face brightened when he saw me. "Hey you!"

"Hey. Any news?"

"No more calls. All quiet. What's in the pan?"

"Chocolate mousse."

"Why?"

"Because Rogan likes it. Good night."

"Good night."

I climbed up another flight of stairs and tried Rogan's door. The door handle turned in my hands. I walked in. He sat at a desk, his face illuminated by the glow of the computer. He wore sweatpants and a white T-shirt. His feet were bare. This was Rogan in his off mode—relaxed, tired, and unbearably hot.

He turned and saw me. Surprise slapped his face. He didn't think I was coming over. He thought I was mad at him. Foolish, foolish Rogan.

I walked to the small fridge in the corner, which, as I discovered last night, he used for drinks, and slid the pan in there. It was a tight fit, but I managed. I went to the closet in the right wall, shrugged off my shoes, peeled off my stockings, got out of my dress, and took off my bra. Finally. There was nothing quite as good as getting out of a bra at the end of the day. I pulled on my sleeping T-shirt, went to the sink, and washed the war paint off my face. It took a while. The cold floor felt so good under my toes after they had been squished into those terrible shoes for two hours.

Finally, face clean, teeth brushed, I grabbed my laptop and flopped on Rogan's bed, backwards, with my feet toward the headboard. I had neglected my email box for the last week and a half. There were things in there that couldn't wait, like bills and invoice payments.

About a minute later, Rogan moved across the floor, opened the fridge, and looked inside.

Silence stretched.

I concentrated on the emails. Usually there would be at least one or two new cases in there, considering I hadn't checked it for at least ten days, but there was nothing. Houston was waiting to see if we would pass the trials. If we failed, our business would take a serious hit and I wasn't sure it would recover. Yet more pressure, because I clearly didn't have enough of it in my life already.

An email from Bern. I may have something for you in the morning. Well, that wasn't cryptic or anything.

An email from Rivera. Odd. Good evening, Ms. Baylor. You asked the hospital to notify you when Edward Sherwood awoke. He is awake. I escorted Rynda Sherwood to visit him this evening. House Sherwood has a new security chief and Edward Sherwood is under 24–7 guard.

House Sherwood stonewalled me again. Of course. I typed a quick thank-you note.

Rogan climbed into bed next to me and sat cross-legged, his laptop in front of him. He had one of the mousse cups in his hand, and he'd spooned a small mountain of whipped cream on top of it.

"It's not set yet," I told him.

"I don't care."

His laptop showed a picture of a yellowed page, the kind that came from a notebook, covered in precise neat cursive.

"What are you reading?" I asked.

"My father's notes," Rogan said, spooning more mousse into his mouth. "He kept a file on every potential threat. This one is on Sturm. You said you couldn't cook."

"I can't. I don't have the time, but it doesn't mean I don't know how to cook some things."

I nodded, scooted closer to him so we were touching, and went back to my emails. His fingertips brushed my back. He did it without looking away from his laptop. Just checking that I was still there.

This is what it would be like, I realized. We could come home to each other every night.

It didn't have to be all blood and gore and fancy dinners. It could also be this, and this felt so good.

CHAPTER 9

ꟼ WAS SITTING in Rogan's kitchen, drinking coffee and eating another bear claw. The bear claw was dipped in a thin sugar glaze that crunched under my teeth with every bite and then melted in my mouth. It was probably ridiculously bad for me, but I didn't care.

Across from me, Rogan was drinking his coffee. Last night, after I was done going through my emails, Rogan decided that we both needed a bit of exercise before bed. He was very convincing. I could've used another hour of sleep today. Instead I was up, drinking coffee and wearing my semi-professional work clothes: jeans, a T-shirt, and a soft oversized sweater that was big enough to obscure my gun.

Heart, Rivera, and Bug sat around the island, drinking coffee and talking in low voices.

"Where are we with surveillance?" Rogan asked.

Everyone went silent.

Bug cleared his throat. "No sign of Vincent. He's laying low. I've been keeping an eye on the Harcourts. No movement there. No sign of Brian."

"Sturm?" Rogan asked.

"He went back to his house after the restaurant and hasn't left."

"Victoria Tremaine?" Rogan asked.

Bug shook his head. "If she's moving, I can't see it."

It was unlikely that Brian was being held at Sturm's house. Too obvious and too damning if Brian's presence was discovered. Most likely Brian was secured somewhere else. Vincent, on the other hand, would be at Sturm's house, because if I were Sturm, I'd want him on a short leash after his last fun outing.

Rogan looked at Heart. "Fortification analysis?"

"I've sent people out to install additional lightning rods," Heart said, "but there is not a lot we can do against a tornado. This building is solid and has a basement, and so do the two others we designated as barracks. I had the three basements stocked with first aid, water, and rations. We're installing reinforced doors. We'll drill evacuation procedures today."

"The warehouse?" Rogan asked.

"It's properly anchored and the steel walls will bend rather than break apart," Heart said. "Technically, it's rated to withstand 170-mph winds. Practically, it depends on who you talk to. If you ask steel building manufacturers, they'll tell you stories of people who survived F-4 in one. But nobody knows what will happen if Sturm spins off a tornado and then holds it in one place."

If Sturm did that, our warehouse would crumple like an empty Coke can.

"We need a shelter," I said.

Heart nodded. "There are issues with that. The ideal shelter would be sunken into the floor; however, it would require engineering and careful construction to do it properly, because the shelter has to bear the weight of the warehouse and soil. That will take time, which we don't have. The other option would be to construct a reinforced shelter within the warehouse; however, the warehouse is filled with heavy vehicles. When picked up by a tornado, they will become airborne projectiles, which have a high probability of crushing any shelter within the warehouse."

"So our best option is to run to your basement," I said.

"Yes," Rogan and Heart said at the same time.

"Great."

"Sturm and I are both offensive mages," Rogan said. "Defenses are our weak point, so whoever throws the first punch has the advantage."

And we couldn't throw the first punch. We had no proof and no probable cause. Neither could Sturm, for that matter, not if he was hoping to keep his public image intact. It would be an unprovoked attack either way. The question was, who would snap first.

"We're installing an early warning system," Rivera said. "He can create a tornado out of thin air, but he can't mask the drop in air pressure and change in the air movement. We'll have several sirens ready."

"I'll brief your mother this afternoon," Heart said.

My phone chimed. It was a text from Leon. Fullerton is here.

"I have to go." I jumped off the chair, carried my cup to the sink, rinsed it, and stuck it upside-down into the dish rack. Rogan reached out and I let him catch me as I walked by.

"What's the plan today?" he asked.

"I'm going to keep digging. The clock's ticking, and we need to come up with the ransom by tomorrow."

"Where do you expect to go today?" He'd asked the question very carefully.

"I'm going to meet with Fullerton at the warehouse now, and then I'll go to the hospital to speak with Edward. Depending on what he tells me, I may be out in the city longer. I'll have to play it by ear. I will be home in time to get ready for my dinner with Garen."

"About that thing you asked," Bug said. "Three, but only one offers an unobstructed view of the street."

He was talking about the cameras facing Memorial Drive. Curiouser and curiouser.

"What's that about?" Rogan asked.

"I'll explain when I have something solid." If I explained it now, he might tell Rynda, and I wanted to be one hundred percent sure before I dropped that kind of bomb on her. "I'll know more after I talk to Edward."

"Do you want to take backup?" Rogan asked quietly.

"No. I can't run around Houston with armed guards, Rogan." Especially if they were his armed guards.

"It's better to have protection and not need it," Heart said, sounding reasonable. "What's the harm in taking a couple of people with you?"

"She doesn't want to be seen with my people," Rogan said. "She's being watched. House Baylor must emerge as an independent House, not a vassal."

Heart looked at him. "I thought that was settled."

Rogan shook his head, barely. "No."

"My apologies. I misunderstood the situation," Heart said.

What were they talking about?

"I'll take Cornelius with me," I said. If I could pry him away from Zeus.

Rogan's face told me he didn't like it.

"My grandmother isn't going to try anything in broad daylight, not after you took Dave apart. Sturm gave us forty-eight hours. I'm trying to find the thing he wants. It isn't in his best interests to impede me, and I doubt he'd let Vincent out of his sight now. Trying to grab me off the street is risky and wouldn't make sense. He already has all the leverage he needs. Bug will keep an eye on me and warn me if anything weird comes up."

All the words I was saying made total sense, and they were bouncing off Rogan without making any impact. I had to redirect this before he thought up some creative ways to keep me safe and hamstring my investigation in the process.

The best defense is a good offense. "Where will you be today?"

"I'm going to see House Ade-Afefe in Austin," Rogan said.

Ah. Now the paranoia made sense. He would be out of town, so if something happened, he couldn't drop everything and rush over to my side to murder everyone in sight. "What kind of House is it?"

"They are weather mages," Rogan said. "Very powerful House. We've done business before. I'm going to ask for help. I know who I want, but I doubt I'll get her, so I'll take whoever they'll let me have. If they let me have anyone. I'll be back in time for the dinner."

Primes never did anything for free. "What will it cost you?"

For a second weariness claimed his face, then vanished so fast that if I wasn't looking straight at him, I would've missed it. "It's not the cost. I'll have to explain the full extent of what we're facing. I'll have to do it in person."

That meant explaining the conspiracy and the ramifications of picking a side. This was a no-way-back kind of decision. Once the choice was made, you were either against Caesar or with him. Either way, the choice wouldn't be forgotten. What was it Sturm said yesterday? A man can often assume that he's in the right, only to find himself unexpectedly on the wrong side of history. History was written by the winners. House Ade-Afefe would likely need a lot of convincing.

"Do you need me to come with you?" I asked.

"No."

Yes, on second thought, bringing Victoria Tremaine's granddaughter to deal with sensitive negotiations wouldn't endear him to any House. It signaled he expected them to lie and he needed me to tell him when they did. My presence would shatter any illusion of trust like a wrecking ball swinging at a glass house.

"Okay," I said. "Let me know if I can help."

His arm was still around me, and he showed no signs of letting me go. His eyes brimmed with power, calculating, smart, and worried.

"Fullerton is waiting," I reminded him quietly.

"He will wait." Rogan reached for his laptop. "I want to show you something."

I'd tell him I heard that line before but Bug, Rivera, and Heart were right there.

Rogan opened his laptop and clicked a file. An image of my mother filled the screen. She lay on the carpeted floor in some building, her gun pointing at a small perfectly circular hole in the window. Leon lay next to her. The Harcourt building loomed in the distance.

"Go to three alpha, three o'clock, ten mils," Leon said.

The sector game. I remembered playing it in the kitchen when I was a child. You divided your field of vision into sectors by reference points. From doorway to table, sector one. From left table edge to centerpiece, sector two. From centerpiece to the right edge of the table, sector three . . . Then you moved on to depth. From the table to the island, sector alpha. From the island to the fridge, sector bravo. Then Mom would call out, and we'd identify. Salt on the left side of the table became two alpha, nine o'clock. When each of us got older, Mom took us to the firing range and the game got slightly more complicated.

Leon was playing it for real now.

"Contact," Mom said. "Second window from the left. No target."

"Bottom right corner. Little more to the left. Little more."

Leon was breaking protocol. That wasn't how you talked the sniper onto the target.

"Little bit more."

He should be telling her to check parallax and mil. Once she got the mil, she would say it out loud, he would plug it into the ballistic computer, give the hold over, wait for the "Ready," and then give wind call. None of that was happening. And my mother wasn't correcting him.

"Fire," Leon said.

Mom squeezed the trigger. The window shattered.

Leon laughed quietly under his breath.

"Did she hit the target?" I asked.

"The best we can figure out," Rivera said, "the bullet struck something inside the building, made an almost ninety-degree turn, and took out the shooter at the other side. Leon can literally shoot around corners. The kid is magic."

"Two bravo, six o'clock," Leon said. "A little to the left."

I would've never gotten away with that "a little to the left."

Wait. We *all* had made trips to the range, including Leon. My mother knew. She had to have known about his magic before any of us. It would've come out at the range. When I had told her my big revelation about Leon's talent, she had already figured it out.

Clearly, I was a brilliant detective. Mom and I were overdue for a talk.

Another shot rang out.

"How many confirmed kills?" I asked.

"Thirteen," Heart said. "It's difficult to determine exactly, because as Rivera said, your cousin lines up shots that kill people two rooms over. Your mother fired twenty-one times. Your cousin laughed or smiled seventeen times, so we estimate the actual kill count at seventeen."

Leon smiled when he killed people. I rubbed my face. "Maybe if I can get him some therapy . . ."

The four men at the island stared at me.

"He laughs when he kills people. He thinks it's funny."

"I don't care if he laughs," Rivera said. "As long as he's next to me shooting out, I'm good."

Rogan glanced at him. Rivera clamped his mouth shut.

"He isn't laughing because he's killing someone," Rogan said gently. "He's laughing because he's finally using his magic. This is what he was born to do. In the moment the bullet hits the target, he doesn't feel small, or weak, or useless, because it works. He would laugh the same way if he was shooting at sandbags. Think about how it felt when you used an amplification circle for the first time."

When I sent my magic into the circle and that first rush of power came back, surging through me, twice as potent as before, it felt like I had learned to fly. Leon had wanted magic so badly. He didn't even realize he had it.

"I hope you're right."

"Ask him."

"I will."

Rogan closed his laptop. "Please take Leon with you."

"You want me to bring my baby cousin with me in case I get into a firefight?"

"Please consider it," Rogan suggested.

"I'll think about it."

Rogan studied me. His power uncurled around him and wound around me, as if it too didn't want to let me go.

"Be careful out there," the dragon said.

"I'll bring my sword and shield," I murmured, brushed a kiss on his lips, and headed to the stairway.

Rynda stood on the stairs, just out of sight. She hurried up, pretending that I caught her walking up the stairs, but I would've heard her moving. No, she'd waited on the steps until I was leaving.

"How are you this morning?" I asked.

"I still don't have my husband," she said quietly.

"I'm working on it."

"I know."

There didn't seem to be much left to say after that, so I took the stairs down.

On the bottom floor, to the left of the open doors, someone had rigged a big-screen TV. Sergeant Teddy sprawled in front of it. Matilda sat in the crook of his paw, a big bowl of trail mix on her lap. Jessica and Kyle leaned against Sergeant Teddy's side. I rubbed my eyes to make sure I wasn't seeing things.

On the screen, Bear in the Big Blue House sang a song about cleaning. Matilda picked some dried apples out of the bowl. Sergeant Teddy opened his mouth, and she put the fruit on his tongue. The enormous grizzly chewed. The children watched the show, content.

I snapped a picture with my phone and went home.

FULLERTON WAITED IN my office, as lanky and grim as I remembered. I stopping humming "Come on everybody, let's clean up the house," nodded at him through the glass, retrieved the cooler, and brought it to my office.

"I've received a request from House Sherwood," Fullerton said. "Specifically, from Rynda Sherwood. She asked me to give you my full cooperation and assistance."

I opened the cooler and let him look inside. "Could you sequence the DNA and determine if this ear belongs to Brian Sherwood?"

"Yes." Fullerton looked at me, his long face thoughtful. "Is time of the essence?"

"Yes."

"Do you require confirmation or proof that would stand in a court of law?"

"Confirmation will be sufficient."

Fullerton pulled back his suit sleeve and held his hand above the ear, fingers splayed. Magic pulsed from him in a short, controlled burst. He raised his hand and tugged the sleeve back. "The ear doesn't belong to Brian Sherwood or any other member of House Sherwood."

I knew it. "Are you certain?"

"I'm never wrong," he said.

"Thank you for your services. Please bill me."

"I will," he said.

"Have there been any inquiries on our account?"

"No. I would've immediately notified you. Is there a particular inquiry you're waiting for, Ms. Baylor?"

"Yes. House Rogan."

Fullerton paused, his face thoughtful. "You can receive requests for the genetic profile. You can also make them. They wouldn't be honored until after your trials and the formal establishment of your House, but they can be made now. Good evening, Ms. Baylor."

I saw him to the door, packed the cooler back into the fridge, and walked to Cornelius' office. He wasn't in it.

I could request Rogan's profile.

What if he said no?

More importantly, did I really care if his genes aligned with mine or did I just want him the way he was, without any qualifiers?

Yes. I just wanted him.

I returned to my office and checked my laptop. Bern wasn't up on the family network. I pushed the intercom. "Does anybody know where Bern is?"

"He left with Cornelius to check something out," Leon responded.

"Where is everybody?"

"Your mom is with Grandma helping her in the motor pool. The control freak and evil incarnate are in the control freak's room."

Control freak and evil, huh. Someone was sore about something.

"What are they doing in there?"

"They won't tell me. Something happened on Instagram. I looked at their accounts, but I can't see anything."

Ah. Leon had the curiosity of a cat. When you locked him out, it drove him nuts.

Everyone was busy. It was just me and Leon. The stars had aligned. I sighed.

"Come to the office."

"Why?"

"I'll tell you when you get here."

I unlocked the small gun safe I kept hidden in the bottom drawer of my desk and took out my Sig 210 and a magazine.

Leon sauntered into my office and flopped into my client chair, a picture of teenage apathy.

I showed him the magazine. "Eight rounds, 9mm."

Leon's eyes lit up. He leaned forward, his eyes fixed on the gun.

"Manual safety. The barrel is machined from a solid block of steel. It's an older gun, but it's durable, reliable, and it's very accurate. That's what I practiced with and that's what my dad shot."

I pushed the gun and the magazine toward him. He swiped it off the table, slid the magazine into the gun, and sighted the hallway with it, all in one blink. One moment the gun was on the table, the next it jumped into his hand.

"Get a holster," I told him. "And a zip-up hoodie. I shouldn't see the gun under your clothes. I'm going out and you're my backup."

He leaped out of the seat and took off. I sighed. This was probably the wrong thing to do. Leon would turn seventeen in twelve days, right behind Catalina, who would be eighteen in three. I still needed to buy them both a gift. The way this was going, Catalina would end up doing trials right on her birthday. All the holidays were screwed up this year. First Christmas, now her birthday, and probably Leon's birthday. Ugh.

In a year, Leon could legally enlist in the military, where he would be given a firearm and conditioned to use it. In a year and a half, he could be out in the field, killing people left and right. Nothing magical happened to separate your eighteenth birthday from your seventeenth. You became an adult, but you didn't feel like one.

It's time he knew. We couldn't shelter him forever.

I pulled out my phone and texted Bern. **Where are you?**

> **Checking on a lead with Cornelius. Where are you?**

Asking about what lead would spark a chain reaction of explanations, and knowing Bern, he'd start with him getting up this morning and then spend the next twenty minutes presenting it in a logical fashion.

> **Going to see Edward in the hospital. Leon's with me. Be careful.**

> **We will.**

I texted Arabella. **What's going on with you two?**

> Alessandro Sagredo followed Catalina on Instagram. She's freaking out.

Who the heck is Alessandro Sagredo and why did his name sound familiar?

I pulled my laptop closer and typed in the name. **Alessandro Sagredo, second son of House Sagredo, Antistasi Prime . . .** Oh. He was the Italian Prime the Office of Records was bringing in to test Catalina's magic.

So he followed her on Instagram. What's the big deal? **He's going to test her in the trials. Tell her it's nothing weird.**

> She's FREAKING out. I'm trying to calm her down. I may have to get wine. Or pot. Can I buy some pot?

No.

> It's medicinal.

No pot or I tell Mom.

Leon reappeared, wearing a loose blue hoodie. He was lean bordering on skinny, and the sweatshirt hung on his sparse frame. He could've hidden a bazooka under there and I wouldn't be able to tell.

I fixed him with my serious stare. "You're going as my backup. I don't expect trouble, but if it happens, you shoot only when I give you the order. If you fire before I give you permission, I'll never take you with me again, and I'll make sure you don't get anywhere close to a gun for the next year and a half. Do we understand each other?"

Leon frantically nodded.

"Good."

THE HEAD OF Edward Sherwood's guard detail stared at me. He was a stocky, muscular man who looked like he could run through a wall, and he was doing his best to be intimidating. I had a feeling I was supposed to wilt under that stare.

"We won't be surrendering our firearms," I told him.

"Then you won't see Mr. Sherwood."

"Please ask him if he will see us anyway. This matter concerns his brother."

"You're not getting into that hospital room armed," he said.

"The last time I saw Mr. Sherwood, I was armed, and I put myself between him and the creature that was trying to eat him."

"We're aware of your role, Ms. Baylor. House Sherwood is grateful for your assistance."

It was time to pull out the big guns. "Before I arrived to the incident that resulted in this situation, my associate called to House Sherwood and informed your head of security that we believed Rynda Sherwood was in danger. We were told to mind our own business."

The guard's ice-cold composure cracked a little. "That person is no longer employed by House Sherwood."

"I'm so glad to hear that. It's very disheartening when you try to offer important information only to be brushed off. Please ask Edward if he would see us anyway. It's important and urgent."

The man stared at me. A switch clicked in his head. That's right, the last time your people blew me off, your Prime was hurt and your chief of security was fired.

"Please wait here." He turned around and walked down the hallway, leaving us in the waiting room under the watchful eyes of a man and a woman in House Sherwood uniforms.

Leon winked at them. They remained stoic.

My phone chimed. Cornelius. I answered the call. "Yes?"

"We've gone through Brian's receipts," Cornelius said. "On December 21st, he stopped at Millennium Coffee House. Brian doesn't drink coffee or tea. Millennium Coffee House is located near the intersection of Gulf and the 610. He drove fifteen miles. There are sixteen coffee shops that are closer to BioCore."

It made no sense for him to drive fifteen miles in Houston traffic for a coffee he doesn't drink.

"Was he alone?"

"No. The barista remembered him because he ordered a fruit tea and then made a fuss because she wrote Bryan with a Y instead of Brian with an I on his cup. He met a man there. They sat outside and spoke for about forty-five minutes. She could see through the window. We showed her some pictures, and she picked Sturm out."

And the pieces had fallen into place. "Thank you."

"Does that help?"

"It's exactly what we needed."

"Fantastic. Here is Bernard."

"Nevada?" my cousin said into the phone.

"Yes?"

"Bug and I tracked Brian's logins. Someone used his credentials to log into his home network on December 21st. According to their emails and Rynda's Facebook, they spent the evening with her mother-in-law and Edward."

"Is there any way to trace what was accessed? Did they copy anything?"

"No. To a computer system, opening a file and copying it is pretty much the same thing. It doesn't record the difference. All I can tell you is someone who wasn't Brian Sherwood had complete access to his network."

"Thank you."

"We're going home."

"Be careful."

"We will."

I hung up.

The head of security emerged from the hallway. "He'll see you now."

Edward lay in a hospital bed, his skin only a couple of shades darker than the stark white of the sheets. Sunlight streamed through the open drapes, falling on a beautiful bonsai tree on the table next to him. A compact woman, her hair pulled back into a severe ponytail, waited discreetly in the corner, watching me and Leon like a hawk. She carried a Beretta. Leon parked himself next to her, looking like he didn't have a care in the world. She gave him a once-over and dismissed him.

The head of security stood guard by the door and showed no signs of moving.

I pulled up a chair. "How are you feeling?"

"Like a man who dodged a bullet," he said quietly. He touched the controls on the armrest of the bed, and it slowly moved to bring him into a semi-sitting position. "Have you found Brian?"

"No."

"How's Rynda?"

"She's holding up."

"She came to see me last night." He reached out and touched the leaves of the bonsai.

"Did she bring the tree?"

"Yes. Satsuki Azalea, seventy-two years old. Flowers from May to June. The blossoms are beautiful pink and white. They have a really diverse range of flowering patterns, even on the same tree. I've wanted one for a while, but I've been so busy lately. She remembered." He smiled, then caught himself. "Thank you for saving her and the children. And me. Us."

"You don't have to thank me. Anyone in my place would've done the same."

"I doubt it."

There was no easy way to say it. "How much do you trust your security people?"

I had to give it to him; even on his sickbed Edward managed a glare. "I trust them."

"What I'm about to say can't go past this room."

"Say whatever it is."

I kept my voice low. "Alexander Sturm is involved in the kidnapping of your brother."

A heavy silence descended. Every time Sturm's name was mentioned, people paused.

"Are you sure?"

"Yes. We can't prove it yet, but we're certain."

"But why?"

"Alexander Sturm and Vincent Harcourt are part of a conspiracy that involved Olivia Charles. They belong to an organization of Primes that's trying to destabilize Houston so they can put their leader in power. They call him Caesar. Adam Pierce was also part of this conspiracy."

Edward gaped at me.

"Sturm is under the impression that Olivia hid something in Brian and Rynda's house. Something vital. He wants it back, but he refuses to state clearly what he's looking for. He wasn't happy with our failure to find the ransom, so he sent a severed human ear to Rynda to try to convince us to expedite our efforts."

"Dear God." Edward tried to rise.

"Please don't get up," the head of security said. "Please, sir. We need you to get well."

Edward lowered himself back onto the bed.

"On December 21st, your brother visited Millennium Coffee House about fifteen miles from BioCore. He met Sturm there."

I let it sink in.

Edward frowned. "Are you sure?"

"Yes. We found an eyewitness who picked Sturm out of a photo lineup."

"Brian had no reason to meet Sturm. BioCore doesn't do business with Sturm Enterprises. And if he wanted to meet him, why go alone? Everyone knows Sturm's reputation. Why didn't he tell me about it?"

Those were excellent questions. "Later that night, when Brian and Rynda met you and your mother for dinner, someone used Brian's credentials to log into his home network."

He didn't say anything.

"Brian's kidnapping occurred in seconds. The people who perpetrated it were efficient and professional. Brian is predictable. He drives the same route to work and back at about the same time every day, along Memorial Drive, which is mostly wooded. There are three cameras along the route Brian takes to work, but only one offers an unobstructed view of the road."

Edward still didn't say anything. I couldn't tell if he had connected the dots or not.

"They managed to force him to stop at the exact spot along his route where his kidnapping was guaranteed to be recorded. Thirty feet in either direction, and the crime would never have been caught on camera. It's highly unlikely that a crew that efficient hadn't done their homework and didn't know where the cameras were located. It's also interesting that once they tapped his bumper, Brian drove into the guardrail, conveniently marking the location of his kidnapping."

Edward's eyes turned dark. It was time to deliver the final blow.

"When Rynda asked Brian if he was okay, after the ear was delivered, he stated that he was in pain. When she asked him if his wound was treated by a doctor, he said it was. We contracted Scroll to perform a DNA analysis on the severed ear. It doesn't belong to your brother."

Edward looked up. His face tightened. His jaw set. He stared at the ceiling as if he were going to burn a hole in it with his gaze. His hands curled into fists, crushing the sheets. Edward Sherwood was monumentally angry, and he was doing all he could to contain his rage.

I waited.

He unclenched his jaw. His voice was a low growl. "I'll fucking kill him."

The bonsai creaked. Its trunk thickened, its branches thrust up, growing. Roots writhed under the soil.

"I'll strangle him with my bare hands."

Buds formed on the branches.

"I always knew he was a coward. But this is . . ." He shook with fury.

The ceramic planter cracked and burst. Pieces of it showered my clothes. Behind me Leon must've moved, because the security chief drew his gun.

The azalea spread its roots, grasping the table like some monstrous octopus. It had quadrupled in size, its branches hanging over the bed.

"This is beyond anything he's ever done before. That scumbag. That cowardly, weak scumbag."

The buds snapped open. A riot of flowers blanketed the tree, the delicate blossoms in all shades from white to intense pink so dense, you couldn't see the leaves. A sweet scent filled the room.

Edward closed his eyes and breathed in, deeply.

The azalea bloomed harder, as if trying to comfort him.

"Put the guns away," I murmured.

The security chief slowly lowered his weapon.

"He nearly killed his own children, that selfish prick," Edward snarled. "He almost murdered his wife. He almost killed me. He ruined the future of our House. Now, when people talk of Sherwoods, they'll think of murder, treachery, and conspiracy."

His eyes snapped open.

"Fourteen years. Fourteen years I kept BioCore afloat. I pulled it back from the brink of bankruptcy after our senile asshole of a father drove it into the ground. I kept it afloat when Brian's research stalled, because he needed time for himself, because he was too overwhelmed and under too much pressure. That little fucker, what the hell does he know about pressure? We all shielded him from it since he was a baby. *I* kept the creditors at bay. *I* made deals. *I* put my own future on hold to keep the House afloat. Olivia was only marginally connected to us, and the effect on our business was catastrophic. Olivia's betrayal hurt us, but given time, I would've pulled us back from it. But now it's over. He is the fucking Head of our House. His involvement will get out. Rynda's already a social pariah. With her husband and her mother connected to this mess, nobody will believe she's innocent. There is no way to overcome the taint. It will strangle the future of his children. He's finally killed us. We're done."

I didn't know what to say. That was decades of resentment spilling out.

The room was quiet as a tomb.

"Colin," Edward said.

"Yes, sir?" the chief of security asked.

"Inform my mother that in light of the recent events, I'll be assuming leadership of the House. What's left of it. Explain to her that the golden child has driven us into the ground. Also, advise her to prepare for the BioCore bankruptcy filing."

"Yes, sir."

The security chief stepped out into the hallway.

Edward looked at me.

"I need to find out why," I told him. "Could he have done it for money?"

Edward shook his head. "Rynda is independently wealthy. Last night she offered to bail out the company. She views all of our current problems as her fault."

"Did you take her up on it?"

"No."

True.

"Not only that, but I made sure that our personal wealth was at least partially shielded. If . . . when BioCore goes under, Brian will still have ample funds to live his life in comfort. Not extravagantly, but in comfort."

"Is it possible that he did it to keep BioCore afloat?"

Edward laughed.

"I take it that's a no."

"No."

Brian had very few ambitions. That left only one possible motive. "Did your brother ever express dissatisfaction with his marriage?"

Edward sighed. "He came to me about a year and a half ago and told me he wanted to divorce Rynda. He said his children were defective."

Well. "What did you tell him?"

"I told him I would pretend I never heard what he said. Then I explained that Jessica and Kyle were his children and that as a father, he was supposed to love them unconditionally. He was supposed to protect them and take care of them. That they couldn't be discarded or traded in for a new model like last year's car. If he couldn't bring himself to be proud of them, because they didn't have the kind of magic talent he was hoping for, he still couldn't abandon his responsibilities. I also reminded him what a charmer our father was, and how tragic it would be if Brian turned into our old man."

"What did he say?"

"He asked me what would happen if he did it anyway. He said that the marriage was stressing him out." Disgust dripped from Edward's voice. "I reminded him that Olivia Charles had powerful friends. The effect on BioCore and his social standing would be devastating. I also told him that if that idiocy ever came out of his mouth again, I would retire and leave the running of the company to him, so he could fend for himself. That last one did it."

"Is social standing that important to him?"

"Yes. Our parents made sure we had clearly defined roles. He is a brilliant researcher, and I'm his older brother, destined to be his caretaker. He doesn't like when people talk about him in any way other than his assigned role. He tolerated Jessica because she is, in all likelihood, a Prime empath like her mother. But Kyle conflicted with Brian's view of himself. Brian was a gifted Prime herbamagos, therefore his son would also be a gifted Prime herbamagos."

If Rogan and I ever married and our children weren't Primes, would he resent me? My heart squeezed itself into a tiny painful ball.

"My brother isn't dense. He knows perfectly well that his position as the Head of the House lets him float through life. Doors open. The maître d' always finds his reservation, and if one hadn't been made, a table is miraculously found anyway. People treat him with respect. Everyone minds his feelings. He doesn't have to deal with investors and creditors. He doesn't have to make painful decisions about firing people. He delegates his problems to me and his wife. Kyle threatened that. What happens when Brian retires? Who takes over? Does BioCore even have a future? It calls the very essence of who Brian is into question. There is nothing worse than a failing vector. The stigma of it is like poison. It stains the whole House."

I'd heard the term before. A failing vector meant a person whose ancestors possessed potent magic, but who fails to pass it on to his children, so the family's magic grows weaker with every generation.

"Do you think Brian is a failing vector?"

"I don't care," Edward said. "But no. I think Kyle will come into his own. And even if he doesn't, he's a bright child. Anyone who talks to him for longer than a minute can see it. My mother never cared much for children, even her own, but Olivia saw it. She adored him. She framed every painting he made."

"Thank you for your time." I rose.

He looked at me, his eyes haunted. "Have you told Rynda?"

"Not yet."

"It might break her. I want to be there."

"I'll do my best to make sure you're there, but I can't promise anything. I don't know what will happen."

I left the room. Leon trailed me.

I wanted to take a shower to wash the stress off.

"He's in love with Rynda," Leon said. "His whole face lit up when he talked about her."

"Yes."

"Why didn't he marry her? Why did she marry Brian?"

"Probably because Brian was the Head of his House, and Olivia Charles wouldn't have seen Edward as a winner. She was very proud."

We took the elevator down to the lobby.

"If we become a House, you'll be the Head of House Baylor."

"Yes." And what joy that would be.

"We'd be a serious House," he said. "You're a Prime, Catalina is a Prime, Arabella is probably a Prime. Bern might be a Significant. We'd have four higher-tier magic users."

"Mhm." He'd obviously given it some thought.

"Are you going to marry Mad Rogan?" Leon asked. "You'd both be Heads of the Houses."

Um. "He hasn't asked me."

I walked through the doors outside and blinked against the bright sunshine.

"Maybe you should ask him," Leon said.

If only it were that easy. We headed to my car. The parking lot was half-deserted. I had parked on the side because the lot at the front entrance and ER was full.

"You just want to be related to Mad Rogan."

"No," he said, his dark eyes serious. "I want you to be happy."

"I'm sorry?" I stopped.

"I want you to be happy," he repeated. "He makes you happy."

"Rogan and I may not be compatible."

Leon looked like he had bitten into a lemon. "Like . . . sex . . . ?"

"Children, Leon. He's a telekinetic and I'm a truthseeker. Our children might not be Primes. You saw how Brian dealt with it."

"Does Rogan care?"

The last time we openly talked about it, Rogan told me that even though I thought it didn't matter, it would. "I don't know. He said he doesn't—"

My phone rang just as a massive armored truck swung into the parking lot in front of us. *A Vault vehicle* flashed in my head. Grandma had worked on one before. It looked like an armored security truck from the outside and a stretch limo from the inside. Seating capacity of twenty-five. Shit. We'd never make it to our car. The hospital and Sherwood's security was our best bet.

"Run!" I barked, and sprinted toward the hospital. Leon shot past me like I wasn't even moving.

Magic punched the ground in front of me. The blast knocked me back. I stumbled.

A man popped into existence two feet from me. He was almost eight feet tall, slabbed with muscle and naked. His skin was bright red, the bright red of the biological armor of House Madero, and he had Dave Madero's face. But that couldn't be right, because Rogan had broken Dave like a toothpick.

Someone had teleported him flashed in my head.

The man's hands clamped my shoulders. He jerked me off my feet. My bones groaned.

"House Madero says hello, bitch!" He shook me like a rag doll. "Where is your boyfriend? He hurt my brother!"

Not Dave. Frank or Roger Madero.

"Where is he?" He shook me. My teeth rattled in my skull. "Your grandma said to bring you alive. She didn't say in one piece."

That was too much. All the stress, worry, and fear combusted into fury inside me and burst into an inferno. He had my shoulders but he didn't have my hands. I jerked my forearms up and clamped my fingers on his face. Pain flared inside me and rolled down my arms, turning into pure agony. Lightning shot out of my fingers and sank into the armored skin.

Madero screamed.

Welcome to the shockers, bitch. Someone snarled like a pissed-off animal and I realized it was me.

Madero howled and dropped to his knees. I clung on to him. My nails cut into his skin, drawing blood. His armor was failing.

The pain was almost too much to take.

Madero ran out of air. His scream broke into weak, desperate yelps, his voice hoarse.

A glowing light swung into my view. I had to let go, or I would spend all my magic and die.

I jerked my hands away. Madero collapsed at my feet, face-down, convulsing.

I reeled back. People were running from the truck toward us. The world was swimming, out of focus. I'd spent too much magic.

My cousin thrust himself into my view, his gun in his hands. "Now?"

"Now!" My hand found my Baby Desert Eagle.

Leon fired. There was no pause. He didn't wait to sight. He didn't breathe. He jerked the gun up and fired all eight shots in what felt like a single second.

Eight people dropped. Four remained. For a moment they paused, shocked, then spun around and dashed back to their truck.

I thrust my gun up, lined up a shot, and took it. The truck's front left tire shuddered. Another shot, another tire. The four fleeing attackers veered away from the vehicle, running deeper into the parking lot.

I exhaled.

None of the eight bodies moved.

Madero lay at my feet, breathing like he was about to have a heart attack. He'd shrunk some and his skin turned an almost normal color.

"Five," I said.

Leon looked at me, wild-eyed.

"House Baylor will have five higher-tier magic users. This is what you do, Leon. This is your magic."

Leon stared at the eight bodies in the parking lot. "Oh my God. Oh my God. They're dead. They're *dead* dead."

"Yes."

He spun to me. "I killed them."

"Yes."

Leon's expression crumbled. He bent over and vomited onto the pavement.

CHAPTER 10

ONCE LEON FINISHED throwing up, I told him to go inside and tell the hospital staff we needed help. It took six people to load Dave 2.0 onto a gurney and wheel him into the ER.

A hospital administrator, a plump Hispanic woman in her mid-forties, ran up to me, her face pale, her mouth a thin, tense line. "Should I call the cops?"

What would Rogan say? "It's House business."

She straightened. Some of the frantic agitation went out of her face. I'd said the magic words absolving her of all responsibility.

"I'll notify the authorities," I said. "Please see to the wounded."

"What wounded? Everyone is dead."

"See to my cousin, then."

She turned around to where Leon sat on the curb. His skin had acquired a sallow greenish tint.

"Okay," she said. "We'll do that."

I walked over to Leon, crouched, and hugged him. He didn't struggle or make disgusted noises. A really bad sign.

"You did great," I told him.

"It wasn't real before," he said quietly.

"When you lined up shots for Mom?"

He nodded. "It's real now. I killed them. They're dead because of me."

I had to fix this now, or it would break him. "No, I killed them.

I ordered you to shoot, and you obeyed my order. This is on me, not on you."

His hands were shaking.

"Leon, these people were attacking us. If you didn't stop them, they would've dragged me off to Victoria Tremaine. They might have killed you. Our whole family would be in danger. You did the right thing. You didn't run away. You saved me, and Mom, and Grandma, and your cousins and your brother. You saved all of us."

A man in hospital scrubs came up and wrapped a blanket around Leon. I gently tucked the blanket around him.

"You did great."

He looked up at me. "I did."

"Yes. Mom will be so proud. My dad would be so proud. You defended us."

"Okay," he said.

Victoria would pay for this. I would make her pay.

"Did you get sick?" he asked.

"The first time I shot someone? I felt sick."

"But did you throw up?"

"I didn't have time. The building exploded and I passed out. But if I'd had a chance, I would've thrown up for sure. The first time I saw Rogan kill someone, I almost got sick on him. We were in the Pit and he dropped a building on this scumbag. Just cut a chunk of the building off and crushed him with it. It took me a long time to get over it."

"Is it always this bad?"

"No. You grow numb to it." The sound of David Howling's neck breaking popped in my ears. Leon didn't need to know about that. He didn't ever need to know how that felt. I would move heaven and earth to make sure he never found out.

Two armored SUVs pulled into the parking lot and ejected Rivera and six of Rogan's people. The cavalry had arrived in record time, but they were too late.

They raced toward me, Rivera barking orders. "Guard here, here, and there. I want no blind spots. If something aims for this parking lot, I want to know about it before it gets here."

People peeled off from the group. He crashed to a halt before me. "Are you okay, Ms. Baylor?"

Define okay. "Everything is fine."

"Where is Frank Madero?"

It took me a second to remember that he would be in constant contact with Bug and Bug would've identified Frank the moment he popped into existence. "In the ER."

"Should we take him into custody?"

"No."

Rivera looked uncomfortable. "Do you want guards on his room?"

"No." He wouldn't be getting up anytime soon.

"Bug said there were survivors. Do you want us to chase them down?"

"I don't think that's necessary."

The four remaining ex-military badasses looked almost desperate.

"The Major was very specific." Rivera's face had the expression of a man walking across hot coals. "We're supposed to render assistance and keep you safe. We weren't here."

Now it made sense. Rogan told them to guard me and they let me get attacked and got here after the fight was over. That's why they were sweating bullets.

"When the Major returns, you can tell him that you did your job. There was an altercation, it's over now, and I'm safe. If he asks about details, tell him to ask me."

Rivera didn't look convinced.

I sighed. "Would you like to render some assistance?"

"Yes."

"What exactly did Rogan say you could help me with?"

"Anything you need."

"Please gather the dead people and identify as many of them as possible. Someone teleported Frank in front of me, and it would be good to ID the teleporter mage. Please follow whatever protocol Rogan uses and notify the authorities that a violent confrontation took place between House Madero and Baylor family. If we could get Rogan's legal department involved, it would be great, because I need to be home in the evening, and I can't spend the rest of the day in the police station being interrogated. I also need phone numbers for the Madero family and Victoria Tremaine. I'd like new tires for the Vault. It's worth two hundred and fifty grand and we're going to take it home to my grandma. And once everything has been taken care of and the authorities release us, I would appreciate an escort home. That should keep the Major happy."

"Yes, ma'am."

In less than a minute Bug texted the two phone numbers, one for House Madero, ruled by Peter Madero, and the other for Victoria Tremaine's rented penthouse office suites at Landry Tower. I sat on the curb next to Leon and watched Rogan's people move the corpses.

Madero or Tremaine first? Tackling Madero would be simpler. I'd looked them up after Dave's attack. House Madero consisted of Peter Madero, the patriarch, who was in his seventies; his daughter-in-law Linda; and her sons David, Frank, Roger, and fourteen-year-old twins, Ethan and Evan. Roger was married and his wife was pregnant.

Judging by Dave and Frank, their grandpa Peter would be nasty and tough as nails. First, he sent his grandson after me and

Rogan, then after Rogan made an origami crane out of Dave, he sent his other grandson. Peter didn't give up easily, but he didn't survive this long without some wisdom.

I dialed the number and put the call on speaker.

"House Madero," a woman chirped into the phone.

"This is Nevada Baylor. Let me speak with the Head of the House."

"And who the hell are you?"

"I'm the person who just put Frank into the ER. Put the call through."

There was a pause, then a gruff male voice came on the line. "So you're the bitch Tremaine wants."

Aha. I've got your number. "Charming. Your family is short on brains, so I'll say this slowly. Frank is in the Houston Memorial ER. I put him there. If he makes it, he'll tell you that he brought twelve people with him against me and my sixteen-year-old cousin. Eight of your people are dead. Four ran off. I'm taking your fun wagon as spoils of war."

"You fucking whore."

"That will be Prime whore to you."

Peter Madero choked on his own spit.

Rivera and Leon stared at me.

"I don't know if Tremaine promised you money and you're just greedy and not that bright, or if she has something on you and you're scared, but I'm her granddaughter. Flesh and blood. Think about it."

"I ain't scared of you or your memaw."

"So far one of your grandsons has both arms in casts, and the other might be dying. I need to know if you're going to drop the contract or try again. Because if you're trying again, I'm going to let Mad Rogan's people take custody of Frank."

"I'll tear your throat out and shit down your neck."

"You didn't survive to your seventies because you made bad business decisions. You send Roger after me, his baby will grow up without a father. You know it, and I know it. Who's left? The twins?"

"I'll do it myself."

"No, you won't. You had a triple bypass three months ago. Frank and Dave both could barely breathe three minutes into the fight. I won't have to fight you, I'll just run circles around you until your body gives out. And then where would the family be?"

"You stay out of my business!"

"I need a decision about Frank. I can't sit here all day. Also, what do you want to do about your dead people?"

"You give me my bus back, and I'll think about dropping the contract."

"No, that's my bus. I earned it fair and square."

He swore.

"Just admit you're beat, you cantankerous old bastard."

"Fine. Leave our dead at the hospital; we'll pick 'em up. And don't let me find you there, or I'll wring your scrawny neck."

I hung up. Rivera was looking at me like he'd never seen me before.

"I had a client like that once," I told him. "The only way to win his respect was to meet him on his playing field and give as good as you got."

I stared at my grandmother's number. Some sort of response had to be made. She attacked us for the second time. Do I call and issue an ultimatum? Do I call the Office of Records and complain? Would this make us look weak or would we look weaker by not complaining and just letting her continue to terrorize us?

Leon huddled next to me. Rivera studied him for a moment and spoke into his headset. "Kurt? Find me."

A moment later a gruff-looking man walked up to us. He had a dense red beard and shoulders that wouldn't fit through the door. He glanced at Leon and nodded. "Come with me."

Leon got up and followed him.

"What's going on?"

"Kurt is our PTSD specialist," Rivera said. "He's an ex–Navy SEAL, highly decorated."

"And with a high kill count?" I guessed.

Rivera nodded. "Leon needs help, and Kurt will be able to help him. He knows the right things to say."

"Thank you," I said.

"He's a talented kid," Rivera said, and walked away.

I looked at my phone. I needed some advice. If Rogan was here, I might have gone to him, but even if I did, he could decide to go and have a personal chat with Victoria Tremaine. So far he had been almost painfully careful about not stepping on my toes, but he nearly lost it when I came to him to ask about how to handle Augustine. He came close to killing his friend—probably his only friend—for my sake.

No, I needed a neutral third party. Someone who had no trouble navigating House waters, but had no personal stake in the matter. I scrolled through my contacts. There it was, Linus Duncan. Once the most powerful man in Texas. He said to call if I needed any advice. Cornelius thought the world of him, and Rogan respected him.

I dialed the number.

"Hello, Ms. Baylor," Linus Duncan said into the phone in his rich, slightly amused baritone. "How may I help?"

"I need some advice."

"Is the matter urgent?"

"Yes."

"Where are you?"

"I'm at Houston Memorial."

"Are you injured?"

"No. But I just survived a second attack by Victoria Tremaine."

There was a small pause.

"You're right," Linus said, a note of concern slipping into his voice. "The matter is urgent. As I recall, Houston Memorial has a quiet coffee shop. I will be there in forty minutes."

SERGEANT MUNOZ PEERED at me. A stocky dark-haired man about twice my age, he looked like a cop, which is exactly what he was. Career cops had that odd air of ingrained authority and jaded world-weariness. They'd seen it all, they expected the worst-case scenario and ridiculous crap, and nothing surprised them anymore. If an alien landed in the parking lot and leveled a blaster at us, Sergeant Munoz wouldn't bat an eye. He'd order it to raise its limbs and lie down on the ground, but he wouldn't be surprised.

The parking lot had rapidly filled with cops. Sergeant Munoz took charge, and he clearly didn't like what he saw.

"I know you. Longhorn Hotel, enerkinetic cheating on his wife."

"Yes, sir." It was a routine cheating spouse case until the wife showed up at the hotel to confront her husband against my explicit instructions. I had a strong feeling that if the cheating husband got his wife into the car, nobody would ever see her again, so I stepped in and got thrown into the wall for my trouble, before I managed to tase him.

"And now we have this." He turned to the eight bodies laid out in a row. Each of them showed a single shot in the same exact spot.

"This is what we call a T-box kill. Do you know what a T-box is?"

"Yes."

If you drew a vertical rectangle around the nose and a horizontal rectangle over the nose bridge that ended at the center of each pupil, you would get a T-shaped area. People thought that head shots were always lethal. They weren't. Sometimes bullets bounced off a skull, or caused some brain damage but failed to kill the target. Sometimes they penetrated the skull but caused only a minor injury. But a shot to the T-box was always lethal. A bullet to the T-box scrambled the lower brain and brain stem, which control the automatic organ processes we require to live, such as breathing. Death was immediate. It was the surest and most merciful way to drop your target. The victim would never realize they were dying. Their last memory would be of a gun and then their brain would explode.

Leon had put one bullet into each of the eight people exactly between their eyes. Eight shots, eight instant kills.

A Harley-Davidson pulled into the adjacent parking lot. Its rider, in a black leather jacket and jeans, jumped off, pulled the helmet off her head, revealing a halo of dark curly hair, and sprinted toward us. A Black woman with medium brown skin, about thirty-five or so. A patrolman got in her way and she barked something at him and kept going.

"Did you line them up?" Sergeant Munoz asked. "Was this an execution?"

"No. This was self-defense. They were shot while running at us with their weapons out."

Munoz looked at the corpses and back at me. "From how far away?"

"Don't answer that!" the woman in leather snapped.

Munoz turned to her.

"Don't answer anything." She pulled an ID out and thrust it in front of Munoz. "My name is Sabrian Turner. I'm the legal counsel to House Rogan and future House Baylor."

"We have multiple homicides. Your client needs to answer my questions."

"You're asking for information that's privileged under the House Protection Act. And you're doing it in the middle of the parking lot, where you can't guarantee the information won't be overheard. My client is under no obligation to disclose the exact extent and nature of her magic or the magic of her family members unless you can guarantee its confidentiality."

Munoz clenched his jaw. "Your client isn't a member of a House."

"My client is registered to undergo the trials. Until she fails them, House protections and rights extend to her."

"Excuse me," I said.

"Under the same act, your client is supposed to offer full cooperation in cases where the safety of the public is in question."

"What public? These people were hired by House Madero. This is House warfare."

"Excuse me," I said louder.

"I will be the judge of whether this is House warfare."

Sabrian crossed her arms. "Oh really?"

"Hey!" I barked.

The two of them looked at me.

"There is a camera above us," I said. "I'm sure it caught the whole thing."

"We'll get to that," Munoz promised, and turned back to Sabrian. "Maybe I'll just have to take your client somewhere more private."

Sabrian narrowed her eyes. "My client will answer your questions when she chooses."

"You should just get some swords and have it out," I said.

"Oh, I don't think that will be necessary, do you?" Linus Duncan said.

Munoz stepped aside, revealing Linus Duncan in a flawless

black suit. A long blue scarf hung from his shoulders. He smiled, showing even white teeth against his dark beard, touched with silver. "After all, House Madero was involved, and we all know what that means. Excuse me."

He stepped between Sabrian and Munoz and offered me his hand. I took it, and he helped me off the curb. "Ms. Baylor owes me a coffee. We'll be in the hospital cafeteria if you need us."

"Yes, sir," Sergeant Munoz said.

The coffee shop was small and intimate, furnished in rich brown and soothing beige, and only a third full. Linus and I stood in a short line. He ordered espresso and I settled on an herbal tea. My hands were trembling slightly, the aftereffect of adrenaline and nerves.

We took our order number and sat at an isolated table by the window. From there I had an excellent view of the pandemonium in the parking lot. At least Leon was safe. I seriously doubted that anyone could get past Kurt to talk to him.

"I didn't mean to interrupt your day," I said.

Linus winked at me. "Please. Invitations for a coffee with an interesting young woman are rare at my age. How could I pass it up?"

I smiled. Something about Linus made me feel at ease. You knew that he was sincere and whatever he told you wouldn't be a lie.

The barista brought our drinks and departed.

Linus sipped the jet-black brew out of a small white cup and tilted his head from side to side, thinking. He must've decided the espresso was adequate, because he took another small sip.

"Shall we talk about your grandmother?"

"What is she like?"

"Victoria? Smart. Ruthless. Determined. She thinks she's al-

ways right and frequently is. This"—he glanced at the window—
"is very unlike her. She prefers to operate quietly. She must be
getting desperate."

"Why?"

"You're family," he said. "Family is all any of us have. You're
her hidden legacy, the future of her House. Her parents died
when she was only twelve. She wanted a child so badly. I saw her
shortly after James was born. She seemed happy for the first time
since I'd known her. She practically glowed."

"She was horrible to my father."

"I don't doubt it. She's demanding and difficult. She holds
herself to the highest standard and never stops to consider that
perhaps not everyone possesses the ability or will to match
hers."

"This is the second time she attacked us."

"When was the first time?" he asked.

"Two days ago. Dave Madero chased Rogan and me in his
Jeep."

He sipped his espresso. "How did it end?"

"Rogan broke Dave's arms in five places."

Linus smiled. "If Dave Madero chased the woman I loved, I
would've broken his legs as well."

"Oh, he tried. I asked him not to."

"You should've let him. House Madero has waged a war on
subtlety for the last fifty years. They understand brute strength
and clear messages."

"That is almost word for word what Rogan told me." I drank
my tea through a straw. It tasted sour, but it was better than the
metallic coppery patina on my tongue.

Linus sighed. "Rogan is well-versed in House politics. He's
been playing the game for a long time. He was born into it, and
his instincts are usually right. However, he's in a delicate posi-

tion. Pardon me for inquiring, but have you discussed your potential future?"

I coughed.

"I'll take that as a no." Linus fixed me with his dark eyes. "Allow me to hazard a guess: he pushed and you pushed back. He
pushed harder, and you set some boundaries and refused to back
away from them."

I managed to make a word. "Yes."

"That was likely a new experience for him."

"Yes." I had a sudden urge to crawl under the table. It felt like I
was twelve again and my mom decided to have the Talk with me.
"Do you know him?"

"I knew his father when he was Connor's age. We had business dealings together, mostly military contracts. Connor was
twelve at the time, and I could tell by the way they butted heads
that the apple didn't roll far from the tree."

True. I tried to imagine two Rogans and failed.

"Rogan is very conscious of the fact that you'll soon be the
Head of an emerging House. As the Head of his own House,
he has certain ethical obligations, and he can't obviously steer
your entrance into our society, because he cares about you and
he wants House Baylor to emerge as an independent entity, not a
vassal of House Rogan. As a man who loves you, he doesn't want
to impose his will on yours, even when it's in the interests of your
safety, because he wouldn't allow himself to be treated that way.
He knows if he pushes too far, you'll leave him. Unfortunately,
you're obviously a target in both the physical and emotional sense
of the word. People want to kidnap you, manipulate you, and take
advantage of your inexperience. He sees all of it, so he's fighting
a powerful urge to shove you into full body armor, lock you in a
windowless room, and stand guard by it until the trials are over. I
sympathize. I once had to go through a similar thing."

True.

"It was a uniquely frustrating experience. It gave me grey hair. See?" He pointed to his temple.

I didn't know what to say.

"My unsolicited advice would be to continue on your present course. You've terrified the Harcourts, stood up to Madero, and resisted Tremaine. You seem to be managing quite well."

"What do I do about my grandmother?"

"What do your instincts tell you to do?"

I sighed. "She's attacked me twice. It requires a response."

He nodded. "Yes."

"I thought about complaining to the Office of House Records, but it may make us look weak."

"Do you want to be the child who runs to the teacher because someone pushed her on the playground?"

"No."

"I didn't think so. You have a choice. You can be seen as a House who relies on others or a House who handles its own problems. Leave your grandmother a message. Make it short and to the point."

I flicked through my phone and dialed the second number Bug sent me.

"Trust your instincts," Linus said, and smiled.

"TRM Enterprises," a cultured male voice answered.

"Take a message for my grandmother," I said.

He didn't even pause. "Yes, Ms. Baylor."

"House Madero is out. Your move."

I hung up.

"Good," Linus said, and sipped his espresso. "Things would be much easier if the two of you could sit down and talk."

"She doesn't want to talk. She wants to kidnap me and force me to serve her."

"Victoria is practical. Eventually, she'll come to the realization that she must settle, just as you'll come to the realization that you can't completely escape her. Surely the two of you can find some middle ground. Your grandmother just needs a slight push. If you met somewhere public and talked things out, you would come to a compromise."

"What if she won't compromise?"

"Then you're no worse off than when you started."

True.

"Would you like me to nudge her in the right direction?" he asked.

"Yes, but how do I know she won't try anything?"

"You know because I'm giving you my word and personally arranging for your safety with Victoria. If she doesn't agree to my terms, then there's no meeting."

"Okay."

"Then it will be taken care of. And here comes the avenging angel with her flaming sword."

Sabrian marched toward us and stopped. "Frank Madero came to and confirmed that this matter was House business. You are free to go."

"Thank you."

She nodded to me and walked away.

"Thank you," I said to Linus.

"Of course. This is what I'm here for. It's my function as your witness." He grinned again. "Besides, things around you have a way of turning interesting. I do hate to be bored."

WE MADE IT home a few minutes after 4:00 p.m. Mom was in the kitchen, cooking dinner. Arabella sat at the kitchen table with her nose in her phone.

Mom saw Leon—he still looked a little green—and pinned me down with her stare. "What did you do?"

"I took him with me as backup," I said.

"What happened?"

I made big eyes in Arabella's direction. Mom refused to take the hint. "What happened?"

"Victoria Tremaine attacked us. She sent Dave Madero's brother. And some people. I took care of Frank. Leon took care of the other people."

There, that was nice and neutral.

Arabella got up and walked across the kitchen.

Mom opened the cabinet, pulled out the decanter filled with whiskey, and poured three shots into small shot glasses. "Are you okay?"

The intercom came on. "Leon killed somebody!" Arabella's cheerful voice announced.

"I'm going to murder her," I growled.

"Too late," Mom said. "Brace yourselves."

Doors opened and slammed shut inside the house. The Baylors had mobilized.

Mom put one shot glass in front of Leon and pushed the other toward me. "Drink."

We drank. Liquid fire slid down my throat. Leon coughed.

Bern made it first. He tore into the kitchen, grabbed his brother by the shoulders, and shook him. "Are you okay?"

"He won't be if you keep squeezing him like that," Mom warned.

Catalina marched into the kitchen, her face outraged. "What happened?"

Grandma Frida came next. "Details! I want details!"

Arabella slunk back into the kitchen behind her.

I pointed my finger at her. "You're dead."

She shrugged.

"Will someone tell me the details?" Grandma Frida demanded.

"Ask Leon," I told her.

Everyone looked at him. He gave an awkward one-shouldered shrug. "I couldn't let them take Nevada."

"Well?" Grandma Frida spun to me. "Is he as good as you?"

"Oh no. He's better. Much, much better." I took a USB stick out of my pocket. I made sure to get a copy of the footage from the hospital's camera before I left. The hospital didn't object. House business and all that. "Leon, do you want to let them see it?"

He thought about it. "Kurt said it might help to deal with it."

I held up the USB stick. "We need a TV."

We all stampeded into the living room, where I plugged the USB stick into the TV. The images of Leon and me walking filled the screen. The Vault vehicle charged into the parking lot. I paused the video.

"We got the Vault bus. It's parked out back."

Grandma Frida's eyes lit up. "Good girl."

"Press play!" Arabella ground out.

I pushed the button. On screen we spun around and ran for the door, Leon sprinting past me. Frank Madero popped into existence right in front of me. The family gasped.

On screen the shockers' lightning looked like feathers. Fine white feathers that flickered into existence and licked Frank's skin.

It was so quiet, you could hear a pin drop.

Frank dropped to his knees. I let him go. He collapsed facedown. I stumbled, groping for my gun. People were running toward us.

Leon dashed into the frame next to me, the Sig 210 in his hands. He raised it and fired. I thought it took only a second. It was more like two or maybe two and a half. He fired as fast as he could pull the trigger.

Eight people dropped as if cut. The rest turned around and fled for their lives.

Nobody said anything.

"One shot, one kill," Mom said finally.

"You think he ranks around Notable, like your father?" Grandma Frida asked her.

Mom squinted at the recording. "That's what, fifty meters between them?"

"He's higher." I got out my phone and showed Mom a picture of two of the bodies.

Her eyes widened. "Every single one?"

I nodded.

"What?" Catalina asked.

"He shot them all between the eyes," Mom said. "Instant kill. He did it at a fifty-meter distance, rapid fire. He is at least Significant."

Grandma Frida whistled.

Bern grabbed Leon and crushed him into what could've been an excited brotherly bear hug or a judo submission hold. It was hard to tell for sure.

"This is special, Leon," Mom said. "You're special."

Leon turned red in the face.

"You're choking him," I told Bern.

Bernard let go.

"Are you going to register for trials?" Arabella asked.

"No," Leon said.

"What the hell is wrong with this family?" Arabella waved her arms. "Why would you not register?"

"Because I don't need to," Leon said. "It's better that I don't."

"Why?" my sister wailed.

"Kurt explained it to me."

Mom looked at me.

"Ex–Navy SEAL," I explained. "Rogan's PTSD specialist."

"Sometimes bad shit happens, and you have to protect the people you love," Leon said. "It would be nice if you can do that and keep your hands clean, but life doesn't work that way. Life is messy, and sometimes you must do what needs to be done to keep your family safe. It doesn't make you a bad person."

I'd have to thank Kurt.

"One day some other Prime will threaten our House, and when that day comes, I'll kill him."

What?

"I'll do it quiet and clean, and nobody will ever know." Leon smiled. "I'm going to be a dark horse, House Baylor's secret. I'll be the best assassin. A legend. They'll never see me coming."

I would kill Kurt. I would strangle him with my bare hands.

I STOMPED UP the stairs to the second floor of Rogan's HQ, where Heart and Bug waited for me. Napoleon saw my face and ran behind Bug's chair to hide.

"Where is Kurt?" I growled.

Bug blinked. "I'm not sure I should tell you this information."

"Bug!"

"Kurt is a valuable member of the team, and you have murder on your face."

"What did he do?" Heart asked.

"He talked to Leon, and now my sixteen-year-old cousin has decided to be an assassin when he grows up."

Bug pondered it. "Well, you have to admit it's not a bad option for someone with his particular skill set."

"Bug!"

"What else is he going to do? Competitive shooting?"

262 • ILONA ANDREWS

I looked for something to throw at him, but nothing was close.

"I doubt Kurt would suggest Leon become an assassin," Heart said. "That's not Kurt's philosophy."

"And, before you go on a warpath," Bug added, "your dinner is in seventy-two minutes, so you'll have to hunt Kurt down after your date with Garen."

"It's not a date."

"Pardon me, your worship. I meant your business meeting in a romantic French bistro with a young, single millionaire Prime for which you're wearing a sexy pantsuit," Bug said.

"I'm not wearing a sexy pantsuit, I'm wearing a run-away-fast-if-necessary pantsuit. For your information, I bought it at Macy's, on sale, for two hundred dollars, because occasionally I have to do surveillance in the city and it makes me look like I'm on my way back to my cubicle. Garen Shaffer probably finds two hundred bucks when he empties loose change from his pockets."

"Fine!" Bug raised his hands in the air. "I was wrong. What equipment are you carrying?"

"Why would I tell you that?"

"I just want to know if you're packing good stuff or one of those cheap-ass ten-frames-per-second garbage cameras."

"I'm a PI. Surveillance is my bread and butter." Dad had always stressed the importance of good equipment, which was why I updated ours every year. "I'll transmit live feed to Bern."

"But I want to watch."

"You can watch with Bern."

"But my screens are bigger."

I ignored him. "Where is Rogan?"

"Somewhere on I-10," Heart said.

"I thought he said he would take a jet to Austin."

"He did. There is a hailstorm and the planes are grounded. He's driving back," Bug said.

I really wanted to see him before the date. "Okay."

"What precautions are you taking?" Heart asked.

"I'm bringing Cornelius, and he's bringing Bunny."

"Who's Bunny?" Heart asked.

"Doberman." Bug raised his hands, right hand above, left below, fingers curved and touching, imitating opening and closing jaws. "Teeth."

"Molly's Pub is in the same plaza," Heart said. "Three of our people will be there. One of them is an aegis. How will they know if something goes wrong?"

"If I need help, I'll cover the camera with my finger and hold it for a second. Bern knows what it means."

"Good," Heart said. "Then we're ready."

"I still say my screens are bigger," Bug muttered.

I WALKED INTO Bistro le Cep at five to six. The reviews described it as cozy, quaint, traditionally European, and they didn't lie. White walls offering French-themed art; white ceiling, crossed by golden pine rafters; large windows. Elaborate pine shelves showcased dark wine bottles. Rows of tables, each covered with a red tablecloth, topped with white linen, and flanked by padded chairs, offered comfortable seating. The stagecoach lanterns glowed softly with intimate light. The busy streets of Houston faded. It was like stepping into a different world.

The restaurant was two-thirds full. Cornelius sat two tables down from the entrance, on the left. Bunny discreetly lay at his feet. Normally, getting a dog into any restaurant in Houston would be out of the question, unless it was a service animal, but people made exceptions for animal mages.

A manager smiled at me. "Good evening. Mr. Shaffer's party?"

"Yes."

"This way, please."

He led me around the pine shelves to a different section of the restaurant. Garen sat at an out-of-the-way table, engrossed in his menu. He wore a grey suit that fit him like a glove. His blond hair had that slightly tousled look that happened when you casually dragged your hand through a thousand-dollar haircut. He held himself with a quiet, effortless self-assurance; there was nothing flashy about him. When Rogan walked into the room, his presence punched you. He emanated danger. Garen emanated . . . I wasn't even sure what it was. Charm seemed too smarmy to describe it. You just knew that this was a man who was perfectly comfortable in his own skin and sure of his place in the world. He was always where he was supposed to be, he wasn't easily rattled, and if he showed up to a formal event in jeans and a T-shirt, they would let him in without a pause. He would still look elegant, and everyone else would feel horribly overdressed.

He raised his head. Our stares connected. Garen smiled.

Wow.

I bet he would order in French.

Garen stood and held out my chair. The royal treatment. I smiled and sat.

"You came," he said.

"I said I would."

"I wasn't sure."

True. I took out my phone and put it on the table next to me. He glanced at it.

"Sorry," I told him. "Work." Also, the hidden camera in the side of the phone case now had an excellent view of him and sent live feed to Bern. It was a better camera than the one hidden behind the left lapel of my suit, but it was best to have the feed from both in case one of them decided to suddenly die.

"No worries."

A waiter appeared, smiling, introduced himself, and brought complimentary toast and pâté. I ordered water. Garen did the same.

"Wine?" he asked.

"Your preference."

He glanced at the wine list and murmured something to the waiter, who nodded and departed.

"I always feel uncomfortable ordering wine for the table," Garen said.

True. "Why?"

"Because it's so subjective. The taste of wine has very little to do with the price. Some people train their palate for years to become connoisseurs and some just want a delicious drink. I've been at a dinner where the host opened a five-thousand-dollar bottle of Riesling. It tasted like oak bark soaked in vinegar."

I laughed.

"And the man looked straight at me while I tasted it. I knew I had to say something."

"What did you say?"

Garen leaned forward, nodding. "Oh I lied through my teeth. I think I told him it was exquisite."

Oh my, Mr. Wolf. What lovely eyes you have and delightful stories you tell. I can barely see the fangs. "One-word lies are the easiest."

"Yes, they are."

The drinks arrived. The waiter opened a bottle of white wine and poured some into the two glasses.

"Please," Garen invited me.

The wine tasted clean and sweet. "I like it."

I felt a light flick against my skin. Garen had truth-checked me. He was smiling.

The waiter filled our glasses and politely asked for the starter order. I went for the seared scallop.

"Make that two," Garen said, and we were again alone.

He studied me, smart green eyes careful. "Let's make a pact for tonight."

"Mmm?"

"Let's be honest with each other."

"How honest?"

"Brutally. Ask me any question, and I'll answer honestly. No shields, no attempt to block the probe. I ask the same in return."

I swirled the wine in my glass. "That's a dangerous game."

"I realize that."

"You won't like my questions," I said.

"I like to live on the edge."

We faced off across the table, like two gunfighters, armed with glasses of wine instead of six-shooters.

"Go ahead," he dared me.

"Have you or a member of your family ever lifted a hex with the purpose of finding the third piece of an artifact, which was located in the statue in the Bridge Park?"

I had considered that question carefully. That's how the conspiracy showed itself the first time. They made a deal with a rogue Prime called Adam Pierce. Pierce wanted to burn Houston down, but he needed an artifact to amplify his power. The location of the artifact was a closely guarded secret, entrusted to the Emmens family. All members of that family, trusted with this knowledge, had a hex implanted in their minds to protect them from disclosing their secret. The members of the conspiracy had kidnapped the youngest member of the family and pried that knowledge out of his mind, despite the hex, the same way I had done with the oldest member of the family, except in my case he had volunteered to help me save Houston.

A truthseeker had cracked the hex in the younger Emmens, and I wanted to know if Garen was that truthseeker. Asking him about the Emmens family was useless. He may not have been told the name of the man whose mind the conspirators wanted unlocked. However, if Garen had anything to do with breaking the hex, he would know the location of the object.

"I don't know what this is about, but that is oddly specific. No."

True. Relief washed through me. Surprising. I didn't realize that on some level, I liked him. I didn't want him to be connected to the conspiracy.

He studied me, a hint of predatory anticipation in his eyes. Despite all his charm and disarming honesty, Garen was a Prime. "My turn. Are you really Victoria Tremaine's granddaughter?"

"Yes."

The waiter appeared with our appetizers and asked for our orders.

"Red snapper," I said.

"*Medallion de Marcassin à l'aigre-doux.*"

I won the bet. He did order in French.

The waiter departed.

"Let's continue," Garen said. "Your move."

"What is the significance of a wavy line?"

"I don't follow."

"When you're facing someone with hard mental defenses, and you want to loosen their will instead of bashing through it by brute force, you draw a wavy line inside the amplification circle. Why do people freak out when they see it?"

Garen stared at me for a second, picked up his glass, and gulped all of the wine in one swallow. "Have you done this?"

"Yes. Answer the question."

"They freak out, because it's a spell of House Tremaine. Nobody else does it." He leaned forward, focused on me. "How do you determine the pattern of the waves?"

"You tailor it to the specific defenses of the person. By feel."

"I knew it." He slapped the table lightly. "I knew it. We've been trying to duplicate it for years. Will you show me?"

"Maybe. It's your turn."

He thought about it. "In the office, when I asked you the last question about me being an only child, did you know I was lying?"

"Yes." I cut a small piece off my scallop. It was getting cold, and it looked delicious. It would be a shame to waste it.

He leaned back in his chair. His eyes were shining and it wasn't all wine. "Your turn."

"Why did you come here, Garen?"

He paused. "I came to find out if you were the real thing."

"I know that. That's not what I meant."

"That's a more complicated question."

Our food appeared. The red snapper looked divine and smelled even better, but I barely noticed.

Garen waited until we were alone again. "As I said, I came to find out if you were the real thing. If I determined you lied or your magic wasn't of high enough caliber, I would have been on a plane home already."

"But you're still here."

"I am."

He pondered the meat medallion on his plate.

"What is that?" I asked.

"Wild boar. Would you like to try?"

"No, thank you."

"I understand you and Rogan have a history," he said. "A tumultuous, violent history, very exciting but full of danger, fear, and uncertainty."

"Yes."

"Has he requested your profile?"

"No."

"Then he is a complete fool."

I tried my snapper to keep from responding. It melted on my tongue.

"I probably shouldn't have said that," he said, "but it's too late now."

I smiled. "Are you afraid he overheard?"

"No. But you obviously care for him, and I don't want to alienate you. I've made some inquiries. I'm sorry about your father."

Well, that was a 180-degree turn. "Thank you."

"You took over a struggling PI firm on the brink of failure and you saved it. You didn't overextend and grow too fast, hiring people to churn through as many cases as you could. Instead you concentrated on quality. You were instrumental in saving Houston from Adam Pierce, yet you stayed out of the limelight. I suspect that being quietly competent is much more important to you than being the flavor of the month. Am I right?"

"Yes. We didn't need that kind of attention. Our caseload is small but perfectly manageable. Our business puts food on the table."

"You take care of your family. I do the same thing. I took over after my father was diagnosed with early-onset Alzheimer's."

"I'm sorry."

"Thank you. I was eighteen. When I'd done an audit and realized how deep the problem lay, our firm was in serious jeopardy. For the next twelve years I lived and breathed Shaffer Security. I know exactly what it costs. You put your life on hold, and you get up every morning and plow through it, fixing it, building it up block by block, case by case, client by client. You lay awake at night, wondering how you'll pay the bills. It takes dedication and perseverance. So when some dunce with a microphone comes along and shoves it in your face, wanting you to give him a good ten-second sound bite about a case you worked for eight months, you walk away, because that's not what your work is about."

"Baylor Investigative Agency prides itself on discretion. Our clients expect confidentiality."

He nodded. "Going on TV and making the talk show circuit would send the wrong message."

"Yes." He did get it. "Did you save your company?"

"Yes. We're the second-biggest security firm in the United States. MII is the third. Augustine Montgomery has been snapping at my heels for years." Garen smiled. "Unfortunately for him, he's destined to stay an ankle biter."

The snapper went the wrong way down my throat. I coughed.

Garen grinned. "I thought you might like that. On a serious note, my personal net worth is over four hundred million and it's rising. The company is valued at over a billion."

"Why did you tell me that?"

"Because we promised to be honest with each other, and I want you to have all of the pertinent information, so you can make an informed decision."

I paused with the glass in my hand. "Is there a decision at the end of all of this?"

"Yes. I'm asking you to marry me."

It was so good that I wasn't drinking when he said it. "You don't know me, Garen. I don't know you. Help me understand this."

"Marriage is a partnership. I think we will be good partners. We're similar. We both value family, integrity, and competence. We do the same type of work, and we dedicate ourselves to it. We care about reputation rather than fame. We're both careful, because we know what's at stake. I think we would be a good match."

"And genetics have nothing to do with it?"

He sighed. "Genetics have everything to do with it. If you were a flighty opportunist, I still would've seriously considered it, given your set of genes."

"The pickings are slim, I take it?"

"Yes. We're a rare breed, and when we step outside of our own type of magic, there is always a risk of diluting the power."

"Wouldn't it have been wise to at least wait until the trials, so you would know for certain?"

He put his fork down. "I don't need the trials. I know you're a Prime. You drew the Tremaine wave without even knowing what it is. That suggests that your ability is genetic, and it will be passed on to your children. That is gold."

"Mhm."

"Does it bother you that we're discussing this as if the two of us were a rare type of cattle we're considering breeding?"

"Of course, it bothers me. I'm a human being, Garen. I have dreams and expectations. I want to marry for love, not for my genes."

"So do I."

True.

He sighed. "But there is always that catastrophic moment when expectations meet cold, hard reality. I can guarantee that our children will be powerful Primes. That's a rare opportunity for both of us. You're an emerging House. You'll need to form alliances to survive. You'll need to invest in security and person- nel for yourself and your family members, which means startup capital. You'll need to learn to navigate the shark-infested waters of the Houses. You'll need training. You may be naturally stron- ger than me. We won't know this until we truly grapple. But in a life or death struggle, I would kill you. I have the knowledge and experience of using my magic, and you lack both. Marriage to me would guarantee that all of those needs would be taken care of."

A lot of what he said made sense. "And what's in it for you?"

"A partner who truly understands me. Someone who will be loyal, who will work with me toward common goals. Someone who will grow with me, who will be an asset. A fascinating, intelligent woman. Someone who will be a remarkable mother." He paused. "The relationship with me will be honest, Nevada. I won't lie to you. I can't, but even if I could, I wouldn't want to. We both know it's a double-edged sword, but it's best we put it all out here now."

"I don't love you, Garen," I said gently.

"I know. Like you said, we don't know each other. But you're attracted to me. I'm attracted to you. It's a good start. Given time, we'd come to love each other. I've seen it happen before. That's the way it happened for my parents. My childhood was idyllic, because my father loved my mother and treated her with respect, and she loved him and offered the same respect back. Neither of them had affairs. They lived happily, until my father's illness and eventual death three years ago. Arranged marriage can succeed."

"I don't want to marry because I tick all of the right boxes."

"Isn't that the criteria for all marriage? You marry someone precisely because they tick all of your boxes."

"I'm in a relationship with someone else," I said.

He pushed his plate away and leaned forward. "I said I didn't want to criticize Rogan, but I may have to go back on my word. I really want this, Nevada. This is my opportunity of a lifetime."

Wow. So slick.

"Rogan is larger than life. High impact. Dangerous, and that danger can carry a certain allure. But he's also unpredictable and ruthless. He measures everyone by his own standards. He'll put you in danger assuming you can handle it, and he'll fail to notice the moment you can't. I would do everything in my power to keep you from being put into a dangerous situation in the first place, because that's what a husband is supposed to do. Ask yourself, would he be a good husband? A good father? Would he be able to control his temper? We both come from large families. You know how deranged your younger siblings can make you.

Think of him in the role of a caregiver. Think of all that stress. Would you feel safe leaving the children with him? Would you feel safer leaving them with me?"

He was really good at this. Much better than I expected.

"I offer security, stability, and comfort. He offers excitement, danger, and risk. I offer marriage, a formal agreement which gives you rights and protections. He hasn't even considered it."

Garen leaned forward and touched my hand with his elegant fingers. The personal connection.

"Nevada, the bottom line is that Rogan and I want two different women. I want the smart, confident, cautious woman who built her own business, who understands loyalty and integrity. He wants a warrior, someone who can go toe-to-toe with him into whatever latest high-risk venture he wants to plunge into. He wants someone people will be afraid of. To put it crudely, he gets off on it. If you accept me, you'll become the head of a Fortune 500 corporation with me, with all of the influence and security that position brings. If you stay with him, you will become your grandmother. You have to decide who you want to be. In the end, it's all about family."

CHAPTER 11

GAREN OFFERED DESSERT, but I declined. He didn't insist. He did walk me out to the parking lot and watched over me while I got into my car. He missed the three people who conveniently exited Molly's Pub at about the same time and got into a silver Range Rover.

I pulled into traffic. "Call Bern."

The car dialed the number.

"Here," my cousin said.

"I survived. Where is Cornelius?"

"He just left the restaurant."

"Did Rogan make it back?"

"Yes." There was a hint of amusement in my cousin's voice. "We're all in the back, in the motor pool."

"I'll be there shortly. I need to make a brief detour." Something Garen said ate at me. It was all about family. If I had a secret, a terrible secret that I didn't want anyone to know, I would trust my family. Olivia Charles was a Prime. She would trust her family. The ransom had to be somewhere in Rynda's house.

Traffic was surprisingly light. My escort stayed about a car length behind me the whole way until I pulled in front of Rynda's house. I stepped out. The doors of the SUV behind me opened and three people jumped out: an Asian man in his early twenties with a faded scar on his left cheek; a dark-haired, serious-looking man in his thirties; and Melosa, Rogan's personal aegis.

"Why aren't you in Austin with him?" I asked her.

"Because he considers your safety a higher priority," she said. "Why are we here?"

"I need to search Rynda's house."

"It's already been searched," the dark-haired man said.

"I know." I headed for the door.

"Oh no, you don't." Melosa ran in front of me and blocked my way. "Delun?"

"On it." The Asian man moved toward the door and punched in the code. The door swung open under the pressure of his fingertips. He moved inside, stepping lightly, and paused.

A long moment passed.

"Clear," he said. "It's empty."

He turned and flipped the lights on. I walked into the house. Someone had cleaned the mess. The bloodstains were gone from the tiles and the overturned Christmas tree had disappeared.

I stopped in the living room. Bits and pieces of past conversations floated up onto the surface of my memory.

. . . *She was a wonderful grandmother to my children. She loved them so much* . . .

. . . *It's not in the computer. It's somewhere in the house* . . .

. . . *but Olivia saw it. She adored him. She framed every painting he made* . . .

. . . *in the end, it's all about family* . . .

I stepped over to the nearest painting on the wall. Two trees, standing close to each other, their trunks almost touching. The lines of the painting were obviously drawn by a child, slightly shaky and basic, but the colors, the vibrant greens and rich browns, drew the eye. The sunlit crowns of the trees almost glowed. It made me want to go outside to breathe in the air and run my hand across the bark. I would hang it in my office and smile every time I looked at it.

I took it off the wall. A plain black frame, rectangular, wooden, the kind you could get in any craft or art supply store. Gently I pried it open and pulled the frame apart. No secret code, no writing on the mat, no piece of translucent rice paper hidden between the mat and the painting itself. I plucked the heavy piece of watercolor paper out and held the painting up so the light shone through it.

Paint and paper fibers. Even if I reached into left field for some improbable spy solution to this mystery, an invisible ink still left traces. A pen would've left scratches on the smooth dense paper. A brush would've left patterns as it soaked into the texture. Watercolor paint came in varying pH and posed a significant risk to reacting with the ink, not to mention that watercolor painting required a lot of water. Soaking the paper with the hidden message on it was risky. No, the painting was exactly what it pretended to be.

I knocked on the frame, looking for hollow spots. Only solid wood answered.

"What are you looking for?" Melosa asked.

"I'll know it when I see it."

"I'll go see if I can find more," the dark-haired man offered.

I laid the painting on the floor and tried the next one. A picture of the house, two adults and two children, and a ghostly outline of a dog. Was the dog dead? Was Kyle wishing for a puppy? I took the painting off the wall, just as the dark-haired man and Delun brought in four more. They moved on upstairs, while Melosa and I took the next frame apart.

Half an hour later all twenty-four paintings lay on the floor.

I had gone through every inch of paper and wood with a fine-toothed comb. Nothing.

The disappointment crushed me. I had been so sure.

The paintings ticked all the right boxes, ranking right there with hollow books as a cliché hiding place: most people wouldn't think of it, so those who did thought they were being really clever and enjoyed knowing that their valuables were hidden in plain sight. It was just the kind of thing I would've expected Olivia Charles to do. She framed all of Kyle's paintings.

"Do you want to look anywhere else?" Delun asked.

"Not tonight." I'd come back in the morning with an ultraviolet light and give it another go. "Let's go home."

The escort faithfully followed me all the way to the parking lot in front of the warehouse, then they veered toward Rogan's HQ. I parked the car, got out, and walked around the warehouse. It was easier than punching the code in and going through all the doors inside.

I turned the corner. A twisted wreck that might have been a car at some point lay mangled in the street. Someone had taken a car frame, crushed and twisted it, like a piece of aluminum foil, and then tossed it onto the street. Odd.

Ahead the commerce-size garage door stood open, spilling yellow electric light onto the street and another dented wreckage. This one looked like some giant pressed the car into a ball and decided to practice soccer tricks with it.

I sped up.

The motor pool was mostly empty. Someone had conveniently moved the vehicles to the side, leaving an open space in the center. Smaller chunks of metal, wrenched and twisted, littered the concrete floor. Grandma Frida leaned against Romeo. He was Grandma Frida's pet project. He'd started out his life as an M551

Sheridan, a light armored tank, armed with nine antitank Shillelagh missiles, and other fun things. However, Grandma Frida had made modifications, and ever since Romeo saw some action almost two weeks ago, she'd been tinkering with him nonstop.

At the far end, near the inner wall, Rogan loomed, like the living embodiment of manly darkness, by two large screens, studying the footage of Garen. On the left, Bern sat in a chair a few feet away from the screen with his keyboard on his lap. Bug had straddled a chair backwards on the right and leaned over the back of it, his chin on his forearms. My mother sat near Bug, Grandma Frida's knitting on her lap. As I approached, she picked at it with a crochet hook and unraveled another tangled row. Two blankets lay on the floor, next to a half-finished bowl of popcorn. My sisters must've been in attendance.

I paused by Grandma Frida and nodded at the metal carnage.

"He was watching your date and the walls started buckling. I needed some old frames scrapped so I gave him something to do."

"And the girls?"

"They went to bed. While you were having your adventures, we've been running tornado drills all day. They're sick to death of running across the street into the basement. Don't worry, they watched the whole thing. You'll get an earful tomorrow."

I rolled my eyes. That's what was missing in my life, the teenager perspective. "What's Mom doing?"

Grandma Frida gave me the evil eye. "That yarn cost thirty-eight dollars a skein. I want her to salvage it. I tried doing it myself, except I have frayed nerves today. I was going to set it on fire for closure, but your mother took away my blowtorch."

I nodded and went to stand by Rogan. "Did you catch all that?"

"Yes." The voice was glacially cold.

"I especially liked the part where he casually threatened me."

"I caught that too," he said.

I leaned forward to look at his face. The dragon was out in all his terrifying glory. I grinned. "What are you thinking about?"

"Nothing."

Lie. "You can't kill Garen Shaffer."

"Technically, I can. I choose not to. And I wasn't thinking of killing him."

"If you go over to his place and break his arms in five places, it would look bad. People will be afraid to do business with me."

"I wasn't thinking of breaking his arms either. I was thinking of hamstringing his corporation, ripping it apart, and selling it piece by piece while he watched."

Mad Rogan, the Scourge of Mexico. A civilized and considerate enemy. "You can't ruin every man who threatens me."

"Yes, I can. Besides, I would only have to ruin the first couple and the rest will get the hint. Except for the Maderos, who are particularly dense, apparently."

"It's okay. I had a nice chat with Frank and Dave's grandpa. We understand each other now."

On screen, Garen reached out and touched my hand. The carved biceps on Rogan's arm visibly tensed. Behind us, a chunk of metal rose in the air and crimped, contorting with a harsh screech.

I had to thaw him out. "See how he maintains eye contact. A gentle yet firm touch, just brief enough to underscore sincerity. Reassurance that he's on my side, he's in charge, and he will take care of everything."

Bug turned and looked at me, his face surprised.

I winked at him. "Garen knows how to read people. He watched them lie his entire life. It gives you a unique perspective. He knows how to obtain a confession. You do it by convincing the person you're on their side. He started with that charming confession about being uncomfortable with choosing the wine and it only got better from there. He was sincere, disarming, and logical."

"Is that magic?" Bug asked.

"No, it's human nature. Shaffer is a professional interrogator. But so am I." I gave Bug my best reassuring smile. "I can see into your brain, Bug. I know what makes you tick."

He shuddered. "Don't do that."

Bern laughed in his chair. Rogan remained stoic. Still no dice.

"The good news is, Garen isn't involved in the conspiracy, so he isn't our problem. We can set this aside and move on."

Rogan gave no indication he heard me.

"I have something to tell you, Rogan."

His expression didn't change.

"Rogan." I touched his arm.

He came to, turned, and looked at me, his attention completely focused on me. The effect was overpowering. For this moment nothing existed in Rogan's universe except me. I loved when he did that.

"Yes?"

"I have a strong reason to believe that Brian Sherwood is working with Alexander Sturm."

"Fuck."

"Yep."

"Why?"

"He wasn't satisfied with the way his family turned out. His daughter is an empath, which is useless as far as he's concerned. Kyle has no magic, and it threatens Brian. His parents raised Brian as their golden child, whose only value was in his talent, which would ensure he would inherit BioCore and become a Prime of a certain standing. His entire self-worth is tied up in being Brian Sherwood, the brilliant herbamagos Prime and Head of House Sherwood. Brian knew since birth that he is special and he has grown accustomed to the world acknowledging it. He hates the idea that someone might question his ability to sire Prime children. He wanted out for a while, but as long as Olivia Charles was alive, he didn't dare to make any waves in that placid pond. And since his wife became a social pariah, now he views her as a liability."

He thought about it. "Olivia is dead. Why not just divorce Rynda?"

"Because Edward told him that Brian has certain responsibilities as a husband and father and if he shirked those responsibilities, Edward would retire, leaving BioCore in Brian's hands. Brian can't run that company. He has no idea how to do it. If Edward retires, all of Brian's prestige evaporates. He knows he will run BioCore into the ground. He would no longer be treated with deference. Nobody would think he was important."

Rogan's eyes darkened, his expression harsh. "But if something happened to Rynda, and Brian became a widower, things line up rather nicely."

"Yes. He wouldn't hire a hit man. It's too risky and he doesn't even know where to look for one. He's probably terrified that if he tried to find someone, they would turn out to be an undercover cop and he'd end up in prison. This way everything is taken care of: his new violent friends get what they want while he cools his heels in some mansion, and when the time comes to make the exchange, Rynda is tragically killed."

Rogan nodded. "If not at the exchange, then shortly after. Perhaps the children die with her."

"Yes. He's then free to pursue his new life, and nobody is the wiser."

"It's plausible. How solid is this?"

"We know that the kidnapping occurred in view of one of only three cameras facing Memorial Drive," Bug said.

"We can put Brian and Sturm together in a coffee shop two days before the kidnapping," Bern said. "We also know that someone accessed his home computer that night, using Brian's credentials, while Brian and Rynda were out."

"We have Edward Sherwood, who told me about the conversation he had with his brother. He didn't lie. And, the ear they sent us doesn't belong to Brian," I finished.

"Have you told Rynda?" Rogan asked.

"Not yet. But I will. She's my client, and her life and the lives of her children may be in danger."

"If she's so empathic, how come she didn't see this coming?" Grandma Frida asked.

"I listened to the initial interview," I said. "She never said, 'Brian loves me.' She said Brian takes care of her and the kids. She talked about how much the kids miss him. I think she sensed the resentment. What I don't understand is why the marriage happened in the first place. Rynda didn't need his money, and as much as she craved stability, I find it hard to believe she saw something irresistible in him."

"I can explain that," Rogan said.

"How did you figure it out?"

"I asked my mother. Rynda is an NPTN WC variant."

"What does that mean?" I asked.

"NPTN is a gene responsible for coding neuroplastin, a protein. Some variants of the NPTN gene are linked to higher intelligence," Rogan explained. "Normally magic is passed on from parents to children, and it's hereditary in power and type, which is why we have Houses."

That made sense. If the parents were aquakinetics, water

mages, their children likely would be water mages as well. There was some variation, but the talents didn't vary widely. Two water mages might have a child who is psychrokinetic, able to control ice, or mistukinetic, able to control mist and fog. But they wouldn't make a truthseeker, for example.

"People with NPTN WC variant roll the dice," Rogan said. "WC stands for wild card. Their children may or may not be magic, and those who have power are unpredictable. If Rynda's children have magic, it will likely be of a mental type. They might be empaths, telepaths, precogs, or harmonizers. There is no way to predict the exact nature of it. My father was willing to roll the dice with Rynda, because he was confident in our genetic line. He figured that at least one of my children would be a strong telekinetic, and if anyone could produce a telekinetic telepath, it would be Rynda."

"But most Primes don't want to play," I guessed. "Rynda could jeopardize the line."

Rogan grimaced. "Yes and no. Some Houses would jump on the chance for variation, but most of these marriages wouldn't be to the Head of the House. Heads of the House want their children to inherit the family throne. According to my mother, Olivia wouldn't settle for anything less for her daughter, which is why she hated me. I ruined her perfect plan by breaking the engagement."

"Brian offered all the right things," I thought out loud. "He was the Head of his House. He owned a thriving corporation which would secure income for the House. He was stable, focused on safety, low-key enough to not upset Rynda with wild emotional swings, and susceptible to pressure. I bet Olivia had invested in BioCore."

"You're thinking like a Prime again," Rogan said, appreciation in his eyes.

I nodded. "If he stepped out of line, she could apply pressure socially and financially. She was trying to keep her daughter safe." Olivia must've loved Rynda so much.

My mother sighed. "Your world is screwed up, Rogan."

"I know," he said quietly.

"And now my daughter is in it." Mom put the half-unraveled scarf down. "I'll finish in the morning."

She left.

"It's late for me too," Grandma Frida declared.

"Okay, okay," I grumbled. "We can take the hint."

Bernard got up and shut down the equipment. The screens went black. Bug jumped off his chair and trotted outside. Rogan dipped his head to look at me. The mask slipped, and Connor was looking at me. I caught a flash of the upstairs room, with the shroud of night sky spread above us. It was quick and faint, a mere shred of projection. He must've crushed it the instant he thought of it, but I caught it anyway.

Come home with me.

Of course I will, Connor.

I slipped closer to him, fitting myself in his arm. "I'm tired and my feet hurt."

He chuckled. "Want me to carry you?"

He could and probably would if I asked. "No. I have an image to maintain."

We walked out of the motor pool. The door rumbled shut behind us.

"What image is that?"

"According to Garen, I'm a young Victoria Tremaine, terrible and glorious."

"Would you like me to commission a golden palanquin for you?"

"Possibly." The night sky was endless above us. "I searched Rynda's house. I thought whatever they were looking for might be in the paintings Kyle made. It wasn't."

"Sorry," he said.

"The deadline is up tomorrow at four. We still have nothing."

"I know. One good thing came out of this mess. At least we don't have to worry about keeping that bastard alive. They're not going to kill him."

"And if they do, they would be doing us a favor," I finished.

"So vicious."

"This is the worst betrayal. It's worse than an affair. He's Rynda's husband. He didn't even have the guts to ask for a divorce."

"We'll get him," Rogan promised.

"How did it go in Austin?"

"The Ade-Afefe are thinking about it. That was the best I could do." His voice dripped with disappointment. "You win some, you lose some."

"Stellar day for us both, huh?"

"Yes." He fell silent. "Shaffer is right about one thing. When it comes to assuring the hereditary stability of truthseeker talent, his genes win."

That's what true love looked like. Shaffer wouldn't know it if it was staring him in the face.

"I'll take it under advisement."

Everything was screwed up. The deadline was almost up, and I still had nothing. Sturm wouldn't let it go. There would be repercussions, and we had very little protection against his magic. Tomorrow I'd have to explain to Rynda that her husband most likely plotted to murder her. My evil grandmother was still trying to kidnap me. Leon still wanted to be an assassin when he grew up. The trials were growing closer.

I just wanted a break from it all. I wanted to put it away until tomorrow, because if I thought about it too much, I'd collapse like an imploded building.

We took the stairs to the second floor. I thought about the room under the night sky, and the massive bed, and him naked, his weight on me, the feel of steel-hard muscle, the way he looked at me, the intoxicating taste of his magic dripping on my skin and setting my nerves on fire . . .

"Nevada," he said, his voice gaining a harsh edge.

"Yes?"

"Move faster."

I let him chase me up the stairs. He caught me on the landing and kissed me. I tasted Rogan, man and coffee, inhaled the scent of sandalwood on his skin, and felt his arms around me. Magic caressed my neck, hot and velvet-soft, and then the world no longer mattered.

THE MORNING CAME too soon.

"You're lying." Red blotches appeared on Rynda's cheeks.

"Unfortunately, no. Everything I told you is backed up by evidence and personal accounts. Edward will verify his part in it. He didn't lie to me."

She looked away from me. We sat on the balcony off the second floor, as far away from any audience as we could. The raw pain on her face made me ill. I had half convinced myself that she had to have known or at least suspected that Brian was in on the whole thing. I was wrong. She had no idea. It hit her like a ton of bricks.

"Why?" she said, her voice broken. "How? How could he do this to us? To me and the kids?"

"He's selfish and manipulative. Adults don't run away from stress and problems. We deal with them. The first time he ran away, someone should've sat him down and explained to him how much he worried everyone. And then they should've grounded him, so he wouldn't do it again. Instead they encouraged it and he fell into a pattern. He's afraid of confrontations. Killing you and the kids is easier than facing Edward or dealing with the divorce. You're the empath, Rynda. You know him better than anyone."

"I stopped," she said. Her eyes were haunted.

"You stopped what?"

"I stopped scanning him years ago, after Kyle was born. The indifference was too much to take. I couldn't handle it. Indifference from him, derision from his parents, disappointment from my mother. I shut it out. I hadn't used my talent in years."

Not using magic was like cutting off a chunk of your soul. It must've hurt so much to know what Brian really felt for her. For their kids.

"The only people safe to scan are the children and . . . the children."

And Edward. She'd almost said it.

"And I don't need empathy to know what they are feeling. They're my babies. I grew them inside me, and I gave birth to them. They are a part of me and a part of him. And he wants them dead. How do I tell them that?"

"I wouldn't."

"I'm a pity fuck."

"I'm sorry?"

Rynda turned to me, her eyes red. She was on the verge of tears. "I'm the daughter with the useless magic talent, a disappointment to my mother. She loved me, but she couldn't hide it. An abandoned bride. A match nobody wanted because of her wild genes. A wife whose husband didn't love her. A mother who didn't manage to pass the right DNA to her children."

Well, that progressed into a complete catastrophe. I had no idea what to say.

Rynda sniffed.

I got up and brought her a box of Kleenex.

"You have no idea what it's like to be an empath. People look at you like you're some horrible freak."

I leaned forward. "Victoria Tremaine is my grandmother."

Rynda drew back as if I had thrown a venomous snake on the table between us.

"I don't need to be an empath to know you're horrified." I smiled.

"I . . . I didn't mean . . ."

"The first time I made a man tell me his secrets against his will, he curled up on the ground and cried. He was an experienced mercenary, but he cried like a hurt child, because I'd violated his mind. So you and I have things in common. You're not a disappointment to anyone. You don't need anyone's approval."

She closed her mouth and sat up straighter. "Does Rogan know about Brian's betrayal?"

"Yes."

"Who else?"

"My family, Cornelius, Bug, Edward, and Edward's security chief. Possibly your mother-in-law."

"What happens now?"

"We proceed as if we don't know about Brian. We still have to find the thing they want. They're not going to stop until we do, or until we end the whole organization permanently."

She got up. "I'll have to tell the children. They must know that they can't trust their father."

"Rynda . . ."

She walked away.

Well, that went well.

I picked myself up and went across the street to our warehouse.

We had hours until the deadline was due. I could practically feel the time ticking away. It ate at me. We had to find Olivia's secret. I had to find it. Rynda and her little family wouldn't be safe until I did. If Sturm didn't get what he wanted, he would retaliate. He'd probably retaliate anyway. Rogan almost killed him in the steakhouse. Sturm wouldn't let that go.

Everything went wrong for Rynda. Everything went wrong in this investigation, period. This one thing had to go right.

Inside, Catalina's shrill voice sliced at my eardrums. "I don't want to talk about it!"

Whenever she got upset, her voice shot up into piercing notes.

I rounded the corner.

"Catalina!" Arabella chased her. Matilda trailed her, her fluffy white cat following her. I didn't know she was still here.

"I don't want to talk about it!" The door to Catalina's room thudded shut.

"You're being ridiculous," Arabella growled.

"What is it?"

"She deleted her Instagram account."

"Why?"

"Alessandro Sagredo." Arabella put her hands on her hips.

"Did he say something to her?" If he said something mean to my sister, I'd skin him alive.

"No."

"Then what's the problem?"

Arabella whipped out her phone and stuck it under my nose. "He looks like that!"

The man on the phone looked about twenty and he was stunning. Square jaw; full, perfectly drawn mouth; strong nose; narrow, almost green hazel eyes under dark eyebrows. A mass of chocolate-brown hair, trimmed in an expensive haircut, framed it all, setting off the strong lines of his face that promised to become chiseled with time. Life hadn't beaten him up yet, and there was still something fresh about his face, but the harshness had begun to break through. He looked like he was the son of a Roman gladiator about to enter the arena for the first time. And he stood leaning against a beautiful silver and blue Maserati.

"He follows like three people on Instagram," Arabella said. "And Catalina. She woke up with six thousand followers, so she deleted the account, because she is an idiot!"

"Are you going to marry him, Catalina?" Matilda asked seriously.

The door swung open, revealing Catalina. She stabbed her finger at Arabella. "Stay out of my business, you little weirdo. You too, Matilda."

She slammed the door shut.

Matilda looked at the door, looked at me, and laughed like little silver bells ringing.

"I don't have time for this." I started down the hallway. It was morning, therefore Bern would be in the kitchen, eating his second or third breakfast.

"Nevada, do something!" Arabella snarled behind me.

"No time."

"I hate this family!"

"We hate you too."

"Hehe!" The silver bells rang.

Bern sat at the kitchen table, putting away a bowl of cereal.

"Will you please come with me to Rynda's house? I want to look through it one more time in case I missed something. I don't want to go by myself, and I don't want to ask Cornelius because he'll bring Zeus and I have trouble concentrating when he's around. I don't want to take Leon either, because I don't want to be responsible for him shooting anyone. I just want to think quietly."

Bern got up and took his bowl of cereal to the sink. "Let's go."

RYNDA'S HOUSE STOOD quiet. Bern and I walked through the front entrance into the living room, our steps loud on the tiled floor. Houston decided that we really needed some rain, and the light filtering through the dense blanket of clouds was watery and dim. The air felt oppressive.

"Gloomy," Bern observed.

"Yes." The house felt like a crypt. "I wonder if Rynda will sell it."

"I would," Bern said. "Where do you want to look?"

"I'm not sure," I said. "Divide and conquer?"

We split up. I headed for the kitchen. Rogan's people had already swept through the place. I'd reviewed the search report. They were thorough and efficient. But they might have missed something.

I started with the pantry. An hour later I was done with the kitchen. Coffee proved to be coffee, rice turned out to be rice, and a container of sugar contained only sugar. No hidden Ziploc bags containing mysterious evidence. I shook the cans one by one. None showed any signs of tampering. No hidden spots in the dishes. Nothing taped to the inside of the cabinets. We were wasting time we didn't have, but every instinct I had told me that whatever we were looking for was here somewhere.

"Nevada?" Bern called.

I walked into the living room. He stood over Kyle's paintings. I came over to stand next to him.

"What are these?" he asked.

"Kyle's paintings. Olivia Charles had them framed. I've gone through them. No hidden ink. Nothing in the frames. I was so sure that there was something hidden here."

Bern crouched and picked up the top painting. A curving road flanked by trees.

"There is something about them," I said. "It makes you want to keep looking at them."

Bern wandered to the center of the room where the light from the back window shone on the carpet, and put the painting down.

"Give me the rest?" he asked.

I picked up a stack of paintings and handed him the next one, a tiny sea with a too-big pirate ship on it. He took a few steps backwards and placed the painting to the left and below the first one. "Next."

A playground with a cute monster holding a red balloon and peering out of the bushes followed, then the curve of a road with a bright yellow sports car, then the clouds with a white, almost transparent flying ship. Another road with a knight in armor riding on his horse. Bern put it between the first painting and the yellow car. The road connected.

The tiny hairs on the back of my neck rose.

We went through the stack, Bern placing the pictures one by one into a six-by-four grid, like pieces of a puzzle clicking together. We finished and stood back. A road wound in a wide arc around a house that was part suburban home, part castle, and part magic tower. A playground lay to the right, a pond just below, mountains to the left, and in the bottom left corner, four paintings came together to form an X near a gnarled tree.

"A map," I whispered.

"He isn't a dud," Bern said. "He's Magister Examplaria. A pattern mage, like me."

Grandma gave Kyle a treasure. He hid it and then he drew a map to it, because he couldn't help himself. And Olivia must've known. I'd helped to take away the only person in Kyle's life who understood him.

"I'm incompetent," I said.

Bern glanced at me.

"I should've questioned the children. Instead I let Rynda do it, because they were traumatized by Vincent. I let it get personal, and it blinded me." This is why Dad always cautioned about getting too involved.

"We have it now," Bern said. "You can beat yourself up later. The sea is the pool. We'll need a shovel. He must've buried it. Pirate treasure is always buried."

I snapped a picture of the map with my phone. We found a pair of shovels in the garden shed and tracked our way through the lot down to the back of the property, where the woods stood dense. We pushed through the brush into a small clearing.

The sky broke open, sifting cold rain on us. I surveyed the clearing. On the right a big oak spread its branches, on the left two stumps and more brush. No signs of digging marked the forest floor.

If I were a little boy, where would I bury my treasure?

He'd made sure to point out the tree on the map. The tree was important.

I circled the big oak. Little round marks punctured the bark on the north side, two in a row, at about even intervals.

"What is it?" Bern asked.

"This was a climbing tree. These are nail holes. They must've nailed planks to it and then someone pulled them off."

Bern took a running start and jumped. His hands caught the thick lower branch and he pulled himself up.

"Anything?"

"A hollow. Hold on."

He jumped back down, a canvas bag in his hands. He set it on the ground, and I gently pulled the strings open. A plastic pirate chest, the kind you could get in a craft store or online, the plastic made to look like dark aged wood. A skull sat where the lid met the box, with two plastic swords thrust through the skull's eyes. Smaller skulls decorated the surface.

Bern carefully pulled the swords free and opened the chest. I took the objects out one by one, carefully placing them on the canvas. A Swiss Army knife. A little velvet sack containing ten golden dollar coins, each with a different president. Three bullets. A yellow sports car. A flashlight. And a small cardboard jewelry box, the kind you would use to store a necklace.

Gently I opened it. A single USB stick lay on the velvet cushion. Inside the lid in a confident feminine cursive, someone had written, "Grandma's Secret."

I hugged the box. I felt like crying.

I DROVE THROUGH Houston's traffic.

"It's encrypted," Bern said, his fingers flying over the keyboard of his laptop.

"Can you break it?"

"I'll need time. It's not one of the commercially available cyphers. This is a custom job and it's very good."

"Call Rogan."

The car obediently dialed the number.

"Yes?" he answered.

"We have Olivia Charles' USB. We can meet their demands."

"What's on it?"

"It's encrypted. We're bringing it home, but Bern's uploading it to our home server as we speak."

"Good. Great."

"Okay, bye." I hesitated for a moment. Why not? "Love you."

There was a slight pause. "I love you too."

I hung up and grinned. The Scourge of Mexico just told me he loved me. I never got tired of hearing it.

"What's going to happen when this is over?" Bern asked.

"What do you mean?"

"What will happen with you and Rogan once this emergency is over?"

"Then we'll have to do the trials."

"You're avoiding the question."

"What exactly is the question, Bern?"

"Once all of these crises are over, what will happen with you and Rogan? Will you move with him into his house? Will you commute to work? Are you planning to marry him? Do you want to marry him?"

Well, that was unexpected. "You've been hanging out with Grandma Frida for too long. Are you worried I might take advantage of Rogan's virtue and shack up with him?"

"No, I'm worried that you have no plan. You're not thinking about any of these things, and you need to figure them out, not for us, but for yourself. What is it you want?"

That part was easy. I wanted to wake up next to Rogan every morning. Sometimes he would be Connor, sometimes he would be Mad Rogan, and I was good with that. I loved all of him.

"I don't know how it will turn out. I'm taking it one day at a time."

"We'll be fine," Bern said. "You don't need to worry about us."

"What do you mean?"

"I checked the accounts. We have enough money to survive on for about ten months. Maybe a year if we stretch. With no new cases coming in."

"I know that."

"You don't need to worry about money. We can wait on things like House security. Don't jump into something because you think that the family needs things, because we've become a House."

Thank you, Garen Shaffer. "It's not like that. I love him, Bern. I mean that."

"I was afraid of that," he said quietly. "I don't want you to be hurt."

"Thank you. Rogan won't hurt me."

"You weren't there when he was watching you with Garen. His face was flat. Cold. He stood there, without an expression on his face, and twisted solid metal into bows like it was Play-Doh."

"He didn't prevent me from going to that dinner. He never asked me not to go. When Garen walked into my office, he didn't storm over and try to throw him out. He put himself on a chain for my benefit, because as much as he wants to wrap me in bubble wrap and kidnap me to his lair, he knows I wouldn't stand for it. He's trying to make sure I see all choices available to us as an emerging House. As we were walking home, after he watched me and Garen, he told me one more time that from a genetic perspective, Garen was the better choice."

"Is Garen the better choice?"

"No. Because I don't love him. Even if love wasn't a factor, I would choose Rogan over him. When we were naked and freezing in David Howling's cistern, Rogan sacrificed himself for me. He fully expected to die. If Garen and I were in danger, and only one of us could make it, Garen would rationalize why he was the better choice to survive and leave me."

"Just be careful, Nevada."

It was too late for that. I was all in. "I will."

The phone rang. An unfamiliar number. I accepted. "You've reached Nevada Baylor."

"You wanted to talk," a cultured female voice said. "I will meet you at Takara in fifteen minutes. If you do not show, I'll know where we stand."

The call ended.

"Was that . . . ?" Bern blinked.

"That was Victoria Tremaine." When Linus Duncan made you a promise, he kept it. She'd picked Takara, the place where I often ate. It was a dig at me. *See, I know where you eat and what you like to order. I have your whole life under surveillance.*

I locked my jaw and took the exit.

"You can't be serious," Bern said.

"She tried twice and failed both times. She wants to talk, I'll talk to her."

"This isn't wise."

"If we don't talk, she'll just keep trying and we can't afford that. Eventually the girls and Leon have to go to school. We have to live normal lives. Our House status will protect us, but she's determined. I don't want her throwing wrenches into it."

"How do you know it's safe?"

"Because Linus Duncan arranged it. Do you want me to drop you off?"

"No." Bern pulled out his phone.

"What are you doing?"

"Texting Bug. I want to know what we're driving into. I want him to get eyes on the restaurant, and I want him to get us some backup."

TAKARA SERVED AS our go-to sushi place when we wanted a treat. Its listing said Asian Fusion, which in their case meant authentic Japanese cuisine and bulgogi on the menu. A quiet place, furnished in rich tones of brown and green with elegant but comfortable décor. When Rogan invited me to our first lunch, I decided to meet him there, because Takara sat right in the middle of a large shopping plaza off I-10 that had everything from Toys "R" Us and Academy Sports, to Olive Garden and H-E-B, the trademark Texas grocery store. Nonstop traffic, lots of people, and very little privacy. The perfect place to meet someone you don't trust.

Despite the two-thirds full parking lot, I recognized Victoria's car immediately. It was the only Mercedes with a human Rottweiler in a suit stationed by it. I parked at the opposite end of the parking lot.

"Do you want to come in?" I asked Bern.

"No. She doesn't want to see me. I'm going to stay here and keep the car running in case you come running out."

I handed the keys to him and stepped out of the vehicle. Victoria's bodyguard watched me as I crossed the parking lot. Twenty yards separated me from the door, and each step proved harder than the last. I could barely move. Finally my hand fastened around the door handle. Made it.

I took a deep breath and walked into Takara with my head held high.

The restaurant was empty, except for one patron. Victoria Tremaine sat in the back by the window. Almost the same table Rogan had chosen. She wore a beautifully tailored black suit. A stunning blue and turquoise shawl, gossamer thin and embroidered with peacock feathers, hung off her left shoulder. It gleamed, catching the light from the window, with what was probably real gold thread.

A hostess smiled at me.

"I'm with the lady in the shawl," I told her.

Her smile faltered slightly. "Please, this way."

"No need. I see her."

I marched to the table and checked the floor for traces of an arcane circle, just in case.

Victoria Tremaine scoffed.

"One can never be too careful." I sat in the chair.

A waiter approached us.

"Bring hot tea," Victoria ordered. "Green or black, whatever is best in the house. Two cups. Leave the kettle and keep it refilled. My granddaughter and I will be talking. Don't disturb us."

The waiter took off at a near run.

When I thought of *grandmother*, I thought of Grandma Frida, with her halo of platinum curls and the comforting smell of machine grease and gun oil that seemed to follow her everywhere. To me, that word meant safety and warmth. No matter how badly I screwed things up with Mom and Dad, Grandma Frida would always be there to listen, to make me laugh.

Victoria Tremaine couldn't be more different. She was taller and heavier than Grandma Frida, who was always bird-boned, but it was a formidable kind of heaviness. She was solid, as if the age accreted around her. Lines crossed her face. Unlike most aging wealthy, she hadn't bothered with either plastic surgery or illusion magic. Her hair, styled the last time I saw a recording of her, had been artfully chopped into a shorter cut that emphasized the severe lines of her face. I looked at her eyes and wished I hadn't. They were the exact blue of my father's. But my father's eyes had been kind, laughing, sometimes stern. Victoria's eyes were those of a raptor. She wasn't an evil witch, she was the aging queen. Instead of mellowing with age, she had only grown more dangerous, ruthless, and merciless.

"You look like James," she said.

"I also hold his values."

"And what are those?"

"I take care of my family, and I try to be a good person."

"A good person?" She leaned half an inch forward. "Do tell."

If we took that exit, we'd be at it for a while. "You wanted to speak to me. I'm here."

"I want you to drop this House Baylor nonsense. You belong to House Tremaine."

"No. Was there anything else?"

"You have no connections. You have no finances, no work-force, and you don't even know enough to realize how much you don't know."

"I'll learn."

The waiter brought the tea and placed it in front of us with two cups.

"At what cost? You have no idea how deep these waters are. We are related by blood. Blood is the only thing in this world you can trust."

The waiter poured the tea and took off.

"I know exactly how deep they are. I know that there is an organization which is attempting to destabilize Houston with the long-range goal of installing an authoritarian government based on the Roman Empire. I know that the man at the head of it calls himself Caesar. I know that this plan began with Adam Pierce. I know that Olivia Charles and David Howling were part of the same conspiracy, which also includes Vincent Harcourt and Alexander Sturm. David Howling told this to me before I snapped his neck. I know that this conspiracy repeat-edly targeted my family, going as far as to hire mercenaries to assault the warehouse where we live. They had orders to kill me and my sisters. I also know that you were the one who lifted the hex on the mind of a young man to find the artifact for Adam Pierce. And that you hexed Vincent Harcourt to keep him from spilling Caesar's secrets. You're in this conspiracy up to your elbows."

I took a breath. "So I'm a little confused. You tell me that I'm supposed to trust you because you and I are blood. When was blood the most important thing to you? Was it when the mer-cenaries arrived in the middle of the night to butcher us, when Howling iced the overpass while I was in the car behind him so

I would wreck and die, or when Adam tried to burn me to death in the middle of downtown?"

Victoria narrowed her eyes. "Clever girl."

I sipped my tea.

"You have no proof."

"I don't need proof. A truthseeker hexed Vincent's mind. There are only three truthseeker Houses in the US. I met Garen Shaffer and eliminated him as a suspect."

"You cracked Garen Shaffer?" Skepticism filled her voice.

"I didn't have to. He wanted to play a game, and he lost."

"He didn't cloak?"

"He did at some point, but I picked through it. Garen Shaffer is too focused on the welfare of his family and his corporate health to become involved in a conspiracy. He's quite content with things as they are. House Lin is up to their throats in government contracts." Rogan had shared that handy fact with me one night, while we discussed the future of House Baylor. "Involving themselves with the conspiracy would be too risky, as they're under heavy scrutiny. That leaves you. You fit the profile."

"Oh, so there is a profile?"

"Yes. Everyone involved comes from an old powerful House, at least four generations deep. Everyone is dissatisfied with the status quo. Pierce wanted to burn the world free of repercussions and constraints of the law. David Howling wanted to destroy his brother and take over his House. Olivia Charles hated to see her only daughter stuck in a loveless marriage because of her genes. She had reached the apex of her social climb, but it wasn't enough. She wanted the kind of status that would allow Rynda to pick and choose her husband among the elite of the elites, no matter her genes. Vincent Harcourt is a sadist, who is almost never given free rein by his House. Not sure what Sturm's issues are, but he definitely has some."

"And me?" Her voice was deceptively mild.

"Your only son ran away when he was still a teenager. You never had another child, probably because you can't. Without heirs, House Tremaine will die with you."

Victoria's face showed no emotion. Nothing at all, as if she were carved from rock.

"You looked for him and terrorized everyone you thought might be connected to his disappearance. But you went too far, and you were made to stop. You wanted the freedom of looking for your son. You wanted access to every database, every information bank, every person you decided to question without such pesky limitations as criminal code or rulings of the Assembly. You wanted more power. What you did is treason. My father wouldn't stand for it and neither will I. I want nothing to do with you."

I got up, turned away, and took a step.

"The middle one is a siren," Victoria said behind me. "Like her grandfather. But the youngest is neither a siren, nor truthseeker. She is something else. Something you can never let out."

Catalina and Arabella. I spun around.

Victoria pointed at the chair. "Sit."

I sat.

"I had twelve miscarriages. It runs in the family, something you may need to worry about in the future. We get one offspring per generation, and we count our lucky stars if the child survives. I was my mother's ninth and final pregnancy. She died when I was twelve. My father followed her two years later. I am House Tremaine. Alone. I wanted a child. The future of the House required it, but I wanted one. And that child would need to be a strong one. A weakling would be killed. The father had to be a Prime. I tried with three different Primes, each carefully chosen, cajoled, seduced, bribed. Whatever it took."

Her hands curled around her cup like talons. Old pain flared in her eyes.

"Why not marry?"

"Because the man I loved died three weeks into our engagement. He was a precog from the House Vidente. He never foresaw his own death. His business rival commissioned the hit. He was shot as we were walking out of the theater." She brushed her cheek. "It took me a long time to stop seeing the blood on my skin. It went away, finally, after I killed the last of them."

"You killed the entire rival House?"

"Yes. All of them, the husband, the wife, the children. Their dog."

Ice claws pierced my spine.

"For me, there was only one man. But my child required a father. I tried twelve times before I finally saw the writing on the wall. It had to be an in vitro fertilization. Do you have any idea how difficult it is to convince a Prime to donate his sperm? How afraid they are that their precious DNA will grow legs and take off into the world? You can seduce a man into your bed and tell him comfortable lies about how much you desire him and how your contraception is flawless, so he comes inside you, but ask him to ejaculate into a tube and you can't hide the true purpose of that request. They realize that you intend to have their child, and they run, because they're cowards."

I should have walked away, but I couldn't now. I had to know. "What did you do?"

"In the end, I found one. Formerly of House Molpe. They call themselves something else now. I suppose Molpe was too on the nose. The Office of Records is delighted to call Catalina's talent siren. They think they are clever and came up with something new, but the truth is, your grandfather's family called their magic that for generations."

"How did you convince him?"

She grimaced. "Money. They'd excised him. He was a siren, a true Prime, terrified to use his talent because it brought him nothing but misery."

"I thought the siren talent only manifested in females."

"They'd like you to think that, but no. Believe me, I checked. I had far too much riding on it. The father was the lesser hurdle. I also had to find a surrogate. She had to be a Prime. Anything less than a Prime, and I ran the risk of lessening the child's magic or her failing to carry to term. I couldn't afford either. Finding a Prime surrogate was impossible."

Oh no. Oh my God, no. "You didn't."

She smiled for the first time, a quick parting of lips and a flash of teeth. "I did."

"How?"

"Blackmail and money. Two of the oldest levers one presses when trying to move people to her purpose."

I just stared, horrified.

"Your father wasn't just special. He was one of a kind. There will never be another. I had them neuter her."

"What?"

"She's kept under constant sedation. That's the only way they can keep her contained. She never knew the pregnancy happened. The cost was astronomical, but it was worth it."

"That's horrible. You are horrible."

"I am."

She sipped her tea.

"Your father was a triple carrier. His own magic failed to express, which was expected. I never held that against him. I had enough magic for us both. His real value was in the children he would produce. I always had faith that the genes would sort themselves out. But to do that, to be a successor, he had to be shaped and molded. There were lessons he had to learn. Practical, useful lessons that would keep him alive after I was gone. He hated them, and he hated me for teaching them."

Considering what I just heard, those lessons wouldn't have been the gentle kind. "He left."

"He did. I underestimated him. He kept his spine so well-hidden. I pushed and pushed, expecting him to learn or break, but he did neither. He planned his escape and executed it so well that even all of my power couldn't find him. I was so proud. My son had outsmarted me. I should've expected it, but I was so focused on making sure he survived. I had so much to teach and I was in a hurry."

"You're a monster," I told her.

"An abomination. I believe that's the preferred term."

I flinched. She smiled again.

"I see you've run into it."

"I can't believe you did that."

"I would do it again."

"What?"

"Look how wonderful it turned out. James made not one but three—three!—children. All of them Primes. He did so well. House Tremaine will go on. All I have to do is convince you to see things my way. And we've just established that I can be very convincing. What will it take, Nevada?"

"The answer is still no."

"You will do as I say." The power of her magic clamped me. I shrugged it off.

"No, I won't."

Victoria laughed. She actually laughed. "You're everything I ever wanted."

My phone chimed. I checked it. A text from Bern. **Get out of there.**

I jumped to my feet.

Five men walked into the restaurant, guns drawn. "On the floor," the lead one ordered. The hostess dropped down. On my left, the two chefs behind the sushi bar hit the floor.

"Hands where I can see them," the leader ordered.

They hadn't fired, so they wanted me alive. I held my hands up and glared at Victoria. "Really?"

She was looking past me at the men. "What is the meaning of this?"

"Alexander says he's sorry," the lead man said. "He needs the girl. This is for the cause. He said you would understand."

"Oh no, my dears," my grandmother said. "This isn't about the cause. This is about family."

Magic snapped out of her. When I clamped people with my will, my magic turned into a vise, a net that smothered and bound them. Victoria turned hers into a blade and stabbed the leader with it. He cried out, a weak fading sound, his eyes rolled back into his skull, and he collapsed.

I jerked my Baby Desert Eagle out.

In the same instant, the man to the left of the leader yelped and clawed at his eyes. The man on the right fell to his knees and hit his head on the floor.

I got off four shots before I realized the two remaining targets stood completely still. My bullets ripped into their chests. Slowly, they toppled over. Five dead bodies lay on the floor. There was nobody left to kill.

Someone shoved me from behind. I stumbled forward. The sound of shattering glass cut at my ears, impossibly loud. I swung right, toward the broken window. A man stood with his rifle up, taking another shot. A Ford Explorer exploded out of the parking lot and smashed into him. The shooter went down, a rag doll under the wheels. Bern drove over him, his face bloodless, reversed and backed over the body.

I turned to Victoria. A dark wet stain spread through Victoria's shoulder. She'd pushed me out of the way. The bullet with my name on it had torn into her instead.

"You need an ambulance."

She grimaced. "I'll be fine. I have a private physician."

"You'll bleed out. You need paramedics now." I grabbed my phone to dial 911. "Why did you do it?"

"Because you're my granddaughter."

My phone died. What the hell, I had fully charged it in the car . . .

"Wait . . ." Victoria turned pale, looking at something past me.

I glanced over my shoulder. A darkness spread through the restaurant, expanding from the entrance, climbing over the walls, claiming the space. An ancient darkness that took me into its maw and made me still.

Michael from the Office of Records walked into the restaurant. He still wore the sharp suit and a crisp shirt, blindingly white against his tattooed neck. His hands burned with blue fire.

He didn't look like a gangster at a funeral today. He looked like the twenty-first century Grim Reaper.

"I didn't break the rules," Victoria squeezed out through her clenched teeth. Sweat broke out on her forehead. She strained, locking her teeth again.

Nothing happened.

I tried to grab hold of my magic. It flowed out of me. The darkness pounced and devoured it. It hurt. The pain ripped a gasp out of me. Oh, it hurt.

Michael held up the phone. On it the Keeper of Records smiled. "But you have, twice indirectly and now in public. It is time for punishment, Victoria. So sorry."

Michael raised his right hand. The blue fire leaped across the space and splashed onto my grandmother.

Victoria Tremaine screamed.

The blue fire poured on.

Victoria slid off the chair and dropped to the floor. They weren't just hurting her. They were killing her.

I heard my own voice. "Stop! Please stop!"

"Michael," the Keeper of Records said.

The blue flames ebbed. Victoria strained to breathe, her skin ashen.

"Are you asking us to stop, Ms. Baylor?"

"Yes."

"Why?"

"She's my grandmother. She saved me. I don't want to start our House with her death."

The Keeper of Records considered it. "Is it a formal request, Ms. Baylor?"

"Yes."

"The Office of Records will grant it, provided you will grant us a favor in return in a place and time of our choosing."

"Don't take it," Victoria squeezed out, her hand on her chest, blood dripping from her fingers.

"I agree."

"Very well," the Keeper said. "We will see you at trials, Ms. Baylor."

The phone went black.

Michael opened his mouth. "A mistake."

He turned around and walked away, taking the darkness with him.

In the distance sirens wailed, getting closer.

An ambulance shot into the parking lot and screeched to a halt. Paramedics ran out, carrying a stretcher through the broken window.

I crouched by Victoria. "If I peer under Vincent's hex, will I find your name there?"

"Yes."

"You should run, Grandmother. I won't shield you from the consequences."

She bared her teeth at me. "I'm too old to run. Do what you have to do."

My phone flared into life and screamed at me. Bug.

I swiped my fingers across it to answer.

"Get on the freeway! Get on Katy now!" Bug screamed into the phone.

"What's going on?"

Something thumped and Catalina's voice filled the phone. "Vincent kidnapped Kyle and Matilda! He has Matilda!"

I sprinted to the car.

CHAPTER 12

"WHICH WAY ON Katy?" I barked into the phone.

"West!" Bug answered.

Bern made a hard right, cutting off a Honda. The driver laid on the horn, but we were already speeding through the entrance lane. It was 11:00 a.m. Rush hour traffic. Bern merged into the densely packed lane, and we chugged forward at a breathtaking thirty miles per hour.

Adrenaline pounded through me. My skin felt hot, my whole body wound so tightly, I was like a loaded gun just waiting to pull the trigger. He took the children. That fucking scumbag. I'd twist his head off.

"What am I looking for?" I put the phone on speaker.

"A white truck," Bug said.

You've got to be kidding me. "Make, model?"

"Chevy Silverado. Anywhere from 2011 to 2015."

The second most common truck in Texas. "That's it?"

"All I've got to work with is a shot from the side."

I craned my neck. My vision, kicked by adrenaline, could see three white trucks. Yelling at Bug about it would do no good. He was doing the best he could.

"What happened?"

"Edward showed up and wanted to talk to Rynda. Catalina vol-

unteered to watch the kids. Kyle, Jessica, and Matilda wanted to
play in the evac basement. We set up a fort for them in there so
they wouldn't be scared during the tornado drill. Jessica wanted
to go to the bathroom, and Catalina took her, because Jessica was
too shy to go upstairs by herself. Kurt was watching the kids.
That dick fucker summoned something that could dig. It tunneled under the basement, broke through the floor, and grabbed
Kyle and Matilda."

Cold gripped me. "Kurt?"

"He didn't make it."

Damn it. Damn it, damn it, damn it. Poor Kurt. Poor Leon.

"Catalina found him when they got back down there. By the
time it got to me, all I caught was Vincent speeding off from
Hammerly onto Sam Houston. I tracked him all the way to I-10,
then lost him."

"You sure it was him?" Bern asked.

"I saw the white cat in the window."

Matilda never went anywhere without that cat.

We passed Addick's Road.

"Where is Rogan?" I asked.

"Look above you," Bug said.

I dipped my head to look out the windshield. A helicopter was
flying low overhead.

"That tunnel would've taken awhile," I thought out loud.
"Vincent had to have watched us drill for tornados. He would've
tunneled under there in advance and waited. He knew the exact
moment." All of which meant Vincent Harcourt or his people
were watching us, or someone betrayed us. Rogan would just love
that.

"Good strategy with the truck," Bern observed in a detached
way.

"Yes. Vincent knew he wouldn't be able to outrun Rogan, so he didn't try." Even if Vincent had a helicopter of his own, nothing would stop Rogan from getting into striking range.

"Why Matilda?" Bern wondered.

"Because Jessica wasn't there. Whatever creatures he sent probably knew they had to grab the boy and the girl, so they did."

Minutes dripped by. Bern wove in and out of traffic with inch-narrow margins of error. Asking Bug if he had anything was pointless.

"Think he is foolish enough to take the HOV lane?" I asked.

"I wouldn't," Bern said. "He'd be trapped in it."

A row of white metal poles separated the High Occupancy Vehicle lane from the rest of the traffic. The HOV traffic moved faster. Fewer cars, more visibility. I'd hide in the slow-moving right lane or in the middle. I'd want to exit if things got too hot.

The helicopter veered left.

"What's going on?" I said into the phone.

"A white truck took the exit to Barker Cypress. The camera caught something white in the window." Bug's voice vibrated with tension.

"Should I take the exit?" Bern asked.

To exit or not? Swinging off the highway onto the side street was a good strategy. It would get Vincent away from the focus of our search.

"Nevada?"

The exit waited just ahead. I would get off the highway in his place, but I wouldn't do it with the chopper overhead. Too risky. And if it was the right truck, Rogan would handle it.

"I need an answer," Bern said.

"No. Stay in the lane."

We crept forward. This was awful, even for Houston. Something had to be going on ahead, roadwork, an accident, some disaster to account for this crawl.

"The truck sped up," Bug reported. "They are chasing it down."

Greenhouse Road.

"I'm getting the feed now. It's the right truck."

If Bug said it was the right truck, it was the right truck. He had one of the best visual recognition capacities on the planet.

It just didn't feel right.

The Fry Road exit veered off ahead.

Bern looked at me. I shook my head. We would stay put.

I wanted to run, punch, scream, do something, but instead I had to sit. We rolled forward.

A blue flash dashed by me on the shoulder. I stuck my head out of the open window. Zeus.

"Follow the cat! Bern!"

He swung the car onto the shoulder and barreled down the lane to the symphony of outraged honking, between the line of cars and the waist-high concrete barrier bordering the edge of the highway.

The blue tiger charged down the highway, massive legs pumping, its tail curling up and straightening with each leap. The fringe of tentacles spread upright from its neck like a glowing corona with a turquoise star on each end of the ray. If I lived a hundred years, I'd never forget this.

Zeus leaped, forward and to the left, and landed on top of a car in the middle lane. His paws slid. He teetered, jumped forward, and crouched in the back of a black Ford 150 truck. Bern screeched to a halt.

Zeus' fur stood on end. His muzzle wrinkled. His lips rose in a ferocious snarl, revealing curved dagger fangs. The fringe pulsed with crimson. Magic thumped. A pulse of crimson ripped into the cab, biting at it. The Ford tore out of the lane, ramming into a blue Honda Civic. The impact pushed the Civic out of its lane, blocking us. The massive Ford screeched free and swung onto the shoulder and roared off with Zeus snarling.

Crap.

Bern laid on the horn. The woman in the Civic waved her arms, spinning around. Stuck.

"Bug, it's not a white Chevy, it's a black Ford!" I stuck my head out of the window and screamed. "Get out of the way!"

The woman flipped me off.

"Get out of the way!"

People behind the Civic honked. The woman picked up her cell phone. Damn it. She would sit right here until the cops arrived.

Bern laid on the horn.

Something thudded against our car. The Ford Explorer rocked and groaned, accepting a massive weight. I spun around and saw something dark in the rear window. The top of the cab bent inward. I pulled my gun out.

An enormous shaggy paw lowered onto the hood, then another, and then a giant bear belly blocked out the sun. Sergeant Teddy slid off our roof and landed in front of the car. He lumbered over to the Civic.

The woman dropped her phone.

The huge grizzly leaned against the Civic and pushed. The small car slid back into its lane. Sergeant Teddy took a running start and landed on our hood. The Ford creaked. The grizzly slid over us and landed on the pavement, his huge head taking up the entire rear window. Claws scraped against metal. The hatchback rose and Sergeant Teddy climbed into the back. Even with the third row of seats stowed away, he barely fit. Suddenly the car was full of bear.

Bern turned slowly and looked at me, his eyes as big as saucers.

"They're getting away!" I yelled at him. "Drive!"

He shook himself and stepped on the gas. The Ford jerked forward. We sped down the shoulder.

Ahead, crimson magic flashed again.

"Bug?" I resisted the urge to shake the phone. "Bug?"

". . . Yes?"

"Black Ford F-150, driving on the shoulder of I-10 just west of Fry Road exit. Get eyes on it."

There was a pause. "Drone launching now. It will take a few minutes from the helicopter."

The highway climbed as the road picked up altitude for an overpass. If we went over the side now, it was all over.

Ahead the black truck veered wildly, scraped the side of the concrete barrier, bounced off, skimmed the line of cars, and slammed on the brakes. Zeus flattened himself in the cab. He was trying to shake off the tiger.

"There are children in that truck," Bern growled.

"I don't think he cares."

Gun shots popped like firecrackers. The deep roar of a pissed-off carnivore answered.

Bern sped up to forty-five miles per hour. Our Explorer grazed the concrete on the right with a sickening screech. He straightened it out.

The distance between us shrank.

"Almost got him," Bern said, his face savage.

The sign for the exit for Westgreen Road came up ahead.

"Take the exit," I prayed.

The truck laid on the horn. The line of cars parted and he tore through the gap.

"Damn it."

Bern laid on the horn. Sergeant Teddy roared. The cars slammed on their brakes and we shot through the same gap. I stuck my finger into my left ear and shook it to clear the ringing out.

The Ford was only a few dozen yards ahead now, but picking up speed. It grazed the cars on the left and bounced into the concrete barrier. My heart skipped a beat.

The barrier held.

The truck looked old, the back of the bed chipped. Likely stolen. Stolen truck probably meant it didn't have the fancy run-flat tires.

"Keep it steady." I leaned out of the window.

"Kids," Bern reminded me.

"I remember."

Either I shot the tires now, or they would wreck and go off the highway. I aimed at the right rear tire and squeezed the trigger.

The shot popped off.

"Did it hit?" Bern asked.

"It did."

At that distance and at the relatively low speed, .40 caliber ammo would punch through the tire and likely exit on the other side. The tire would gradually deflate.

Seconds ticked by.

The tire went flat. The black truck slowed slightly.

"I have eyes on the black truck," Bug said. "The children are in it. I repeat, the children are in it."

Another burst of red magic flared in the truck bed. Zeus wasn't done yet.

Mason Road exit. He didn't take that one either.

"The chopper is coming," Bug said.

"ETA?" I asked.

"At least four minutes."

A hell of a lot could happen in the next four minutes. It would only take a second for the black truck to hit something and roll over that concrete barrier to the ground far below. The image of a crushed, overturned truck flashed before me. We couldn't let it happen.

Sergeant Teddy growled low.

"If we go any faster, we'll wreck," I told him. "Or he'll wreck."

"Do you understand what he says?"

"No, but I can guess. We have to keep the kids safe. We just need to follow him."

Frontage Road exit flashed by. An electronic sign offered words glowing with orange. Exit Closed Ahead. An orange sign followed. Right Lane Closed Ahead.

Crap.

Road Work Ahead.

Traffic Fines Double.

A white and orange roadwork barrier went flying ahead. The black truck tore through the flimsy plastic barricades and shot onto the overpass exit to the Grand Parkway. What the hell was Vincent doing?

Ahead the black truck turned right sharply and screeched to a stop, blocking the lane, the passenger side toward us.

A man jumped out of the truck, holding Matilda with one hand and a gun in the other. She was still clutching her white cat.

Bern slammed on the brakes. The Ford Explorer slid to a stop. I jumped out of the car before it even stopped moving and aimed my gun. "Don't move!"

"I'll blow her fucking head off!" The man aimed the gun at Matilda's head.

Matilda dropped the cat. The white beast yowled and lunged at the man's legs, clawing his way up. The gunman cried out and spun, trying to shake the little cat free. Matilda fell to the ground. The cat ripped at him in a feral frenzy, writhing too fast to give me a clear shot. Zeus leaped out of the truck bed and crushed the man beneath his bulk. The huge maw gaped open and the saber teeth sank deep into the side of the man's neck. His feet drummed the ground and went limp.

Zeus spun toward us, his muzzle bloody.

Sergeant Teddy charged past us, heading toward the truck.

Zeus snarled, grabbed Matilda by her sweater as if she were a kitten, and sprinted past us, back the way we came. The white cat chased them.

I ran to the truck. Bern and I reached it at the same time. Behind us the thumping noise of the helicopter rocked the air.

Magic punched me, a terrifying avalanche of power. I struggled to draw a breath and couldn't. Bern and I gasped at the same time.

I craned my neck and looked around the truck's rear. Sergeant Teddy was backing up toward me one foot at a time, snarling. In front of him Vincent stood in the middle of an amplification circle, clutching Kyle to him. Behind them the overpass split, one exit going to North Grand Parkway, the other to the South. Construction vehicles and concrete barriers blocked both. The only way out was on foot.

Above Vincent an angry darkness churned, shot through with purple lightning, growing larger. It flashed with bright purple and tore. A giant spilled into existence. Upright, vaguely humanoid, and completely hairless, it towered above us, its cloven feet bigger than the black truck. Its skin, the color of duct tape, stretched too tightly across its frame and formed what looked like rocky outcroppings on its shoulders and the top of its round head. Black, three-foot-long claws tipped its paw-hands. The creature had no nose, only a wide gash of a mouth, filled with long slender teeth and two slanted red eyes, glowing as if lit by fire from within.

It had to be seventy feet tall.

The huge hand reached down. The claws caught the corpse of

the dead kidnapper, pulled it up, and the creature tossed it into its mouth. Bones crunched. It looked down onto the sea of cars and took an enormous step. The overpass shook.

It was heading down to the traffic below and there wasn't a damn thing I could do about it. I glanced back. People were running between the cars. The creature focused on them. Its mouth gaped open, and an eerie, high-pitched shriek rang out.

Rogan's chopper hovered above the abandoned vehicles. The quick staccato of a machine gun echoed. The bullets ripped into the creature. It didn't even notice.

There was nothing for Rogan to throw at it. Chucking cars at it would be like throwing pebbles at a bull.

Rogan's chopper swung to the side, where an empty field and the big rectangular building of a Cinemark theater bordered the highway.

The creature took another massive step, crushing several cars that had been waiting to merge into the middle lane, and shrieked again.

"Nevada!" Bern screamed at me. "What do we do?"

I don't know.

"Nevada!"

I never felt so helpless in my whole life.

Something fell from Rogan's chopper, a dark flash that plummeted to the earth and exploded into a colossal shaggy shape. Oh no. No . . .

A monster landed by Cinemark. Stocky, huge, covered with long strands of jet-black fur, with muscled arms armed with talons, and a blunt head, shielded by a bone carapace. Two thick horns shielded the sides of its head, curving forward as if someone had taken two enormous ram horns and turned them sideways. Thick meat-eater's fangs filled its mouth. Its two round eyes glowed with yellow.

"Fuck!" Bern spat.

People stopped running and gaped. Everyone had seen the footage. Everyone recognized this.

The Beast of Cologne that was my sister roared a deafening challenge, lunged at the grey creature, and jerked it off the overpass into the field. The creature fell. An earthquake shudder shook the overpass. The red *C* in Cinemark fell off and crashed down.

The grey thing clawed at Arabella, trying to fight back. She landed on top of it, a huge, muscled, shaggy nightmare filled with rage, and ripped at it in a frenzy, punching, smashing, clawing, throwing wet chunks of it wherever they would land. The terrible temper volcano that powered Arabella had erupted and there was no stopping it.

Mom would kill us. Mom would kill all of us. We could never go home.

The grey thing screeched again, desperate now. My sister squatted on it, clamped its head with one arm, its right shoulder with another, and bit its neck. I didn't want to see, but I couldn't look away. She gnawed at it, severing muscle and tendon. The grey giant flailed, kicking feebly, weaker and weaker. My sister bit one last time, jerked the head she had chewed off into the air, tossed it behind her, and roared.

And dozens of people recorded it on cell phones.

Arabella rocked back, sat on her butt, stuck her claws into her mouth, and pulled a long fleshy strand out. She spat it, her mouth wrinkling, spat again, her muzzle twisted as if she'd just bitten into slimy fruit.

Under control. Everything was under control. She hadn't lost it. I turned. A few feet away Vincent stood frozen, his mouth hanging open.

I raised the gun. He saw me and jerked Kyle in front of him.

He was holding an enormous handgun, so big it looked like a movie prop. The barrel had to be ten inches long.

He pointed the gun at me and began backing up.

The concrete barriers behind him slid together, cutting off the narrow space the workers used as a clear path. A heavy construction vehicle scraped across the pavement, joining the barriers. I didn't have to look to know Rogan was walking up the overpass behind me.

Vincent turned pale and chanced a quick glance behind him. Yes, you're trapped.

Rogan loomed next to me, a handful of coins hanging in the air in front of him. I'd seen him launch these before at a near-bullet speed.

The coins didn't move. He'd come to the same conclusion I did. If we had any chance at all against Sturm, we'd need Vincent alive.

"Stay where you are," Vincent called out.

"It's over," Rogan said. "Put down the gun."

"Don't come any closer or I'll shoot you." The barrel of the enormous cannon trembled.

"You're holding a Magnum BFR," I told him. "Big Frame Revolver. Otherwise known as Big Fucking Gun. It weighs over five pounds loaded and has horrible recoil. The only way to fire it is to grip it with both hands and brace yourself. Your hand is shaking from the weight. If you try to squeeze the trigger, you'll miss and hit yourself in the head with your own gun. Then I'll shoot you where it counts."

Vincent gripped the gun tighter, which only made the barrel dance more.

"You'll hit the kid," Vincent squeezed out.

"I won't. I'm Magus Sagittarius."

Vincent shifted his grip and pointed his cannon at Kyle's head.

"The child is keeping you alive," Rogan said. His voice was ice. "Kill him, and I will kill you on this overpass, slowly, piece by piece."

Vincent swallowed.

"There are two ways this can go," Rogan said. "Let go of the child and you live. Harm the boy and you die."

"Decide quickly," I told him. "You killed Kurt. I liked Kurt."

Vincent swallowed again and opened his hand. The oversized revolver clattered to the ground.

"Let go of the boy," Rogan said.

Vincent squeezed Kyle to him. His eyes went wild. He looked like he would dash to the nearest edge and jump over it. If he sprinted, I had to shoot him in the head. Anything else was too risky for Kyle.

Rogan's voice snapped like a whip. "I don't have all day, Harcourt!"

Vincent let go of Kyle. The boy ran to me and I picked him up. Rogan strode toward Vincent. The summoner took a few steps back, put his hands up, and took a wild swing at Rogan. The punch missed him by a mile. Rogan reached out, almost casually. His fingers locked on Vincent's wrist. He twisted and Vincent bent over, his eyes watering. Rogan grabbed Vincent's shirt with his other hand and half dragged, half walked him down to us.

Out of the corner of my eye, I saw Arabella stalk to the Frontage Road exit curving below us. A familiar silver Range Rover pulled up. My sister shrank into her normal human self, naked and covered in arcane blood. The passenger door opened. She jumped inside and the Range Rover sped down the curve of the road, heading north.

"Thank you," I told Rogan.

"We need to talk later," he said.

Rogan's people handcuffed Vincent and put him into the helicopter. Rogan and I watched him being loaded. Bern backed our Ford down the overpass. Sergeant Teddy climbed inside.

In the distance a cacophony of sirens shrieked and wailed, getting closer.

Another from Rogan's fleet of Range Rovers arrived with Troy behind the wheel. Rogan held the passenger door open for me. His face told me that he expected me to get into the damn car and if I didn't he would put me in it. A storm was gathering on the horizon and I was about to be in the epicenter of it.

Bern saw the hurricane too. "I'll take Teddy home."

I got into the car and buckled Kyle in at the center of the seat. Rogan got in on the other side, Troy stepped on the gas, and we were off.

We rode in silence for almost five minutes.

"The Beast of Cologne?" Rogan finally said.

"Yes."

"How?" The word cut like a knife. "How can she do this, how long, how many times, how many people know?"

"She can do this because it's her magic. She has done it since she was a baby. She has transformed a total of twelve times. Nobody knows except the family and her pediatrician."

"So she can control it."

"Yes. It was touch and go between the ages of eleven and fourteen, but she's slowly maturing. We're cautiously optimistic she will achieve complete control by the time her hormones settle down, which should be around twenty or so."

"Cautiously . . ." Rogan choked off the word. His blue eyes were hard like a glacier. "Is it genetic?"

"Yes."

"Is there a possibility of your children manifesting it?"

"Yes."

"How?"

"Victoria Tremaine couldn't carry a child to term, so she paid off a Prime to obtain his sperm, had her egg fertilized and implanted into Misha Marcotte, who is being kept under sedation somewhere in Europe. Misha was the only Prime available to be a surrogate. My father carried the truthseeker gene from his mother, the siren talent from his father, and, apparently, the Beast of Cologne abilities from the surrogate. I don't know how it's possible, since talents are supposed to be genetic, and none of Misha's genetic material would've made it into his DNA, but here it is. We are his daughters. We all carry his legacy."

Rogan squeezed his eyes shut for a long moment. Well, here it was. His head would explode.

"Is there anything else you would like to tell me?"

"I forgot to mention that Victoria Tremaine also knows. She admitted it when she and I had lunch together earlier today."

He stared at me.

"The Office of Records sent Michael to kill her, but I talked them out of it, because she's my grandmother and because she pushed me out of the way when one of Sturm's thugs tried to kill me. She was bleeding from her shoulder and I couldn't bring myself to watch Michael fry her to death. I now owe them a favor."

Rogan's face snapped into an impenetrable mask.

"Connor . . ."

He held up his hand. I shut up. He clearly needed a minute.

Rogan looked at me, opened his mouth to say something, clamped it shut, and shook his head wordlessly. A terrible internal struggle was taking place.

"Use your words," Kyle suggested helpfully.

Rogan glared at him for a second, then looked back at me. "It's nice that you saved your grandmother, but if she ever comes for you, I'll kill her."

"She won't hurt me. I'm family."

Rogan made a noise that might have been a snarl or a growl, it was hard to tell, and pulled out his phone.

"Good afternoon, Keeper," he said. "Due to unprecedented circumstances, I, as a witness, urge the Office to move up the Baylor trials. Ms. Baylor and her family will need the immunity immediately. . . . Yes, related to the I-10 incident. . . . Yes." He turned to me. "Will Arabella register? Say yes."

I hesitated.

"If she demonstrates ability to reason during the trial, her status as a Prime of your House will protect her from federal authorities. Otherwise, they will take her into custody under the Danger to Public Act," Rogan said.

"Yes." She would be overjoyed.

"She will register. . . . Sealed demonstration. . . . Thank you."

He hung up and pulled up another number. "Mother? I have a favor to ask. I'm sending a young girl to you by car. Could you please keep her hidden until I come to get her? . . . No, she isn't my secret love child. I'll explain later. Thank you."

He dialed a third number. I heard Sergeant Heart's crisp hello.

"We're about to get federal visitors. Lock it down. Nobody goes in, nobody goes out, nobody knows anything."

He hung up and looked at me. "No more surprises. At least for the next twelve hours."

"I'll do my best."

"You had one job," my mother fumed. "One."

Bern, Catalina, and I stood in the kitchen. Grandma Frida sat at the table, resting her chin on her hands, her expression grave. Leon had stormed off because I refused to let him kill Vincent.

"You had to keep her hidden. You know she has no sense. And you failed."

326 • ILONA ANDREWS

I waited. There was no point in talking.

Mom glared at us. "Do you have anything to say for yourselves?"

I opened my mouth. Catalina beat me to it. "You let her get into the helicopter."

Mom blinked. Catalina almost never got into a fight with anyone except Arabella and me.

"I was taking care of Jessica. You let her run out of the house and climb into the helicopter, Mom. What were we supposed to do? Was I supposed to telepathically make her behave? Were Bern and Nevada supposed to magically make her stop while they were being shot at?"

Mom opened her mouth.

"No," Catalina said. "I'm sick and tired of everyone making excuses for her. She's special. She's under a lot of pressure. She's a spoiled brat who's used to getting her way. She acts like a five-year-old and you want all of us to compensate. Well, she's too old for us to do that. I'm not going to listen to any more of this. I'm done. Seriously, I'm fucking done."

She turned and marched away. A door slammed somewhere. The pressure of the upcoming trials was getting to her.

"What is happening to this family . . ." Grandma Frida murmured.

"Arabella did what you taught her to do," I said to Mom. "She turned, took care of the problem, saved hundreds of people, turned back, and split. She didn't linger, she didn't show off, and she didn't pose for any photos. She did her job and vanished."

"Once she got into the helicopter, there was no way to stop her," Bern said.

My mother landed into a chair. She looked defeated and old, older than I'd ever seen her. It was like being stabbed in the heart. I came over and crouched by her. "Mom?"

She looked at me, glassy-eyed.

"It will be okay."

Mom didn't answer.

"Mom? You're scaring me."

"I just can't stop it," she said softly. "I've done everything I can and I can't keep you all safe."

I took her hands. "It will be okay. I promise."

"How?"

"The trials are being moved up. She'll do a sealed trial, where she will be in front of a small group of witnesses. She'll demonstrate reason during the trial, which we all know won't be a problem. She's still herself when she transforms. She just can't speak. Once we qualify as a House, she will be protected under Emerging House Law."

Mom stared at me.

"Emerging House Law states that no member of the House can be pressed into military service or be held by federal, state, or local authorities absent of clear evidence of committing a criminal act," Bern said. "If we make it as a House, they can't touch her."

I wasn't sure she heard us. "Mom?"

"What if they get her before the trials?"

"They won't," I told her. "She's with Rogan's mother. They're not going to violate the privacy of House Rogan. They have no cause and no proof. If they try, she will make them regret it."

"It will be on TV," Grandma Frida said.

"Let it be on TV. I trust Rogan and his mother to keep her safe. It will be fine."

My phone chimed. I answered it.

"I'm sorry to interrupt," Rivera said. "We're ready for you."

"I'll be right there."

I hung up. "I have to go now, but I'll be back. Don't worry." I hugged my mother and went outside. Crossing the street to Rogan's HQ only took a few seconds, but I wasn't going to his HQ. I was going to the one-story building behind it. Before Rogan bought it, it held a printing shop, and some traces of it still remained, including the granite counter at the front, now manned by one of Rogan's employees, a tall, golden-haired woman. I nodded to her and went past her, through the heavy door to a large rectangular room. It had been gutted and painted with charcoal-black chalkboard paint. In the center of the room, Vincent sat, handcuffed to a chair. He saw me and sneered. Apparently, he was back to his old self.

At the wall closest to the door, Bug perched in a chair, with two screens in front of him. A row of chairs had been set up. Rogan sat in one, Heart in another, Rivera in the third, and Rynda in the fourth. Her spine was ramrod straight. Cornelius sat in the fifth chair, Matilda in his lap. His sister, Diana, the Head of House Harrison, sat next to him. Their gazes were fixed on Vincent. Cornelius' eyes glowed blue, Diana's green, and when Matilda glanced at me, an eerie amber light rolled over her irises.

Between the chairs and Vincent, two pieces of chalk waited for me.

I walked over and picked one up.

"What do you think you're going to do with that, huh?" Vincent asked. "You don't even know how to use it properly. We know all about you. No training. No education."

My magic spilled out.

"Poor little cast-off from the family tree with a dead daddy. Your dad was a piece of shit. The two go together in your family."

I drew a simple amplification circle on the floor.

"Ugh. Are your fingers broken? Rogan, come and do this for her. This is embarrassing."

"Sir?" Bug murmured.

I stepped into the circle and concentrated. The room dimmed, the figure of Vincent in a chair dimming with it. A vague silver glow flared in his head—the hex reacting with my magic.

I needed to get a closer look. I needed to dive deeper, all the way into the place I had once reached when Olivia Charles attacked me.

"Nevada?" Rogan asked next to me.

"Yes?" I concentrated on the glow.

"Your family would like to watch. Your mother, sisters, cousins, and grandmothers."

"That's fine."

"Both your grandmothers," he said.

His voice dragged me back to the real world. I looked up. Bug had set a laptop on the desk to the right. On it, Victoria Tremaine reclined in a plush chair, her arm in a sling.

Behind me someone drew a sharp breath and I knew it was my mother.

"That's fine."

I crouched. I needed more power. I drew a second, smaller circle, joining the first, pivoted and added a third, the same size as the second, then a fourth. The tetrad, also known as Mother and Triplets. I had found it in one of the books Rogan had secretly sent me a while ago. It wasn't that much more powerful than the perfect simplicity of the usual amplification circle, but when I practiced with it, it let me hone my magic with the precision of a scalpel. I would need a scalpel today if I hoped to break my grandmother's hex and leave enough of Vincent intact to interrogate him.

"You're a fucking traitor," Vincent snarled at Victoria.

She smiled like a deep-water shark.

I fed power into the circle. It pulsed pale blue. The current of magic punched me, clear and strong. I concentrated on the hex, letting everything else fade.

The light grew dim.

Dimmer.

Dimmer.

The darker it grew, the brighter was the glow in Vincent's mind. A pattern began to form in the glowing haze. A spark flickering in a straight line, like a glowing silver thread, as thin as a hair.

I fed more power into the circle. The room grew completely dark. More sparks, more silver hairs.

A bit more power.

"She's committing too much," Rynda warned.

"She can handle it," Rogan said.

I was falling, falling down through a black well toward the glowing hex at the bottom.

A little more power.

"Rogan!" Rynda's voice spiked somewhere far away.

"You're distracting her," Cornelius said gently.

I crashed to the bottom, somehow landing on my feet. The hex glowed in front of me. It was an arcane circle, a dazzling, glowing creation of pure power woven into gossamer lace. Its complexity made me dizzy.

How do I pull it apart?

The magic flowed through the pattern, a complete circuit. Interrupt the flow, and it would collapse. What would happen . . . ?

It wasn't a single circle, but three, layered on top of each other. Within the second layer, nine triangles stretched toward the center. If I attacked, trying to force my will over Vincent's, the top circle would collapse onto the center, the triangles would point down, like dagger blades, puncture the bottom layer, and the power of the entire hex would then surge into the daggers. It would plunge down and stab into Vincent's psyche. It was a genius trap, impossible to disarm.

Breaking it was out of the question.

Could I shift the pattern? Maybe I could pull it apart . . .

Too risky.

If I broke the hex at any point, the collapse was inevitable.

When David Howling trapped us inside an arcane circle, Rogan had altered it. A hex was basically a circle. A really complicated, difficult to understand circle, drawn with pure magic in someone's mind. Could I draw on it?

A dull pain came from somewhere deep inside me. I had expended too much magic and I would likely need more.

"This is too much for her." Mom's voice. "You're asking her to take apart something that . . . woman built with years of experience."

"She's right."

Shaffer. Who let him in?

"I can feel the hex in his mind. It is exceedingly complex. It's a trap and she's too inexperienced to realize it." Shaffer again.

"But is it breakable?" Rynda asked.

"No," Shaffer said. "It's a perfect trap. Get her out of there before she overextends."

"She's fine," Rogan said. "She knows her limits."

They all needed to shut up.

The hex was too complicated to alter. There were loops within loops, twisting magic onto itself.

But I didn't need to alter it. All I needed to do was shield Vincent's mind from the daggers.

I pulled on my magic. It came from within me, stretching into a thin line glowing with silvery blue. I slipped it under the bottom layer and began to weave. A direct shield wouldn't work, no more than a blunt approach would've worked with Vincent's father. There was too much power in the hex. I had to redirect the energy of the spell away once it collapsed. I had to . . . Yes. That would work.

"If you want your daughter to live, you will stop this," Shaffer said. "Look at him. He doesn't care if she lives or dies, as long as he gets what he wants. I care. I want to marry her."

"Nevada knows what she's doing." Mom's voice. Cold. She didn't like him.

The pattern grew more complex, spreading under the hex like a snowflake, unfurling from the center.

An insistent pounding began in my head, a sure sign that my magic resources had grown low. I was walking a tightrope.

"Have all of you lost your minds?" Shaffer demanded.

"Will someone shut that weakling up?" Victoria snapped.

The last stroke of my bottom layer. It was all or nothing.

I molded my magic into a blade and severed the top layer of the hex.

The blackness broke. I was back in the room, with the glowing pattern in front of me. I had drawn it in chalk on the floor, a circle of rivulets with nine points within it locked in the spirals. The ghostly radiance of Victoria's hex flared above it, an echo of the real hex.

Someone gasped.

The top layer collapsed, flowing into the second, like sand or water spilling from a hole in the bottom of a vase. Its power flowed into the triangles, bending them down, feeding into them, stretching them into razor-sharp blades.

The second layer collapsed into the third. The daggers punctured through it and met the soft rivulets of my circle. Their points touched the nine spots where the lines twisted together. They flared with silver, channeling power out. The silver glow spread through the blue, overpowering it. The lines grew thicker, channeling the magic. The spirals I had made rose, fed by the hex's collapse, stretching higher and higher, glowing, beautiful, unfurling as they grew. An ethereal carnation bloomed in Vincent's mind, its nine petals delicate and shimmering with magic.

It glowed for a long moment and vanished, the hex's power expended.

A vicious sound echoed through the silence and I realized it was Grandmother Victoria laughing.

I turned. Shaffer was on his feet. His hands shook. He stared at me, turned, and fled.

Rogan smiled at me. There was pride on Mom's face, shock on Grandma Frida's, and respect on Catalina's. Leon looked slightly freaked out, while Bern acted like nothing had happened. Rynda sat very still.

I turned back to Vincent. He swallowed.

My magic snapped out and gripped him in its vise. My voice dropped into an inhuman register, suffused with power.

"Where is Brian Sherwood?"

CHAPTER 13

I BLINKED. THE ceiling looked familiar. I lay in Rogan's HQ, on one of his second-floor couches. Gloom shrouded the room, the windows dark and full of night. A warm blanket covered me. Someone had taken my shoes off, and I curled my toes under the blanket. Mmm, comfy.

The interrogation went as expected. Vincent answered all my questions. Alexander Sturm owned a ranch outside of Houston. Brian Sherwood was cooling his heels there. They had contacted him intending to offer him the financial bailout of his company in exchange for Olivia's files. When they found out that he had no idea where Olivia's files were hidden, they struck a bargain. Brian would be their willing victim, but he didn't want money. He wanted his wife dead instead. Prior to contacting Brian, Sturm and Vincent had briefly considered kidnapping Kyle or Jessica, but Sturm was afraid that Rynda would snap, and taking a child carried more risk. Brian turned out to be perfect for the task. He knew Rynda, he knew which buttons to push, and he was sure that the threat of his death could pry Olivia's files out of her.

Rynda was supposed to die during the ransom drop. Failing that, Brian wanted her killed in a tragic car accident. According to Vincent, Brian didn't care if the kids were in the car with her or not. Apparently, he'd said, "Whatever is more convenient."

Vincent had no idea what was in Olivia's files, just that Sturm referred to it as "vital." Vincent was under the impression that unless the files were recovered, all of them "would go down." They had to get the files back and they would do anything to get them. Sturm had directed every aspect of this plan, except for the attack on Rynda's house, where Vincent had decided to take the initiative.

They watched Edward Sherwood, and once he moved to declare himself Head of the House, Sturm realized that we must be aware that Brian was in on the whole mess. They needed new hostages. There was no traitor. They had watched our tornado drills through some high-tech equipment, which was how they figured out where the kids would be. Vincent's creatures had tunneled for two days to grab the children.

Rynda listened to it all, politely excused herself, and left.

After I pried everything Vincent had out of him, I released him. He slid to the floor, curled into a fetal ball, and cried. I didn't feel sorry for him. Fatigue had mugged me. I remembered wanting coffee. I made it out of the room and up the stairs, and then everything went blank.

Now I was on the couch.

Voices came from the kitchen area.

". . . and now I have nobody," Rynda said. "I'm truly and completely alone. Do you know what that's like?"

"Yes," Rogan said.

I should've sat up. Instead I quietly turned on my side. They were standing at the kitchen island, illuminated by the soft glow of the kitchen lamp. A cup of coffee sat in front of Rogan. He looked slightly tired and a little rough around the edges. A dragon in his off mode. I liked when he looked like that.

Rynda stood close to him, her slender body almost touching his. And I got a small stab of jealousy right in the heart. It never failed. They looked good together.

"I don't know how we're going to survive," she said quietly.

"You always were more resilient than your mother gave you credit for. You will persevere, Rynda. I'll help you. I'm not going anywhere."

"Thank you. Thank you for saving my son. Thank you for everything."

She stepped closer, slid her arms around his neck, stretching herself against him, and kissed him on the mouth.

That was going too far. Half of me felt heartbreaking sadness at her desperation and the other half wanted to run over and punch her in the face.

Rogan didn't move. He didn't put his hands around her. He didn't push her away. He just stood there.

She dropped her arms and stepped away. "This was a mistake," she said in a broken voice.

"Yes," he said.

"Why, Connor?"

It was absurd to hate a woman just because she used Rogan's name.

She searched his face with her gaze. "We know each other. We have a history. We have things in common. Same background, same set of friends growing up. I'm pretty. There would be no learning curve."

Thanks, Rynda.

"I would be a good wife."

"I'm in love with someone else."

"But why, Rogan? What is it about her? Is it because she's violent like you?"

"I was asleep," he said. "And she woke me up."

"I don't understand."

"That's okay. You don't have to. I care about you, Rynda, and about your children. But you and I will never be together. We would be miserable."

She turned away from him and leaned against the island with both hands, as if afraid she would fall. "You're right," she said. "You're like wildfire, Connor. You'd rage and burn me until nothing was left but ashes."

He didn't say anything.

"I feel so pathetic right now," she said. "Don't pity me. I don't think I can handle that."

"I don't. Check for yourself."

She shook her head. "All I ever wanted was for someone to love me."

"Someone does love you. Quietly and desperately. You just haven't noticed."

She glanced at him. "I don't understand."

"It's time to stop hiding," Rogan said. "You're a Prime. Olivia is gone. Nobody's judging you. Use your talent."

She raised her chin. "Maybe I will."

They stood quietly for a long moment.

"Are you going to marry her?"

"I'm going to ask."

"When?"

"After she is confirmed as a House."

"Does she know?"

"No."

"And if she says no?"

His voice was controlled and casual. "Then it's a no."

"This isn't like you. You go after what you want, knocking obstacles and people out of the way."

"That's not true. Occasionally I dodge."

"You know what I mean." She leaned back. "Have you told her?"

"No."

"Why not?"

"Because she will be asked at the trials about alliances and associations with current Houses."

"You don't want her to be in your shadow."

He nodded.

"That's very noble, but she should have time to look over the contract. She doesn't have the experience, and once she is declared a House, she'll be bombarded with offers. It's easy to become overwhelmed."

"There won't be a contract."

Rynda frowned at him. "Are you intending to enter this marriage without a prenup?"

"Yes."

"Have you lost your mind? You've known her less than three months."

"Four."

"You're worth over a billion. That's your family's wealth. What if she divorces you after a month? Are you going to give her half of your money?"

He didn't answer.

"Have you even run a genetic compatibility match?"

Silence.

"Connor, this is ridiculous. You're acting like you're a normal person. You're not. You have to protect the interests of your House."

"You followed all the rules and jumped through all the right hoops. How did it work out for you?"

She drew back. "That's a hit below the belt."

"She'll have me or she won't, Rynda. I'm not going to force her. I won't shackle her into a contract that will penalize her if she attempts to leave me. I don't care if our children will be perfect at conception according to a gene chart. This is how it is."

I felt the faintest whisper of magic from Rynda.

"Oh, Connor," she said softly. "I hope you're right. I hope she doesn't hurt you and you don't hurt her."

She reached out, touched his cheek gently, and walked away.

He stood at the island for a while, drinking what had to be cold coffee by now. He rinsed the mug, set it on the counter, came over, and crouched by me.

"Hey."

"Hey," I said.

"You're awake."

"Have I ever told you that you have keen powers of observation?"

He smiled. "No."

"You do. You should be a detective."

"How much did you hear?"

"Everything that mattered."

He nodded, his face unreadable. "It is what it is. All cards are on the table."

"Not quite." I sat up.

"Oh?"

"The real Rogan hasn't asked me."

He frowned.

"I want the dragon to ask me."

"Be careful," he warned.

"I know what the Head of House Rogan wants. I heard all of his noble warnings about the future of House Baylor. I saw him hold himself in check. I want to know what you want, Connor. What do you want of me? Ask me."

Something changed in his eyes. Before I could figure it out, he yanked me off the couch as if I weighed nothing, and carried me off up the stairs. Okay then.

The door flew open in front of him and slammed shut behind us all on its own. He tossed me on the bed. His face was savage, his blue eyes hungry. I shivered.

Magic brushed me, shredding my clothes. He grabbed a handful of fabric that used to be my T-shirt and jeans and tossed them aside. My bra followed. My panties fell apart. Excitement dashed through me, quick and electric, mixed with alarm and anticipation. An insistent low heat began to pool between my legs. My body knew what was coming and every cell in me wanted it.

He stripped naked. Hard muscle corded his frame under golden skin. He was big and erect, and when I met his eyes, he nearly set me on fire. He pinned me to the bed, his huge body caging me. His hand slid under my head. He grabbed a handful of hair. Breath caught in my throat.

His mouth closed on mine. There was nothing gentle or beguiling about that kiss. He kissed me like I belonged to him. His tongue invaded my mouth, and I tasted him, the echoes of coffee and the deep male scent that said *Connor* to me. It made me shiver. He kissed me like he could do anything to me and I wanted to let him. I would beg him to do it.

He broke the kiss. His eyes were dark and borderline feral. The heat between my legs turned liquid. I was suddenly in a terrible hurry.

"Look at me." His voice was harsh.

I looked at him.

"You wanted to see me? Here I am."

He seemed barely human, all raw male power, intense sexual need, and dark magic. It boiled all around him. The muscles on his arms were rock-hard. If he squeezed me, he could crush me. He never would, but knowing he could, watching all that power arrested in a moment, waiting to be devoted to making love to me, was the most erotic thing I'd ever seen.

I tried to arch my back to press against him and couldn't. He held me in place.

"Are you scared?" the dragon asked.

"No."

"You should be."

I smiled and let my own magic out.

His eyes shone.

He drew his thumb across my lips. The first intoxicating drop of his magic fell in the hollow between my breasts, hot, molten, velvet. Every nerve in me hummed in response. I was an addict who had smelled her favorite drug. I needed him inside me.

He slid his hand under my ass, squeezing it, feeling it, and dragged me closer, shifting my hips where he wanted me. The blunt head of his shaft pressed against me.

The magic split into two currents, winding around my breasts, and slid up each peak, warming my skin. My nipples were suddenly cold and erect, and then the magical heat crested over them. The jolt of pleasure rocked me, just as he tilted his head and sealed his lips on mine. I gasped into his mouth. He kissed me as the magic twisted around my nipples, sending tiny sparks of bliss through me, and then the stream moved lower. He kissed me while it flowed over my stomach, over my lap, into the crease between my legs. It licked my clit with its tongue, no longer merely hot and velvet, but slightly rough. My whole body contracted in response. It was too much. Waiting was too hard. I fought against him, bucking with everything I had and not moving an inch.

He let me take a breath. The harsh need in his eyes had turned to an all-consuming hunger.

"Why should I be scared?" I asked.

The magic squeezed and licked my clit, slipping in and out of me. It was an exquisite torture. He dipped his head and sucked on my left nipple. I almost came.

"If someone threatens you, I'll kill them. If you're not there to stop me, I'll torture them first."

"I can handle that," I managed. That part of him would never change and I'd made my peace with it.

The magic grew hotter. He moved on to the right nipple. If he didn't thrust into me now, I would either yell at him or start begging.

"When you look at other men, I want to kill them. If you cheat on me, I may. No more dates with other men, Nevada. I don't care what the reason is."

"Deal. No more kisses from other women."

His tongue worked my nipple. His right hand slipped between my legs. His fingers dipped inside me. My head was spinning. My body grew hot and heavy. I needed a release. I wanted all of him.

He made a harsh male noise. His fingers brushed the sensitive bud of my clit. I jerked.

"You'll live with me. You'll sleep with me in our bed," he growled. "Every night."

"Let me go."

He released my arms and I wound my left around him, worked my right low and let my fingers glide up and down the silken hardness of his shaft.

"Mmmm . . ." He kissed me again, thrusting himself into my hand.

"No other woman is going to call you Connor," I breathed. "Only me."

Connor grinned, a scary baring of teeth.

"You're my Connor. I'm not sharing."

"Deal. I love you. You are all I want out of this life. Marry me, Nevada."

I kissed his lips, then his jaw, and whispered in his ear. "Yes."

He thrust into me, his girth gliding in and stretching me. He filled me, deep and hard. It was more than I could take. The pressure stoked by his magic crested like a wave and drowned me. Climax gripped me in its delicious bliss, blocking out the world. I floated through it, that first moment of pure ecstasy stretching into eternity, and I spent it with my arms wrapped around Rogan, watching his eyes as the echoes of my orgasm rolled through him. Pleasure rocked me in waves. I couldn't even talk.

Finally, the aftershocks faded. He kissed me and thrust again, deep and hard, building to a fast, savage rhythm. I matched him. It wasn't gentle or soft. It was fierce, because that's what we were. We gripped each other as another climax rocked me and then again, wrapped in magic, united by pleasure, and when he finally emptied himself inside me, I felt whole.

WE LAY IN bed, wrapped in each other. By all rights, we should've passed out, but for some reason both of us were awake. I lay on his chest and looked at the stars above us. His hand brushed my arm. He did it unconsciously when he was thinking about something.

"Why did you let Shaffer in?" I asked.

"Because I'm a selfish bastard."

I glanced at him, raising my eyebrows. He smiled.

"You want to assign all these altruistic intentions to me, but I want to be with you more than anything else. I'm ruthless when it comes to your safety, your happiness, and being with you." He grinned again. "It's too late to change your mind. You said yes."

I kissed him. "How did you know that showing me off to Shaffer would make him run away?"

"Something he said during the dinner. He was very careful to specify that it wasn't clear that you were stronger than him. A few other things he mentioned confirmed that underneath all that pretty hair and expensive clothes, he had some insecurities about his own place in the world. The way he spoke about Augustine, for example. He desperately wants everyone to see him as a powerful head of the family, in charge of his little empire and his family. He left himself vulnerable and I exploited it. I gambled that if he found out how powerful you really are, he wouldn't be able to handle it. I was right."

"I was never interested in Shaffer."

"And now you never will be." He gave me a self-satisfied smile.

"You're terrible."

"You already said yes," he reminded me again.

"I remember."

"The Keeper called while you slept," Rogan said. "Your trials are set for tomorrow night."

"Does it scare you that I'm Victoria's granddaughter?"

"No."

"You know you can't ever lie to me."

"I know." He squeezed me to him.

"What happens when I'm old and wrinkled and I ask if you still think I'm hot?"

"You will always be hot. Besides, I'll be old and wrinkled by then too."

"I still don't understand what the big deal is about declaring the intent to marry."

He squeezed me to him. "Because once you declare it, our Houses will be tied together. You will inherit all my friends and my enemies. An engagement announced at the trials is almost never broken. You can never undo this, Nevada. Even if you refuse to marry me, nobody will ever be able to think of House Baylor without thinking of House Rogan. I want you to come out with as few obligations as possible. You don't have to declare it at trials. In fact, I advise you to not say anything."

He was still trying to give me an out.

"I love you," I told him.

"I love you too."

Rogan's phone rang in the pile of his clothes. I sat up.

He jumped off the bed, pulled the phone out, and answered it. "Yes? . . . I'll be right down."

"What is it?"

"Adeyemi Ade-Afefe is downstairs. She says we're in danger."

ADEYEMI ADE-AFEFE WAS a short, black woman about my age. I had looked the family up after Rogan first mentioned them. They were of Yoruban descent, came from Nigeria, and the name of their House translated to "Crowned by Wind." Adeyemi wore a white blouse with blue jeans. A gele, a head tie of shimmering grey and blue silk the color of clear sky, hid her hair, crowning her head in an elaborate knot. She looked at the world through big brown eyes and thin-framed glasses, and you instinctively knew that if she smiled, her whole face would light up. She wasn't smiling now.

"You have to get out." She made a short cutting motion with her hand. "Get out and evacuate the city."

Sergeant Heart, Rivera, Bug, Rogan, and I crowded around her downstairs.

"What happened?" Rogan asked.

"Sturm moving the winds in place. You have to get out."

"I thought Adepero said you didn't want to get involved," Rogan said.

"No, Father said we would think about it. We thought about it. We're not going to help you fight a private war, but this is bigger than that."

"How bad is it?" Rogan asked.

Adeyemi pushed her glasses back up her nose. "It will be the worst tornado we've ever seen. He will level this part of the city. He may level the whole city. I don't know if there will be anyone left."

"Is it an F4?" Rivera asked. "F5?"

"An F5 tornado has speeds greater than two hundred miles per hour," Adeyemi snapped. "This will be over three hundred. This storm will rip buildings off their foundations, throw cars like baseballs, and tear down trees. It will bend metal, sever power lines, and dig trenches. Do I need to draw you a picture so you will understand?"

I walked ten feet through the doors into the street. A dense blanket of dark clouds churned in the sky, hiding the stars. Wind gusts pulled at my hair. I ducked back inside.

"Can you fight him?" Rogan asked.

Adeyemi hunched her shoulders. "Weather spells take time and preparation. The atmosphere is wrapped around our planet like a big blanket. It's continuous. Everything is connected. If you make it rain somewhere, that means there will be drought in another place, which would've naturally gotten the rain or the moisture. That nightmare outside is the result of weeks of work. Sturm's been manipulating weather patterns for a month at least. The spells used are so complex, it would take days just to draw the circles properly. I can stall him, but I cannot stop him. Nobody can stop him now."

"So you knew he was doing this?" I asked. "Why didn't you say something?"

"Because it's one thing to create weather conditions for a

storm and another to initiate one." Adeyemi squeezed her hands into fists. "I didn't think he would do it. None of us thought he would. This is . . . The loss of life will be catastrophic. This will be a national emergency."

"Why now?" Rivera wondered.

That, at least, was obvious. "He knows we have the files," I said. "He knows that sooner or later we will decrypt them and that Brian is now worthless as a bargaining chip. He wants to bury us. If everyone's dead and the city is in ruins, nobody will care about the conspiracy. Can we prove that he's the one responsible for the storm?"

Adeyemi shook her head. "Not unless we see him. Weather spells are untraceable, just like other magic. One could make a guess, but a guess wouldn't be good enough to stand up in court or before the Assembly. You have to decide fast. We're running out of time."

The three men stared at Rogan. The question was obvious on their faces. *What do we do?*

He looked at Adeyemi. "How long do we have?"

"An hour," she said. "I can buy you maybe another thirty minutes."

"We hit him first," Rogan said, his face savage.

Rivera grinned.

Rogan pivoted to me. "What is House Baylor's position in this matter?"

Do I go back and ask my family?

They were looking at me. It dawned on me that I was the Head of the House. I had to make the decision now. "House Baylor will render all necessary aid to House Rogan on and off the field."

Rogan grinned. "Thank you. Heart, I want the plans for the Sturm family compound up."

Heart turned and walked away.

"Rivera, I want everybody out of their racks and in full battle rattle in ten minutes in the motor pool with team leaders in the briefing room."

Rivera took off at a run.

"Bug, take Ms. Ade-Afefe and get her whatever she needs to start working, then notify Diana and Cornelius and Rynda Charles."

Rogan pulled his cell out of his pocket.

I took off for the warehouse. Behind me, Rogan said into the phone, "Lenora, we have a problem."

I ran into the warehouse. It was just past eleven, and the light in the kitchen was on. I pressed the button on the intercom and said, "I need everyone in the kitchen now, please."

In twenty seconds, Mom, Grandma Frida, Bern, Leon, and Catalina stared at me in the kitchen.

"Sturm is making a storm that will hit Houston in an hour," I said. "Everything will be destroyed. I don't know if the warehouse will survive. Our only chance is to hit him fast now. Rogan asked me what we will do. I told him we will fight."

Silence claimed the table.

"If anyone would prefer to evacuate instead, now is the time," I said.

Nobody said anything. I looked at Catalina. My sister bared her teeth at me. It was the kind of expression I would've expected from Arabella. "I'm coming."

"Third rule," Leon said. The Baylor agency had only three rules, and the last was the most important. At the end of the day we had to be able to look our reflections in the eye.

I studied their faces. They gazed back at me with grim determination. Baylors made strategic retreats when occasion demanded, but when push came to shove, we didn't run.

"Bern, is everything backed up?"

He nodded. "All of our business records are stored on a server in San Francisco. Our personal records too, the photos, copies of documents, and all that."

"Then we'll have to operate as if our home will be destroyed. Everyone grab anything you can't live without. We'll meet back here in five minutes and go over to attend Rogan's briefing."

Shock slapped Catalina's face. It finally sank in.

"But all of our things are here. Our whole lives are here," my sister said. Her voice almost made my heart break.

Mom smiled at her. "They are just things, darling. We'll get new things. Go. There is no time."

The family scurried off.

I dashed up the stairs to my loft. My entire life was in this room. The last echoes of my childhood. If we failed, and even if we didn't, it could still disappear. I spun around. All my little treasures: my pictures, my books, the stuffed toy dog named Trinity I had kept since I was a kid, who now rested on the shelf . . . What do I do? What do I take?

There was too much. I grabbed the picture of us. It was about ten years old, Dad, Mom, Grandma Frida, my sisters, and my cousins, all crowding into the same shot. I pulled it out of the frame, folded it, stuffed it into my pocket, and headed for the door.

Shoot.

I spun around, dropped to my knees, and pulled the ammo box out from under the bed. The Tear of the Aegean sparkled inside. I slipped the chain around my neck—it was the safest place I could think of—dropped the beautiful stone inside my T-shirt, and ran downstairs.

CHAPTER 14

ALL OF BUG'S nine screens were on. He sat at his workstation like a wizard cooking potions in his arcane laboratory, glancing at the screens arranged three to a row.

The three monitors on the right showed an aerial view of what looked like a concrete mushroom cap, circled by two rings of walls, the inner being stone and the outer a chain-link fence, probably electrified and anchored by four guard posts. The views slid and turned, as the birds of prey carrying cameras fought the wind gusts. House Harrison had sent their scouts. Even if Bug's drones could've handled the rising winds, Sturm's people would detect them and shoot them down.

The place was lit up like a Christmas tree. Massive lamps flooded the interior of the compound around the dome with white light, and industrial lights banished the darkness a full fifty yards past the outer electrified fence. It was pitch-black outside, but inside it might as well have been broad daylight. Sturm clearly expected an attack.

His electric bill had to cost a small fortune.

The top two center screens showed the schematics of the same fortress, while the screen under them offered highlights. Outer fence: electrified fence, eight guard posts. Inner wall: barracks, roughly one hundred personnel, fortified concrete, machine guns. The dome in the center: reinforced concrete monodome, twenty-eight steel pilings driven into the ground, over seven miles of steel reinforcements; earthquake, hurricane, and tornado resistant, the kind of home that a storm mage would build to withstand the worst the planet and magic could throw at him.

The place was a damn fortress. Sturm also owned the neighboring ranch and some additional buildings, but they were of little interest. The fight would center on his fortified base.

The two bottom left screens showed atmospheric readings and live feed from Doppler radar. The top left screen showed Lenora Jordan. She was in her late thirties, with medium brown skin that had a rich red undertone. Her dark brown hair, normally pulled back from her face, fell around it in long, tightly curled locks. She looked like a paladin about to ride into battle. If her eyes could shoot fire, the room would be burning. Behind her, people hurried back and forth, some frantically speaking into a phone.

Our room was full too. Both Cornelius and Diana sat on the couch. Rivera, Heart, and three of Rogan's team leaders, two women and a man, studied the base. My family parked themselves near a wall. Rynda and Edward Sherwood, still pale, sat in the two chairs on my right. We'd all heard the ten-minute briefing. Sturm's fortress could hold off a small army.

The faint sound of drums floated in the air, underscored by a powerful current of magic. Behind the screens, at the outdoor space where Rogan had performed his Key, Adeyemi danced in a furious rhythm, the lines of the arcane circle around her sparkling with lightning.

"How soon can you get there?" Lenora ground out.

"Twenty minutes," Rogan said. "Sooner if you stop asking me things every thirty seconds."

She glowered at him.

"Sir," Bug said. "I have an incoming call from Alexander Sturm, sir."

"I want complete silence," Rogan barked, his voice snapping like a whip.

Everyone froze. The room turned so quiet, you could hear a pin drop.

Rogan glanced at the doors leading to outside where Adeyemi danced. They slammed shut, smothering the drumbeat.

The entire workstation pivoted on its axis toward the kitchen, the only thing Sturm would be able to see. Rogan strode to the kitchen counter. A coffee mug shot out of the cabinet and landed in his hand. He leaned against the counter, mug in hand, and nodded at Bug. He appeared completely alone in an empty room, just a man enjoying a late cup of coffee.

"Rogan," Sturm said from the screen. "Did I wake you?"

"Yes." Rogan's voice was nonchalant. "I was having the best dream. I was wrapping my hands around your throat, and you were begging. I was embarrassed for you, actually."

There was a momentary pause. "I had no idea you devoted so much time to thinking about me."

"Not really. What do you want, Sturm?"

"What I always wanted. Olivia's files."

Rogan pretended to consider it. "No."

"Why do you have to be so tedious? What do you want for them?"

"Nothing you have."

Sturm sighed. "I have a lot of things you don't want. History shows that when our Houses fight, yours loses."

Rogan smiled. The hair on the back of my neck rose.

"Try me."

"I intend to," Sturm said. "There will be enormous losses in personnel and property, and at the end, I'll win. I have one simple advantage, Rogan. I can direct the destruction, while you just emanate it. It's clear I have the tactical advantage. Why don't we skip all that and discuss our options?"

"You have no options," Rogan said, his voice harsh.

"Let me guess, you have a Boy Scout plan. You'll crack the cypher and then what? Turn it over to Jordan?"

"The thought crossed my mind."

Sturm laughed. "Come on. Even if I humor you, and we suppose that I'll sit on my hands while all of this happens, even you can guess about the caliber of people involved. Nothing will happen, Rogan. They will bury it, and if Jordan tries to hold on to it, they will bury that uppity bitch with it. They've been talking about cutting her down to size for months."

I slapped my hand over my mouth, so nothing would escape.

"Then you have nothing to worry about."

"Except my reputation. Which is precisely why I won't be sitting on my hands. While your geeks are trying to break the cypher, I will be demolishing Houston."

"And this helps you how?"

"By the time I'm done, there will be no city left. Do you know what happens in the wake of a natural disaster of such proportions? There is no law and order. There is no accountability. There is only chaos. By the time they get around to sorting out who may be responsible for what, nobody will be able to implicate me. Weather spells can't be traced. In fact, credible proof may surface that you were responsible for the destruction of the city. Of the two of us, you're the one with the cute nicknames, Huracan."

"I had no idea my powers expanded to atmospheric manipulation," Rogan said.

"Perhaps you hired a storm mage, and used the storm as a cover to level the city. Whenever something like this happens, people look for a narrative, Rogan. And a former hero, who never came back from the war and finally snapped, makes for a great story. I'll even shed a tear for you."

"You do realize that I'm recording this call?"

"Good. Play it back and listen to it until you realize I don't care. I'm not concerned. I'm not worried about you. Ask yourself why. When you figure out the answer, call me. I'd wish you good night but I doubt you'll be sleeping."

"He hung up, sir," Bug reported.

The workstation turned toward us, the top right screen dark.

Rogan tossed the cup aside—it floated into the sink—and nodded at Lenora. "Did you catch all that?"

"Yes," Lenora Jordan said, her voice cutting. "I did."

"He's playing for time," Rogan said.

"Do whatever the hell you have to do to stop that tornado from hitting Houston. I can't evacuate the city in an hour. We'll see you there. And Rogan? Sturm is mine. I'm the law. Nobody is above the law."

Her screen went dark.

"Right. We have a base to crack," Rogan said. "We have an outer wall with eight guard towers. I'd like to get through that wall with the least noise possible. That means taking out four sets of guards."

"That won't be an issue," Diana said.

Everyone looked at her.

"He took my niece," she said. "And he's trying to destroy the city." She rose.

"Thank you," Rogan said.

Diana nodded. "House Harrison will meet you in the field. We need time to dig."

She walked out and Cornelius followed her.

"Assuming the outer perimeter is down, we'll need to get

through the inner wall," Rogan continued, "which houses the barracks and the bulk of the personnel."

"I'll take care of it," Catalina said.

Everyone turned to her. My sister raised her chin, her face pale. "If you get me inside, I will walk them out. As long as you can guarantee that they will be taken into custody and get me out of there before they attack me."

Rogan glanced at me. I nodded. If she wanted to do it, then I would help her do it in the safest way possible.

"We'll take care of it," Rogan said. "Melosa."

Melosa stepped forward.

"Your team will walk Catalina into that wall and get her out. Once she is outside, she will need immediate evac, by air or car. Gear and safety protocol as for a highly effective psionic or dominator. Noise dampeners, no direct eye contact."

"Understood."

"I will handle the dome," Rogan said. "Heart, once we're through the inner wall, you will assume command and evacuate all personnel . . ."

"Major," Bug said.

The right screen zoomed in. On the wide stretch of clear ground between the inner wall and the dome, three huge odd shapes waited. Rogan squinted.

"Zoom closer."

The three shapes rushed at the screen. Three statues, frozen in mid-movement, built together from pale metal, gears, and oddly shaped plastic parts. One resembled a horse with crocodile jaws filled with metal teeth, the second was vaguely rhino-like, and the third reminded me of a tiger, a massive beast with talons and saber-tooth fangs.

"How large are these?" one of the team leaders asked.

"The tallest is about twenty-five feet," Bug answered.

"That's some weird lawn decorations," Leon murmured.

"They're not decorations," Mom said, her voice hard.

Rogan's eyes were dark. "They're constructs. Military grade, assembled and animated by a Prime zoefactor."

"Is that like the construct we fought before?" I asked.

That construct was put together with random pipes, bolts, and small metal things one would typically find at a construction site. Every time Rogan would break it, the construct reformed itself. It nearly crushed Rogan. Afterward he looked like he'd been hit by a car.

"No. These are better," Rogan said. "That one was made on the fly. These have been designed."

"Don't they need a Prime animator?" I asked.

Rogan shook his head. "Once a Prime has made them and animated them, an Average and above can activate them."

"We've had Sturm under surveillance since his name was mentioned," Bug said. "There is no indication an animator Prime is in residence."

"Will they reform when struck with conventional ammo?" one of the team leaders wanted to know.

"Yes," Rogan answered. "You can toss a grenade in the middle of one. They'll fly apart and reform."

"Awesome," Leon said, his eyes lit up.

Mom fixed him with a parental glare.

Constructs weren't robots. Robots were interconnected structures, driven by a power source, where each part was attached to and depended on the other parts to function. Destroy enough parts or the right parts, and the structure became useless. A construct was held together by magic. Destroy a part, and it simply reformed, with magic compensating for the loss. It was the difference between building a horse with an Erector set, with metal plates, bolts, and nuts, and tossing all these parts into a horse shape defined by magic.

"How do we kill them?" I asked.

"The only way is to reduce the number of particles below critical," Rogan said. "Usually that number is twenty-five to thirty percent. There are three ways to do that. Destroy the particles, jettison them beyond the reforming radius, or isolate part of the construct to prevent it from reforming."

Jettisoning the parts wouldn't work. He'd tried that before with the construct we fought. It wrapped around him and tried to crush him. He would push it back, then it would crush him again. Of course, that time we had an active Prime manipulating the construct. This time we probably wouldn't, but we had three constructs instead of one, and they wouldn't be standing still while Rogan played telekinetic baseball with their particles. If they were made of a single piece, he would toss them so far and so fast, they'd make a sonic boom as they flew by. But they were made of many small parts, which meant targeting each part individually.

"Isolation is the most efficient," Rogan said. "I need to bury them under something with sufficient mass and weight, so they can't reform."

"We could crack the wall for you, sir," one of the team leaders said. "With the right charge placement, we can split it into chunks instead of blowing it up. We can't guarantee that they would all be the same size, but we will do our best, sir."

Rogan frowned. "I'd need a circle and time. We have to occupy the constructs until then."

Occupy them . . . "Do they have target priority protocols?" I asked. "Would they be able to differentiate between a high- and low-priority target?"

Rogan's face shut down. "No."

"No, they don't?" I clarified.

"No, I won't let you do this."

"Last time I checked, I wasn't a vassal of House Rogan." I smiled at him. "I can do whatever I want. And you know Sturm thinks I'm a high-priority target. Even if they don't have target prioritization, the animator mage that's going to activate them will recognize me."

His blue eyes darkened. "No, you can do whatever I judge to be strategically sound. I have the numbers advantage in this operation, I'm in charge of it, and I'm telling you that's too dangerous. You're not playing bait."

"Rogan, what exactly are you going to do if I don't listen to you?" I asked. "Refuse to fight Sturm?"

"I can physically prevent you from approaching Sturm's fort," he ground out.

"No, you can't," Catalina said quietly.

Rogan's magic splayed out around him, a furious elemental thundercloud. The magic-sensitive people in the room sat up straighter, unconsciously trying to put some distance between themselves and the churning power. It shot out and met the cold wall that was my magic.

We stared at each other. The tension in the room was so thick, you could slice it with a knife and serve it with tea.

Leon whistled a melody from a gunfighter Western.

Rogan crossed his arms, regarding me. "Just out of curiosity, how are you planning on surviving long enough?"

"She's going to let her grandma handle that," Grandma Frida said.

"I would like to help," Edward Sherwood said.

The room turned to him.

"You're not a combat mage," Rynda said softly. "And you're still recovering."

"But I am a Prime. My brother is at the root of all this mess." Edward's jaw was set.

"Thank you," Rogan said. "We can use your help."

I CROUCHED IN the field. Rogan waited like an impassive statue next to me. A few hundred yards away Sturm's compound glowed, a bright electric jewel in the midnight fields. We'd doubled around the compound, across the pastures. The only road leading to the compound lay on our left, where it ran into the gate and the main guardhouse inside the electrified fence perimeter. Another, smaller guardhouse waited to the right, and two more were behind the ring of the inner wall, out of sight.

The place looked like a prison.

Around me Rogan's people waited, quiet shadows in the dark night. I checked my watch. Fifteen minutes left on the deadline Adeyemi gave us. We had cut it too close. The wind was rising, the air thick as soup with violent magic.

Behind me, Cornelius stood with his head bowed. Behind him, Diana and Blake, Cornelius' older brother, waited quietly, eight jaguars sitting at their feet, three black and five golden. The big cats watched the night with their bottomless eyes. Matilda sat with the cats, a human child somehow part of their pack. I couldn't figure out why everyone insisted on bringing her with us despite the danger. When I asked Diana about it, she just smiled.

Edward Sherwood stood by himself on a level stretch of ground. He'd been sprinkling seeds out of a large packet around himself for the last five minutes.

Nothing left to do but wait.

"Are you sure you want to use that old tank?" Rogan asked me for the third time. "I can still get you a better one . . ."

"Hey!" Grandma Frida reached out and poked him with her finger. "You can get her a newer tank, but not better."

Another minute dragged by.

"The badgers are through," Cornelius said, and wiped the sweat off his forehead.

The jaguars dashed into the night. Above them two owls soared. Both Diana and Blake looked into small tablets, whispering into their communication sets.

Cornelius came to sit by me. He looked haggard.

"Will the cats go through the badger tunnel?" I asked.

"Not under ordinary circumstances," he said. "But they will do whatever we ask of them."

The cats reached the edge of the light and slunk forward, moving silently.

Another long moment.

"What if they are seen?"

"They won't be," Cornelius said. "The word *yaguar* means he who kills in one bite. They don't suffocate their prey. They pierce its neck with one bite. Their jaws can crush a human skull. In terms of an ambush predator, they are perfect."

Another minute.

Tension rode me. I had to squish the urge to run into that field of light screaming just to let it out.

Another minute . . .

"They are through," Cornelius said.

Nothing changed. From all outward appearance, the base appeared untouched.

Talon landed on Cornelius' arm. Cornelius looked at Edward, who nodded. The animal mage handed a small sack to Talon. The hawk clutched it in his claws and flew off.

Time to get in position. I got up and moved across our perimeter to take my place with the small team in tactical gear. Six people formed up around my sister. Rivera was in front, Melosa behind Catalina, and Leon on Catalina's left. I took the spot on her right.

Catalina looked down at her ballistic vest. She looked twelve in that helmet, vulnerable and delicate. The worry in her eyes punched me.

"Are you sure?" I asked for the fiftieth time.

"Yes."

I put my helmet on.

On the far right, Edward Sherwood straightened and held out his hands. White grass sprouted around him, its stalks forming a complex arcane circle. Wow.

Seconds dragged by.

"It's done," Diana said in my ear.

"Team Alpha, go," Heart said.

We took off through the field, aiming for the nearest guard-house and its gate. A few breaths and the sheltering darkness ended. Suddenly we were in the light, exposed like sitting ducks. My sister was right next to me in a ridiculous helmet, and if there was a sniper on the roof, they could shoot her right in the face.

Don't think about it, don't think about it, just do it.

I ran, trying to cover as much of Catalina with my body as I could.

Heartbeats echoed through my head, one, two, three . . .

We crouched by the gate. Rivera pulled out big wire cutters. Behind the fence, a guard slumped over the console inside the guardhouse. A wet red smudge marked the window.

The gate swung open. We dashed across to the wall and the door within it. One of the other ex-soldiers slapped a small charge on it. Rivera pushed us back, and we flattened ourselves against the wall.

The charge popped like a firecracker.

Rivera checked the door. Gunfire tore the silence. A siren screamed somewhere.

Rivera pointed to Leon and Melosa, and nodded to the door.

Leon lunged into the doorway, Melosa behind him, her magic screen flaring to shield them from the hail of bullets.

"Now!" Leon barked.

Four shots blended into one.

"Clear," Leon called.

We filed into a narrow hallway, prone forms in the two guard cages on both sides of us.

A female ex-soldier slid a camera onto a flexible wire, checked the hallway, and drew back as bullets answered. "Long hallway. Rooms on both sides."

The hallway probably ran the entire length of the wall.

"Marko, give me head count," Rivera barked.

An older male soldier closed his eyes. "Three dozen in the room on the left, about five dozen on the right."

They had pulled all of the personnel from the wall to box us in.

Catalina stood against the wall, her face bloodless.

A small metal object rolled into the hallway.

"Grenade!" Melosa lunged forward.

I threw myself over Catalina.

Magic flared in front of Melosa in a blue screen. An explosion shook the building. Melosa flew backward. Something burned my back. Debris pelted us.

Melosa rolled off the floor, snarling. "Fuckers."

We were pinned down here. There were a hell of a lot more of them than of us. We couldn't go forward. We couldn't sit here, because they would come calling with superior firepower and flush us out. If we ran outside, they would shoot us.

"Now," I told Catalina.

My sister pushed me aside and stepped forward. Her hands shook.

"You have to do it now. You can do it."

She pushed from the wall. Magic coursed through her. I felt it. Like heat from a stove.

"Initiate deaf mode," Rivera snapped.

I didn't hear anything, but if everything went well, right now the helmets' noise-canceling software was pumping sound into the soldiers' ears.

Catalina turned to the hallway. Melosa followed Catalina, the blue screen shielding my sister. Magic coursed through her. The breath caught in my throat. So much power . . .

Bullets ripped into the barrier, sending waves through it. Catalina opened her mouth. Her skin glowed, as if a golden light warmed her from within. She raised her hands palms up in the mage pose. Her voice, impossibly beautiful, rolled through the building, an intimate whisper that somehow sounded as loud as a church bell, carrying a heart-stopping pulse of magic with it.

"Come to me."

Too strong. She'd poured so much magic into it.

The gunfire died.

I moved next to her, blocking her from Rogan's people.

A man walked into the hallway. He dropped his gun, pulled his helmet off, and knelt before my sister.

Rivera stared at me, trying to catch a glimpse of Catalina. I shook my head.

Men and women were coming through the hallway, dropping their weapons, and kneeling.

"Follow me to safety."

"Face the wall!" I barked, and pointed at the wall. Rogan's squad turned and put their faces into the wall.

I stepped aside. Catalina turned and walked past me outside.

People followed her, single file, moving past us smiling.

"Go!" I told Leon.

He pushed through the column of people outside, trailing Catalina, his gun up. If any of them tried to touch her, he would shoot them.

They came and came and came. I tapped my helmet's comm link. "Rogan, she used so much magic. She will need immediate evac. Don't let them kill my sister."

"She'll be safe," his voice said, reassuring and calm. "I promise."

Two of Rogan's people followed the column. Marko and Melosa jumped on them.

The column marched through the fields. Above them the sky raged, shot through with lightning. Wind tore at their clothes. We had minutes until the storm hit.

The last person left the wall. They kept walking, oblivious to another shape speeding in the opposite direction on its tracks, the massive gun pointed straight at the wall, and Team Bravo, Rogan's sappers, running next to it. Catalina had done her part. It was my turn.

I ran out of the building. Rivera's team followed me.

Romeo tore through the chain-link fence. I ran up to it, climbed on top, and into the hatch. The inside of the tank was cramped and dark. I groped about for the weapon I told Grandma Frida to leave for me. My hand brushed the heavy cold metal. There.

Romeo lurched.

"Ready to do this?" Grandma Frida yelled.

"Ready."

Romeo fired, shuddering. Another shot, another shudder.

"We have us a hole!" Grandma Frida laughed. The tank lurched forward. "Old tank, my foot. I'll show him an old tank."

I grabbed my firearm and popped out of the hatch. The bright electric light blinded me for a second. The wall was a dark barrier behind us. I blinked and saw the nearest construct, an enormous horselike beast, gleaming in the light of the floodlights. Its eyes flared with bright electric blue. It opened its jaws, testing scissor-like teeth as big as my forearm.

This was a bad idea. This was a horrible, ridiculous idea.

The XM25 in my hands weighed a ton. I leveled it at the construct, braced myself, and squeezed the trigger. The airburst grenade launcher spat a grenade. The recoil jerked me.

The grenade smashed against the horse's chest and exploded, ripping a hole in its center and sending metal and plastic flying into the air. The construct faltered. Ha! They didn't call it the Punisher for nothing.

Parts torn away by the blast streamed back to fill the hole. Crap.

"Go!" I yelled at Grandma. "Go!"

Romeo sped forward, circling the dome. The horse snarled, a harsh metal roar.

Holy crap.

It snapped its fangs and gave chase.

The little tank charged as fast as it could go, which wasn't fast enough. The horse hurtled toward us.

I lobbed another grenade at it. It ripped through the bottom part of its stomach and blew apart its legs. The horse stumbled. Behind it, the massive tiger construct rounded the bend.

"Get down!" Grandma Frida screamed.

I whipped around just in time to see the massive rhino construct bearing down on us from the opposite direction.

I ducked inside. The construct smashed into the tank, sending me into the bulkhead. My helmet smacked into something hard, rattling my skull. Things went blurry.

Romeo shook. Grandma Frida fired another missile.

Steel teeth blocked out the light in the hatch above me. I saw metal guts glowing with magic. The horrible screech of metal ripping metal lanced my ears. The tiger was on top of us and trying to dig in.

Metal groaned. It was ripping our armor.

When I shot the horse, the explosion should've carried the particles out, but it didn't. They shot out a few feet and fell back in. The magic contained the explosion.

I thrust the grenade launcher straight up, into the metal throat, fired, and dropped down. Metal teeth snapped, nearly scissoring my arm off.

The blast wave punched me, but not nearly as strong as it should've been. Suddenly light flooded through the hatch. I scrambled up. The tiger was rolling on the ground, a quickly reforming mess where its head used to be. The rhino had managed to come around and tore after us. The horse was only yards away.

I fired and kept firing, trying to buy us time. Massive gouges scored Romeo where the tiger had carved at it. We couldn't take another attack. If we let the tiger get to us, the construct would open us like a tin can.

An explosion rolled through the air. We rounded the dome and I saw the wall collapsing in huge chunks.

We rocketed down the grass, the small tank and three giants following it: the horse, the tiger, and the rhino.

The horse leaped onto Romeo, looming over me. Enormous teeth ducked down.

I fired my last grenade into its gut and dropped into the tank, hearing it blossom into a beautiful explosion. That's it. Out of ammo. I had three regular grenades left. I grabbed them and thrust into the open. The horse had faltered and the tiger took the lead.

I pulled the pin and tossed the grenade. The tiger dodged and leaped, metal tail snapping, claws spread for the kill.

That's it. We're done for.

A huge chunk of the wall rose and smashed into the tiger, knocking it aside in midair. The tiger crashed, the section of the wall on top of it, its tail flailing frantically, sticking out from under the wreckage. A second chunk landed on top of it.

Ahead, Rogan stood in the circle he drew on the paved driveway. He flexed, his hands clawing the air.

Another massive section of the wall rose in the air and flattened the horse. It didn't rise, buried under the rubble.

Romeo rolled past Rogan.

Behind us, the rhino was coming up, unstoppable, massive, pounding the ground with its feet.

Rogan thrust his hands up.

A twenty-five-yard section of the wall shook. He was trying to break it free from the rest, but it held.

The tank stopped, turning.

"Jump!" Grandma Frida ordered.

"What?"

"Jump!" she snarled.

I pulled myself out of the hatch, jumped and rolled into the grass. Romeo sped toward the rhino.

Oh no. No . . .

The small tank rammed the construct. The rhino veered at the last moment, throwing all of its bulk against Romeo's flank. The tank rolled on its side. The rhino tore at it with its feet, punching holes in the armor. Fear turned my insides liquid. I ran toward it, because that was all I could do.

A shadow fell on me. The section of the wall slid above me and swept the rhino aside, burying it.

The heap of rubble shook and exploded. The rhino sprang free, reforming.

The ground underneath it split. A forest of shoots sprang up, spiraling up to the sky, fed by magic, straight through the rhino. The construct flailed, trying to break free, but the shoots caught the particles that made its substance and kept growing, thicker and thicker, becoming branches, their wood encasing the captured parts. Magic shook the lawn. The tree swept the rhino off the ground, trapping the stray pieces as they fell. An enormous tree spread its branches, a hundred and fifty feet tall, its trunk twenty-five feet wide. The colossal Montezuma cypress shook once and became still, towering over the lawn.

Wow.

Grandma Frida crawled out of Romeo, her face stained with blood. She ran for the remnants of the wall.

The sky tore. A funnel spun from the clouds, reaching toward us. We had run out of time.

"Nevada!" Rogan snarled.

I turned. He was running toward me. I sprinted to him. We collided. His arms closed around me.

The wind disappeared. It was suddenly calm and peaceful. I looked up. Rogan's eyes had turned a glowing turquoise. He'd accessed his ultimate power. We stood in a circle of null space. Nothing would penetrate. This was how he broke entire cities, reducing them to rubble.

Around us the storm raged. An enormous tornado was forming just beyond the dome, as if someone had taken the storm clouds from the sky and spun them into a maelstrom.

The wall of air cut at us and stopped, severed by the perfect circle of the null space around Rogan. Beyond it another tornado touched down. Then another.

Dear God . . .

The circle containing us pulsed, the echo of it rattling my bones. The dome in front of us cracked.

Another pulse.

Pieces broke from the dome's top, crashing down.

Rogan was looking into the distance. He began rising.

I clamped him to me. If I didn't, he would keep going until he ran out of magic. Nothing would be left and our people wouldn't be able to get away. They were too close.

He kept rising.

"Connor! Stay with me."

His hands were still locked around me. My feet left the ground.

The third pulse. The dome cracked like a broken egg.

"I love you, Connor. Please come back to me. Come back." I kissed him. "Come back."

He turned his head slowly and looked at me, his eyes still distant, as if waking up from a deep sleep. Recognition flared within the magic-saturated turquoise.

"I'm here," he said.

The fourth pulse hit the dome. It broke apart, the pieces of it crashing down.

Alexander Sturm hung within it, caught in the column of spinning air, his hands raised, his hair pulling with the wind.

He brought his hands together. A tornado moved toward us, a wall of enraged air digging a deep trench in the torn-up lawn. It slid over us, and for a moment I saw the clear sky above. Then it passed and we were still there, floating in the column of Rogan's power.

Rogan smiled at Sturm.

Alexander bared his teeth. A second tornado swung over us and passed.

Sturm snarled something. I saw his lips moving but I couldn't hear the words.

Magic sparked in a flash of crimson. Lenora Jordan appeared between us, nude and unafraid, her head held high. She'd risked a teleport. Oh wow.

Lenora looked up at Sturm and raised her hands.

Silver chains as thick as my leg shot out of the ground, pierced Sturm's private tornado keeping him afloat, and wound about his body. He screamed, his face a mask of agony. The chains wound, squeezed, and dragged him down. He crashed onto the grass at Lenora's feet.

She regarded him for a long moment, derision on her face, and raised her hand. Magic flashed from her in a wide circle. Another null space. She stood within it, Sturm bound at her feet, and waited until a new twister, light and transparent, brought Adeyemi Ade-Afefe over the wall and deposited her between us. Adeyemi raised her hands and began to dance.

She danced and danced, striking a quick rhythm, bending forward, then straightening again. As her feet moved, the tornados lost power. They spun slower and slower, breaking free of the ground, until finally they dissolved into the sky. The storm clouds tore open, revealing the first light of the sunrise.

Adeyemi smiled, lay on the grass on her back, and fell asleep.

A FOREST OF swords studded the lawn. The tornado had picked up Sturm's collection and seeded the grounds with them. For some freaky reason, all of the blades landed point down and now rose at a diagonal, like razor-sharp mutant flowers.

Rogan was holding me. He'd refused to let go of me and so we stood together, watching the flurry of activity on the lawn of Sturm's fortress.

To the left my mother was trying to administer some first aid to Grandma Frida. Grandma Frida didn't want to be aided.

"Will you stop fussing over me?' Grandma Frida pushed my mother's hand away.

"Be quiet, Mother. You're bleeding."

Around us Lenora Jordan's people were processing the scene. They had already taken Sturm off, bound, gagged, and sedated. Lenora was still here, fully clothed now, striding through the scene and shouting orders in a crisp voice.

Sturm's people sat on the ground in handcuffs. Two psionics moved between them, broadcasting calm and happy thoughts. A helicopter had taken Catalina out of the area just before the storm broke, and faced with the several dozen hardened mercenaries crying and wailing because she was gone, Lenora Jordan resorted to the big guns and brought in psionics.

A few feet away from us, Rynda was trying her best to take care of Edward. He slumped on the ground, against the trunk of his cypress. Growing the massive beast of a tree must've taken every last reserve he had. The expression on her face wasn't just concerned, it was tender.

An armored vehicle drove through the hole Romeo had made and stopped. The door opened, Rivera jumped out, and held the passenger door open, holding it deferentially. Brian Sherwood emerged into the light. Same height and build as Edward, broad shoulders, sturdy frame, long limbs. He looked like his brother and at the same time he looked nothing like him.

"Rynda," he called out. "Oh my God, Rynda. Here you are."

She turned and glared at him like she saw a snake.

"I missed you so much!" Brian started across the lawn toward his wife. He didn't know that we were aware of his betrayal.

"Nobody told him?" I murmured.

"No." The smile on Rogan's face was frightening.

Rynda rose, her spine perfectly straight, her face iced over, every inch her mother's daughter.

"Did you miss me?" she asked, her voice as cold as a glacier.

Brian halted. "Yes."

"I missed you too, Brian. I endured so much while you were gone."

He took another tentative step forward. "It's okay. I'm here now. Everything will be okay now."

"Yes." Rynda started toward him. "It will. I'm so glad you

are here, Brian. Let me share with you everything I've been through."

Magic lashed out of her in a torrent, so potent, I felt it from yards away. Terror, panic, despair, anxiety, worry, crushing sadness, and rage. So much rage. It merely brushed me and I nearly cried just to release the pressure.

Brian shuddered. His mouth gaped open. He crumpled to his knees.

"Stop! Rynda, stop!"

She kept walking, her face merciless. "Why aren't you running away now, Brian? Are you stressed out yet?"

"Please stop! Please!"

"You wanted to murder me and the children. You wanted us dead. Our children! You should've shot me in my sleep, Brian. Because now, I will make you suffer. Feel, husband. Feel every drop."

Tears streamed down his face. "Stop! Stop, you fucking bitch, stop!"

"No."

Brian turned bright red, his eyes crazed. He jerked up, his face a furious grimace, and charged at Rynda, his hands stretched out toward her throat. Edward Sherwood lunged in his way, a huge sword in his hands. The blade rose and came down with awful finality. Brian Sherwood crashed to the ground, blood soaking his clothes. Edward raised the sword, thrust it straight down through his brother's chest, and twisted it with a sharp tug.

Everyone stood completely still.

Edward straightened, his face impassive, like a medieval knight over the body of his enemy. "House Sherwood has resolved its internal conflict," he said. "We are now whole."

$\mathcal{E}$PILOGUE

THE ARENA OF trials lay in front of me, a cavernous room with a clear space two hundred feet long and one hundred feet wide at its center, ringed by rows and rows of seats. Bern, Catalina, Arabella, and I stood at its edge. Midway down, a podium was placed to the side, like a referee's chair. The Keeper of Records stood at it. To the right and left of him, three chairs waited on each side. Six people sat in them, the Primes who served as the arbiters of the trials. One of them was Sylvester Green, the current head of the Assembly. Two seats down from him sat Lenora Jordan, the Harris County District Attorney. She looked surprisingly serene, not peaceful, but imperturbable, as if nothing in this world could get a rise out of her right now. Between the arbiters, flanking the podium, our two witnesses stood, Rogan on one side and Linus Duncan on the other. "You will do fine," Rogan had told me before walking out there.

I touched the Tear through my T-shirt. I was still wearing it.

My mother, Grandma Frida, and Leon sat on the opposite side in the chairs reserved for friends and family. We had opted for the sealed trials, which meant no audience except for family, and our entire family wouldn't miss it for the world. Everyone was present, including Grandma Frida, who had a huge smile on her face and a bandage on her arm.

While Lenora's people had sorted out the arrests of Sturm and his personnel, and first responders had pulled Grandma Frida from the rubble of the wall, Bern had broken the cypher on Olivia's files. It detailed the entirety of what she knew about the conspiracy: names, details, crimes committed in the name of the cause. We knew everything except for the identity of Caesar. That remained a secret.

Just before the trials, Rogan and I made a deal: we would turn over the information on the conspiracy to Lenora if she put the weight of Houston behind Arabella's registration. If my sister registered as a Prime, Houston would defend her against federal authorities. Lenora didn't like it, but she agreed to do it.

Grandmother Victoria's name was among those listed in Olivia's files. I had already warned her and I stood by what I said. The files were turned over to Lenora intact and unedited.

It was now all up to the four of us.

"I can't do this," Catalina whispered next to me. She took a step back. "I can't."

I hugged her and told her the same thing Rogan had told me. "You will do fine."

"Let us begin," the Keeper said into a microphone. "The Office of Records calls Nevada Frida Baylor. Present yourself and be tested."

I walked down to the podium. It was only about a hundred feet, but it felt like a lifetime.

"Declare yourself," the Keeper of Records said.

"I'm Nevada Frida Baylor. I come to be recognized as an Elenchus and to seek formation of House Baylor."

"Before we begin, are there any affiliations and alliances to other Houses you wish to declare?"

"Yes. In the event of the formation of House Baylor, House Baylor intends to sign a Mutual Aid Pact with House Harrison."

"So noted," the Keeper stated.

"Also, I wish to announce my engagement to Connor Rogan of House Rogan."

Everyone sat up straighter and looked at Rogan. For the first time since I'd known him, shock showed on Rogan's face. It was there only for a fleeting second, but I saw it and I would savor it for the rest of my life.

Linus Duncan laughed quietly.

"Has anyone pressured or threatened you into making this engagement?" the Keeper asked.

"No. I agreed to marry Connor Rogan, because I love him."

"Does House Rogan confirm the engagement?" the Keeper asked.

"Yes," Rogan said, his face again a neutral mask. "I love Nevada Baylor and want to marry her."

"So noted," the Keeper said. "Let us proceed."

A woman walked into the arena. She was tall and Asian. She looked to be about my mother's age. She stopped on the other side of the white line drawn on the floor.

"Face your tester," the Keeper stated.

I walked over and stopped on my side of the white line. The woman raised her hands. Her mind disappeared behind a dense curtain. A truthseeker, using the same trick as Shaffer. But her shield wasn't quite as dense.

"Nevada Baylor, you must determine truth from lie," the Keeper stated. "Your tester is a registered Elenchus. Voice your answers only once. If you change your mind, your second answer won't be counted. Do you understand?"

"Yes."

"Prepare your magic. Are you ready?" the Keeper asked.

The woman nodded.

376 • ILONA ANDREWS

I wrapped my magic around her defensive cocoon and began slipping tendrils of it inside. I only needed one to make it through. And there it was.

"Yes," I said.

"Begin," the Keeper said.

"*Mein Bruder hat einen Hund,*" the woman said.

My magic buzzed. I had no idea what she said, but it didn't matter. "Lie."

The woman blinked, startled. She poured more magic into the cocoon. I fed a little more of mine into the tendrils.

"*Ich besitze ein Boot.*"

"Truth."

"*Rosen sind meine Lieblingsblume.*"

"Lie."

"Are the arbiters satisfied?" the Keeper asked.

"No," Lenora said. "Let her continue."

"Lie," I told her.

Linus Duncan laughed again, showing even, white teeth.

"I'm forty-two years old," an older arbiter said.

"Truth." Although he looked a decade older.

"We are satisfied with her diagnostics," Sylvester Green said. "We wish to see the demonstration of the voice before making the final decision."

The Keeper bowed his head to my tester. She turned and departed. A man in his thirties replaced her, his face carefully neutral. I reached out to test the waters. His mind was closed off, wrapped in a nutshell of protection. It was very subtle, but it was there.

I looked at the Keeper. "Compelling another person to answer my questions against their will is traumatic."

"The Office of Records understands your concern," the Keeper said.

"This man has a protective shield around his mind. I can break through it by brute force, but if the Office would allow me to use chalk, I can compel him to answer with minimal damage."

"No chalk," the forty-two-year-old arbiter said.

I turned toward the man. "I'm sorry."

"Stop stalling," the man said.

I concentrated and stabbed with my magic, turning it into a dagger. The shell cracked and split. Thank you, Grandmother Victoria.

My magic snapped out and gripped the man's mind into its fist.

"Tell me your name."

My will crushed his.

"Benjamin Cars."

"The shell on your mind isn't yours. Who put it in place?"

"Orlando Gonzales."

A commotion broke out behind me, but I couldn't turn around. *"Why?"*

"He doesn't want you to become a House."

"Why?"

"He didn't tell me."

I turned around. Everyone was looking at one of the arbiters, the one who told me his age.

I released the other man and clamped the arbiter with my will. Behind me Benjamin collapsed, weeping.

The shell around Orlando's mind was thicker and stronger. I stabbed at it. It held. I stabbed again and again.

He got off his chair and staggered back.

Another stab. He fought me, his will bucking, but if I didn't do this now, there would be some doubt about the legitimacy of my trial. I couldn't afford doubt. Our family's survival depended on it.

Stab. The shell cracked. I poured my magic through the gap and wrenched it open.

I thought about Sturm and Vincent and dead Kurt. Anger surged through me. The arbiter's will snapped under my pressure.

"Why did you protect Benjamin's mind?"

His whole body shook from the strain. I squeezed. The world wavered. So much magic spent so quickly.

They wouldn't keep me from protecting my family. I didn't care how much they sneered, how many obstacles they put in my way, I would become a House today.

"Answer me."

The words came out one by one. "I . . . did it . . . because . . . Colleen Shaffer asked me."

Colleen Shaffer was Garen's mother.

"Why did Colleen ask you to interfere in my trials?"

"Because . . . she wants . . . you to accept her son. If you fail the trials, you . . . will be . . . vulnerable."

I released him. Another second, and I would've blacked out.

Orlando collapsed on the floor in a heap. Tears rolled from his eyes.

"Interfering with the trials is a mortal offense," the Keeper said.

Michael stepped forward as if materializing from thin air. He fastened his hand on Orlando, pulled him to his feet, and led him away.

"Are the arbiters satisfied?" the Keeper asked.

A chorus of yesses answered.

"Let it be known that Nevada Frida Baylor was tested and found to be an Elenchus. Congratulations, Ms. Baylor. You may sit down."

Someone had replaced the muscles in my legs with wet cotton. Somehow, I made it to the chairs and sat down.

"Kick ass," Arabella whispered in my ear from the right.

"You did it," Catalina said from the left.

"The Office calls Bernard Adam Baylor."

Bernard sorted a complex pattern out in record time. They registered him as upper-level Significant.

Catalina was next. She walked out to the line on wobbly legs.

Alessandro Sagredo was just as devastating as his Instagram photo.

"Catalina Baylor," the Keeper announced. "To be certified as Prime, you must use your powers to make Alessandro step over the white line. If you are unable to compel him to do so, we have a mage of lesser ability ready for you."

My sister swallowed. She was visibly shaking.

"Are you ready?"

"Do your worst," Alessandro told her with a grin.

Catalina covered her face with her hands.

You can do it.

"Are you ready?" the Keeper repeated.

"Yes." She lowered her hands and looked at him. "Do you live in Italy?"

"Yes."

"There are nice beaches in Italy. One time I went to the beach with my family in Florida. The beaches there are not like they are here. The water is crystal clear, and the sand is white, and you can float for hours and hours, looking at little fishes. They dart around in the water and sometimes you can reach out and almost touch one."

Sweat broke out on Alessandro's forehead.

"Do you like the beach?"

"Yes," he said through clenched teeth.

"I like swimming. One day I would like to go out on a boat. I was going to try the Jet Skis, but a storm came. We have terrible storms in Florida, and here in Texas, too. Do you have storms in Italy?"

"Yes."

"Come and tell me about it?"

Alessandro took a step over the line and headed for my sister.

Four people tackled him. He threw two of them off and punched the third one in the face.

"I'm so sorry," Catalina said.

"It's fine." Alessandro stopped struggling. "Let go of me. I said, it's fine."

The handlers let go of him. Alessandro shook himself, turned to the Keeper, and said, "The young lady is a Prime."

"The Office of Records thanks House Sagredo for their services."

Alessandro gave a short nod and walked off to the other door. Wow. That was the first time I had ever seen anyone besides us shrug off Catalina's magic.

My sister was pronounced a Prime. She came and sat by me. I hugged her.

It was now Arabella's turn. The arbiters stared holes in her as she walked to the white line. She wore a white robe and nothing else. She seemed so tiny, just a short, petite blond girl standing on the line.

"The Office will test your ability to reason," the Keeper told her.

A massive blackboard slid from the ceiling and stopped, suspended high above the floor. A piece of chalk as wide as a telephone pole hung from it on a chain.

"Once you transform, you will flip this blackboard. You will see a series of mathematical equations. You must solve them. This will demonstrate to us that you are truly a Prime Metamorphosis and you are in control of your abilities."

"Does it have to be math?" Arabella asked. "Can I write a short essay?"

"Math is the ultimate test of reason," the Keeper said.

My youngest sister sighed. "Okay."

"Transform at will."

My sister held up her robe. "Don't look."

The Keeper lowered his eyes.

The Beast of Cologne tore out of my sister.

The arbiters froze. Some gasped, petrified, others tried to move and slid their chairs back.

The shaggy nightmare shook herself, stomped over to the blackboard, and flipped it over.

$$67 + 13 =$$
$$7 \times 11 =$$
$$981 / 8 =$$

She pointed at the last one with the chalk, turned, and looked at the Keeper.

"Do your best," the Keeper said.

Arabella heaved a sigh. The first one gave her no trouble, although at some point she counted on her clawed fingers. The second she solved in seconds. The third . . .

"It's baby math," Catalina growled. "I could do this in my sleep in second grade."

Arabella ran out of blackboard space, crouched, and began dividing on the floor.

"This is what we get for teaching them Common Core," one of the arbiters said.

"There is nothing wrong with Common Core," someone else said.

Arabella wrote, "This sucks!" on the floor and kept dividing. Finally, she stood up, wrote 124 on the board, and glared at the Keeper. Catalina slapped her hand over her face.

"I say we take it," Linus said. "Otherwise we might be here all night."

Fifteen minutes later, House Baylor, triumphant, emerged from the Office of Records. Finally. We won. Nothing was hanging over our heads. The conspiracy was thrashing in its death throes. We secured immunity for our family for the next three years. Rogan asked me to marry him. There were things to solve in the future: me moving out, a new base of operations, finding money to keep up with our new status. But those things would wait.

I wanted to celebrate.

My family walked to the cars. Rogan turned to me.

"Take a ride with me?"

"Where to?"

"I thought we'd go to the country for a couple of hours."

"What's in the country?"

"My mother."

"You're taking me home to meet your mother?"

"She can't wait to meet you. In fact, if I don't bring you over, I might be in danger. Will you come with me?" He held out his hand.

"Always." I put my hand into his. I wasn't sure what the future would bring, but I knew I wouldn't face it alone.

Connor smiled at me, and we walked together to his car.

"Would you like a formal engagement celebration?" he asked.

"No."

"So just a ring then?"

"A sensible ring."

"Define sensible."

"Something I could wear every day while doing my job and not be afraid to lose, because it's too expensive."

He didn't say anything.

"I mean it, Rogan. Do not buy me a one of a kind diamond the size of a grape."

He laughed, my mad, mad dragon.

"I'm serious!"

"Of course, dear."

This was going to be one wild ride.

VICTORIA TREMAINE STROLLED through the garden path, painfully conscious of the man next to her. Roses bloomed on both sides. She never cared for roses. She preferred simpler, sturdier flowers. Like carnations.

"You have to admit, for a prison, this is rather posh," the man said.

"A prison is a prison, even if it comes in the shape of a country club."

"Think of it as a long-deserved vacation. Something tells me it won't last long."

They strolled on.

"Your granddaughter sent shock waves through H-town."

Victoria smiled.

"Last I heard, they are beginning construction of a new family home. Not far from House Rogan's country place, from what I understand."

"Who wants a long commute to visit the family," Victoria said.

"Indeed."

"Whatever happened to that little weasel, the one who started this mess. Brian Sherwood? I heard his brother killed him."

"He did. Disemboweled him with one of Sturm's swords apparently."

"I didn't think he'd have the guts."

"Victoria! You're terrible."

"I thought that was quite clever. What about the wife?"

"Edward and Rynda are engaged. They are retiring to the West Coast. Apparently, Edward wants to grow apples on an orchard, and she can't wait to go with him."

They strolled some more.

"Do they suspect you?" she asked.

"No. They've made their last round of arrests from Olivia's files. I'm in the clear. The cause isn't dead, Victoria. We will build New Rome. It will take time, a few years perhaps, but we will persevere."

"Without me."

"That would be a shame."

"There is nothing you can offer me," she said.

"Oh, I don't know. You might change your mind. You're like me, Victoria." He grinned. "You like to do things that make life interesting. We both do so hate to be bored."

Nevada Frida Baylor and Connor Ander Rogan
cordially invite you to join their wedding
celebration . . . Read on for the next installment of
Ilona Andrews' Hidden Legacy series, the novella

DIAMOND FIRE

Ramirez Family Tree

Mrs. Rogan's Siblings

Mattin, Inigo, Miren, Arrosa, Mirkel (half-brother), Ane (half-sister), Zorion (half-brother)

Guests of the West Wing

Paul and Isabella have no blood ties to the family.

PROLOGUE

NEVADA

ALL FAMILIES HAVE odd moments. Our family just has them more often than others.

I sat at our family kitchen table and stuffed my face with pancakes.

Arabella, my youngest sister, peered at me from across the table. "Why are you here? You don't even live here anymore, Nevada."

I had officially moved out yesterday. I'd spent the last nine years of my life in the second-floor suite of the warehouse that served as both our home and our business. Given that I now spent most of my time with Connor, otherwise known as Mad Rogan, and we recently became officially engaged, I decided to move out. There was surprisingly little fanfare. I hadn't accumulated much, and it took me less than a day to pack my belongings into boxes. Rogan's people got them last night and delivered them to his house, on the outskirts of Houston. Grandma Frida cried a little bit and Mom made a lot of grumpy noises, so I'd stayed the night in Rogan's HQ across the street just in case they decided to have a nervous breakdown about it.

I shouldn't have worried.

"Leave her alone," Mom told Arabella. "That's her third pancake."

"So?" Arabella glanced at me.

I stuck my tongue out at her and cut another piece of pancake with my fork.

"She's stress eating," Grandma Frida volunteered. "Rogan's picking her up in five minutes. She's scared to meet his mother."

Thank you, Grandma. I choked on my pancake and gulped my coffee. "I'm not scared."

I was totally scared. He'd wanted to take me to see her right after the trials, but I begged off for three days. There was no escape now. I had to meet my future mother-in-law.

Arabella squinted at me. Grandma Frida was past seventy and Arabella was still fifteen, but in that moment, they looked remarkably alike: both blue-eyed, both pale-haired—although Grandma Frida's curls were white because of her age—and both wearing identical sly expressions.

"You're wearing a pair of new jeans and your favorite green blouse," Arabella said.

"So?"

My sister dipped her blond head under the table. "And pretty, strappy sandals. And your toenails have polish."

"I can have polish on my toenails." Usually I wore sneakers because I occasionally needed to run in the course of my job, but I owned three pairs of sandals too.

"You better brush your teeth," Grandma Frida said. "You don't want coffee breath."

My toothbrush was at Rogan's HQ. Damn it.

"Stop it, the two of you," Mom growled and turned to me. "You'll be fine."

After Dad died, Mom became an unmovable rock in our turbulent sea. No matter what happened, she would be there, fixing it. It took me a long time to learn to look past that armor. The last year made that especially clear. But today I needed that rock and so I grabbed on to it.

"Mom says I'll be fine," I told them. "You've met her, Arabella. You could just tell me what she's like."

Arabella smiled. "I like watching you squirm."

My phone chimed. A text from Rogan. You're missing the show.

What show?

Come outside.

I really wanted to run upstairs to my old room and lock the door. I couldn't do that for two reasons. One, I was an adult, and two, my other sister, Catalina, moved into my room, so it wasn't technically mine anymore.

It was absurd. I was a trained private investigator with almost ten years of experience. Baylor Investigative Agency existed today because I took it over when Dad got sick and made it successful against all odds. Not only that, but I was a Prime, the highest level of magic user one could reach. My paternal grandmother had the same talent, and people cringed when they heard her name. I had stood up to her and to a dozen other Primes. In the past year I've been shot at, hit with a car, burned, teleported, and frozen nearly to death. I had a bus almost dropped on me, I faced a psionic who nearly destroyed my mind, and I told Connor Rogan, the Scourge of Mexico, "no" repeatedly and stood my ground. I should be able to meet my fiancé's mother.

I could do this.

I got up, put my plate into the sink, hugged my mom, and went to the door.

A gunmetal grey Range Rover waited in front of our ware-

house. Unless you looked closely and knew what you were looking for, you would never guess that the car was armored.

Rogan leaned against the vehicle. I've seen him in a twenty-
thousand-dollar suit and in dirt-stained jeans and a T-shirt. No
matter what he wore, he always had a kind of rugged masculinity
about him. You got a sense that nothing would knock him off his
stride. Whatever came up, he would handle it and he wouldn't
panic. The fact that he was huge—over six feet tall and built like
he fought people for a living—only added to it. Today he wore a
pair of jeans and an olive T-shirt. With his bronze skin and dark
hair, he looked like some sort of jungle explorer.

Oh no.

I stopped.

"What?" he asked.

"We match," I ground out.

"So?"

"I'm going to go change."

He caught my hand and drew me to him. His dark blue eyes
were laughing as he leaned down and kissed me. He tasted of
mint and coffee and the touch of his lips anchored me. You know
what, it would be fine.

"You look great. Also, if you leave, you'll miss the best part."

He nodded to my left. I glanced in that direction.

A sapphire-blue Maserati GranCabrio was parked at the curb.
Next to it, directly under my—no, my sister's—window stood
Alessandro Sagredo.

When I first saw Alessandro's picture shortly before the trials, I thought he looked like the son of a gladiator ready for his
first match. That impression was even stronger in person. His
face still had traces of softness, but they were quickly disappearing. The lines of his face were becoming hard and precise, but
whichever form they would take, one thing remained certain—

Alessandro was cursed to spend his life being ridiculously handsome.

My shy quiet sister was leaning out of her window and seemed clearly agitated.

"No!" Catalina declared.

"Why not?" Alessandro's voice held just the slightest trace of an Italian accent.

"Because what you're feeling for me isn't real."

"Who says I'm feeling anything? I'm just suggesting we go for a drive." Alessandro nodded at the Maserati gleaming bright blue in the sunlight. "I have the car right here."

"No."

Only a few days ago, our family had to undergo the trials to prove that we possessed at least two Primes and therefore could be declared a House. We needed the protections granted to the emerging houses desperately, which meant that I and my sisters had to demonstrate our magical abilities before a panel of Prime judges. Alessandro was Catalina's test. A powerful Antistasi Prime, he could nullify others' magic, while my sister possessed the ability to make people love her. They had stood facing each other, with a white line between them. Then Catalina told him a story about our vacation in Florida and by the end of it, Alessandro crossed the line and fought the four people who tried to stop him. He'd shrugged it off in seconds, but my sister was declared a Prime.

"I thought Catalina's magic wore off with time," Rogan said quietly.

"It does. I don't think he's here because of her magic. He followed her on Instagram before the trials."

Rogan's dark eyebrows crept up a fraction of an inch. "And that's significant why?"

"He is a teenage heartthrob and Herald's darling with a couple million followers. He followed three people and Catalina. She became Instagram-famous overnight and deleted her account."

In our world Primes were the most prominent of celebrities. There was an entire social network dedicated to the obsession—the Herald, where members posted speculation, rumors, and fan fic. Alessandro Sagredo, being young, unmarried, and devastatingly handsome, was Prime groupie magnet, and Catalina hated attention of any sort. She had good reasons for it. I would've given anything to make it easier on her, but all magic came with a price and my sister had drawn the short stick.

"You need distance," Catalina declared. "It will wear off with time and distance."

Alessandro hung his head, his longish brown hair falling over his face. *"Per l'amor del cielo!"*

I turned to Rogan. "What did he say?"

"No clue."

"I'm not under the influence of your magic. I'm not climbing the walls to get to you. I'm just here to invite you to go for a quick drive."

A long pause ensued.

Alessandro tilted his head and gazed at the window. Modern-day Romeo in luxury jeans next to his one-hundred-and-seventy-thousand-dollar steed.

Silence stretched.

"Is there going to be an answer?" Rogan asked me.

"No."

"She's just going to leave him standing there?"

"No, I meant that the answer will be no." I smiled at him. "Let's go. This is hard enough for Catalina as is, and we're not helping."

"I hate that window," Rogan said, as we got into his car.

Across the street, a heavy crate rose a few inches off the ground.

"Don't you dare," I told him. The memory of the last time we had an argument at that window was still fresh. Rogan was a Prime telekinetic and he didn't like fighting with me from the street. He'd stacked half of the contents of his motor pool against the wall of our warehouse, so he could get to the window and talk to me face-to-face. "Seriously, this won't help."

The crate landed back on the pavement. Rogan drove out of the parking lot. "Poor count."

I glanced at him. "What do you mean?"

"Alessandro is a count. Conte di Sagredo. They date back to the twelfth century."

"Don't tell Catalina," I said.

My sister was self-conscious enough around regular people. Carrying on a conversation with someone who came from an old noble family would cause a complete shutdown. She would obsess over every word trying to make sure she didn't say something embarrassing or draw attention to herself.

It was enough that Alessandro was handsome, a Prime, and a verified teen heartthrob. Throwing a title in there would only make things worse.

THE LONG ROAD veered gently between rugged hills rising from the green cushion of ashe junipers and live oaks. We were climbing our way northwest, into Texas Hill Country. The ground looked dry, with big limestone boulders thrusting through the thin layer of topsoil. After the humidity of Houston, looking out of the car window made me thirsty.

"Why here?" I asked.

"She says the hills remind her of home," he said.

"Where is home?"

"Spain. Basque country, near Navarre, in the mountains. I've been there. It's not a perfect match, but it's dry and rugged in places, like here."

The road turned, and as Rogan smoothly took the curve, I saw the house. It crowned the hill, a beautiful Mediterranean mansion, its adobe walls interrupted by tall gleaming windows. We kept turning and the house kept going and going . . .

"What if she doesn't like me?"

"She will like you. I love you and that's all that really matters. But my mother will like you."

The road brought us to the apex of the hill, to a stone wall topped by a red clay roof. A sturdy metal gate guarded the entrance. It swung open at our approach and the Range Rover smoothly rolled down the long driveway, past the landscaped lawn to another arched entrance. We passed through it to the courtyard with a beautiful fountain in its center. Rogan brought the car to a stop.

"That's a giant house," I said.

"Mountain Rose. Twenty-two thousand square feet. Ten bedrooms. Twelve bathrooms. Two swimming pools. Tennis court, gardens, the works." Rogan grimaced. "I once asked my mother why she needed a house that large, and she said, 'For the grandchildren.'"

"You don't have any siblings, do you?"

"No." He moved his hand, indicating the length of the house. "One bedroom for her, one for us—that leaves eight bedrooms' worth of grandchildren, all on our shoulders."

"Great." It wasn't my shoulders I was worried about, but if I told him that, it would take him another ten minutes to get all of the funny innuendo out of his system.

We sat for a long moment. I didn't want to get out.

"Chicken?" he asked.

People lied every day, sometimes a dozen times a day, often for the best of reasons, but every time they bent the truth, my magic warned me. So I had long ago made it a point to lie as little as possible, and to Rogan not at all. He couldn't lie to me, and we had to come to this relationship as equals. "Yes."

"It will be fine." He reached over and kissed me. It was a quick kiss, meant to reassure, but about half a second into it, Rogan changed his mind. His hand caught my hair. He tasted like sandalwood, mint, and Connor. I sank into it and kissed him back. There was nothing like kissing Rogan. All my worries vanished and it was me and him, his taste, his smell, his touch . . .

We broke the kiss. His blue eyes turned darker. He looked like he was going to go in for seconds.

We couldn't just stay in the car making out. Arrosa Rogan was a Prime. She lived in a mansion with Prime-level security, which meant our kissing was likely splashed in horrifyingly HD detail on the internal security screens.

I opened my door. He grinned at me and we got out of the car.

The inside of the house was as impressive as the outside. The walls, covered with delicate swirls of beige and cream plaster, swept up to tall ceilings. The floor was travertine, laid in large slabs rather than typical tiles. The furniture had the same timeless quality as the pieces in Rogan's house, but where his furnishings were solid and almost plain, with a lot of square angles, the couches and chairs here were more ornate. There was something undeniably feminine about it.

Nobody came to greet us. Odd. Was this a power play of some kind? Was she putting me in my place by making me wait? All my nervousness came right back.

Rogan strode to the kitchen and opened the huge fridge. I almost called to him to stop but caught myself. To me it was a mansion. To him it was his mother's house, and like any kid returning home, he made a beeline for the fridge. I did the same thing when I walked through the door into the warehouse this morning.

"Would you like a drink?"

"What are my choices?"

"Sparkling water, iced tea, juice . . ."

"Tea. Thank you."

The kitchen was vast, with dark brown cabinets and beautiful granite countertops. State-of-the-art appliances waited to be used. The cooktop looked like something out of a kitchen competition show.

Rogan poured us two tall glasses of tea. I slid my butt onto a stool at the other end of the island and he pushed one glass toward me. I picked it up and drank.

Eight bedrooms' worth of grandchildren. Right.

I always wondered why Rogan was the only child. Primes warred with each other like medieval city states, and most Prime families took pains to ensure an heir and a spare. There was no spare. There was only Rogan. I've been meaning to ask him why but kept forgetting, and right now didn't seem to be the best time.

A mechanical whisper made me turn. A woman in a motorized wheelchair rolled into the kitchen. She was middle-aged and beautiful, with dark hair touched by grey, bottomless dark eyes, and bronze skin.

Oh.

Rogan walked over to her, leaned, and kissed her on the cheek. "Hi, Mom."

She smiled at him. They looked so alike.

"There is smoked brisket in the fridge," she said.

"I saw."

Arrosa turned to me. "Hello, dear."

"Hi." I remembered to get off the chair, took a few steps forward, and stopped, not sure what to do with myself.

"She's nervous, because you're scary," Rogan told her.

You traitor. I would remember this.

My future mother-in-law leaned her head back and laughed.

WE SAT UNDER the roof of a balcony on the second floor. Rogan had gone inside to make tea for his mother. The rain finally came, and the air felt crisp and cold.

"He didn't tell you about the chair, did he?" Arrosa asked.

"No."

She smiled. "Silly boy. It happened when he was three years old. His father was a target of an assassination. He was supposed to have been alone in a hotel room in New York, but I went with him. I'd had a bad feeling about that trip. He and I survived, which was all that mattered."

She got hurt trying to protect her husband. "I'm so sorry."

"I'm used to it. And my magic makes matters a lot easier. Are you cold?"

"I'm okay."

"You look cold. Here."

The big wooden chest on the side of the outdoor sofa opened and a blanket floated to me. Like Connor, Arrosa was a Prime telekinetic.

"Thank you." I tucked the blanket around myself.

"Most men in Will's position would have divorced me. Connor was our only child. It was a risk to rely on only one heir to carry the line forward. But Will loved me very much and here we are."

"Rogan said that yours was an arranged marriage." I probably shouldn't have said that.

Arrosa's eyes sparkled. "He did, did he? Connor is very angry at my father. Yes, it started out that way. My family isn't a House.

The bloodline frequently produces magic users of Significant and Average caliber, but my grandfather was a Prime. The family always hoped that another would be born and when I tested as a Prime, my relatives threw the biggest party. Hundreds of people were invited. My father, Rogan's grandfather, had great hopes for me. I was not to be married off; I would remain with the family; my spouse would join the family and take my name; and the two of us would be expected to have as many children as possible in hopes that we produced more Primes."

Made sense. I had looked up the Ramírez family. To be considered a House, they had to produce two Prime magic users in three generations. Arrosa's grandfather died before she was born, but if Arrosa had a child who tested as Prime, the Ramírez family could petition to become a House.

Arrosa pulled her shawl tight around her shoulders. "All those plans . . . And then Will Rogan showed up. My genetic profile matched his requirements and he traveled to Spain to meet me. I remember the first time I saw him. I was standing in the library, trying to sort the books, so I had several books floating over my head, and he was walking by and stopped in the doorway. We just stood and looked at each other. I had never seen anyone like him."

She smiled at the memories. I had a moment like that too. The first time I saw Connor, he was walking toward me through the park and I just sat there and watched him and wished that one day I could find someone like him.

"What happened?" I asked.

"My father told him no. Not many people told Will Rogan no. He was a third generation Prime. His magic was off the charts. He had military contracts, civilian contracts, foreign contracts, and half of the world owed him a favor. It is fair to say that in some respects Connor is a lot like his father."

In my experience, Connor acted as if the word no meant nothing unless he was the one saying it.

"Will made sure to run into me when I was in town. We talked. Then I met him again. And again. It was so easy talking to him. We were different, but it was effortless. So, he came to see my father again, and my father, who by that point realized that offending House Rogan wouldn't end well, told Will that he would have to compensate the family for the loss of a Prime. He named an outrageous amount of money. Will wrote the check on the spot. Nearly bankrupted himself." Arrosa's eyes narrowed and I saw a glimpse of power, sharp and frightening. Alarm shot through me.

"My father called me into his study and told me that Will bought me, and I had to go with him. And you know what my Will told him?"

"No."

"He said, 'Aren't you going to ask her if she wants to come with me? It's her decision.' And my father told him I would do what was best for the family. He didn't get it. He never did."

I was 100 percent with Rogan. I didn't like his grandfather either. "Did you ever regret it?"

"Never. Will was everything to me. We came home. His family wasn't thrilled that he signed away nearly three-quarters of his assets. His father once called me their Louisiana Purchase. It didn't matter. We worked together to rebuild what he had lost. We were a great team. He loved me, Nevada. I got to experience the kind of love very few people do. I miss him every day. Sometimes I wake, and I reach over, expecting him to be in bed with me. But he is never there. I do still talk to him. He is buried in the gardens, next to his parents."

This could be me. If I married Rogan, in a few years I could be sitting in her spot, mourning my husband. Primes swam in dangerous waters. It was almost enough to make you reconsider, but I wanted Connor too much. A week or fifty years, I would take whatever time we could have together.

"Do you love Connor?" Arrosa asked.

"Yes." It wasn't even a question.

"And what about children? You are probably not genetically compatible. Does that bother you?"

"I want to have his children. I will love them whether they have magic or not."

Arrosa's eyes narrowed again. "Connor, you, and your children will be in danger much more frequently than most people. You are Primes. We live by different rules and my son has made powerful enemies. Some women would take an easier path."

Okay, I didn't like what she was implying. I raised my head. "I may not be a telekinetic, but I promise you, anybody who thinks they can harm Connor or our children will have to go through me and they will change their mind fast. If they have a mind left by the time I'm done."

She scrutinized my face. "What if I decide that I don't like this marriage?"

My heart made a flip in my chest. I was afraid of that. "Then I'm very sorry. I have the deepest respect for you and I will still strive to be the best daughter-in-law I can be. But I love him, and I will marry him."

Connor chose that moment to walk out on the balcony, carrying a platter with three steaming coffee mugs filled with tea. "Are you done torturing Nevada?"

"I like her," Arrosa said.

What?

"How in the world did you manage to get her?"

"He kidnapped me and chained me to the floor in his basement."

"What?!"

"It was a misunderstanding," Rogan said and shot me a look. Yeah, payback is a bitch. Deal with it.

"I am going to need the whole story," Arrosa said.

"Does this mean you will attend the wedding?" he asked.

"What kind of a question is that?"

And my future husband just successfully derailed his mother's train of thought and sent her into a new direction. *Nice.*

Arrosa floated her cup to her and sipped. "Have you set a date?"

"In a couple of weeks," Connor said.

"Out of the question. It will take that long just to inform all of the family."

Family? What family? I glanced at Connor. "I thought you didn't have any family?"

"Oh, he does. He has a grandfather, four uncles, two aunts, fourteen cousins, some of them with their own children, and that's not counting the extended family. Most of them are from my side and they live in Spain. He just doesn't like some of them very much."

I pivoted to Connor.

"Some of them are vultures," he said and drank his tea. "I want a simple wedding, Mother."

"Connor Ander Rogan."

Oh-oh. Middle name. Never a good sign.

"I was planning to invite Uncle Inigo," he said. "And Uncle Mattin. What if we only invite the ones I like? If we're inviting everyone, perhaps we should invite Kelly."

Oh, that was a low blow. Kelly Waller was Connor's cousin and she and her son were the only surviving blood relatives from his father's side. In a family of magic users, she was born with a weak talent, while Connor's power was off the charts. She'd married for love instead of genetics, and her parents cut her off. From her point of view, she had lost everything. She and her husband struggled, and she had expected Connor, her baby cousin, to set things right when he became an adult. Instead Connor enlisted in the Army and went to fight his own war. She felt twice betrayed.

By the time he came back and tried to reach out, her jealousy and resentment had gone toxic. She hated him and the family so much she'd tried to kill Connor on multiple occasions. For this purpose, she gave her only son, Gavin, to a psychopathic Prime, who used him to murder an off-duty cop. Now Gavin sat in prison, and only Connor's influence and a great deal of investigative work on my end had kept him from being shot on sight.

We would probably invite Gavin and his father. I was reasonably sure that the Rogan family name would buy Gavin a day pass. Kelly was a fugitive, from both the law and the House Assembly. If I saw Kelly, I would put a bullet between her eyes without hesitation. I wouldn't try to apprehend her or talk to her. I would shoot her until I ran out of bullets.

Arrosa looked at him. "Is this a practice marriage for you? Are you planning on divorcing Nevada and doing this again?"

Rogan's face took on that look of intense concentration that usually meant he expected someone to shoot at us. "No."

Magic snapped out of my mother-in-law and I nearly fell out of my chair.

"You are my only son," Arrosa Rogan declared.

The loving mother had vanished. Her expression hardened, her eyes narrowed, and the tone of command in her voice made me want to snap to obey. She would give Grandma Victoria a run for her money.

"If fortune smiles on us, this will be your only wedding. This will be a formal affair. Your bride will be wearing a breathtaking gown, you will be wearing a tuxedo, and I will watch you two exchange vows and kiss in front of our entire family and all of our friends, and I will glow with pride at this moment. You will not rob me of that joy. Later I will talk to your father about it and tell him how beautiful it was. Am I making myself clear?"

The Scourge of Mexico and the most terrifying Prime in Houston unhinged his manly jaws and said the only thing he could, "Yes, Mother."

"Wonderful. We will set the date three months from now. That will give everyone time to rearrange their schedules." Arrosa turned back to me and smiled, all warmth and sunshine again. "I'm so excited! My dear, the dress, the hair, the flowers. You have so many wonderful decisions to make."

CHAPTER 1

CATALINA

Two months and two weeks later

I FOUGHT MY way through the hallway of Mountain Rose house trying to dodge the children. Everything I ever read about my future brother-in-law on Herald suggested that Connor Rogan was a loner with no immediate family besides his mother and his cousin, Kelly Waller, who didn't count.

Herald lied.

The gaggle of children was coming right for me.

I clutched my tablet to my chest and braced myself.

They ran around me in circles, giggling, and dashed down the hallway, leaving a little girl holding a stuffed unicorn in their wake. I let out a breath.

Rogan had oodles of relatives, scattered all over the Mediterranean, and all of them descended on his mother's house to attend the wedding. I liked kids, but there were somewhere between twenty and thirty children under the age of twelve on the premises and they traveled in packs. The last time I ran across this gang of preteens, they knocked the tablet out of my hands. Nothing could happen to the tablet. All of the wedding files were on there.

The little girl and I looked at each other. She was probably five and supercute, with brown hair and big dark eyes. She wore a pretty lavender dress decorated with tiny silk flowers. If Mom had put me into that dress when I was her age, it would be covered with mud and engine grease in about five minutes. When I was five, I either played outside or in Grandma Frida's garage, while she repaired tanks and field artillery.

"Hi," I said. "I'm Catalina."

"Mia Rosa García Ramírez Arroyo del Monte."

I had seen her before, I realized. She always seemed to follow Mrs. Rogan around. She trailed her to the porch, to the study, to the media room. She even wanted to sit next to her in the dining room.

Mia Rosa thrust her unicorn up. It was almost as big as she was and decorated with blue and silver plastic jewels the size of grapes and way too many sparkles.

"This is Sapphire."

"She is very pretty."

"She lives in the midnight clouds and her horn glows with moonlight."

Of course. *Jewel Legends*. It was a popular kid cartoon with mythical animals. I was too old for it, but Arabella, my younger sister, caught the very beginning of it. Everything had to be *Jewel Legends* for a while: notebooks, backpacks, phone cases . . . and then she went to high school and that was the end of that.

"I want a sparkly gun," Mia Rosa announced in a slightly accented voice.

"Um, what?"

"There is a gun that lets you put more sparklies."

"You want a bedazzler?"

Mia Rosa nodded several times. "Yes. My mommy said you were the go girl and I should ask you."

Go girl. I hid a sigh. "I'll see what I can do. What is your mommy's name, so I know where to deliver the bedazzler?"

"Teresa Rosa Arroyo Roberto del Monte. Thank you. But don't give it to mommy. Give it to me."

Awww. She said thank you. "You're welcome."

She curtsied and ran after the kids, dragging her unicorn.

My phone chimed. I glanced at the text message. Arabella had written, **Where are you??? Get here!!!** and added a gif of a crying baby with photoshopped rivers of tears. I took off at a near run.

It all started with Nevada firing the wedding planner. The first wedding planner.

Usually my older sister was a perfectly reasonable person. Well, as reasonable as someone can be when she is a human lie detector. However, two weeks ago Simon Nightingale disappeared, and House Nightingale hired us to find him. Just three months ago our family registered as a House, and our small PI firm went from Baylor Investigative Agency to House Baylor Investigative Agency. The Nightingale case was our first investigation. The entire Houston elite was watching us, and it drove Nevada a little nuts. A lot nuts. She was pretty much a nutcase.

The first wedding planner was fired because she argued with Nevada. My sister would explain the way she wanted things done and the planner would tell why they couldn't do it that way. Most of the time "couldn't" meant "we won't do it because it's a Prime wedding and it's not the way things are done." Finally, the planner explained to Nevada that it wasn't really her wedding, but a wedding of House Rogan and she needed to stop impeding it with "ridiculous demands," such as serving *queso* as an appetizer at the rehearsal dinner. The planner was promptly escorted from the premises.

The second planner was fired because she kept lying. Her approach to wedding planning was to pacify the bride by pretending that everything was under control even when it wasn't. She didn't want to be micromanaged. But, my sister was an epic control freak and her attention to detail was legendary within the family. Nevada would ask if something was a problem, and the planner would repeatedly assure her that things were fine, despite being warned that Nevada could sense her lies. Things came to a head when Nevada asked her point-blank if she and Mrs. Rogan had come to an agreement on the caterer. After being told for the tenth time to not worry about it, Nevada snapped. I realized that the second planner was let go when I saw her running to her car in five-inch heels with a look of pure panic on her face. My sister had burst onto the porch behind her, yelling, "Is it fine now? Is it still fine?"

We didn't bother with a third wedding planner. Arabella and I took a weekend, armed ourselves with takeout, and after thirty odd episodes of *Whose Wedding Is It Anyway?* and four seasons of *Bridezilla*, we decided to plan the wedding ourselves. It was that or there would be no wedding.

Unfortunately, while Rogan and his mother treated us with perfect courtesy, the rest of his family wasn't quite sure about our status. Both Arabella and I were registered as Primes, but our records were sealed. Also, our family wasn't wealthy, and Rogan was a billionaire. With me being eighteen and Arabella turning sixteen, they didn't feel we had any authority. I had a feeling we ranked as "poor relatives who run errands," somewhere just above hired help. Apparently, I was the go girl. I didn't even want to know what Arabella was.

Just what I needed. I already felt like a clumsy trespasser in all of this beautiful luxury. This wasn't my home. My home was in the loft of the warehouse. If there was any way to not be here, I would've taken it. But I loved my sister.

It would be a lot easier if we could do all this in Rogan's house, but Rogan and Nevada declared Rogan's home a wedding-free zone and hid there whenever they could.

I turned the corner and walked into a room where Nevada stood on a dais, wearing high-heeled shoes and the in-progress wedding dress, which currently was muslin marked with blue pencil lines. Two people crawled around her, pinning the hem.

Arabella stood in front of her, her arms crossed over her chest. Both Nevada and Arabella were blond, but Nevada's hair was closer to clover honey, while Arabella's resembled gold corn silk. I was the only brunette in the family, besides Mom. Right now the similarities between my two sisters were really apparent, and if you didn't look at their faces, Arabella seemed like a shorter smaller copy of Nevada.

Ooo, I should tell her that next time we fought. She would hate that.

"What is it?" I asked.

"She wants lilacs in her wedding bouquet."

"Okay . . ." Nevada had said she wanted carnations, but we could stuff some pretty pink lilacs in there. I didn't see the problem.

"Blue," Arabella squeezed out. "She wants blue lilacs."

No and also no. "Nevada . . ."

"I had to hide in a bush of French lilacs yesterday and they were very pretty and smelled nice. The card on the tree said, 'Wonder Blue: prolific in bloom and lush in perfume.'"

I googled French lilac, Wonder Blue. It was blue. Like in your face blue. "Why were you hiding in a bush?"

"She was being shot at," Arabella said with a sour face.

"So you stopped to smell the lilacs while people were shooting at you?" I couldn't even.

"Mmm. I was in a greenhouse and they made a lovely hiding spot."

I decided to go with logic. My sister was a logical person. "You asked for a spring wedding. You chose pink, white, and very light sage green as your colors. There is no blue anywhere in the wedding."

"Now there is."

"Your bouquet has pink carnations, pink sweet pea flowers, white roses, and baby breath." *Three* varieties of pink carnations, because she couldn't pick one. And Nevada would never know the panic in the floral designer's eyes when we told her it had to be a carnation bouquet. Apparently, carnations weren't upscale enough for Mad Rogan's wedding. Poor woman kept trying to suggest orchids.

"And blue lilacs," Nevada said.

"It will clash," Arabella growled.

I googled sage bridesmaid dress, held the tablet toward Nevada, and scrolled through images. "Look at the flowers. Pink and white. Pink. Pink. White. Pink and white."

"I don't care," Nevada said. "I want blue lilacs."

And I want to fly away from here, but that wouldn't happen anytime soon, would it?

"Anyway, I have to get back to the office," Nevada said. "Text me if anything."

"The queen has dismissed us," Arabella announced.

I dropped into a deep curtsy. "Your Majesty."

"I hate you guys."

"We hate you back," Arabella told her.

"We hated you before the wedding."

"Before it was cool to hate you."

"Get out!" Nevada growled.

I walked out of the room.

Arabella caught up with me. "We can't do lilacs. It ruins the theme."

"I know."

"What are we going to do?"

"Sleep on it," I told her. "Let's go home."

"Catalina," a woman called.

I turned toward the sound. Arrosa Rogan, Nevada's future mother-in-law, waved at me from the doorway, from her wheelchair.

"May I speak to you in private, dear?"

Uh-oh. This couldn't be good. "Yes, ma'am."

"I'll wait for you outside," Arabella said.

CHAPTER 2

I FOLLOWED MRS. Rogan deeper into the room. The large office spread before me, walls and walls of bookshelves filled with books of every age, thickness, and color. Daylight spilled from the large arched windows on the right, and the polished floor of cream marble gleamed where sun rays touched it. Each window came with a reading bench equipped with turquoise cushions and ornate pillows. Mexican blankets, white, black, and lavender, were folded on each bench. Delicate Moroccan lanterns hung from the ornate ceiling that was painted with an intricate geometric pattern of pink, white, and blue.

It should've clashed, but instead it all melded into a perfect blend of Texas, Spain, and Morocco. There was something magical about it. Like opening a book of fairy tales and stepping through the pages into some fantasy castle. And Mrs. Rogan glided through it all with effortless elegance, a graceful queen of the palace. Even her wheelchair somehow fit.

I looked down on the floor. Of course, she fit here. She belonged here. It was her house. It wasn't anyone's fault that this house made me feel weird. Being here was like walking through an expensive furniture store or a museum filled with priceless antiques and being afraid to touch anything. It was someone else's space and I just wanted to get out of it and go back to the familiar space of our warehouse.

"I would like to show you something." A heavy leather-bound volume slid from the top shelf and floated to Mrs. Rogan's hand. She opened it.

I came closer and stood on her left. On a thick page, an old, yellowed photograph showed a man in a dark uniform and a beautiful woman in a black dress with a black veil, holding a bouquet of white flowers in her hand. A beautiful tiara secured the veil. In its center, under the highest peak, sat a stunning jewel shaped like a heart. It had to be the size of a walnut and it glittered even through the old, worn paper.

"My great-grandmother at her wedding," Mrs. Rogan said.

"Oh wow. But the dress is black."

"Traditional Spanish wedding dresses are black." Mrs. Rogan smiled. "Catholicism has this slightly morbid part to it. By wearing a black dress, Catholic women promise to love their husband until death."

That was a little morbid. Who wants to think about death during a wedding?

"Black dresses for devotion and orange blossoms for fertility and happiness. The white wedding dresses didn't come into fashion until British royals adopted it in the 19th century. Elite European families followed suit, but my great-grandmother was a holdout."

Mrs. Rogan turned the page. Another beautiful bride, in a white dress this time, next to a groom in a black suit. The gown's silk train was fanned out in front of them across the floor. The same tiara secured a beautiful veil.

"My grandmother."

"She is very beautiful."

"Thank you."

Another turn of the page. A third bride in a white dress cinching her waist next to a man in a tuxedo, with a 1960's hairstyle. The same crown holding back a veil that blew in the wind, but this time the photograph was in color and the blue green of the jewel took my breath away.

"My mother," Mrs. Rogan said.

"She is also very beautiful."

Why don't we have this? As soon as I got home, I would buy a photo album online and get Grandma Frida and Mom to cough up their wedding pictures.

"Thank you."

Mrs. Rogan turned the page and I saw her, young and radiant, next to a man who looked like Mad Rogan. She was glowing. Her gown was delicate like spiderwebs. The tiara perched on her dark hair as if it always belonged there.

"Wow."

Mrs. Rogan laughed. "Thank you so much for cheering me up. I'm going to add Nevada's picture to this album. Rogan is my only child, but I will be gaining a daughter and her picture will belong in this album."

"She will be very honored," I told her.

"Did you notice the tiara?" she asked.

"Yes. It's gorgeous."

"It's called the Sealight Crown. Technically it's a kokoshnik, not a crown, but crown sounds more impressive. The jewel is an aquamarine. Most people don't know this, but natural aqua-marine is often found in sea foam color. They heat it to achieve the light blue. But this stone hasn't been altered in any way. This particular shade of blue-green is important to our family."

Rogan had given Nevada a beautiful necklace with a pendant. She thought it was an emerald at the time, but it turned out to be Tear of the Aegean, a one-of-a-kind blue-green diamond. Now it totally made sense.

"Will you let Nevada wear the tiara?" I probably shouldn't have asked that. It was rude.

"I was counting on it. After the wedding, the Sealight will belong to her and she can pass it on to her and Connor's children." Mrs. Rogan sighed. "One small problem."

"Yes?"

"The crown is missing."

"WHAT DO YOU mean it's missing?"

Concern flickered over Mrs. Rogan's features. "It was in its usual place two days ago and it's not there today. Unfortunately, we have to conclude that it was stolen."

Considering how many people had been in and out of the house, it wasn't shocking. We vetted everyone, but background checks never told you the whole picture. A landscaping crew prepared the grounds for the wedding, carpenters were building the custom arbor, another crew was raising an enormous clear tent, at least eight people were hanging lights on the trees, the interior designer and her people, the furniture delivery people . . . That would be a lot of people to interview. It would take Nevada at least two hours. Getting her to sit still for that long would be a challenge.

"The Sealight is tagged with a sensor," Mrs. Rogan said. "It's embedded into the crown and cannot be removed without destroying the tiara. The system can track it through a satellite with the accuracy of up to one mile. Right now, it's telling me that the tiara is still on the premises. I would like you to find it."

Me? I had worked for our agency since I was twelve, first doing small things like surveillance and answering phones, then moving on to my own jobs, but none of my cases were that significant. Mostly, I dealt with insurance fraud because it was low risk, and runaway teens because kids told me things they wouldn't usually tell an adult. This was a big leap.

"We would . . ." I was a rude idiot. I should thank her for her confidence. "I mean, thank you for trusting me. But we must sort through at least a hundred employees, many of them new to the estate. Nevada can do it in a fraction of the time it would take me, and she would do so with complete accuracy. My sister never had a false positive."

"I don't think the culprit is an employee." Mrs. Rogan looked like she'd bitten into a lime. "I'm confident it's a member of my family."

"Why?"

Mrs. Rogan turned to the bookcase. A section of it—six feet wide and twelve shelves high, all crammed to the brim—rose about one-eighth of an inch off the floor and moved toward us.

I held my breath. The weight had to be enormous.

The bookshelves slid past us and gently landed on the floor, revealing a short passage leading to a round chamber. The lights came on, highlighting persimmon-colored walls pitted with alcoves and niches, each holding a treasure: statues, jeweled daggers, scrolls and books in vacuum-sealed cases, and in the center, in the place of prominence, a niche with a bare jewelry holder.

I remembered to breathe.

"Moving the bookcase by normal means would take several people," Mrs. Rogan said. "They would have to unload the books, slide it out without damaging the floor, then slide it back in and fill it with books. I was in this office for the entire afternoon yesterday and almost the entire day the day before that. At night the office is locked and secured by several alarms installed by Connor's people. To disarm them, the perpetrator would have needed the code and my thumbprint. The windows here face the cliff, and they are secured by alarms as well."

Although most biometric security systems were difficult to bypass, it could be done. Fingerprints and even irises could be digitally cloned by using pictures, sometimes the ones taken with a regular cell phone. "Who knows the code?"

"Connor and I. The house server logs every time the door opens, and there were no log-in attempts after I locked the office for the night."

"Do you lock the office during the day if you leave it for a short period of time?"

"No. Children like to play here, and since only a powerful telekinetic can open the vault, I didn't think anyone would touch it."

I glanced at the corners where the security camera watched over us. "What about the security feed?"

Mrs. Rogan looked sheepish. "The cameras aren't on."

"Why?"

She sighed. "Because a woman has a right to privacy inside her own house. The cameras that cover ingress and egress points are always on and the security footage is monitored by Connor's people, but I don't want strangers watching me inside my home. We compromised."

Knowing my future brother-in-law, he wouldn't have liked that one bit. Connor Rogan was deeply paranoid when it came to security. Nevada was too. I shuddered to think what their kids would be like.

"You see now," Mrs. Rogan said. "There was no opportunity to remove the Sealight by ordinary means. The culprit is a powerful telekinetic, which makes this a family affair. And that's exactly why I don't want to involve your sister. I've had an opportunity to observe Nevada over the past three months and I have both respect and affection for your sister."

"Then why not let her handle this?"

Mrs. Rogan folded her hands on her lap. "My son doesn't care for some family members on my side. He has perfectly justifiable reasons for it. They are difficult, entitled, and often ungrateful.

However, they are still my relatives. I remember playing in the garden with my brothers and sisters, the trips to the beach, and the family celebrations. I have hopes that we will mend the gulf widening between us. If we ask your sister to handle this theft, she will interrogate the family."

Made sense to me. "And you don't want that?"

"No. Nevada's first introduction to the family can't be that of interrogation and suspicion."

Not to mention that when my sister really used her magic, she could paralyze her target and pry all of their secrets out of their minds. Those who experienced it never forgot it. That's why our paternal grandmother, Victoria Tremaine, was so feared by other Primes.

"I know that you have a lot on your plate already," Mrs. Rogan said. "I'm sorry, but I don't have anyone else to ask. If I go to Connor, my son will hold his relatives upside down one by one and shake them until they confess."

Which would be a lot of fun to watch.

"You have investigative experience and I want to keep this within our family. Will you do this for me? As a favor."

"Of course," I said. "And it's not a favor. Family members don't owe favors to each other."

Those assholes stole my sister's crown. Nevada would wear the Sealight to her wedding even if I had to tear the house down to the slab to find it.

I faced Mrs. Rogan. "I understand that your condition is that Nevada can't know?"

"Yes."

"I have some conditions too. First, I will need access and authority to question your relatives. I can't get very far if they refuse to answer me."

"Not a problem," she said.

"I will need access to your security footage. I would also like to place some additional surveillance cameras inside. They will be monitored by my cousin, not an outsider, and we will remove them once the tiara is found."

"Can this be avoided?"

"No." One of the first things I learned about investigation is to gather as much information as I could.

"Very well." Mrs. Rogan nodded.

"Lastly, I have to tell Connor."

"As long as he doesn't interfere."

"I also have to warn you," I said. I've heard Nevada give this speech before and it felt odd to repeat it. "When an investigation includes members of one's family, we often find something that everyone wishes would've stayed buried. You have to be prepared for that possibility."

Mrs. Rogan considered it. "If one of them jeopardized my son's wedding, I want them found. And punished. The family will forgive the embarrassment, but not the betrayal."

Chapter 3

I CLIMBED INTO the blue Honda Element we borrowed from Mom. Our car options were limited. Most of the cars we owned were older and nondescript, so they wouldn't be noticed during surveillance, and the Element was the best-looking available vehicle we had.

"What's going on?" Arabella asked.

"Mrs. Rogan wants my help with a theft."

Arabella's eyes lit up. "What got stolen?"

"A wedding tiara."

"Does Nevada know?"

"No. And we are going to keep it that way. We have to stop by Rogan's."

"What am I, a chauffeur?"

"I drove here, you drive back."

The trip between our house and Mrs. Rogan's mansion ran about three or three and a half hours, depending on traffic. Normally, we could do a lot of things remotely, but as the wedding drew closer, we ended up making the drive more and more often. And because we were a new House and our sister was marrying Mad Rogan, both of them insisted that we never take the trip alone.

Arabella wrinkled her nose. "Yes, but Rogan's is half an hour out of the way."

I pulled out twenty bucks. "Fine, you've been formally retained." I would expense the agency for it.

Arabella snatched the money out of my hands. "Mine."

"Let's go."

My sister's eyes narrowed. "In a minute."

I looked in the direction of her stare. A young guy was walking toward us. He was lean, with a dark wavy haircut long on top. He had a handsome face with chocolate-brown eyes, wide eyebrows, and full lips. His jaw was clean shaven. He had to be at least my age, but there was something slightly teen idol about him, something deliberately messy but at the same time polished, as if he got out of bed, tousled his hair, accidentally rolled into designer clothes, and now he was just wandering around, not sure what to do with himself and being slightly apologetic for being so handsome.

"He is walking this way," Arabella said.

"If you drive off now, we won't have to talk to him."

"I want to talk to him. He's cute."

Ugh. "Drive."

"No. You're like an old lady sometimes."

Ugh.

The guy reached us. For a moment I thought he would go on Arabella's side, but he changed his course and knocked on my window. Oh great. Just great. I wished I could melt into the car seat.

My window slid down. I would kill my sister.

He leaned on the roof of our car so he could look into the window, and smiled. He had such a nice smile. It lit his face.

No. No, you can't like his smile. You know what happens when you like people. Stop it.

"Hi," he said.

"Hi," Arabella said.

He was looking at me. "Hello," I said.

"I keep seeing you around," he told me. "And keep trying to say hi. You're always so busy."

You said it, now go.

"I'm Xavier," he said.

I waited for Arabella to jump in, but for once in her life she suddenly decided to keep her mouth shut. Traitor.

"I'm Catalina," I said.

He smiled again. "I know."

This was a stupid conversation.

"Do you like tennis?" he asked.

Who what? *Say something . . .*

"She loves it," Arabella piped up.

"Maybe we could play sometime." He shrugged. "Sorry, I know it's lame, but the nearest town is an hour away and they won't let me drive. There isn't much to do here. So, what do you say?"

"Sure." This was the quickest way to get rid of him.

"Great. See you around."

He stepped back, gave me another dazzling smile, and walked away. I raised my window. Arabella drove out of the courtyard.

"*She loves it?* I don't even know how to play!"

"He doesn't care about tennis. He knows your name."

"I know that," I growled. "You know I can't."

"No, you won't. You've been controlling your magic much better."

"I can't take the risk."

"No, you won't even try." Arabella shook her head.

"It's irresponsible!"

"Hanging out with a cute guy is irresponsible. Listen to yourself. You're eighteen, not thirty."

"I can't treat people like toys. I might start liking him. I might want to hang out with him."

"And?"

"And sometimes that's how little it takes."

"Why don't you give up and be a nun, then!"

"Maybe I will!"

We rode in silence.

"I'm not saying you should fall in love or make out with him or chase him around screaming, 'wife me now!'" Arabella said.

"I know."

"All I'm saying is that you could give him a chance. A tiny chance. A sliver of a chance. What's the worst that can happen?"

"My control might slip a hair. My magic might leak. He'll become besotted because of my magic and follow me around with a slack look on his face listening to my every word and doing creepy things like stealing hair from my brush so he can hide it under his pillow and sniff it at night when he gets lonely."

Arabella looked at me. "That was oddly specific."

"Michael Sanchez in my freshman year. Eyes on the road."

"Suppose this happens." My sister merged into the middle lane. "Let's say he becomes 'besotted.' So what? He is leaving in a week. Your magic wears off with time and distance. Even if the worst happens, in a month he will be fine. People take that long to get over normal summer flings."

"It still isn't right." I had no right to manipulate other people's feelings. It didn't matter that I wouldn't have meant to do it. The possibility existed.

"Do you remember the ranch?"

The ranch was owned by one of Mom's friends, two hundred acres of scrub and rocks in the middle of nowhere. We would take Arabella there, so she could metamorphose without anyone freaking out.

"We went to the ranch so I could practice. And I went every time and I did my best. Even when I was twelve and a crazy ball of rage, because I knew that if I wanted to have any kind of life, I had to learn my magic. I had to figure out what I could do, how long I could do it, what I couldn't do. It's like driving and learning where the car ends and how quickly it can stop. You don't practice."

I glared at her. "I practice all the time."

"Yes, you practice not using it. You're excellent at not using your power. You've got that part down."

"I *am* excellent at not using it. I have to be."

Arabella's eyes narrowed. "Then Xavier is in no danger, is he?"

She got me. "I hate you sometimes."

"You hate that I'm right. Seriously, what's the harm in talking to Xavier? You're going to college in the fall. There's going to be all kinds of people there. Guys, Catalina. There will be cute *college* guys."

"Maybe I won't go to college."

"Sure," Arabella said.

I didn't say anything.

"Wait, are you serious?"

"Yes."

"Why?"

Why was complicated. There were many reasons. It was expensive. I didn't know what I wanted to major in and I didn't want to waste my time and the family's money. But most of all, I had spent the last four years racing to the graduation finish line trying to get the highest score in everything. I had existed in a state of constant pressure, where something was always due and once I finished it, I was already behind on the next paper, the next exam, or the next project. When they finally ran out of courses to give me and I finished this Christmas, I felt like I had breathed fresh air for the first time since I started high school. They were still making me come back for the graduation and walk across the stage. I would graduate this May. I would finally be free.

And when I told Mom and Grandma Frida that, there would be hell to pay. I had scored 1580 on the SAT out of a possible 1600. I was in the top one percent nationwide. I had my pick of schools. I could get a scholarship almost anywhere. They would tell me I was throwing away my future.

"Even if you don't go to college, you have to interact with people outside the family eventually. I don't want you to be alone, Catalina. If you want to be alone, that's fine, but I don't want you to be forced to be alone because you think you have no choice. If it was just about magic, then you could've gone out with Alessandro. He is an Antistasi Prime. He could've resisted you."

She had to bring that up. "He had been exposed to the full power of my magic."

Arabella grimaced. "Oh don't give me that. I've seen people after you charmed them. He had none of the symptoms. All he wanted to do was take you for a drive in his fancy car and to talk to you. You threatened to call the cops on him. Seriously, what are you afraid of?"

"That it wouldn't be real." The words dropped like bricks. "Nobody ever likes me for me, Arabella." And I had really wanted him to.

Silence stretched.

Arabella reached out and petted my hand. She kept petting it, like I was a dog.

"Quit it."

"There there."

"I said quit touching me."

"How can they ever like you for you if you never talk to them? Who outside of the family knows you? It's a serious question. Are people supposed to telepathically scan you to make friends?"

I groaned. "If I give Xavier a chance, will you shut up?"

"Yes!"

"Then fine. If he comes up to me again, I will talk to him. Happy?"

"Ecstatic."

"Good."

She had a point. I couldn't keep complaining that nobody liked me for me if I didn't give anyone the opportunity to see who I was. Maybe if I started small. Just one boy. Just one conversation. I would keep a steel hold on my magic.

Maybe it wouldn't be so bad.

I LIKED ROGAN's house much better than his mother's mansion. It was still filled with expensive furniture, but it felt different—simpler, rugged. More like a home and less like a palace. Being here was almost like being in the warehouse. I had called ahead to make sure Rogan would be there, but we could've just showed up and nobody would have been surprised.

I rang the doorbell. The door swung open, revealing a sturdy man with broad shoulders and short blond hair. Like most of Rogan's people, he was ex-military.

"Ladies," Troy said. "I'm authorized to tell you there is sushi in the kitchen."

"Ooo." My sister veered off and made a beeline for the kitchen.

"The Major is waiting for you in the office," Troy said.

"Thanks." I climbed the stairs, crossed the balcony, and entered the business part of the house, where Rogan conducted his affairs. I waved at people I knew on the way until I got to the surveillance room, where a thin, wiry man with dark hair sat in front of nine monitors. He spun his chair around when he heard me coming. His face twitched.

"Hi, Bug."

"Hi."

Bug was a swarmer. Swarms existed in the arcane realm. Nobody knew much about the arcane realm or the creatures within it. Summoners and other arcane mages could reach into it and draw things out, but they didn't really understand it.

For example, it was an established fact that implanting a swarm in a human would skyrocket their surveillance capabilities, allowing them to process visual information at an insane rate. It was also an established fact that these augmented humans died within a couple of years. Bug had volunteered for the procedure during his time in the Air Force. Everything went as planned. He survived the implantation process, became a swarmer, and received a substantial bonus. There was just one snag—Bug didn't die. When Nevada first found him, he was borderline insane. Somehow Rogan managed to fix him and now Bug presided over all of Rogan's surveillance.

"Xavier Ramírez Secada," he said. "Age nineteen, first son and heir of Iker Ramírez Madrid and Eva Secada Escudero. Rated as a bottom tier Significant Telekinetic. He likes to tell people that he is Rogan's *Sobrino*."

"So?"

"He is not Rogan's nephew. His father, Iker Ramírez, is Rogan's cousin, which makes Xavier *Primo Segundo* or first cousin once removed. Hard pass, Catalina. *Hard* pass."

"Stay out of my life, Bug." I kept walking.

"His Instagram is called Boss Moves," he yelled.

"Stay out!"

I took another turn and came to Rogan's office. Most of the time he used the room adjacent to Bug's nest, but once in a while he hid in the back, in his study. I knocked on the heavy red oak door. It swung open, inviting me inside.

Like his mother, Rogan devoted the entire wall, floor to ceiling, to books, but here the wood was dark, the chairs were soft chocolate leather, and the floor was old weathered wood. Rogan sat behind a large desk, his fingers dancing over the keyboard of a laptop. A chair slid out for me. I sat. A large glass with an extra wide straw floated over and waited in empty air, motionless. I took it and sipped. Mmm, lychee boba tea. My favorite.

I didn't know if Rogan genuinely liked us, or if he treated us well because we were important to Nevada and he loved her. I liked to think he liked us.

Rogan looked up from his laptop. "Budget update?"

"In your inbox."

He checked the file. "A bedazzler for $19.99?"

"It's a small gun that attaches rhinestones to fabric."

He frowned. "Is that for her veil? Because you know I can't have anything to do with that."

My sister and Rogan had reached a compromise. Neither of them had wanted an expensive wedding. Our family couldn't go half and half with Rogan either, not on the scale this wedding was happening, so it was decided that since Mrs. Rogan wouldn't be denied, we would buy the dress, veil, shoes, and the bouquet, and Rogan would pay for everything else. Rogan would've been happy to pay for all of it, but Nevada insisted, and if she found out we went around her in any way, there would be hell to pay.

"No, the bedazzler isn't for the veil. It's for Mia Rosa García Ramírez Arroyo del Monte's stuffed unicorn."

"Okay then. Next?"

"Sealight is missing," I told him.

There was a second of silence.

"Those assholes stole it," he said.

Wow. He went right to it.

"Mrs. Rogan asked me to look into it. She wants it handled quietly, and she doesn't want Nevada involved."

Rogan sighed. "Of course. The less my future wife has to do with those dickheads the better."

"Are all of them dickheads?"

"No. Uncle Inigo, his wife, Emilia, and their three kids have my complete confidence. Same for Uncle Mattin and his family. I don't agree with his politics, but he would never dishonor the family name. We can scratch them off the list. Aunt Miren and her daughter, Cousin Gracia, are women of impeccable integrity, and I trust Gracia's wife and their two children. But the younger of my mother's siblings are perfectly capable of stealing from the bride at the wedding."

I leaned back. "Tell me about it?"

He sighed. "My grandfather is one of those men who believes that children belong to their mothers until they are old enough to contribute to the family business. He is an old cantankerous bastard. He married my grandmother and had four children, including my mother. When mom was ten years old, her mother died, leaving my grandfather with four kids and no idea how to raise them. As soon as he was done with mourning, he remarried. The second wife was only twelve years older than my mother. He married her because she had the right pedigree, the right set of powers, and was young and healthy. I've met her. She was very young when she married, and she had dreams of a loving husband and a beautiful family, and instead she found herself relegated to the role of a glorified babysitter, whom my grandfather mostly ignored."

That wasn't fair.

"My grandfather had three children with her. By the time the last one was born, the older children were grown and assumed their responsibilities, so they received the lion's portion of his attention. The three younger ones were left to fend for themselves and their mother denied them nothing. They grew up hedonistic and entitled. They have a deep disdain for our side of the family and once the old man dies, the family will likely split. But my mother remembers them as the cute babies who she looked after. She is determined to forgive them their faults, and they are perfectly willing to use her. The only time I hear from them is when they want something: money, influence, guarantees, and so on. Aside from that, they don't even bother with basic maintenance like sending her Christmas cards. So you have Inigo, Mattin, Miren, and my mother on one side, and Markel, Ane, and Zorion on the other."

I checked my tablet for the houseguest chart, which I grabbed from Mrs. Rogan's desktop before leaving. They had put the three oldest siblings and their children in the east wing and the three half siblings and their children in the west. That made my job easier. "Your grandfather isn't coming to the wedding?"

"No. He had an odd rivalry with my father. It was one-sided, but now that Dad is gone, he's carried it over to me. His health is failing, and he doesn't want anyone, especially me, to know it."

"Could any of your relatives open Mrs. Rogan's vault?"

Rogan grimaced. "It's possible. They pride themselves on hiding the full extent of their powers. It's a family sport. Curiously, it keeps the peace. Nobody is sure how strong everyone is, so nobody wants to risk a confrontation. Most of that side of the family ranks in the Significant range, but once in a while, usually once per generation, they produce an off-the-charts Prime. My mother is one. My father came to Basque country because she matched the right set of powers he wanted in a bride and once he met her, he refused to let her go. He'd signed off almost half of his capital over to her father to marry her."

"So, your grandfather sold her?"

"Pretty much. Ask her to tell you the story sometime."

Better and better. "Who would know that cameras in the office are nonfunctioning?"

"Everyone. Mother assured everyone that they would have privacy inside the house."

We stared at each other with identical expressions. Sometimes Mom did things like this. Like when we said, "don't climb into the crow's nest today, because your leg is hurting," and she would do it anyway and then spend the evening rubbing Icy Hot into her knee and limping.

"I'm going to bug the house," I told him.

"Did my mother agree to this?"

"Yes, on the condition that nobody except family views the recording. Bern is family."

Rogan leaned back. "You got further than I have in the last twelve years. Congratulations."

"Thank you. She really wants the Sealight found. She showed me the wedding album."

"What do you need from me?"

"I need files on everyone, even people you don't suspect. I need someone to sneak in as part of the landscaping crew and install the cameras. I could get Bern to do it, but if they had done their homework, they will recognize him, and I don't want to take chances. Also, I would like you to take over the monitoring of the Sealight sensor."

"Which is an antique." Rogan grimaced again.

"I want to be notified immediately if the tiara leaves the grounds."

"Very well," he said.

"Also, I need you to convince Nevada that blue lilacs don't belong in her bouquet."

His eyes flashed. "Nice try. You're on your own."

"It was worth a shot."

PEOPLE SAID THAT the kitchen was the heart of the house. If that was true, what would it make the kitchen table? One of the atriums, because food flowed into it, or one of the ventricles, because we ate the food and flowed out? Sometimes weird things like that got stuck in my brain. Usually when I was tired, and my brain wanted to do something else.

I rubbed my face and drank more coffee. The table was covered with tablets and notepads. On my right, my cousin Bern was messing with hummingbirds—tiny waterproof cameras in casings that could be tinted the color of your choice. We decided to hide them in the pretty shrubs. Bern was a huge blond bear of a guy, the cameras were tiny, and he handled them with the precision of a surgeon. He was the oldest of all of us, except for Nevada.

Across the table Arabella was going over the catering menu on her tablet. When Mrs. Rogan was a child, she was almost poisoned at a birthday party. Her little cousin had died instead. Now she prepared most of her food herself, but that wasn't an option for the wedding. Nevada deferred to Mrs. Rogan, and after interviewing seventeen catering companies, she finally settled on one. Now we had to select the menu, and Mrs. Rogan had delayed till the last minute.

Next to Arabella, Bern's brother, Leon, dark and lean, had taken apart some sort of a gun and was cleaning it. Ever since

Leon discovered his magic talent a few months ago it was all guns all the time. Mom didn't even try to stop him anymore. She was by the sink, trying to precision pour melted gelatin into silicone molds. Arabella had told her that there was no way home-made gummy bears would ever taste the same as store-bought. Now half the fridge was occupied with silicone trays.

My brain hummed, trying to sort through the background files on the two branches of the family Rogan suspected.

We all used to sit just like this when we did our homework.

"What's a canapé?" Arabella asked.

"Something with a melon on it," Leon said.

"It's a bread thing," Bern said.

A door swung open deep in the warehouse and a couple of moments later Grandma Frida emerged wearing a pair of heavy-duty twill overalls, smudged with engine grease. Her platinum white curls framed her face like a halo and her blue eyes sparkled. Grandma Frida was almost never in a bad mood. I once asked her why and she said she didn't have that much time left so she didn't want to waste it being miserable. I obsessed over every cough she made for a month after that.

"Grandma, what's a canapé?" Arabella asked.

Grandma Frida landed in her chair and wrinkled her nose. "Isn't it an Italian desert with cream in it?"

"That's cannoli," Mom said.

"Just google it," Leon said.

Arabella growled under her breath. "Every time I shrink their order window, it resets, and my phone is dead."

I passed her mine.

"How is it going?" Mom asked.

"If I eliminate everyone under the age of ten and everyone Ro-gan has vouched for, it leaves me with twelve primary suspects," I said.

"An adult could get a kid to do their dirty deed," Grandma Frida said.

"Yes, but anyone under the age of ten would tell," I said.

"These kids run around the house in packs, unsupervised," Arabella said. "They would blab. Also, Bern was right. Canapé is a bread thing."

I studied my list of suspects. I had them organized room by room in the west wing, going north to south. The Spanish names were terribly confusing and some of them were very long, so for the sake of clarity, I culled them down to one given name and one married name. The main last name in the family was Ramírez. Mrs. Rogan had three siblings housed in the west wing, her two half brothers, Markel and Zorion, and her half sister, Ane.

First, there was Markel, Mrs. Rogan's oldest half brother, and his second wife, Isabella. Markel didn't seem to be employed. He lived off the proceeds from the family's investments. A search of Isabella's Facebook revealed a lavish house and nice cars. However, Rogan's files noted that Markel repeatedly complained in private that his stipend wasn't large enough. None of this stipend seemed to have made it to his son and daughter.

The next room held Mikel Ramírez, Markel's son, and his wife, Maria. Mikel managed Ramírez Capital, a venture capital firm owned by the family, with focus on telecommunications and internet companies. He was a tall, pale, dark-haired man with a prematurely greying beard and sad eyes. His wife was a thin, overly tan woman with bleached blond hair, who liked designer clothes, usually in white, and chunky gold jewelry. I had seen her twice. Both times she had a wineglass in her hand and both times she asked if I had seen her husband. They had four children, three under the age of twelve.

Next were Lucian and June de Baldivia. June was Markel's

daughter, a plump woman with olive skin and a wealth of dark curly hair. Her husband was tall, athletic, and handsome, with dark hair and narrow, startlingly blue eyes. He jogged around the estate every morning. Lucian worked for a computer firm specializing in cybersecurity, while June was heavily involved in a start-up trying to clean up plastic from the oceans. They had two daughters, who looked exactly like their mom.

Then, there was Zorion and Teresa Rosa del Monte, the parents of bedazzler girl. Zorion, Mrs. Rogan's youngest half brother, was forty years old, trim, athletic, and handsome. He lived off the family proceeds and seemed to have two interests: soccer and cars. Teresa was a housewife with an edgy pixie cut. She took care of their two children and was trying to write a novel. A search of her online activity showed heavy Twitter usage where she stalked a number of romance writers and literary agents, both in and outside of Spain. They weren't in great financial distress.

The next room over was occupied by Ane, Mrs. Rogan's half sister, who had arrived with a boy toy, as Arabella put it. The boy toy was in his late twenties, blond, blue-eyed, pretty, and went by Paul Sarmiento. Ane didn't work, relying on her portion from the family investments as income. Paul didn't have a criminal record and Rogan's people couldn't find his fingerprints in any of the databases, but it wasn't clear what he actually did for a living. I put a check mark by his name.

Finally, in the far south, we had Iker and Eva Ramírez. Iker, Ane's only child, had olive skin and dark blond hair and was an architect. He'd been working at his firm for the last four years. His wife was petite and delicate. She had started her career as an actress, but that went out the window when she married Iker. They had only one child, Xavier.

"One thing I don't understand," Leon said, sliding one gun part into another. He did this without looking down, as if his hands were on autopilot. "Why did they steal the Sealight? They're all rich."

"Let me see a picture of it again," Grandma Frida asked.

I pulled up an image of the Sealight and showed it to her.

Grandma Frida squinted and tapped the aquamarine. "There's your answer."

I shook my head. "I don't think it's about money. The Sealight is appraised and insured for two hundred and fifty thousand, mostly because of its age and the small diamonds framing the aquamarine. The aquamarine heart is worth probably seventy-five thousand by itself. The three black sheep siblings each receive over a million dollars annually from the family's invest-ments. For doing nothing."

"Must be nice," Mom said.

Arabella frowned. "So if they're caught stealing the tiara, they will almost certainly be cut off. Would you risk an easy million to steal something worth a quarter of that?"

Bern clapped his hands. "You did the math in your head, I'm so proud."

Arabella flipped him off.

"I saw that," Mom snapped.

"Sorry." My sister didn't sound sorry.

"Even if they did steal it," I said, "what would they do with it? None of them have been in the US in the past five years. They don't know any fences and no legitimate jeweler would touch it. If you google it, the picture of it comes up as 'The Sealight Crown, heirloom of House Rogan.' Nobody in Texas would touch something stolen from Mad Rogan. They couldn't give it away."

"Maybe they're planning to take it home," Arabella said.

"They would have to declare it at the airport," Leon said.

"How do you know that?" Mom asked.

"He checked into transporting guns by air," Arabella said.

Mom stopped filling the dishwasher and gave Leon a hard stare.

"Just trying to be prepared, that's all," he said.

I leaned back and sighed. "They can't sell it and they can't take it home. So, it's not about the money."

"Well, what is it about then?" Grandma Frida asked.

"It's about Mrs. Rogan, Connor, or Nevada," I said. "Either they hate Mrs. Rogan or Connor, and they want to embarrass them, or they hate Nevada and they don't want her to have it. Which is why she can't know, and we have to handle it and never tell her."

"Agreed," Bern said.

"So, basically, you have to figure out who hates Rogan and Nevada the most," Arabella said. "Is Xavier a suspect?"

Die.

Grandma Frida came to life like a shark smelling a drop of blood in the water. "Who is Xavier?"

"Nobody." What a brilliant response I came up with. That will throw them off the scent. Not.

"Xavier is Rogan's cute cousin, aaannd he likes her," the Evil Hellspawn Sister said.

"If you think he's cute, then you should talk to him," I said.

Arabella made big eyes at me. "She told him her name and he said, 'I know.'"

Grandma Frida and Leon made woo-woo noises at me.

My cheeks were getting warm. I hated when my cheeks got warm.

"You should go for it," Grandma Frida said.

That was about enough. "Mom."

"What happened to that handsome Italian boy?" Grandma Frida asked.

"She ran him off," Leon said. "She told him to get off our land or she would call the law." He had growled "the law" like he had a mouth full of gravel.

They were talking about me as if I wasn't even there. "Mom!"

"Let her be," Mom said. "She's trying to do a job."

"Maybe you should give it a try," Grandma Frida said. "You've been doing good with your magic."

"Yeah," Leon said. "And if things don't work out, I can always shoot him, and nobody will ever find the body."

I took my tablet and files and went to my room.

I STOOD NEXT to the ladder in Iker and Eva's room and watched Rivera install a tiny camera into the smoke detector. Rivera was one of Rogan's top guys. Normally he was trim and clean-cut, but today he was wearing a wig under a grimy baseball cap and his jaw sported a dark two-day stubble. He looked ridiculous.

Each of the guest couples had a suite and we were bugging the living rooms. Outside, Simone, one of Rogan's surveillance specialists, was installing hummingbird cameras in the bushes.

"Hey," Xavier said behind me.

I managed to not jump and turned around. He leaned casually against the doorframe. Right. It was his room too.

"Hi," I managed.

"Hi," he said.

I'd spent a long time on the drive over to Mountain Rose thinking about what to do if I saw Xavier. I had promised Arabella I would talk to him. Unfortunately, I wasn't very good at talking to people, especially people my age. In the end, I decided I had to talk to Xavier. Not just because he was cute and seemed to want to talk to me, but also because he was a potential lead. He was a teenager and a member of Rogan's extended family. Adults generally viewed us as children, whether they were willing to admit it or not, and they often said things around us without thinking.

Once I decided that Xavier was work, things became a lot easier. I just had to get him to like me without using my magic.

"Do you need something from the room? We're almost done."

"No, I just saw you through the window and wondered what you were doing in my suite. What *are* you doing?"

He sounded like he suspected we had gone through his underwear drawer. Rivera rolled his eyes.

"We're checking all the smoke detectors and replacing the batteries," I lied.

"Why?"

"Mrs. Rogan is worried that if a fire breaks out, some people might not get out."

"Each room in this wing has French doors that open to the garden," Xavier said. "Don't you think it's a bit extra? We're not likely to get trapped and most of us are telekinetics."

He seemed like the poster boy for the "adults are unreasonable and lame" crowd. I went through that phase too. When I was twelve. "True. But, she's paranoid and I have to do this. You know how it is." I shrugged. "Old people."

Xavier grinned and glanced at Rivera, then back at me. "Do you have to supervise, or can I steal you away for a little bit? I need your help with something."

Rivera's eyes got a dangerous glint. I had to get Xavier out of here before he asked too many questions or said something Rivera would make him regret.

"You got this?" I asked.

"Yes, ma'am," Rivera said.

"Please let me know when you're finished." I turned to Xavier. "Okay."

We walked out into the hallway. Xavier turned left, and we kept going, through a long hallway to the north end of the house, through the French doors and into the other side of the garden.

A path of decomposed granite started at the door and veered right, running through the orchard to the northeast side of the hill bordering the cliff.

Xavier started on the path, turned, graceful, and smiled at me. He really was very handsome. Almost as handsome as Alessandro Sagredo, but it was a different kind of beauty. Xavier looked like he would be perfect for the lead role in some angsty show about rich teenagers in a prep school. There was something sophisticated but nonchalant about him. Alessandro looked like he needed a sword and a hat with feathers.

Xavier was cute, but I had really liked Alessandro. I had liked him the first time I saw his picture. I had sat there for several minutes staring at it, not really thinking about anything at all. It was as if my brain had gone quiet. That almost never happened. And then I met him, and I knew there was no way.

"What did you need help with?" I asked.

"I need help with being beyond bored. You're the only interesting person I've met. Let's do something fun. You do have that here, don't you?"

"I have to work." *You don't know what you're asking. If I have fun with you, it won't end well for either of us.*

"What will happen if you stop working for just a little while?" He shrugged. "Will the house fall down? Will Arrosa fire you? She can't fire you—you're the bride's sister. Come on, at least walk with me. Am I really worse than working?"

No, he wasn't worse than working; he was work. He was a potential source of information, one I had to explore. Or was it exploit?

"One second," I said. I opened the chat window on my tablet and sent Rivera a quick text. **Please change camera placement in Xavier's suite.** Rogan's files pegged Xavier as a low-level Significant, which meant that when properly motivated, he could likely remove the smoke detector off the twelve-foot ceiling with his magic and examine it. I didn't want to take a chance of him finding the camera.

The tablet pinged back. **Got it.**

"Okay." I walked down the steps to the path. "I'm ready. But only until two o'clock."

"What happens at two?" he asked.

"My sister will be presenting the catering menu to Mrs. Rogan and she might need backup." Arabella did not need backup. Most of the time she was the backup, the field artillery, and the air support, but Nevada taught me to always have an exit strategy. I smiled at Xavier, trying to look enthusiastic. "Lead the way."

We strolled down the path.

"Are you worried that guy is going to steal something?"

What? "No, all of the people I hired have been vetted."

"You hired?" He let it hang.

"Yes, well, Arabella and I hired them. We ran an extensive background check, employment history, arrest history, and credit checks. Everyone on the grounds right now has references."

Xavier's nonchalant mask slid off for a second and he stared at me. "How do you know how to do this?"

"It's my job. I work for our family business."

"Yeah, I know. But I thought your family owned the business. I mean, you're a kid like me. Why do they make you work? Are you that . . . poor?" He said the word like it was something dirty or shameful.

I hid a sigh. It wasn't Xavier's fault. He grew up with different standards. It didn't make him better or worse than me, just different. "Nobody makes me work. I like it. Everybody in my family works for the agency. Even my grandmother, who has her own business, sometimes moonlights for us. It's interesting. Sometimes I get to help people. And I never have to ask my mom for money. I get a paycheck, and nobody tells me what to do with it. How does it work for you?"

"We just always have money. If I need something or want something I use my allowance, if I don't have enough, I ask my mom."

"What do you do for your allowance?"

"What?"

"What do you do? Do you get good grades, do chores? Do you help around the house? Mow the lawn?" I winked at him.

"You're teasing me," he said, sounding slightly injured.

"Maybe a little. But seriously, how does it work in your family? I know that Rogan used telekinesis for a lot of military contracts his House has. Are your parents expecting you to use your magic for family business or are they harping about college at you too?"

Xavier shrugged. "I don't think they care. My mother has been making University noises, but it's like she does it because she thinks she has to. My father gets his money from family investments. I don't remember them ever having jobs. Not the kind where they must be there all day. I wish they had jobs. It would get them out of the house."

When I was in middle school, high school scared me to death. I had been homeschooled. So, I researched, and I stumbled onto *How to Win Friends and Influence People* by Dale Carnegie. I took two things away from that book: people liked to talk about themselves and people liked you when you agreed with them.

"Your parents hover, don't they? I hate when adults do that."

"Yes." He snapped his fingers. "They hover. They don't actually care, they just hang about. They only notice me, so they can drag me to some family bore-fest."

"You didn't want to come to the wedding?" I opened my eyes wide in mock surprise.

"No, I wanted to have the house to myself."

"Yes, I get it. To be honest, I don't feel comfortable here, but then I am a poster girl for monachopsis."

"What?"

"Monachopsis. It means a subtle but nagging feeling of not fitting in and knowing that you don't belong in the place you are. This house is too much. Too big, too many rooms. I didn't grow up wealthy."

"My family has money, but I don't feel comfortable here either." His eyes sparked. His face turned animated, like he was about to ride a roller coaster. "There is wealth. This is Wealth. Capital *w*. Do you know, Rogan is worth $1.27 billion? And there's no prenup. Your sister is going to get half of that. If he dies, she gets all of that."

Well, that got morbid fast.

Xavier smiled. "Good time to suck up, huh?"

I thought of telling him how Nevada was paying for her own wedding dress, but he wouldn't get it.

"You're right. Better be nice."

So far nothing about this conversation made Xavier appealing. He might have been simply uncomfortable talking to me and was trying to say things to impress me, but it was coming out wrong. I had been there.

"Is it true your sister is a Truthseeker Prime?" he asked.

"Yes." Unlike my and Arabella's powers, Nevada's was now public record. Both Arabella and I were registered as Primes, but our records were sealed.

"So, you can't lie to her. Like at all?"

"You can, but she'll know." Now was a good time. "Is your family nervous that she's marrying Rogan? Not a lot of families would welcome a Truthseeker."

"She's making them squirm." He grinned. "Your sister walks into the room, and everyone shuts up. Every time Grandma Ane sees her, her face turns green. Cousin Mikel just runs away. I love it."

He hadn't really answered my question.

The path brought us to the front of the house. Two girls my age stood by the fountain, talking. One was tall and blonde, the other was curvier with dark, almost black hair. A third girl, dressed in white, her brown hair braided over her left shoulder, sat on the rim of the fountain, typing on her phone. The tall blonde was Gracia's oldest daughter, Adriana; the one with very dark hair was either Samanta or Malina, one of Lucian and June's daughters. They looked so similar, it was hard for me to tell them apart. The girl on the phone was Mikel and Maria's daughter. Like her mother, Elba dressed in white and liked gold jewelry.

Adriana and Samanta—I was 75 percent sure she was Samanta—waved. Adriana noticed me and her eyes narrowed. Samanta looked uncomfortable.

"Don't you know you're not supposed to talk to the help?" Elba asked without looking up from her phone.

Well, hello to you too, Ms. Bitch. I smiled.

"Does your dad know that?" Xavier asked. "How many people has he paid off now—is it three or four? We've all lost count."

"*Que te folle un pez,*" Elba said.

I hope you get fucked by a fish? What did that even mean? Their Spanish was different from what I was used to in Texas, but I understood it well enough.

Xavier put his arm around me and I had to stop myself from driving my elbow into his ribs. I did not like to be touched. Especially by people I didn't know. He did it in a protective way, but I still didn't like it.

"Don't mind her," Xavier said.

We crossed the courtyard back to the west wing. My tablet chimed. I glanced at it. The cameras had come online.

444 • ILONA ANDREWS
444 • ILONA ANDREWS

"I have to go."

"Really?" Xavier ducked a little to look at my face. "Are you sure?"

"Yes."

"I had a nice time," he said. He sounded like he meant it. Maybe he did.

The thing was, I kind of had a nice time too. Sure, he said some questionable stuff, but he tried to have an actual conversation with me, and that didn't happen every day. And he tried to protect me from his cousin. I didn't need any help, but it was kind of endearing. Also, he told me that his grandmother and Mikel had something to hide.

"I had a nice time too," I said.

"Then we'll do this again, right?" he asked. "Say yes, Catalina."

He said my name. "Yes. We'll do it again."

I went inside, ducked into one of the conference rooms across from the suites, and checked the feed from the cameras one by one. All of the suite cameras were functioning. I switched to the hummingbird cameras outside. One, two, three, four . . . nine? There should only have been six. I tapped the feed from camera seven. It showed a sitting area on the west side, just outside the building. Camera eight covered the path on the east side from which Xavier and I just came. Camera nine was installed at the top of the fountain. Bern must have wanted additional coverage.

Xavier was walking toward his cousins.

My cell phone rang. I recognized the number. Valentina's House Catering. Oh no. No, no, no. Arabella was in charge of the menu. If they were calling me, there was a problem.

I answered the phone. "Catalina Baylor."

Valentina's voice sounded in my ear. "We've had a tiny, little, itsy-bitsy problem. Someone broke into our restaurant."

Crap. "I'll be right there."

CHAPTER 5

VALENTINA'S HOUSE CATERING was in New Braunfels, a very German town in the middle of Texas. We had interviewed larger catering firms from Austin and San Antonio, but Mrs. Rogan decided she trusted Valentina's and so that's who we went with.

I parked in front of an old brick building. Leon got out of the passenger seat. Arabella was still in school, and today she was crash-writing a two-thousand-word essay, which was assigned to her a month ago and which she had started this morning. Leon was my battle buddy for this mission and he was thrilled.

"Cake shop," he said.

"Yes."

Leon let out a long-suffering sigh. "Are you sure that I'll be enough? These places can get pretty rough. You walk into a cake shop and then some gunslinger tells you, 'You ain't from around here, partner,' and the next thing you know, you're in the middle of the street, your horse is dead, the bad guy's got your girl by her hair, and you're down to one bullet."

"What is going on in your head?"

"It's a dark, lawless place, Catalina. So dark."

I rolled my eyes. "It's a small restaurant and bakery. Most of their money comes from catering, but they do have a small cupcake shop about two blocks down. Four full-time employees, besides the owner. They hire waitstaff for large events."

"So, we're hiring someone, and they're hiring someone? Who is screening the waitstaff?"

"We are hiring the waitstaff this time," I told him. Rogan had given me a nearly unlimited budget and I made sure to hire waiters with great references. "This is the only place Mrs. Rogan trusts to cater, so we did what we could to secure the location. Rogan's people installed an excellent alarm and security system."

"I thought you said they discovered the break-in this morning." Leon eyed the building.

"Yes, they did."

"So, they didn't arm their excellent alarm system?"

"Let's find out."

Most of the building inside was taken up by a large kitchen. Long metal prep tables stretched across the floor in two rows. On the left, two industrial-size refrigerators stood against the wall, along with three large sinks, a dishwasher, and a row of ovens. Next to them a door led to a narrow room with two equally large freezers. Straight ahead, directly opposite the entrance, another door offered access to a large pantry. A row of windows in the wall on our right flooded the space with natural light. It was a clean, uncluttered space. The air smelled faintly of sour wine.

Valentina jumped up from her chair when we entered. A white woman in her midthirties, her short blond hair had a streak of wild purple in it. Her glasses kept sliding down her nose and she kept pushing them back up. Red blotches stained her cheeks. She was clearly stressed out and on the verge of tears. Her XO, Carlos, a solidly built man in his fifties, with black hair and bronze skin, stood next to her, hands on his hips.

"They broke in last night," Valentina said. "Three of them in dark hoodies."

Leon nodded at the first window on our right, with the windowsill stained with grey fingerprint powder. "Is that how they came in?"

"Yes," Carlos said. "We open the windows a lot to air the kitchen out."

"Did the alarm not go off?" I asked.

Both Valentina and Carlos looked like they wanted to fall through the floor.

"The wireless sensor on that window keeps going off randomly," Carlos said.

"Why didn't you notify us that the sensor was malfunctioning?" I asked.

"It didn't seem like a big deal. It's a very small window. We usually bypass it," Valentina said. "Otherwise it goes off in the middle of the night."

"It's kids." Carlos growled, his face turning dark red. "Probably tried the window, figured out we forgot to lock it, and crawled in. I bet it's that idiot Hudson. Him and his sidekick are always in the park across the street. Up to no good. They sit in the park, drink beer all day, and look for trouble to get into. When I was their age, I had a job. I had responsibilities. I—"

I had to cut him off before it turned into a full-blown lecture about kids these days. "What did they take?"

Valentina grimaced. "Champagne. They took a case of it. Probably all they could carry. It's heavy. And they smashed the rest."

"Two hundred and fifty bottles, two hundred and twenty dollars per bottle," Carlos spat.

Fifty thousand dollars' worth of champagne. All gone.

"Damn. Sucks for you," Leon offered helpfully.

Valentina looked green.

"Do you have the security footage?" I asked.

A minute later, I watched three figures in dark hoodies with bandannas over their faces spray the security cameras with whipped cream, which they found in the fridge.

"We don't usually use canned whipped cream," Valentina said. "The client had specifically requested it for her bachelorette party. We didn't ask."

The sounds of champagne being smashed came from the screen. I glanced at Leon. He nodded.

I rewound the recording. "Look. They get through the window and they go straight to the fridge. They knew that the window would be unlocked and bypassed, and they knew right where the whipped cream was."

"What are you implying?" Carlos asked. His eyes bulged. "I know everyone who works here. I vouch for everyone who works here."

Humans dealt with risk by pretending it didn't exist. Even though thousands of people died every year in car accidents, we still got into our cars and drove every day. We built illusions of safety around ourselves and believed them or we would go insane.

A home was one of those vital illusions. It was our shelter, the place where we let our guard down. Nothing bad was supposed to happen to you in your house. When our warehouse was attacked by mercenaries, it felt like my world was cracked open. It made me feel weak and helpless.

Valentina and Carlos were feeling helpless now. The financial loss was crushing, but the violation of their kitchen was likely worse. This was a small business. The employees were probably more like family than hired help. They spent a lot of time together in this kitchen, making delicious food and beautiful cakes. Someone had smashed all those happy memories to pieces. The idea that one their own might have done it was too much.

"Are there any bottles left?" Leon asked.

Valentina reached under the counter and pulled a heavy bottle out. Leon grabbed the bottle by the neck and smashed it against the wall. The bottle held.

"Hey!" Carlos yelled.

I held up my hand. "We'll reimburse you."

It took Leon two more tries before the bottle finally broke.

Panting a little, he held the bottle out to me. "Two hundred, like this?"

I turned to Valentina. "If you're just kids breaking in to steal some wine, you'd grab a few bottles and get out. This took a lot of time and effort. The question is why."

"Yes, why? Why would anybody do this?" Valentina asked.

"Two possible reasons," I said. "First, they were covering up the sound of what they were doing, and second, they counted on you concentrating on the loss of the wine. Our contract with you specified that you were to call us immediately in case of any complications. Why didn't you call us?"

"We called the police," Carlos said.

"You don't understand," Valentina said, her face plum red now. "We came in and there were piles of glass on the floor. All this wine, the smell . . ."

And she had wanted to clean it up as soon as possible, to erase the desecration of their beautiful kitchen.

"It's misdirection." Leon nodded at the broken glass on the floor. "Smashed bottles, broken glass, expensive wine on the floor, everything smells, everything is stained and sticky. You see this and if nothing else appears disturbed, you just concentrate on cleaning things up."

I looked at Valentina and Carlos, and my insides tried to squeeze themselves into a tight painful ball. There were things I had to say now, harsh and unkind things, and I had to say them to two people who were already desperate and traumatized. I felt mean and shitty. But it was my job. I promised I would do it.

"You're in breach of contract," I said. "You were hired by House Rogan. This is House business. Normal rules do not apply here. We were crystal clear when we went over the contract with you. My sister and I sat at this table and read the contract to you paragraph by paragraph and you said you understood and you signed it. First, you failed to set the alarm."

Carlos sucked in a lungful of air, about to say something, but Valentina put her hand on his arm.

"Second, you failed to notify us of the break-in. The contract specifically spells out that we are to be informed in the event of any problems prior to any contact with law enforcement, unless it's a life-threatening emergency. Third, you cleaned up, destroying the evidence."

Nobody said anything.

Valentina bit her lip. "If you cancel everything now, we will be ruined."

I knew exactly what she was thinking. She was looking into the future and seeing the death of her business. And I was the person who decided if it lived or died. I had never wanted to teleport more in my entire life. If I could, I would have run away and pretended this never happened.

"Is there anything we can do to fix this?" Valentina asked.

"It depends," I said. "I would like access to your computer. I will be able to tell you more depending on what we find. Under the terms of our contract, I cannot compel you to grant me access. You can refuse."

"And if we do?" Carlos asked.

I raised my hands. "We walk away."

"Go ahead." Valentina waved at a desktop in the corner by a small desk.

I activated the recording function on my phone. "This is Catalina Baylor. Today is April 20th. I am here with Valentina Krueger, owner of Valentina's House Catering. May I have access to your business computer?"

"Yes."

"Thank you."

Leon headed for the desktop. His fingers flew over the keyboard. "Did you shut the computer down before you left?"

"Yes," Valentina said. She sounded like she expected us to hit her with a baseball bat. "We shut it off every night before we leave."

"What was the last thing you worked on?" Leon asked.

"Fishmonger list," Valentina said.

"Well," Leon said. "Somebody turned it back on at the time of the break-in and accessed the Rogan Cake file."

Crap. I turned to Valentina and Carlos. "Can I have your cell phones, please? I don't need you to unlock them, I just want you to put them on the table over there. And not touch them, until I give them back to you."

"Oh my God." Valentina's eyes got big. "They tampered with the cake. But it's not even put together yet. We just started the sponges yesterday."

"Phones, please," Leon said. His tone was matter-of-fact, but there was something in the way he said it that communicated that disobeying him was a very bad idea.

Two phones landed on the metal table.

"I would like you to go to the pantry and review your inventory. Do not touch anything. If something looks wrong, if it has been moved, or the lid is not on just right, tell me immediately. Please keep the pantry door open, so I can see you."

The two bakers went into the pantry. I dialed Rogan's number. He answered on the second ring. "Yes?"

"I believe someone poisoned your wedding cake. How would you like me to proceed?"

IN HALF AN hour, Rogan's troops, assigned to Mrs. Rogan's house, arrived in two armored cars. New Braunfels was only half an hour from Mountain Rose, but it felt like it took them forever. I spent the time trying to figure out who might have wanted to poison Nevada's cake. Rogan and Nevada had made plenty of enemies when they stopped a conspiracy by several prominent Houses to seize power in Texas. Most of these enemies were dead or in jail.

When Primes killed someone in revenge, they wanted the whole world to know about it. They didn't delegate. They wanted to look into your eyes as their magic choked the life out of you. Poison just seemed so mundane. And, because we had just become a House, none of the Primes could legally attack us for the next three years.

Besides, a lot of Primes would be attending. The guest list read like the Powerful and Influential page on Herald. Whoever poisoned the cake would have killed members of Houston's magical elite. There would be no place for them to hide. It didn't feel like a politically or financially motivated attempt. It felt like hate. Blinding hate, so powerful, it made you forget about your own safety.

I had made a list of suspects. One name kept coming up. Someone who hated Rogan. Who was jealous, hateful, and reckless.

Rivera was the first one through the door. Behind him came a woman in the loose fatigues a lot of Rogan's employees wore. A baseball cap was pulled down tightly on her head. The rest of the crew secured the perimeter, spreading out through and outside of the bakery.

The woman took off her ball cap. She was about my age, red-headed, with skin so pale, it almost glowed. One of my grandfathers was black, and we weren't sure about the other. Both of my grandmothers were white, and all the genes mixed together gave me a naturally tan skin and dark brown hair. A lot of my friends were paler than me, but this girl had epic levels of paleness. It's like she didn't even know what the sun was. How did she survive in Texas?

"Runa Etterson of House Etterson, Magus Venenata." She stuck her hand out at me.

Venenata was Latin for poison. Runa was a poison mage and she was smiling at me and holding her hand out. She could probably poison me by just breathing in my direction.

"Catalina Baylor. Of House Baylor." I shook her hand.

She grinned at me. "Aha, took you a second. Don't worry, I only poison random strangers on Tuesdays."

"Today is Tuesday," Leon said.

"Oops. Well, that's okay. You told me your name, so we're not strangers. You should be safe." She turned to Leon. "But I don't know who you are. No promises."

"This is my cousin, Leon."

"Nice to meet you, Cousin Leon. So, where are the potentially poisoned goodies?"

I led her to the refrigerators and opened the doors. Tubs of frosting and fondant in every color filled the shelves. Runa rubbed her hands together.

"Come on, guys, don't just stand there. Grab a spoon and let's get busy."

Nobody said anything or moved.

"What? How did you think this worked? That I would wiggle my nose and sniff out the poison? If only. No, you eat it and if you die, I can say, 'Yes, it's been poisoned.'"

Rivera sighed. "Ma'am. Please take this seriously. According to the agreement between House Rogan and House Etterson . . ."

"Yes, yes. I've been stuck in the guardhouse on a chance someone at this wedding will get poisoned for the last two weeks. Let me have a little fun."

Runa raised her hands. A faint green mist spread from her, passed through the refrigerators, and dissipated. She stepped forward, took a tub of ice-white fondant out, opened it, pinched some fondant off, and popped it in her mouth. "Mmm, delicious cyanide. Old school. Histotoxic hypoxia on you, histotoxic hypoxia on your house, histotoxic hypoxia on your cow. Wait." She held her hand up. "What is this fishy aftertaste?"

Runa ate a little more and smacked her lips loudly. "It's on the tip of my tongue. Ooo. Tetrodotoxin. Sneaky. Cyanide would kill you in minutes, but if you happened to somehow take an antidote, tetrodotoxin would still get you."

Runa held out her hands. "Every tub in here is poisoned. All of the fondant. If the poisoner wanted to simply assassinate the happy couple, they could have used thallium. It is odorless, tasteless, lethal, and it takes several days to kick in. What this person did is about as subtle as taking a hammer and smashing the bride and groom on the head with it. You are looking for someone for whom Connor's and Nevada's death is deeply personal. This person wants to see them suffer and die. They will likely be in the wedding party or near it. They want to inflict pain and witness it so badly, they are willing to risk their personal safety. They can't wait to do it. There is glee in this and a horrible malice."

This aligned with everything I was thinking so far. I pulled up my main suspect and showed the tablet to Rivera and Leon. Rivera's eyes narrowed.

"Makes sense," he said.

A crazy grin tugged at Leon's mouth. "Oh, I hope so. I really hope so."

"Who is responsible for the fondant?" I asked.

"Jeremy," Carlos said. "But he's a good kid. He wouldn't do this."

Rivera spoke into his phone. "Bug, I need a full workup on Jeremy Wagner. Payments, debt history, any connection to Rogan or Baylor. I want to know where he was and what he was doing since Valentina's was hired for the wedding. Anything you can dig up."

We had done a background check on every employee. Jeremy Wagner had come back clean, which meant that either we were incompetent, or his darkness was well hidden. Trying to retrace Jeremy's steps in the last few days, even with Bug's talent, would take time. We didn't have time. Right now, in Mountain Rose, Mrs. Rogan could be serving the children poisoned lemonade.

I had to use my magic. I felt cold and nauseous and sticky, as if I had been poisoned. It was an awful feeling. My heart was hammering in my chest. I wanted to go somewhere alone and quiet, anywhere but here. I wanted this to be somebody else's problem.

They were going to poison my sister. And Rogan. And his mother. And all their friends, relatives, and children. Mia Rosa with her bedazzled unicorn. I could think of only one person who had that kind of hate.

"I will interview Jeremy."

Rivera startled. Leon frowned at me. "Are you sure?"

"Yes."

"The real target is the person who hired Jeremy," Rivera said.

"I'm aware of that. The background will take time and may not turn up anything. It's a simple matter of what would be quickest and produce the best results. If I ask him, he will tell me."

Rivera spoke slowly and deliberately. "If I wanted to poison someone by tampering with the wedding cake, I would watch the bakery to make sure the tampering was not discovered. The moment you question Jeremy, we will have to sit on him. If the poisoner suspects that we know about the cake, they will try again, and this time we may not find it in time. Tracing Jeremy's employer through Bug is cleaner and carries less risk."

"And what if Bug doesn't find anything?" Leon asked.

Whatever happened, my cousin was in my corner.

"If he doesn't find anything, then we squeeze Jeremy," Rivera said.

"I can question Jeremy and make sure he won't remember it."

Leon's eyebrows crept up.

"Are you sure?" Rivera asked.

I wasn't sure, but sooner or later I had to try it. It had to work. My sister's life depended on it.

"Yes. It's plausible that we would talk to all of the employees after the break-in."

"If Catalina says she can do it, she can do it," Leon said.

"Okay," Rivera said.

I turned to Valentina. "Please call in your employees. Let them know that there has been a burglary and they will be interviewed. Meanwhile, I need you to replace all of the fondant with an identical product. If Jeremy is in on it, he will not taste the fondant, because he knows it's lethal, so he'll have no way of knowing it was switched."

"Ahem," Runa said. "Or you could let me purify the fondant for you, no need to replace or dispose of anything."

"But will it be safe?" Valentina asked.

The smile vanished from Runa's face. Suddenly her expression turned cold and harsh. "Let me introduce myself again. Runa Etterson of House Etterson, *Prime* Venenata. I have walked into a house filled with sarin and after I was done, the family hiding upstairs in the safe room, walked out and made coffee for me in their kitchen. Mad Rogan trusts my House with the safety of the people who are most precious to him. If I say the fondant is safe to use, it's safe to use. Stand back please."

Runa pulled out chalk and began drawing an arcane circle on the floor.

CHAPTER 6

I SAT IN the small office on the other side of the building. Normally this room was used to meet with clients and go over menus and cake books. Today there would be questions about cakes, but they would have a different flavor.

Rivera took his job as chief of security very seriously. He and two of his guys wouldn't budge from their position behind me. Runa perched on the chair, flipping through a photo album filled with beautiful cakes, on the off chance Jeremy tried to poison me.

Leon leaned on the table next to me. "Are you okay?" he asked quietly.

"Yeah." I would have to use my magic with finesse. The few times I'd actively used it required power. Finesse was entirely different.

When I was born, the nurse who helped deliver me picked me up out of the crib by my mother's side and ran. They caught her before she made it off the floor, and when they took me away from her, she screamed and cried. In twenty years of nursing, she had never done anything like that. That woman lost her career because I was born with the kind of magic that made people love me.

She was the first but not the last. Over the years, there had been others. A dentist who examined my teeth tried to hide me in his office and then claimed that I ran away. I was two years old. The preschool teacher loaded me into her car and tried to run my mother over when she attempted to stop her. When we would go shopping, strangers would follow me as I rode in the cart and employees would try to give me things for free.

Other babies and toddlers were encouraged to be cute. I was taught to never draw attention to myself, not to smile at strangers, and not to make friends. If I liked another child, they would abandon everything to play with me. But soon playing wouldn't be enough. They would follow me, mesmerized, and then they would want a piece of me, a piece of my dress, a lock of my hair, some skin, maybe a finger. Once it started, I didn't know how to stop it. Only my family and my primary doctor were immune.

I was homeschooled until high school, when it became clear that I could control my power well enough to keep it from leaking. I had practiced controlling my magic since the moment I understood that I ruined lives. My talent was extremely rare, but I studied similar magics, I practiced arcane circles, and I read all about magic theory, but theory, by definition, wasn't practice.

I had experimented before on my sisters, because they were immune, and I had no way of knowing if anything I learned would actually work. Rivera shouldn't have bothered with the lecture. I needed him and his guys here. He knew what I could do. If I failed to control my power and besotted Jeremy snapped, they would pull him off me.

The door swung open and Jeremy Wagner walked in. Just like in his pictures, which I had reviewed when we vetted him, Jeremy was a tall, dark-haired Caucasian man in his midtwenties. He had one of those generic faces, neither ugly nor handsome, but overall pleasant. There was something soft and sheepish about his demeanor. He seemed like a timid man who knew he was timid and decided to use it to his advantage.

He should have been nervous, concerned at the very least, possibly defensive. Most people would have their guard up. Instead he looked slightly sleepy. It might have been because he'd spent the night breaking into the bakery, but his pictures confirmed that he always looked that way.

"Please sit down," I said.

"Hi." He sat and gave me a smile. Even the way he smiled at me reinforced the sheepishness, as if he were trying to say, "Boy, I'm a mess, but aren't I cute?"

"You are here because someone broke into the shop last night."

"Oh yeah? Did they take anything?"

When my magic was evaluated by a panel of Primes, the Keeper of Records, who registered the members of every House in Houston, had to come up with a name for my brand of power. He called me Siren. Most people thought of sirens as mermaids, but in the original myths, they had feathers and wings. I had wings too. Mesmerizing, beautiful wings that glittered with magic. Nobody ever saw them, except me, but when I opened them, people focused on me and forgot about everything else.

For most people using magic required conscious thought and effort. Like punching a bag or doing a push-up. They practiced and got stronger. For me, it was the opposite. Keeping my wings closed when I was around strangers was like always holding my breath. Opening them was effortless.

I didn't need my full power for Jeremy. I only need a tiny bit of it, so I let him see a bare hint of my feathers. He blinked and smiled at me.

I opened my mouth and my magic stretched forward, fused with my voice, and wound about him, an invisible thread that lured him in. The effort to hold back my power, only letting a tiny bit through, was exhausting.

"They smashed some wine bottles. Do you like wine, Jeremy?"

He was focused completely on me now. "I'm more of a beer guy. I like all kinds of beer. I like IPAs the best. You know, when you can really taste the hops. It's a real beer. It's like studying surrealism. You drink an IPA and there is nothing abstract or vague about it. It's citrus and hops . . ."

I had him. In the corner Runa sat up straighter and put her photo book down.

". . . a baseline against which all other beers should be compared. Like is it stronger than an IPA? Is it sweeter or less hoppy? Do you like beer? There is a great biergarten we can go to right now and I will buy you an IPA."

"Jeremy, are you good at decorating cakes?"

"I'm the best at decorating cakes. Better than people on TV." Jeremy's eyes went wide. "I watch *The Cake Tournament* and most of that shit is pure crap. I am a fucking wizard with fondant. If we had some fondant right now, I could really show you something."

"There is fondant in the bakery," I said.

"Oh no, we can't use that. It's poisoned."

Leon smiled.

"That's weird. Who poisoned it?"

Jeremy waved his hand. "My younger bro and two of his buddies from high school. That's not important. I did all the hard work. I set this up."

My voice wrapped around him, seductive and reassuring. "Wow, you must be very smart, Jeremy. Why would you set it up?"

"I never liked Primes. They act like they're so much better than us. Oh, and this woman paid me a hundred grand in cash. I've got it buried in my backyard. I'm rich. I don't have to work here. You should let me take you out. We could go to South Padre."

I turned my tablet on and showed him the picture I had pulled up.

"That's her," he said. "Do you know her? Did she give you money? I would give you money. I've got money."

"Do you know how she's getting into the wedding?" I asked.

"Nah. She just gave me a bunch of syringes with stuff in them and said to inject the fondant. And she told me not to poke myself with them and to wear plastic gloves." He rolled his eyes. "Duh, like I'm stupid."

Now came the most difficult part.

I opened my mouth and sang. The words didn't matter, only the magic did. Jeremy listened, his jaw hanging slack. The magic wrapped around him, like a glittering veil, and he began to sing with me. "Baa baa black sheep, have you any wool, yes sir, yes sir, three bags full . . ."

I fell silent and gently untangled my magic from him, as it whispered into his mind. *Forget, forget, forget.*

His head drooped, his chin falling to his chest. He pitched forward slowly. His stomach touched the table. Jeremy jerked awake. He blinked at me, his eyes looking wild.

"They smashed some wine bottles," I said. "Do you like wine, Jeremy?"

"I'm more of a beer guy."

"Did you have anything to do with the break-in?" I asked him.

"Nope. It's a shame though. I mean, who would be dumb enough to break into a bakery?"

"Where were you last night between one and two?" I was so tired now. My voice was shaking.

"I was home. My brother will vouch for me. We stayed up playing video games."

"Okay, Jeremy, you're free to go."

"Great." He got up and offered me his hand. I shook it. His handshake was limp. "Great to meet you." He walked out.

Nobody said anything. Rivera stared at his phone. Leon was grinning at me like a lunatic and holding two thumbs up.

Rivera looked up. "Okay, he went into the kitchen."

"Well, that was something else," Runa said.

A wild thought occurred to me. I stuck my hand out. "Catalina Baylor, of House Baylor, Prime Siren."

Runa looked at my hand, took it carefully, and shook it. "Stay out of my head."

"Don't poison anybody I know, and I will."

"Is the memory loss permanent?" Rivera asked.

"I don't know," I said.

"We're going to watch him," Rivera said. "My guess is he told you everything he knows, and she's too smart to give him anything that could lead us to her. We're going to proceed as if we bought the teenager wine story. We're going to put guards here, because it's expected."

"If she wants to get into the wedding, it will have to be the waitstaff," I said.

Rivera nodded. "That seems most likely."

Leon stirred. "Carlos will be a problem. If he suspects Jeremy did this, he won't be able to control himself."

Rivera smiled. "We will tell him that he passed with flying colors. You already got them to sign the NDA."

Rogan had emailed me a nondisclosure agreement that forbade Valentina and Carlos to even mention the word *poison* for the next two weeks. If they broke this agreement, we would immediately terminate our contract. If they managed to stick to it, Rogan would pay for the smashed wine bottles. I had to explain to them in excruciating detail that they, their online communications, and their phone calls would be monitored until after the wedding. It made me feel like a corporate gangster. Like I had come into their shop and smashed it demanding protection money, but it was all legal and binding.

"I think I would like to go now," I told Leon.

* * *

LEON DROVE, WHILE I fought my way through my text messages. Mrs. Rogan wanted to know if there was any progress on finding Sealight. There wasn't, so I told her we were working on it. Rogan wanted to know if I was okay. I wasn't, so I told him I was fine. Mom wanted to know if we were coming home for dinner. We were, and I said yes. Arabella wanted to know if she could put a piece of duct tape over Nevada's mouth and fingers, so she would stop changing the stupid wedding. I told her no. I got a very nice email from Mia Rosa typed by her mother, which thanked me for the bedazzler. Which was awesome. Someone had asked me for something, I did it, and they were happy and said thank you.

The last text was from Bern. **Where are you?**

In the car, with Leon.

Are you going back to Mountain Rose?

Yes, but only for a minute. I needed to make sure they finished the tent like they were supposed to.

I need you to find a safe place to pull over. I'm sending you some footage you need to see before you get there.

What? Send it. I'll just look at it while Leon is driving.

No, I need you to pull over.

I sighed. "Your brother is being weird."
"And this is news how?"
"Can you take the next exit and find a good spot to pull over?"

Two minutes later, Leon pulled over from 281 into a gas station lot and parked. I sent Bern a text. My email dinged, and I started the download on my phone. It was taking forever.

"That was awesome back there," Leon said. "I didn't know you could do that."

"I didn't know I could either."

"Does it feel good when you use your magic?"

"It feels good to not hide it."

If we weren't in a parking lot in public, I would open my wings and just rest. I was even afraid to do it while we were driving. I couldn't take a chance on someone fixating on me and wrecking their car.

"He was going to poison all of us, Leon. When I think about it, it kind of freaks me out. Anybody, *everybody* who ate that cake would have died. Little kids would have died. And he didn't care. I could tell when he was talking that part of it was the money, but not all of it. He did it because he hates us. He doesn't even know us. He didn't feel bad about it, Leon—he was proud of it."

Leon leaned back in his seat. "Everybody in our family has magic. Aunt Penelope, Grandma Frida, you, your sisters, Bern . . . I thought I didn't have magic. I thought I was a dud. I used to climb to the top of the warehouse. There is a way to get to the roof from the attic. I would walk on the edge of the roof."

"Why in the world would you do that?"

"I thought maybe if I got scared enough, my powers would come out." Leon grimaced. "You can practice and get good at sports. You can study and get good grades. But with magic, you have it or you don't. That's it. And it's so fucking unfair. Here you are, and an accident of birth, something in your DNA that you have no control over, decides, before you're even born, how your life is going to go."

I couldn't remember a time when I didn't have magic. It was this scary thing that ruled my life. I had so much guilt wrapped up in it. I never told Leon about it, because I knew he would have given up half of his life for some of that power.

"But you didn't poison people," I said.

"Who would I poison? You're my family. I love you. I wouldn't even poison Mom if she showed back up. I did hate her, you know. Still do. First, if she had slept with Bern's dad instead of whoever my dad was, I would have had magic. Some magic. Second, she is a piss-poor mom."

I tried to look for the best things in people. There was nothing good about Aunt Gisele. I used to think that she was just misunderstood but then she showed up and wrecked our life, and now I hated her too.

"Jeremy is a scumbag," Leon said. "He's too stupid to realize he isn't smart. But he sees all the Primes in the news and on Herald, and he envies them. The jealousy is eating him alive. Once the wedding is over, Rivera will make sure he's turned over to the proper authorities."

Rogan could make Jeremy disappear, but he wouldn't. I once asked Nevada about things like that and she said that being a House meant projecting a show of strength. If someone like Jeremy attacked a House, they would want to make a very public example of him.

The file downloaded. I tapped it. The feed from one of the hummingbird cameras filled the screen. Xavier was walking toward his cousins. I turned the sound up.

Adriana, the tall blonde, took a step toward Xavier, her face stamped with anger. Spanish words flew out. "Why are you doing this? She is a nice girl. Leave her alone."

They were talking about me.

"Shut the fuck up," Xavier said.

Elba giggled from her spot on the fountain, the gold bracelets on her tan arms sliding back and forth as she waved her hands.

"I mean it." Adriana crossed the space between them and got in his face. "Leave Catalina alone. She is working really hard. She doesn't know you're a snake. Find someone else to screw around with."

Xavier crossed his arms. Adriana was tall, but he was taller by at least four inches. "Or what? What are you going to do? Let me tell you what you will do: nothing. You've been doing nothing. None of you are doing anything about this wedding. He's going to marry that bitch."

My heart hammered in my chest. My cheeks were getting hot. Adriana was right. He was a snake. And I almost let him bite me.

"What do you care?" Samanta, the one with curly dark hair, said. "Let him get married."

He turned toward her. "If you stopped shoving food in your mouth long enough to think, you'd figure it out. You want to explain it to her, Elba?"

"Rogan leads a dangerous life," Elba said. "He has powerful enemies. Think about it—he's old, like thirty something, and this is the first time he tried to marry someone. His mom is in a wheelchair because people kept trying to kill his dad. On top of that, everyone knows he's a sicko. Then this bitch, a complete nobody, shows up and now he's marrying her without a prenup."

"Exactly," Xavier jumped in. "He dies one day after the wedding, she gets everything, and we get nothing. Let me explain it to you in small words, so you can understand. Our grandparents are drawing money from family investments. They are not getting that much, one-two mil a year each. Our parents have to work. By the time the grandparents die off, and our parents start drawing their share, they will be getting even less money, because there are more of them. We'll have to work and when it's our turn, there might not be anything left over. You know who has money?"

"Rogan," Elba said. "A nice pretty billion."

"Rogan will get himself killed sooner or later. My dad says he made a lot of powerful enemies this last year. Arrosa is old. All we have to do is wait." Xavier snapped his fingers. "And we'll inherit. But for that to happen, there needs to be no wife and no heir."

"What are you going to do, Xavier?" Adriana sneered at him. "Even if you break up the wedding, are you going to follow him around with a rubber to make sure he doesn't make any kids?"

"That will be later. Right now, we have a more pressing issue. He is marrying that bitch."

"They are Primes," Samanta shot back.

"Yeah, last time I checked, Xavier, you weren't a Prime." Adriana crossed her arms.

"Neither are you," Xavier said. "I looked up their records and they just became a House this year. She's a truthseeker, there is a pattern mage, but everybody else's records are sealed. They are upstarts. If they had useful magic, they would've announced it. What kind of Prime doesn't disclose their magic? Trust me, they're trash. Have you seen Catalina scurrying around with her tablet, like a mouse with a piece of old cheese? She's a Prime? Please. A Prime geek. She knows she doesn't belong here. She told me she feels 'uncomfortable.' She'll feel uncomfortable when I kick her and her sister off the grounds."

I saw red. I actually saw red, as if someone suddenly jerked a translucent red curtain closed in front of me.

"I'm going to shove a gun up his ass sideways," Leon snarled. Xavier paced back and forth. "All that's required of you is to keep your mouths shut and stay out of my way, while I romance that rat. She's got the entire wedding and probably half her family secrets on that tablet she carries with her. I'm going to get that tablet."

"You really are an asshole," Adriana said.

"Don't worry," Xavier said. "Even though great-grandfather kicked your mom out of the family for being a lesbo, you and I can work something out when we inherit."

"Xavier!" Samanta glared at him.

Elba grinned. "Don't be jealous. If I were you, I would be doing everything I could to help us. The way Lucian sleeps around, you'll have to share your inheritance with an army of bastards."

"Ugh!" Adriana spun and walked away. Samanta looked after her, glanced at Xavier and Elba, and hurried after Adriana.

"Don't worry," Elba said. "Samanta is a coward, and Adriana won't say anything. She's bought Isabella's pills off me a couple of times. She's got 'anxiety' and if her mom finds out, she'll skin her alive."

Xavier grimaced. "Good, keep them under control and I'll handle the rest."

The recording stopped.

"I'll fucking kill him." Leon growled. "I'll drown him in that damn fountain and then I'll CPR him back and drown him again."

A pit had opened in my stomach. I tasted acid on my tongue and swallowed it back down. Hot tears wet my cheeks, burning the skin. It was as if I had been poisoned and my body was desperately trying to expel it.

"Don't cry, Catalina—he's not worth it. Don't let him make you sad." Leon hovered next to me. "Please don't cry. I'll make it okay somehow. Just don't cry, or I might cry with you, and then you'll tell everybody, and I'll be embarrassed. Do you need tissues? I have tissues."

He grabbed a box of tissues from the backseat and thrust them in my hands. "Don't be sad."

"I'm not sad," I ground through clenched teeth. "I'm angry."

Leon blinked. "You don't get angry."

I turned and looked at him. He shied back.

"That waste of space actually thinks that he has a chance against us. He thinks that I'm so flattered that he paid attention to me for ten minutes that I'll just do whatever he wants. He thinks he dazzled me. That arrogant prick!"

Leon flinched.

"And their brilliant plan! They'll get ahold of my tablet, because that's where we keep all our family's deep shameful secrets."

"Do we have those?" Leon asked.

"No, but they do, and I will find every last one of them. They think they can break up the wedding, so in some distant future Rogan will die alone. I can't even! This is the dumbest thing I ever heard. It's like a TV movie for tweeners."

"Yes, that is some *Parent Trap* level shit, right there."

"It's something a twelve-year-old would come up with. Xavier is an adult! Elba is sixteen years old. They can't take care of themselves, they're petulant, they're immature, they don't know basic things, they're dumb, and their magic is nowhere near ours. Where does this superior attitude come from exactly?"

Leon started the car and locked the doors. "Okay," he said in a soothing voice. "Your face is turning purple and I've never seen it do that before. I really think we should just go home."

"No, we're going back to Mountain Rose and I will feed him this tablet."

"Well, I'm driving so I say we're going home."

"Leon!"

"Just keep in mind," Leon said, merging onto the highway,

"I'm your cousin and you love me. If you attack me while I'm driving, we will both die and then he wins. Don't let him win, Catalina."

I SAT IN the kitchen, going through the background files. Leon had taken off for his room and a shower. Bern was working in the computer room we called Hut of Evil. It was just me, Arabella, Mom, and Grandma Frida in the kitchen.

I had looked at the files some yesterday, but they were a mile long, and I didn't review them as thoroughly as I needed to. Thanks to Xavier's little rant, I had some nice suspects.

I focused on Mikel, who managed Ramírez Capital, and was the husband of Maria of many cocktails, white clothes, and loud gold jewelry and father to Elba, who was a vicious little bitch. When Xavier put on his little performance for me as we walked by the fountain and he told Elba off, he said something about Mikel paying off the house staff. On the way back to the warehouse, I had scoured his file. On paper, Mikel drew a salary equivalent to one point four million dollars. He had no other significant sources of income. Maria spent money at an alarming rate. They lived in a seven-million-dollar mansion; they had a second home in Barcelona, valued at five million; they owned four luxury cars, totaling over eight hundred thousand dollars; a yacht; and they showed no signs of slowing down. Where was all the money coming from?

I had asked Bug to comb through his financial statements and to let me know as soon as he found something.

Lucian de Baldivia was the next on my list. He was married to June, but it seemed everyone in the family knew he was having affairs. I'd been tracking cheaters down for years and I knew that affairs weren't free. They left a trail. Hotels, gifts, dates, luxury getaways disguised as work conferences or conventions, more gifts, this time to the wronged spouse. Rogan's files listed twenty-three women Lucian had slept with since marrying June twenty years ago, and twelve of these relationships were long-term affairs. Every couple of years he got the itch and found someone to scratch it. His last affair ended eighteen months ago. He was about due for a new one, and the Sealight would make a pretty present.

There was still Paul Sarmiento, the boy toy, who appeared to have materialized out of thin air. He was a mystery: nobody knew him, nobody knew how Ane knew him, and nobody knew what he did. Two hundred and fifty thousand dollars might not be a huge windfall for the Ramírez and de Baldivias, but it was an attractive prize for the average thief . . .

Arabella moaned and dramatically slammed her head on the table.

Mom and Grandma Frida put down their utensils and clapped.

"I've had it," my sister announced. "She is not getting those damn lilacs and that's final."

"If she wants lilacs, just let her have lilacs. What's the harm?" Grandma Frida asked.

"Her colors scheme is sage, pink, and white. Blue is going to clash with it. It's going to be ugly. The bouquet will be in all the important photographs and everybody is going to notice how ugly it looks. You don't understand, Grandma. People on Herald are vicious. I don't want Nevada to be torn apart. They're going to be mean. They're jealous. Nobody wants to hear a story about a beautiful wedding, but everyone is going to make fun of a Prime bride who is marrying a billionaire but couldn't afford to coordinate her bouquet. No!"

"Since when do we care what people on Herald think?" Mom asked.

"Since we became a House and everyone thinks we're country bumpkins." Arabella spun to me. "Catalina, tell them."

Everyone looked at me.

"Fuck Herald," I said.

Grandma Frida dropped her fork.

"Fuck Primes, fuck their paparazzi, and if Nevada wants lilacs, she should have all the lilacs ever. I will buy the damn lilacs myself, with my own money." I took my tablet and walked out.

Behind me, Arabella said, "Mom?"

"I think your sister is a little stressed out," Mom said.

I made a left turn to another hallway and walked to the Hut of Evil. When we sold our house to pay for Dad's medical treatment and moved into the warehouse, the original plan was to set it up as homelike as possible. But instead we just threw walls up wherever they were needed and ended up with some unusual spots. To a stranger, our layout wouldn't make much sense, but to us, it worked great. The Hut of Evil was one of those odd places. It was a small room inside a larger space complete with the door and a roof and raised off the ground to accommodate all the cables and the cooling. I had to walk up three steps to get in.

The temperature inside was at least five degrees cooler than in the rest of the house. Bern sat in his usual seat in front of three monitors. I took a seat in Leon's chair.

"Rough day," Bern said.

"They lie, and cheat, and steal. And they think they're better than us, because we work, and we don't have as much money. This is the kind of family Nevada is marrying into."

"Nevada is marrying Rogan. I like Rogan. I like Mrs. Rogan too, and the East Wing side of the family seem decent. Look, most of them will go back to Europe after this, and we will never, ever see them again. We just have to get through the wedding."

"No, Nevada has to get through the wedding. We have to catch a thief and prevent mass murder at the wedding ceremony. Have you seen them doing anything weird? Something that could help us find the Sealight or whoever took it?"

Bern hesitated. "Well, not sure if it's related but you gotta see this. Hang on."

His fingers flew across the keyboard and an image appeared on the middle screen, a table on a patio, flanked by some chairs. The picturesque shrubs rustled, and a tall, lanky man stepped out of them, like some kind of jungle explorer emerging from the bush. Mikel Ramírez adjusted his glasses, looked around, and took off down a path, away from the building into the orchard.

"Keep watching," Bern said.

A long minute crept by.

Maria Ramírez stomped into frame, her chunky heels making clicking noises on the patio. A faint green smudge stained her white dress. There was a twig in her bleached blond hair. She was holding a martini glass in her hand. She took off her sunglasses, paused, like a hound finding the scent, and took off in the direction her husband had fled.

I put my hand over my mouth and shook my head. "This is just bizarre."

"She chases him like this, all over the house." Bern turned his blond head and looked at me. "At lunch, he excused himself from the table, and never came back. I think he crawled out of a window because neither of the exit cameras caught him, and then he was outside. He could have stolen the Sealight. He's pretty good at sneaking around."

"Yes, but he's a lousy telekinetic, barely an Average, and everything in his file says he's desperate for his father's approval, so it's unlikely he is hiding his power. He wouldn't be able to lift the wall. What about Paul Sarmiento?"

Bern tapped a quick sequence on the keys. Ane and Paul came into view. They sat in the soft chairs overlooking the distant hills. Paul reached over to the table, lifted the small kettle, and poured Ane a cup of tea.

"They are joined at the hip," Bern said. "If he stole the Sealight, she would have helped him, because I never see them apart for more than ten minutes. Also, most of them have used their powers since I started watching them. They levitate something minor or open a door with a wave of their hand. I'll double-check on this, but so far, he's done nothing. I don't think he's telekinetic."

In other words, we still had nothing.

"Will you be here tomorrow?"

"Yes," Bern said. "Why?"

"I'm going to poke this snake nest with a stick and I might need a lot of help."

"I'll be here," Bern promised. "Catalina, don't let this get personal. Let's find the jewel, catch the poisoner, and be done with them. What they think of us doesn't matter. This is an investigation just like any other. They are suspects. You only interact with them to get to your objective."

"I know."

We sat together in a comfortable silence, watching Lucian schmooze his father-in-law over some whiskey and cigars.

"Did you like him?" Bern asked.

"Not that much." Not as much as I had liked Alessandro Sagredo. Walking with Xavier had been nice, before I realized he was a two-faced scumbag, but it was nothing special. But when I saw Alessandro, I wanted to snap my wings open as far as they could go and dazzle him with everything I had, so he would be mine forever. I liked him so much, I had to let him go.

CHAPTER 7

IT WAS ALMOST brunch time, and I was walking through the garden of Mountain Rose, carrying a mimosa in each hand.

"Turn to your right ahead," Bern said into my earpiece.

I turned and stopped at the neat little table with two chairs. The grounds were full of these little nooks, pretty places to sit and enjoy the outdoors. I turned toward the path and concentrated, letting just a little of my magic through. It came sluggishly. I was still tired from yesterday. My books said I would get better with practice. I tried not to think about how I would get that practice.

"Incoming in three, two, one."

Maria Ramírez stumbled onto the path. She wore a white sheath dress that had a modest neckline but left her tan shoulders and arms bare. A thick gold chain hung from her neck and a matching cuff bracelet encircled her forearm.

I gave her a peek at my feathers and cast my shiny magic lure with my voice. "Would you care for a mimosa?"

Maria froze. Her expression relaxed and then she started toward me. "I would love one."

We sat at the table and sipped our mimosas.

"It's peaceful here," Maria said. "It's nice."

"It is nice," I said, saturating my words with more magic.

"Have you seen my husband?" Maria asked. "He would like it here."

"No. Tell me about your husband. What kind of man is he?"

"He's gentle and smart. And I love him so much. That's why it hurts so much when he betrays me." Tears welled up in Maria's eyes. "He betrays me with men. I can't compete with that. I can be prettier, I can be thinner, but I can't be a man. And that's what he likes."

Oh God. "How do you know he likes men?"

"He had a secretary and I would catch them sneaking off together. When I would find them, all conversation stopped. And then the secretary was fired, but Mikel paid him five hundred thousand dollars. I saw the record of the payment in his office. Then there was the gardener. I would see them meet when they thought I wouldn't notice. They would pass each other pieces of paper like children in school. Love letters."

"Have you read one?"

"No."

Somehow, I doubted folded pieces of paper equaled love letters. Drugs would be a much better explanation.

"And now he's doing it again. Do you know who he is doing it with?" She leaned toward me. "Lucian. My husband is having an affair with Lucian. I saw Mikel leave in the middle of the night to meet with him."

Maria gulped the rest of her mimosa. "I must find him." Her eyes widened, her lower lip trembled. She looked panicked. All of her emotions were focused on Mikel. I wouldn't get much out of her and it would be cruel to try.

"I think he went down that way." I pointed down the path and pulled my magic back.

Maria jumped up and headed down the path without looking back.

None of that made any sense. If Lucian was bisexual, he would have had affairs with men as well as women. Lucian had a voracious appetite and he denied himself nothing. If he'd wanted men, he would have had men and there was no record of any male companions.

I texted Rogan. Sorry to interrupt. Do you know why Mikel paid a large bonus to his secretary after firing him? There is nothing in the files.

No, I don't, but ask my mother.

I texted Mrs. Rogan the same question. A grey bubble let me know she was typing the answer. It was taking her a while. I drummed my fingers on the table and drank a little more of my mimosa.

That wasn't a secretary, dear. That was Angel. He is what people of my generation refer to as an illicit love child. Mikel had some wild days and managed to father a child at sixteen. The family compensated the mother well, but when Angel grew up, he wanted a relationship with his father. He's a sweet boy, but it didn't work out. Mikel wasn't what Angel was hoping for. Any progress on Sealight?

Not yet and thank you.

You have my full confidence.

The phone chimed. Mrs. Rogan sent me a selfie of her and Mia Rosa in Mrs. Rogan's office. They were giving me the V for victory with their fingers.

If Lucian and Mikel weren't having an affair, why was Mikel sneaking out to meet him?

A thought occurred to me. "Bern, can you send a text message but make it appear to come from someone else?"

"Yes. *Whose number do you want me to spoof?*"

"I'll tell you when I get home." This will work better if I wasn't here. They would let their guard down if all of us were gone.

I couldn't leave yet. I was due to meet with Paul Sarmiento in ten minutes. I had asked Mrs. Rogan to set the meeting up for me, so Paul wouldn't have any excuses to duck me.

"That was impressive," a man said.

I glanced up. Paul was leaning against a tree.

"Are you planning to do that to me?" he asked.

I FACED PAUL. He had caught me using my magic. He knew my secret. Normally I would've tried to escape the confrontation. But something happened in the past few days, somewhere between the poisoned cake and Xavier calling me a mouse. It seared the shyness out of me.

One time our parents took us for a winter vacation in Colorado. We skied and rode sleighs all day and I had the most fun my eight-year-old self could remember. On the evening before we were supposed to go home, I snuck out of our cabin at dusk and rode my sleigh down the hill into the woods. It was so pretty, snow was falling softly, and for a while I wandered around. Then the sun had set, the wind picked up, and it went from magical to being scary. The snow had covered my tracks and I didn't know where to go. I tried calling but nobody came. The cold was biting at my face, and I realized I had to save myself. I picked a direction and I walked. After a while, I couldn't feel my feet or my fingertips. It was so cold, and it hurt so much, that eventually I got used to it. I accepted it and got numb. I just kept walking through the pain, until my dad found me and carried me back to the cabin.

That's what it was like now. Bad, uncomfortable things kept happening, one after the other. Any one of them would have made me panic on its own, but all of them together made me numb. I had to get out of this forest. I had accepted that it wouldn't be easy or pleasant.

I looked at Paul and asked, "Are you going to force me to do that to you or would you prefer to sit down and talk?"

He walked over and took a seat at the table. "How can I help you?"

"I have a problem. According to every background check we've run, you don't exist. You have no driver's license, your finger-prints are not in any of the databases, and the documents that follow most people through life, like birth certificates, diplomas, and résumés, simply can't be found. So, I have two questions: Who are you and why are you here?"

"And if I refuse to answer?"

"I'm afraid I'll have to compel you to. We've had some compli-cations and the safety of the wedding guests is at stake."

"I don't think you are afraid at all."

Paul reached into his pocket, took out a wallet, and pulled a business card out. He slid it across the table to me. It was a pale blue card with two words embossed on it in dark blue—Wishing Well. Under the words was an address located in Seattle, with a phone number.

"My name is Lance Gibson. I'm an employee of the Wishing Well. Our corporate headquarters are in Japan, but I work out of the Seattle office. Ane is one of my clients."

There was no tactful way to ask the next question. "Are you an escort?"

"I'm not a prostitute, but, in a manner of speaking, I am Ane's escort. Our company specializes in wish fulfillment of a very specific nature. Have you ever felt that you are missing an important person in your life?"

I missed my dad every day. "I don't understand. Is it like the boyfriend experience?"

"It can be, but typically it isn't." Lance steepled his fingers. "People come to us because there is a hole in their lives. For example, suppose a father abandons his wife and their young child. The wife divorces him. The child needs a father, yet she can't bring herself to enter another relationship. She might come to us and for a fee, one of us will become her divorced spouse for her child."

"So, you impersonate people? Like an actor?"

"Exactly like that. However, an actor assumes a different persona only for a short time, while we may do it for years. A couple hired me, because they have a daughter who is suffering from lupus. At the time, she was eight years old. She adored her older brother, who was fifteen years her senior. He was a remarkable individual, gifted, compassionate, and adventurous. Due to the nature of his charitable work, he traveled and always made time to call or email his little sister. One day the emails stopped. He died in a conflict in Belize. Her parents were terrified that the news would kill her. So, little by little, they replaced his photographs with mine. We started with emails, then phone calls, and then one day, her brother walked through the door. I'm there for every birthday. I'm the person she calls when she has problems at school or with her parents. This summer I'm taking her on a college tour."

"But you're not her brother."

Lance smiled. "No. But I'm fulfilling his role."

I wasn't sure what to think about that. "Will you ever tell her?"

"No. That is forbidden. Her parents can tell her, if and when they choose. Perhaps, when she no longer needs a brother, I will make a graceful exit. A plane crash, a skydiving accident. But for now, I'm there to provide a shoulder to lean on and the unconditional love and kindness one would expect from an older sibling."

"So, what are you to Ane?"

"Ane is single by choice. She enjoys being single. She was pressured into her marriage, and after her husband died, she was pressured again to remarry. Instead she hired me. Our relationship is not sexual. I escort her to family events and to vacations, I take care of her during these outings in a way a loving partner would be expected to take care of her, and on occasion, I act as her bodyguard. My services come with a guarantee a real relationship can't provide. I will never embarrass her. I will never get drunk, cause a scene, cheat on her, attempt to steal from her or coerce her into a course of action beneficial to myself, all of the things she had experienced in her prior relationships. Ane is in complete control. She engages my services as she wishes and can terminate our business relationship at any time."

"Does it bother you that people think you're a gigolo?"

Lance smiled again. "Why would I care what anybody but Ane thinks of me? The needs of my client are the only thing that matters. I'm paid to anticipate complications and smooth them over, which is why I'm talking to you now. I have emailed my credentials to Mr. Rivera, whom I understand to be in charge of security. You will find all of the necessary documents enclosed. Am I free to go, Ms. Baylor?"

Nobody had ever asked me that before. "Yes."

Lance rose and walked away.

"Did you get all that?" I asked Bern.

"Yeah, I got it."

"I am coming home," I told him. "I think I've had enough for today."

I TEXTED TROY, one of Rogan's guys. Bern and I had decided that we should keep Leon as far away from Xavier as was humanly possible, so Troy was my battle buddy for the day. He would get the car.

I started down the path that brought me to the courtyard. In the center, by the fountain, Xavier and Raul, one of Rogan's cousins from East Wing, sparred with rapiers. Mrs. Rogan and other adults were watching from the shade of the porch. The gaggle of teenagers surrounding them alternated between shouting encouragement and pretending to be bored.

Great. I would have to walk past them to my car. I started moving, hoping nobody would notice me.

"Catalina!" Xavier jogged toward me. The circle of kids parted to let him pass. People were catcalling.

I did my absolute best to ignore him. It was that or punch him in the throat. Usually people aimed for the face, because that's what you saw in movies and TV, but I grew up in a family of veterans. A punch to the throat didn't hurt your hand and it disabled your opponent.

Xavier ran ahead of me and blocked my way. He was holding two rapiers and offered me one. "Let's spar. It will be fun."

Oh, you moron. You colossal moron. If only you knew.

"Xavier!" Raul called. "Are we doing this or what?"

"Come on," Xavier said. "I'll show you."

"I don't know how, and I have things to do." Everybody was looking at me. It was like some kind of nightmare, but it was real and it was happening right now.

"Come on," he repeated. "Don't be an old lady."

I was so angry that my hands shook. This was the worst-case scenario. The whole family was there, all the kids, and all the adults, and just me without anyone on my side.

Xavier waved the rapier in front of me.

Something in me snapped. I took it from him and marched into the circle.

Raul bowed and stepped aside. Xavier took position opposite me and slid into a stance. He probably had fencing lessons in whatever school he went to. I had no lessons, but I had a lot of hate. I had no idea what the point of this was, besides embarrassing me.

"First thing you do is get into *en garde* position. Like this. Turn your lead foot forward, bend your knees, make sure your knees are over your toes."

I just stood sideways, the way I always stood, when we practiced self-defense.

"Bend your knees," Xavier said.

Someone giggled.

"Are we going to fight or are you going to talk all day?" I asked.

The kids oohed. Raul gave me a thumbs-up.

"I'll go easy on you," Xavier said. "I'm going to lunge—try to parry."

The anger and my magic fused together. The world shrank down to just Xavier and me. The sword felt light and flexible in my hand, an extension of me, almost like an arm. I held it in front of me pointing at his midsection.

He lunged.

I shied out of his way and drove the blunted point of the rapier into his ribs on his left.

"Touché," someone screamed.

Xavier jerked back, anger flickering across his face. "I let you have that one. Are you ready?"

"Are you?"

He attacked. I didn't know how, but I knew exactly where he would strike. It felt like the sword itself guided me out of the way.

I sidestepped and brought my sword with all my strength on top of his blade, knocking it out of his hand.

Xavier stared at me.

"You weren't ready," I said. "Your sword is over there. Are you supposed to be good at this?"

Xavier snatched his rapier up. His face was red now. He bared his teeth and lunged. I saw it, as if we were both underwater, the point of his rapier aiming straight for my unprotected face. Somehow I knew there was no time to back up, so I went forward instead, sliding my rapier against his, trying to force it to my right. We collided. The flat of his blade slid against mine, all the way to the guard, and suddenly our faces were very close.

Xavier's eyes were crazy.

He smashed his forehead into my face. I shied back, but not far or fast enough. Dark circles burst in front of my eyes. It hurt. It really hurt.

Raul was running toward us, and so was Adrianna. Xavier shoved me back. Something slammed into him from the right, knocking him aside like he weighed nothing.

The ground under my feet trembled and a terrible voice sounded from everywhere at once. *"Enough."*

Adrianna put her arms around me. "Are you okay?"

I blinked trying to clear the tears from my face. Xavier was sprawled on the ground two dozen yards away, a shocked look on his face. A heavy outdoor cushion pinned him in place. He was struggling to lift it off, his arms shaking with the strain. He should've been able to push it off of him, but it trapped him like it was made of cement.

The courtyard was completely silent. I turned and saw Mrs. Rogan on the porch. Magic emanated from her, like an invisible corona. I couldn't see it, but I felt it and the power in her took my breath away. It was like standing in the eye of a catastrophic storm. You couldn't see the wind, but you could feel it all around you, and if you took a step, it would rip you apart. I couldn't move, I couldn't speak. I just stood there, feeling the terror roll over me in icy waves.

Behind her, her three older siblings and their children looked outraged. The West Wing crowd didn't share the indignation. Markel and Zorion were sneering; Lucian raised his eyebrows, amused; Mikel and Maria looked alarmed; Eva, Xavier's mother, glared at Mrs. Rogan, and Iker, Xavier's father, wore a completely flat expression. The line splitting the family down the middle was never so clear.

Mrs. Rogan turned her head and stared at Eva. Her magic turned with her and stared at Eva, too, like an ancient dragon noticing a trespasser.

Eva looked at her feet. Her bottom lip trembled.

Iker stepped in front of his wife and bowed his head. "Our sincerest apologies. He is young and stupid. We meant no disrespect."

Mrs. Rogan spoke, and her voice reverberated through me, pulsing in my bones. The water in the fountain shook. "Take him to your rooms. He does not come out unless I call for him."

Iker strode to his son. The cushion lifted on its own and moved back to the outdoor sofa on the porch. Nobody moved to help Iker. He grabbed Xavier by his right shoulder and hauled him upright.

"Are you all right, dear?" Mrs. Rogan asked.

The dragon was looking at me. I had to say something, and it was so hard. "Yes, ma'am."

"I am so very sorry," Mrs. Rogan said. "Please forgive me."

I wanted to fall through the ground and keep falling until I was on the other side of the world. "It's okay. I'm fine, everything is fine. It's all good." I clicked my teeth shut before any more rambling nonsense came out.

"Very well. I think I will retire to my office. I've had all the excitement I could stand." The dragon folded her wings collapsing back, and Mrs. Rogan turned her wheelchair and rolled back into the house.

I turned and fled toward the gate as fast as I could. A familiar Honda Element drove through the gates toward me, Troy behind the wheel. I almost ran. The Honda stopped, and I jumped into the passenger seat. Troy was looking at my hand and I realized I was still clutching the stupid rapier. There was blood on the blade. I must have cut Xavier somehow.

"What the hell happened?" Troy asked.

"Too complicated. Could you please just drive?"

Troy turned the car around and drove out of Mountain Rose.

"What took you so long?" I asked.

"We found Sealight," he said and dropped a duffel bag on my lap.

I unzipped the black duffel. The glittering crown looked back at me, the diamonds sparkling as they caught the light.

The heart-shaped aquamarine was missing.

CHAPTER 8

I SAT ON the couch in the dark media room, watching the security feed from the camera. Bern had forwarded it to our TV. The Sealight without the jewel rested on the couch to my left. The bloodstained rapier lay across my lap. My whole face was puffy. A large lump had formed on the right side of my forehead. It throbbed. My skin felt hot and ready to burst. I had an absurd feeling that if my lump healed, a pocket of skin would just sag off the side of my face. Google would probably tell me I was crazy, but I didn't care enough to do a search on it. I stopped caring about a lot of things. It had been that kind of a day.

On the screen, the table and chairs where I had interviewed Maria and Lance waited quietly for the victims of Bern's phone spoofing.

Mom walked into the room and flicked the lights on. "Why are you sitting by yourself in the dark . . ." She saw my face, fell silent, and sat on the couch near me. We sat together and watched the empty table.

"I don't want to go to college," I said.

Mom just looked at me.

"There is so much pressure to go to college. It starts from the first day of high school and never lets up. Every grade, every test, every club, every sport, everything matters, and not because you want to do it, but because it might count toward the college scorecard. You're supposed to do great on your SAT, get a scholarship, graduate with honors, and then leave to have this awesome college experience. Winners go on to colleges, losers stay home and work crappy jobs. Well, I'm a loser, Mom. I think you should go to college if there's something you want to do that can't be done without a degree. I don't know what I want to do. I'm not going to waste your money and I'm not going to torture myself just because someone might think that I failed at life because I didn't move halfway across the country to get a degree I don't want."

I braced myself for the crushing disappointment on Mom's face.

"Okay," Mom said.

Okay? What did okay mean?

We sat some more.

"Someone's poisoned Nevada's wedding cake. There is a man whose job it is to impersonate people's relatives for a fee. Bug says the company has a really good medical plan. Also, I got in a sword fight."

"Did you win?" Mom asked.

"I didn't lose, and he cheated." I looked at her. "Also, I have learned how to use my magic to get people to tell me their secrets and then make them forget that they did. I'm like Nevada and Grandma Victoria, except I don't force people. When I violate their minds, I just dangle my magic in front of them and they trip over themselves to tell me everything they know."

I looked back at the screen.

Mom hugged me.

"Are you mad about college?" I asked.

"No. I've done my job. I've raised you to be a good person. You're kind and smart and when you see a wrong, you try to fix it. That's all a parent can hope for. The rest is up to you. It's your life. You have to live it, and I would be a terrible parent if I tried to do it for you. I have no doubt that if you want a formal education in the future, you will get one. Everyone's path is different, Catalina."

"We found the crown under some bushes," I said. "They took the jewel out of it and left the expensive diamonds behind. It doesn't make any sense, does it?"

"It doesn't make sense, because you assume the thief wanted the crown for the money or because they wanted to embarrass the family. Maybe they just wanted the jewel from the start."

Bern walked into the room carrying his laptop. He landed in the recliner. "Did you see the email from Bug about Mikel?"

"I saw." It explained a lot of things.

"Are we ready for this?" Bern asked.

I nodded. Bern typed in a quick sequence. The camera zoomed in slightly, bringing the table into better focus.

"What's going on?" Mom asked.

"Earlier today we sent Lucian a text from Mikel's number telling him to meet in that spot at eight o'clock." I pointed at the TV. "We sent an identical text to Mikel from Lucian. It's seven fifty-five."

"Mom," Arabella called from the depths of the warehouse.

Mom hugged me again, kissed my forehead, and walked out.

Lucian walked into frame. He looked around, clearly impatient.

A minute passed. Another.

Mikel came striding down the path. He hurried to the table and stepped in close to Lucian. They were the same height, but where Mikel was thin and awkward, Lucian looked fit and athletic.

"What is it?" Mikel hissed. "I've wired the payment. What the hell do you want from me?"

"I don't want anything from you. You . . ."

"Then stay the hell away from me. There's no more. You're bleeding me dry as it is. Leave me alone."

Mikel took off down the path at a near run.

Lucian looked after him and sneered. There was something very familiar about that sneer. Lucian pulled out his phone and typed something.

"Who is he texting?" I wondered aloud.

"No way to tell," Bern said. "The angle is wrong."

Lucian didn't seem in a hurry to leave. We waited.

A slim figure came down the path and stopped by the table, her chestnut hair spilling over her shoulder.

"Have you lost your mind?" Eva asked.

"I miss you," Lucian said.

What?

"Really? Now, here of all places, with all the family here, you miss me?"

Lucian moved toward her, and she stepped back.

"What you and I did is in the past," Eva said. "It's over. It has to be over."

"It's not really over, is it? Some consequences can't be ignored. Especially when they blunder so badly." He took another step toward her. "Come on, Eva. Let me help you escape this house, if only for an hour or two."

She turned around and dashed down the path. Lucian rolled his eyes and started walking in the direction of the house at a leisurely pace.

"Clearly, this is not Lucian's night," Bern said.

"Can you bring up Lucian's image?" I asked.

Lucian's face filled the screen. He was a very handsome man. Dark hair and a distinctive line of the jaw.

I picked up my phone and dialed Rogan's number. He answered, "Yes."

"Can I have permission to request a DNA test from the Scroll database to determine if someone is a relative of House Rogan?"

"Why?" Rogan asked.

I told him.

"I'll make the call," he said.

I thanked him and hung up.

"Well, that is a hell of a thing," Bern said.

I rubbed my face and wished I hadn't. It hurt. "This is a messed-up family."

"I've got a very nice shot of Isabella collecting money from Elba and restocking her with Oxy," Bern said. "Does that cheer you up?"

"We still don't know who took the Sealight."

"You should rest," Bern said. "You'll feel better in the morning."

"I want to look at some more footage. Maybe there's something I missed."

Bern got up and put the laptop in front of me. "The folders are marked by date. Have fun."

It was past 1:00 a.m., when I watched a gang of kids run down the hallway. Behind them Mrs. Rogan followed in her wheel-chair, a happy smile on her face. You would never know she was a dragon. Mia Rosa trailed her, dragging her stuffed unicorn.

I was so tired, I almost missed it. Mom must have heard me laughing like a lunatic, because she came in, confiscated the lap-top, and chased me off to bed.

It was Friday, two days after Xavier had headbutted me and the swelling had finally gone down. I had another bruise on my shoulder, because on Thursday morning Arabella saw my face and we had to physically restrain her from jumping into the car and driving to Mountain Rose to "fix Xavier's face so good, his mom wouldn't recognize him." She accidently punched me while swinging her arms, and then she felt bad, and followed me around trying to get me to eat chocolate she bought for me.

Also, on Thursday Nevada called. She had finally closed the Nightingale investigation. House Nightingale was satisfied, and Rogan and my sister were going to celebrate. Arabella and Grandma Frida wanted to know which restaurant they would be going to, and the answer turned out to be Domino's. They had ordered pizza and spent the evening watching bad movies.

Today was the day of the rehearsal dinner. None of the high-ranking guests were coming, so it would be just the two families, Rogan's and ours. The wedding was on Saturday, and everyone involved would be spending the night at Mountain Rose.

I had driven to Rogan's house and met him in his kitchen, while Nevada was getting ready. Rogan was in a hurry, and so he used his magic to do several things at once. I would never get used to the coffee carafe pouring the coffee by itself.

"What's up?" he asked, as the coffee mug landed in his hand.

"I found out some things about your family which you probably should know. They're unpleasant."

"I've known that for years."

"No, I meant the things I found out were unpleasant."

"I knew what you meant," he said. "Why don't you just tell me what's bothering you?"

"I can either expose all those things, or I can tell you and Mrs. Rogan in private. If I do it in public, it will get ugly."

"Are you afraid?" he asked.

"No," I said. "But I don't want you or Mrs. Rogan to be embarrassed or uncomfortable. You're the client. Tell me what you would like me to do."

"Do any of those things compromise or have the potential to compromise the security of the family?" he asked.

"Yes."

Rogan drank his coffee. "I say let's get it all out there. As much as my mother wants to retain her privacy, she would be the first to tell you that potential security issues override that. Do what you need to do."

"Okay." I just hoped he wouldn't regret it.

THE REHEARSAL DINNER took place in the courtyard.

In twenty-four hours everyone was going to be dressed up, so for the rehearsal we went with casual. Tables were set out, covered with white tablecloths. Pitchers of lemonade and iced tea were distributed. Baskets of rolls were placed on the tables, next to simple centerpieces of wildflowers in plain glass vases. Valentina's House Catering had prepared a traditional Texas barbecue, and platters of smoked meats made their way around each table—moist and dry brisket, smoked chicken and turkey, beef and pork ribs, sausage rings with jalapeno kick, followed by bowls of coleslaw, corn on the cob, and baked beans.

I sat at the head table, with Rogan and Nevada, together with Arabella, Bern, Leon, Mom, and Grandma Frida, and Mrs. Rogan. My seat was on Nevada's left, because I was the Maid of Honor. My sister practically glowed.

I felt so bad. I had warned her that some crazy stuff was coming, but I didn't go into specifics. It was either ruin the rehearsal dinner or the wedding. This was the lesser of the two evils.

Mrs. Rogan smiled at me. "It's time, dear."

I got up and walked to the raised porch where Rogan had set up a huge flat-screen TV. To my right stood a lectern covered with a length of blue cloth.

Rogan's entire family was in front of me. My family too. So many people. They were all looking at me. My skin felt too tight. I glanced around the tables, noting the familiar faces. Lucian and June; Maria and Mikel; Markel and Isabella; Iker and Eva, sullen

Xavier sandwiched between them; Ane and Lance; Zorion and Teresa . . .

I took a deep breath. I had spent a good hour writing the intro to my speech and trying to sound as adult as I could. "Recently we became aware that the Sealight tiara, which is traditionally worn by the brides of the Ramírez family, has been stolen."

The courtyard went quiet, surprise and concern registering on people's faces. The blue cloth hiding the lectern fell to the floor, revealing a blue pillow with the Sealight on it, its jewel still missing.

"We were able to recover the Sealight and in the process of our investigation, several facts have come to light, which I will now share with you."

I looked at Elba sitting at the table with her parents, Mikel and Maria. Elba grinned at me. *Keep smiling. Let's see if you are still smiling when I'm done.*

I smiled back and looked to the table where Markel and his wife, Isabella, sat. "Isabella Ramírez is buying and selling prescription medication and is using Elba and two other children, not related to the family, to distribute it. Here's the footage of her resupplying Elba and collecting the money."

The flat screen came to life showing Isabella counting off Oxy-Contin pills into the jar and handing it over to Elba.

"The authorities in Bilbao are aware of her activities due to one of the parents of the other children filing a police report."

A copy of the police complaint appeared on the screen. Bug really was a wizard.

The smile fell from Elba's face. Isabella went bright red, then white. Markel stared at her. "Why?"

"Because you have me on an allowance like a child," she snapped. "This man rations everything. He wants to know where every euro went. He would ration my tampons if he could."

Maria was glaring at Elba. The next part was going to be even better.

"Maria Ramírez," I said.

Maria jerked in her seat.

"Your husband is not bisexual. He is not having an affair with Lucian. Mikel is running a Ponzi scheme through Ramírez Venture Capital. To date, he has embezzled thirty-four million euros from investors. Lucian de Baldivia became aware of the theft, because his company provides cybersecurity for Ramírez Capital. He has been blackmailing your husband for the last five months. Here are the financial statements to prove it. They have also been sent to all of your email addresses."

The courtyard exploded. Everyone shouted at once. Ramírez Venture Capital was the family's piggy bank.

"I've made some bad investments!" Mikel yelled over the noise.

"You had no authority to make any investments!" Mattin Ramírez thundered. "You were supposed to sit on your ass and watch the money. That's it. An idiot could have done it."

"I will pay back every euro with interest!" Mikel shouted.

"How?" Ane demanded. "With more fraud?"

"There was no affair?" Maria cried out. "Why do you keep running away from me?"

"Because you drive me insane!" Mikel fired back.

Rogan leaned his elbow on the table and rested his chin on his hand, watching the chaos like it was a Saturday morning cartoon. Mrs. Rogan was rubbing her temples. Nevada leaned back out of her mother-in-law's view and gave me a thumbs-up.

"I want a divorce!" Maria announced.

"I am not done," I announced. "Please let me finish."

"There can't possibly be more," Zorion Ramírez said.

The image on the TV blinked, replaced by Xavier at the fountain. I let his rant roll in all of its glory. When he got to the point of how he would inherit, the courtyard went completely silent. Everyone stared, horrified. The look on Xavier's face was pure hate. I pressed pause on the remote and looked directly at him.

"Xavier, do you know why your plan won't work?"

He cursed at me.

I pressed play. Two images appeared on the screen, side by side. Lucian and Eva. A third image, a document with the Scroll logo on it, popped up under them.

"We have obtained permission from Mattin Ramírez, who is the acting head of your family for the duration of this visit, to test your blood, which you left on my rapier. You do not share DNA with anyone in the Ramírez family. Your DNA profile, however, indicates with a 99.999998 percent certainty that these two people are your parents. You will not inherit, because you are not related to Rogan."

The silence was deafening. Everyone was looking at Lucian and Eva.

Lucian bared his teeth while Xavier shot up to his feet. "It's not true! Mom, tell them it's not true!"

Eva swooned and fainted. Iker stared at her as if he didn't know who she was.

"Almost forgot," I said. I picked up Sealight, stepped off the porch, walked over to the children's table, and smiled at Mia Rosa. "May I see Sapphire, please?"

Mia Rosa raised her unicorn up. A bright blue jewel in the shape of a heart glittered in the stuffed toy's forehead, the white fur around it stained with streaks of purple school glue.

"Did you try to bedazzle it?" I asked.

"The bedazzler wasn't big enough," Mia Rosa said. "I glued it."

"I'm sorry, but it's not yours." I plucked the jewel from Sapphire's head and fitted it back into the crown. The Sealight was whole again.

"You should probably give it back to your aunt," I told her.

Mia Rosa, Prime telekinetic, sighed. The tiara floated from my hands, dodging the guests with surgical precision, and came to rest gently on the table in front of Mrs. Rogan.

Behind me a table fell as Iker Ramírez threw himself at Lucian de Baldivia.

THE WEDDING WAS beautiful.

Nevada looked like a princess with the Sealight tiara on her head, while Rogan looked like himself in a tuxedo. The powerful and magically elite of Texas had gathered in full force. The Herald had declared that an invitation to this exclusive wedding was the most coveted in the last ten years. They also snuck a mole into the wedding. I told Rivera to not bust them until after the vows were said. As the woman was gently expelled, her last post on Herald announced that Nevada's lilac bouquet was to die for. Apparently power and wealth trumped the clashing colors.

The wedding ceremony ended, and the reception began. The guest list read like a who's who of Texas Houses. Augustine Montgomery, Best Man, Prime. Linus Duncan, Prime. Lenora Jordan, Prime. House Harrison, House Latimer, House Ade-Afefe, House Etterson, House, House, House . . . Even Grandmother Victoria managed to secure a temporary supervised release. She danced with Linus Duncan and had a civil conversation with Grandma Frida, both of which weirded me and Arabella out.

So many rich and powerful people gathered in one spot. Xavier would have loved it. Unfortunately for him and half a dozen other of Rogan's relatives, their invitations had been revoked and they were even now flying back to Europe. Of the west wing, only

Zorion and Teresa and Ane and Lance remained. June and her daughters were invited but declined to stay.

In the happy commotion nobody noticed me, Rivera, and several of Rogan's soldiers walking into the kitchen, where the waitstaff and the caterers were preparing and plating the various courses for the reception. Nobody paid me any attention as I walked up to a middle-aged woman with recently bleached blond hair. She was straightening her waiter's uniform.

"Kelly Waller?" I asked.

She glanced up, a flicker of panic in her eyes, but I had already cast my magic lure.

"Give me your gun," I said. And she did. And then she and Jeremy followed me meekly out of the house and into a waiting armored vehicle. So ended the story of Kelly Waller, without fanfare, with a whimper, as she deserved.

Whatever happened to her after this, I didn't feel bad for her at all. Her son, Gavin, was at the wedding and would have eaten the poisoned cake. Her hatred was so strong, she was willing to sacrifice her child to it. I wrote an email to Rogan and Nevada outlining the whole thing. It was my wedding gift to them. They would read it later when they had a chance.

I had watched Nevada and Connor dance under the glittering strands of lights hanging from the trees. They looked like they had stepped out of a fairy tale. Happiness lit my sister's face and it made everything worth it. She took care of us for so long. She deserved to have all the happiness in the world.

They were still dancing, but I was worn-out. I wandered through the house, away from the fading music, until I ended up in Mrs. Rogan's study. She hadn't bothered to lock it. I sat on the window bench and looked outside at the moon.

I felt so tired and empty.

I wanted to cry.

A mechanical whisper made me turn.

"There you are," Mrs. Rogan said. "I've been looking for you."

"I'm sorry. I didn't mean to intrude into your private space."

"You're not intruding. I wanted to thank you for helping me. It was a very heavy burden to put on someone so young. If I had known how difficult it would be, I probably wouldn't have asked you to do it."

"I didn't mean to ruin the relationship between you and some of your family members."

"You didn't ruin anything. You didn't cheat, you didn't steal, and you didn't plot to profit from my son's misfortune. You seem so sad, Catalina. You've done so well. Everyone is proud of you. I thought you would be celebrating."

The words kind of tumbled out on their own. "I don't belong here."

Mrs. Rogan frowned. "Here where? In this house?"

"No. In this space." I wasn't explaining it very well. "Before Nevada met Connor, we all pretended that we were ordinary. Even after she met him, when I had to use my magic, I could still pretend that those were isolated incidents. Nobody knew I was a Prime except for people we trusted. And then we became a House. When I was working on this wedding, I had to use my magic. And it worked. I had tried things that were purely theoretical, and they worked."

"Why is that cause for concern?" Mrs. Rogan frowned.

"Because my magic always came with a price. It was only to be used as a last resort. There was no expectation placed on me. I didn't place any expectations on myself. Now I have learned I can use my magic just like any other Prime. There is no hiding from it now. The next time I'm involved in an investigation for our family business, I will likely use it. Sooner or later, people will realize I'm a Prime and that scares me."

"Because being a Prime puts you in greater danger?" Mrs. Rogan asked.

"No. I know how to be Catalina Baylor, ordinary person. I know what's expected of me. I have no idea how to be a Prime. I don't know what the rules are. I need the rules. They make me feel safe. As long as I followed the rules for using my magic, nobody got hurt." I waved my arms. "All my rules are gone. I don't know how to be. I don't know when other people are breaking the rules and how I'm supposed to react to it when they do. Like this room." I pointed at the bench where I sat and the colorful pillows. "I don't know how to mix these patterns together. If I tried, I have no idea if the result would be tasteful or tacky. I feel like I'm drowning."

I should not have said all that.

Mrs. Rogan leaned back in her chair. "When I left Spain and came here with Connor's father, I felt like I was drowning too. I didn't know anyone. I had no idea how to be a Prime in Texas. I didn't know what was expected of me and I couldn't tell if I was making a fool of myself. But I learned. All those things you have listed can be learned."

"I don't have anybody to teach me."

Mrs. Rogan smiled. "That's not true. You have me. And I have nothing but time. I think we should start with fencing. I suspect there is a lot more to the way you move your sword than pure luck."

ABOUT THE AUTHOR

"ILONA ANDREWS" is the pseudonym for a husband-and-wife writing team. Ilona is a native-born Russian, and Gordon is a former communications sergeant in the U.S. Army. Contrary to popular belief, Gordon was never an intelligence officer with a license to kill, and Ilona was never the mysterious Russian spy who seduced him. They met in college, in English Composition 101, where Ilona got a better grade. (Gordon is still sore about that.) They have co-authored four *New York Times* and *USA Today* bestselling series: the urban fantasy of Kate Daniels, rustic fantasy of the Edge, paranormal romance of Hidden Legacy, and the Innkeeper Chronicles. They live in Texas with their two children and many dogs and cats.

DISCOVER
THE HIDDEN LEGACY SERIES

Burn for Me

White Hot

Wildfire

Sapphire Flames

Emerald Blaze

Ruby Fever

PRAISE FOR ILONA ANDREWS

"Ilona Andrews's books are guaranteed good reads."

—Patricia Briggs,
#1 *New York Times* bestselling author

"With heart-pounding romance and non-stop action,
this is Ilona Andrews at her best!"

—Jeaniene Frost,
New York Times bestselling author

"Addictive, imaginative, and incredibly sexy."

—Eloisa James, *New York Times* bestselling author